AMBITION BRINGS
ITS OWN REWARD

To Karen and Arthur,

With Very Best Wishes,

Kathleen and Andrew.

AMBITION BRINGS ITS OWN REWARD

"MY STORY": A WORK OF FICTION

An Ambitious Academic Attempts to 'Protect the Environment'
But His Efforts Do Not Work Out As He Expected...

BY ANDREW GALWEY

Matador
9 Priory Business Park,
Wistow Road, Kibworth Beauchamp,
Leicestershire. LE8 0RX
Tel: 0116 279 2299
Email: books@troubador.co.uk
Web: www.troubador.co.uk/matador
Twitter: @matadorbooks

ISBN 978 1838593 902

British Library Cataloguing in Publication Data.
A catalogue record for this book is available from the British Library.

Printed and bound in Great Britain by 4edge Limited
Typeset in 13pt Gill Sans by Troubador Publishing Ltd, Leicester, UK

Matador is an imprint of Troubador Publishing Ltd

Dedicated with Love to My Dear Wife: Friend, Partner and Life Companion (One Person)

DISCLAIMERS

FOLLOWING BEST CONSERVATION PRACTICE, THIS FICTIONAL story uses exclusively words recycled from other literature. These words have been extracted from all previous contexts before being reassembled into this entirely novel sequence, thereby infringing nobody's copyright. The events described are entirely imaginary and not derived from any source known to the author. The story is presented within realistic contexts imagined from the author's four decades of participation in the day-to-day workings of typical UK academic institutions, including teaching, research and administration.

Similarly, all characters portrayed are entirely figments of the author's imagination: none represents an individual, living or dead. Universities are, however, staffed by real people with diverse personalities, many radically different from any stereotypical portrait of the academic don. Every character in the tale recounted has been synthesised from bits borrowed from innumerable individuals. Of course, it would please me if readers believed that some of these created personalities resemble persons they know! But this cannot be so! It is, however, less of a coincidence that some of the arcane administrative practices, which are described as taking place in the non-existent Linkirk University, resemble those occurring routinely in existing academic institutions…

The story told is for leisure reading, diversion and relaxation, and, hopefully, also offers entertainment and amusement. The action, set in the mid-1990s, concerns academics attempting to develop skills in the increasingly popular (fashionable) area of environmental science (or *jumping onto a topical research bandwagon*). However, the science is not an essential feature of the narrative and need not be understood. It is included as a plausible background for the fictional plot, in which differing academic imperatives result in the tensions and serious conflicts that are played out between the principal characters. This is neither a science textbook nor teaching manual. It does not advocate any partisan or political viewpoint of the author. Technical publications and the media address these topics from their alternative perspectives, promoting their differing, varied, and sometimes changing and/or conflicting interests and agendas. Ideas current at the time of the action are not reviewed here. Some personal opinions expressed by the characters portrayed represent early attempts by beginners to establish themselves in an unfamiliar research field. The research ideas mentioned do have plausible scientific foundations, together with realistic environmental relevance, including speculations about how these concepts might be developed into viable research projects. Academics undertake research on such subjects, and some fashionable (often tentative and changing intermittently) notions are mentioned. Environmental science has since moved on and has become an increasingly prominent feature of everyday life (including global warming). Despite such progress, the disturbing feature is that – without the political will – we are still doing far, far too little to protect our fragile home planet. It should also be emphasised that this history is set in the 1990s, prior to much of the subsequent advances in electronic gadgetry (computers, mobile phones, the web, etc.) that play much more important roles in our lives today. Sex and violence are featured as virtually indispensable components of any contemporary fictional tale involving homicide. The Scottish location provides a regional flavour.

University education has markedly expanded recently; a policy of previous governments has been that up to *half* UK school-leavers should aspire to become graduates. It is, therefore, appropriate and timely to take a critical, though not entirely serious, look at some internal workings of our (august) higher education institutions. Formerly, these establishments enjoyed privilege and privacy, being accorded the status of *ivory towers* and being remote from the (perhaps less educated) wider public. However, with the rising numbers of students and the costs of higher education in our society, this narrative is offered to the increasing population of graduates who may be amused to speculate about the tensions and conflicts that may have beset their Professors.

Bill Green, 1995 (Edited by Brian 'Dickey' Richards, Linkirk)

CONTENTS

WORDS HAVING TWO DISTINCT AND DIFFERENT
MEANINGS (ALTERNATIVE DEFINITIONS GIVEN) **BOTH**
OF WHICH RELATE TO CHAPTER CONTENTS

INTRODUCTION TO
A G(G)REEN STORY

BY BRIAN 'DICKEY' RICHARDS

IT IS PROBABLE THAT, AFTER SO MANY YEARS, YOU MAY NOT remember the extensive publicity given to accidents resulting in the deaths of two of the academic staff of Linkirk University, in the Scottish Borders region. At the time, 1995, these fatal incidents attracted considerable attention from the media, though national interest faded rapidly when the expected sensational developments failed to materialise. As with so many news stories, the most unusual features of these two, almost concurrent, fatalities remained unresolved publicly. Having stagnated, the case was soon eclipsed by other more saleable – or salacious – 'news', and was forgotten by everyone, apart from the hapless individuals involved directly. Now, at last, it is possible to reveal the inside story of academic rivalry that led ultimately to the unfortunate and untimely deaths of academic colleagues, who were supposedly working harmoniously together in a respected university.

In summary, the media reported the following story. Two 'professors' (*sic*), who were colleagues in Linkirk University, died on the same day, in separate accidents (or were they?) and at widely separated locations. The unusual feature of the deaths, prompting the surge of media interest, was that a third academic – a colleague of the two men who had lost their lives – absconded suddenly and inexplicably from his home and place of work a few days after the fatalities. This, apparently premeditated, disappearance of someone who – as hinted by the press – might have been an essential witness was regarded as significant or even sinister. Police appeals for him to come forward to assist with their inquiries remained unanswered then and subsequently. Because all three individuals implicated in these unexplained, and still officially unresolved, happenings were staff of the School of Chemistry at Linkirk University, an anonymous headline-writer dubbed the story 'The Chem-Mystery' – the label by which it might still be remembered.

The inexplicable disappearance of Dr William Green has provided fertile ground for suspicion and has fuelled speculation about his possible involvement in the demise of his colleagues. TV and press reports that purported to be 'informing the public about the incident' carefully avoided using the word '*murder*'. Nevertheless, the suggestion that one, or even both deaths, might have been homicide was widely implied as a plausible reason for this sudden departure of the only person thought capable of providing insights into either or both fatalities (or possibly accidents?). Indeed, speculations about the fate and whereabouts of the missing (perhaps even guilty?) Bill Green featured much more in the national media than details of the incidents involved, which the police withheld. Bill's later death, also apparently accidental, at the Grey Mare's Tail Waterfall, attracted relatively little media notice and contributed nothing to resolve The Chem-Mystery.

Without adequate explanations for the deaths and no prospect of obtaining further relevant information, eventually, the procurator fiscal (coroner) recorded verdicts of 'death by misadventure' for both Professor John Bland and Dr Walter Thompson. There never were two 'professors', as headlined: Dr Thompson held the title 'lecturer'. (Undoubtedly, Thompson would have much preferred that any such promotion to *Professor* had occurred *before* his premature demise. As in all hierarchical institutions, status symbols, most notably titles, are *very important* to academics.)

Events that generate media headlines, attracting the ephemeral interest of their readers, must maintain a high degree of novelty if they are to outlive their first days of notoriety. The Chem-Mystery, although headline news initially, soon slipped from the public eye when the 'missing Dr Green' failed to emerge from his 'self-imposed exile' and was not found by the police. The brief flowering of this top story ended when (if I remember correctly) a pop star was caught smuggling a snake ('answering' to the name of 'Fangs') through Heathrow Airport. Because this breed of reptile was on an endangered-species list, the authorities took a serious view of the crime. The 'scandalised' music industry responded in such a way as to gain maximum publicity for their 'innocent and persecuted star'. Certainly, the unexplained deaths of two Scottish academics, even with the suspicious absence of a third, were obviously of much less public interest than the definite appearance of Fangs. This sensation, in turn, was replaced by a match-fixing scandal that was alleged to have involved another star; this time, a footballer. So the fickle spotlight flickered ever onwards, always finding (even generating?) novel breaking news, often involving self-promoting 'Mini-lebrities'.

The unsolved mystery at Linkirk left many loose ends. Even at the time of writing, unfillable gaps remain in the lives of the families and friends of the accident victims – if 'accidents' they were – and uncertainties remain. The police have reported no progress in their supposedly continuing inquiries, having never established whether a crime or crimes, or even homicide, were committed. Hitherto, no implicated lawbreaker has been brought to justice or even charged. Questions remain as to whether Dr Green was involved, either directly or indirectly, in one or in both accidents, and if so, how? In the absence of facts, speculations could sell papers only for a limited period, but brought no final closure to The Chem-Mystery. These tragedies remain unexplained – *until now!*

I am keenly aware that, even after so many years, memories of these sad events continue to cause pain and grief to many of my friends, ex-colleagues and acquaintances in Linkirk (where I still live, though I am now retired). Consequently, I have decided that I must now make public all I know about The Chem-Mystery. My long silence is easily explained, though certainly not so easily justified. After the accidents, I became involved personally in the events described in this book, in definitely culpable ways. By saying nothing and feigning ignorance, I must admit to having 'perverted the course of justice'. I have dodged the certain censure of my friends, not to mention legal action. I accept that my behaviour has been indefensible, but I will try here to make some small amends by a belated full confession. Again, not to my credit, this action is prompted by my recent diagnosis of a fatal illness: I can expect to live for only a brief time longer.

As told now, more authoritatively and interestingly than I could ever manage, the history of Dr William Green, former chemistry lecturer at Linkirk University, is given here, in his own words. For reasons he explains, the manuscript describing in detail his short and unfortunate academic career became available to me some time ago. With apologies for the delay (for my own entirely selfish reasons), I now publish this 'tale of our time' because it may be of wider interest by it solving The Chem-Mystery, while also being a very human story. This action, revealing all while I am still capable of so doing, is to fulfil overdue obligations to everyone concerned in Linkirk and, perhaps, an innate desire to 'come clean with the cops'.

Brian 'Dickey' Richards, Linkirk, 1995.

Prologue

SECOND WEDNESDAY IN APRIL

# DRIVE	a. Energetic action to fulfil an objective b. Operating a moving vehicle

THAT NIGHT, I WAS CONTEMPLATING MURDER. MY INTENDED target was an academic colleague: Walter Thompson. What still remained unclear was how *exactly* to achieve my mission. Working out how to execute my intention would have to be left to the *very last* moment. I would have to be pragmatic when confronting the unprepared Thompson. My considerable, hopefully decisive, advantage of surprise must be fully exploited to rid the world of this particularly ruthless and nasty individual.

Carefully planned preparations, already in place, would distance me effectively from the 'unfortunate, fatal accident' that Thompson was about to suffer. Just then, he was, I believed, undertaking scientific fieldwork, quite alone in a remote mountain valley. The arrangements already in place would ensure that nobody would ever guess it was possible that I *could* have visited the remote location in the Italian Dolomites at this critical time. Later – after returning home to Scotland – I would, of course, join in the communal shock and horror expressed by my colleagues at our 'frightful and unexpected loss'. Privately, however, I could then hope to advance my university career in much improved circumstances, without the devious competition and ruthless opposition from the hostile Thompson, who was resolutely exploiting his one-year seniority to me in the School of Chemistry at Linkirk University (LU).

Murder is, out of necessity, a secretive activity. One way to perpetrate a successful homicide is to devise circumstances that ensure no suspicion *whatsoever* arises to suggest that *anyone else* contributed to the victim's demise. Such a death can be planned to appear to have resulted from an accident, due directly to actions, risks, etc. taken by the deceased themselves. An additional precaution for the perpetrator can be to create an effective alibi by fabricating an opaque screen completely hiding the possibility that he/she *could* have contributed to the 'accident'. Consequently, the likelihood that the fatality was not an unfortunate accident is never examined properly.

That evening, I believed myself to be within sight of achieving this ideal. It only remained for me to contrive and execute the 'fatal accident' for my unsuspecting enemy. Blame, if ever considered, would focus on the deceased. In my imagination, I could already hear my colleagues' comments: 'Working alone, in mountains... that was dangerous'; 'If he'd taken precautions...'; 'A trained scientist should know better'; 'He disregarded health and safety rules'; and 'It's his own fault'. The possibility that the fatal fall (or whatever other hazard I could exploit) might not have been *entirely* accidental need never be questioned at any inquest. I would never appear to be a suspect.

Recently, by unofficially and *temporarily* 'borrowing' confidential university files, I had learned that Thompson intended to undertake environmental research on rocks in the Italian Mountains, at just this time, and that he would be quite alone. Because, *officially*, there was no (legal) way I *could* know exactly when and where he was working, I had contrived this opportunity to be able to confront him secretly in the remote wilderness, engineer his 'fatal accident' and depart anonymously.

To locate my quarry, I was driving my hire car alone and at night, on the *Autobahn* south from Munich, through Austria (A13) to cross the Brenner Pass into Italy (A22). The Dolomite Mountains, the location of

Thompson's fieldwork, were to my south-east, and, soon, I would reach the town he had specified as his intended base.

It had been comparatively easy for me to absent myself for that night from the scientific conference that I was attending in Munich, to pay this unscheduled (surprise!) visit to 'help' a university colleague complete his scientific research projects. At the conference dinner, which I attended before setting out earlier that evening, I had taken elaborate precautions to convince several other delegates that I had excessively imbibed the alcoholic beverages that had been generously provided. My evident overindulgence would also account for my tired appearance when I resurfaced, late the next day (thereby concealing the truancy that was then enabling me to make this clandestine visit to Italy and thus fabricate my alibi). After my drunken performance, my friends would believe readily that I had been no fit state to drive or even capable of leaving town that night. In fact, by subterfuge, I had managed to avoid drinking any intoxicating liquor whatsoever. Consequently, I was stone-cold sober as I pressed on rapidly towards the opportunity to repay Thompson, in full, for his calculated and persistent undermining of my career – and my fond relationship with Beth...

This was undoubtedly the only opportunity for revenge that I would ever have, thereby enabling me to terminate the many malevolent manoeuvres by which my tormentor was destroying my ambition to establish myself as a successful university teacher. He resented my presence as a colleague and exploited every opportunity to put me in my place. His opposition is spelled out in *My Story* below. Although I had originated the proposal that the School of Chemistry at LU should establish an environmental-research centre of excellence, Thompson had been appointed as its first director. The 'playing fields' in academia are not level, and this excursion, if successful, could correct the unfairness in this promotion of Thompson by removing him permanently from his obstructive position in my life. In addition to this professional setback, I had reason to believe that my rival had started walking out with my girlfriend. My motives were personal and strong: he was effectively annihilating both my university career and my romance. Can a man have more justifiable reasons for revenge? I think not!

My resolve must not falter if I am to retain any prospect of achieving a worthwhile future in academia. Can I dispose of my foe and reinvigorate my academic career? I can! I must! *And I will!*

But *My Story* must start from its beginning, at Chapter 1...

Chapter 1

FOURTH THURSDAY IN AUGUST

CAREER	*a.* Professional progression throughout life
	b. Uncoordinated movements in random directions

'TO GET TO THE TOP OF THE HEAP IN THIS UNIVERSITY, YOU DON'T need brains. There're plenty of bright youngsters here to think up the brilliant ideas. First, you need to find some of those keen types, anxious to show off their skills. Then, you harness their intelligence for your own academic advancement. Share the kudos with them, by all means, but be sure that some of the credits for their achievements also appear on your score sheet…'

Strong stuff indeed! I gave my full attention to my self-appointed informant, listening – with some surprise – to his impromptu, and certainly unexpected, exposure of the inner workings of academia. This generous advice on how best to advance a university career was being authoritatively offered by my table companion, whom I had first met only a few moments ago. There might, indeed, be food for thought in this dining room, though my personal mental digestion and assimilation of the controversial, distinctly nonconformist notions being explained would have to be deferred until later. Just now, other thoughts competed for attention in my already overloaded mental 'in terminal'.

A short time previously, bearing my lunch tray (with a small-but-lean pork chop, incompletely mashed potatoes, mixed veg of varied brightish hues but uncertain provenance, and yoghurt) into the dining room of the university's Staff Club. I found a convenient seat, giving me pleasant views across an untidy garden to the hills beyond. Already at the table was a man in his mid-fifties, who was apparently fully immersed in the sports page of a newspaper. Preoccupied with my own thoughts, I barely noticed him until, after he had folded his paper, I became aware of his stare.

'New here, aren't you?' he asked.

'Well… yes. Is it that obvious?' I replied. This accurate diagnosis of my status was faintly disturbing, prompting me to look more carefully at my unexpected interlocutor. He was a large man with short, greying hair and a matching, tidily trimmed beard. Seated, his muscular bulk suggested former athletic skills; perhaps he had been a rugby player who had maintained some fitness, though now was becoming perceptively overweight. His bow tie and tweedy jacket, which were well-worn to the point of being 'comfortable', gave him a slightly untidy appearance – almost caricaturing the traditional 'venerable and learned academic' – but 'absent-minded professor' he was not. His ready smile set me at ease, though, at times, I found his serious, steady gaze to be indefinably unsettling, with his the gold-rimmed glasses magnifying a piercing, questioning look in his eyes. As our capricious, almost quirky, conversation developed, I welcomed his friendly overtures and listened with interest to his readily shared, if (for me) novel, opinions.

He answered my question: 'It's the season for new staff. You looked a bit lost. Even a bit apprehensive. So I guess you're wondering whether you'll like it here? Or whether we'll like you?' (There was a disturbing thought!) 'Perhaps you're musing on the wisdom of your decision to join our enclave of academic excellence?'

My slight discomfort increased. 'Yes, Yes, you're right. I'm a new boy. It's my first day at this school, and I'm yet to find my way around.' No adequate continuation of this theme came to mind, so I did my trite-sounding best: 'I accepted the university lectureship here, starting officially next month... But... no, I don't regret my decision. Rather, it's the opposite; I'm more than pleased to have got this job. It's not easy to get into universities these days. If, heaven forbid, things don't work out for me here, I can always move on elsewhere.' This horrible thought must not, could not, be entertained; it should never, never have entered my mind before I had even started work here! I needed to be confident (which is not my strong point) and, perhaps to convince myself, I tried to be positive: 'I'm most optimistic. LU has a good reputation.'

'To get to the top of the heap in this university, you don't need brains. There're plenty of bright youngsters here to think up the brilliant ideas...' My talkative companion dunked his biscuit, slurped his coffee and went on: 'What you need to get on here is *craft*: the guile to play the skilled gamesmen, or gameswomen, at their own little schemes...but make sure you're a winner. "Always watch your back," is what I say. Also, your front. Never be backwards in coming forward.'

Ignoring the final incomprehensibility, I started eating because I could find no adequate response to this distinctly unorthodox appraisal of the academic condition. Time was needed to think about the implications of this decidedly unorthodox exposition of the problems that a beginner (such as me) might encounter in my new profession. And I had committed myself recently to a university career – and voluntarily!

My new acquaintance appeared to be a deeply disillusioned man. I sought comfort in the belief that abundant optimism, when starting my career, must improve the chances of realising my initial high hopes. Now, I had just been told that I would have to make and exploit my own opportunities to prosper here. These cynical insights into academia appeared to be a genuine statement of discontent, volunteered by an obviously frustrated academic. Presumably, his own early aspirations had been unfulfilled. While reasons for his academic shortcomings were not explained, he certainly was not shy about expressing views on how to work the system. What troubled me most was that this man was obviously intelligent: his talents included a considerable ability to maintain a conversation that was both stimulating and entertaining, though at times tended towards a monologue. My faltering attempts to make sense of

3

these novel and (to me) unfamiliar opinions were again interrupted by his direct approach.

'I guess you're a scientist,' he declared. It was a statement, not a question.

Again, this was mildly disconcerting. How did he know that? 'Yes… In fact, I'm a chemist,' I confirmed.

'Now you'll tell me that your type of chemist is different from pharmacists, who run drugstores and sell medicines.'

'I wasn't going to say so, but I can't disagree.' I continued eating, finding the food unexpectedly palatable.

My new, still-anonymous friend, having finished his meal, gazed out of the window, providing a rare moment of silence, before redirecting his unsettling gaze to me. 'I should introduce myself. I'm Douglas Montgomery. Call me Doug. Everyone does! I'm also a chemist, so we're colleagues. I'm pleased to meet you and to be the first to welcome you here. You're Bill Green. I heard you'd be joining us. When you sat down, I guessed you might be our new recruit.' His formal handshake was so firm that it was a while before the blood flow in my hand recovered.

'Correct. I'm Bill Green, the new chemistry recruit, but I'm surprised you recognised me so easily.'

'We're a fairly small community here at Linkirk University, which is often referred to as LU. Many faces are familiar, even if I can't always attach names to them. This year there aren't many newcomers and you… you seemed… a bit alone.'

'I'm pleased to meet a colleague. I met some chemists at my interview some time ago, but, like you, I have trouble fitting names to faces. I saw your name on the staff list.'

'Yes. I'm a permanent fixture here and likely to last forever. I started soon after the School of Chemistry opened, in 1969, more than two decades ago. It seems more like a lifetime, and I still have more than ten years to go before they'll let me retire.'

'Surely you enjoy your work?' His negative attitude surprised me.

'Take no notice of my jaundiced views. No one else does. I know I ramble on a bit at times, and you happen to be a sympathetic ear. Just now, I'm suffering from a mid-life crisis or a touch of the blues, whichever you like. I've never been much good at university politics, and, currently, my marriage is going through a bad patch. Besides, my recent application for early retirement was declined, so I can't leave and be bored at home. I'm stuck in my job. I do my teaching with a minimum of effort, observing academia with a critical eye. I draw my own conclusions about what makes men tick. I say "men", but we can't forget the fairer sex in this age of "fairness".'

I wondered if the edge to that last remark was prompted by his marriage problems, but said, 'Don't you still do research?' The wonderful freedom to embark on whatever research interested me most was the main reason why I had applied for and accepted the job here. The idea that someone as intelligent as Doug had simply opted out of such fascinating opportunities offered by the university amazed, even shocked, me.

'Not really. I maintain a façade, but the searches for research money from industry and the problems of finding good students who are capable of thinking for themselves have become too much of an effort these days. It's unrewarding. So, I've become a 'student adviser'. I tell undergraduates which subjects to study and which courses to attend. In practice, most of them make up their own minds about what they'll do and ignore my nuggets of wisdom. Because I'm called an 'adviser', the university fulfils its obligation to provide student guidance, and I get an extra £200 a year. Everyone is happy.'

'But... research?' I could not believe that the prospect of investigating one's own scientific ideas could be set aside so lightly. This was heresy. The golden opportunity to do original research had brought me here.

'My career came off the rails years ago. Maybe I'll tell you the story some other time, perhaps over a pint of beer. I offended the powers that be, and, although they're not particularly powerful, they enjoy exploiting whatever superiority they can muster. One consequence of my alleged offences was that my promotion prospects became zero. I'll never be a "Professor". I remain "Doctor" and will stay that way, no matter how much wonderful research I do. Offended academics have at least one important similarity to elephants: they *never* forget. I cannot pack my trunk either; nobody'll give me a decent reference. So here I am, making the best of the job I have. If I don't blot my copybook too badly, I can go on until retirement, enjoying a comfortable life with minimal effort.'

Some of this sounded a bit over-rehearsed, and its glib presentation suggested others had already heard it or something similar. A matching reply seemed appropriate, but the only response my overloaded brain could then muster was, 'Well, as you guessed, I'm William Green, more usually Bill, LU's most junior chemistry lecturer. I've just arrived and I look forward to living in Scotland, though this is only my second time across the border. These days, universities seem to have a lot in common, so living and working in… er… LU will, I suppose, be much the same as I'd find elsewhere. I've enjoyed the small amount of lecturing I've already done, but the bonus is that now I'm free to do any type of research that interests me. A bit like being my own boss.' It was all a bit trite.

This exchange of personal information seemed to bring our impromptu conversation to a natural conclusion. Although it started spontaneously between strangers, I could perhaps hope that this contact might be a first step towards friendship with a colleague. Clearly, Doug was a man of independent, even eccentric opinions with the ability to express them entertainingly, but without taking himself too seriously. This could make him a stimulating companion, but I wondered how he related to our other colleagues and about his standing within the school. It might be helpful to me to be on good terms with someone so willing to offer unconventional wisdom, though I would always have to assess, most critically, its relevance to whatever future difficulties might beset me.

Doug got up and put these thoughts into words: 'I'll let you finish your meal in peace, Bill. Remember this: academic life is highly competitive and has its pitfalls. Don't pay too much attention to my advice; I'm finding life a bit bleak just now. You decide things for yourself and make your own way in the world. Thanks for your company. I look forward to seeing you round, as they say. Welcome to LU and good luck.'

'Thank you… and… er… good luck to you too, er… Doug.'

After 'self-clearing' my tray, as requested, I left the dining room and went to the adjoining garden. Here, roses bloomed in a flowerbed that required attention from the gardeners: nature was (re)encroaching, with wild flowers appearing. Other patrons of the Staff Club, possibly colleagues, had brought out glasses of beer, and were sitting on rustic benches and relaxing in the late summer sunshine before resuming academic duties.

Here, near the centre of the LU campus, the Staff Club occupied a prime position, enjoying a spectacular southwards panorama. This view was already familiar to me from local publicity material for both LU and southern Scotland, deservedly featuring on postcards sold in Linkirk. University buildings, landscaped into the flatter areas of this hillside, were scattered across this western side of Biggar Heights, which descended in sweeping slopes to the edge of the town of Linkirk. The small urban zone occupied much of the low ground in the valley below. The glint of a river (Meggett Water, from the map) could be seen in places between the grey, slate roofs and the church spires of dark stone. Beyond the built-up area of Linkirk, the ground rose, becoming the rounded uplands of the Scottish Borders, extending far into the distance. I relaxed, savouring the view.

The informative, but now rather worn, *Linkirk University, Map and Guide*, which had been sent to me before my interview, helped me to identify landmarks across the sunny landscape. Mains Road, running north from Linkirk to Edinburgh, formed the western perimeter of LU, passing the main entrance. From this junction, the principal campus road, The Spine, rose steadily upwards in a serpentine series of contoured curves, with branches to all the colleges. Each college into which the university was divided consisted of groups of buildings of varied sizes and architectural styles, some rather obviously older than others. A few areas of trees and grass still remained, giving the campus a few open spaces, but I wondered how soon these would be built over.

Rising from town level, The Spine ended at the most elevated, and certainly the most imposing, campus building: the (immodestly) named Biggar House. According to my guidebook, this impressive laird's residence had been built by the local landed gentry, the Scott family, in Victorian times. This more luxurious accommodation replaced their former ancestral home, which was built around 1400 and was a fortified castle, strategically positioned in the valley beside Meggett Water. Despite later improvements, it must have been an uncomfortable home and eventually, when times had become more peaceful, the family moved into Biggar House, nearer Linkirk. Its dominant position, overlooking the town, could be seen as expressing the family view of their exalted status, as being raised above their fellow citizens. Nevertheless, the Scott Estate, including the laird's residence, had to be sold when family fortunes declined, and it was purchased as the campus for the new LU in 1966. The former defensive stronghold, historic Meggettglen Castle, had since become a notable tourist attraction.

The large and substantial Biggar House, of the Scottish Baronial style, complete with turrets and battlements, was built expensively and to last. Perversely, its architecture recalled their fortified former home, which had been essential only during the earlier, unsettled times. Despite its forbidding exterior, this new accommodation provided an indulgent lifestyle; it was built for comfort and to maintain the dominance to which the family had always aspired, or perhaps regarded as their right. Nevertheless, their declining fortunes – or perhaps the cost of their grand, new home – meant that all had to be sold eventually. The Scott family still lived locally, but in much-more-modest accommodation.

My interview, which led to the offer of my lectureship, took place in Biggar House. While awaiting that stressful experience, another interviewee, who was seeking internal promotion, had eased his personal tension by sharing with me his views on this LU hierarchy's power base. After the already deteriorating Biggar House had become the home of LU, it was refurbished extensively (and again expensively) to renew its full potential as a comfortable, even luxurious, headquarters for the administrative staff to provide their leadership in all important university matters. Now, befitting their seniority, the provost and other worthies occupied offices in this building, in which all governing committees met. Officially, the building was known as the Facilitation Centre, though the aptness of this descriptive label was sometimes questioned by LU staff members upon whom the said *facilitations* were all too often imposed. In recognition of its dominant position, staff sometimes remarked that, 'High people in high places get above their station.' It was also referred to as the Paper Factory, recognising its most prolific product and principal 'export'.

The colleges, with the earliest dating from 1968, were distributed on both sides of The Spine. Some contrasted unfortunately with and fell far below the architectural elegance and solidity of Biggar House. Despite limited attempts to give each college some individual character, many plain concrete walls had discoloured unevenly in the Scottish winters. Evidence of poor finish and the impermanence of some recent buildings was beginning to become all too evident, contrasting with the durable stone of Biggar Hall. Later extensions to several colleges – including clumsy, even ugly, additions to the original designs – did not improve the overall architectural merit or unity of the site. Building continuing at one college testified to further campus in-filling.

Beyond the LU buildings, covering much of this side of Biggar Heights, were open grasslands. This traditional-sheep-farming country, unchanged for centuries, extended from the hills beyond Linkirk through the more distant Southern Uplands. The outline of those green, rounded hilltops seemed unexpectedly familiar. Initially puzzled, I decided that I could sense vague resemblances to the South Downs, in southern England, which was the area I had regarded, until recently, as my permanent home. Although only arriving this morning, this unexpected recognition of superficial scenic similarities triggered a moment of nostalgia.

○

It had not been part of any career plan to work in Scotland, relatively far from my native Sussex. However, my temporary fellowship in nearby Weald University was ending at a time when very few university appointments in chemistry were available. Having obtained the necessary qualifications, I had become fascinated by the challenges offered by environmental research and sought any chance to continue my work in this field, but on projects of my own choosing. The best prospect of achieving this freedom appeared to be by becoming an academic. However, applications for the few suitable posts then advertised did not progress beyond the initial stages, and I became pessimistic. So, when my approach to LU (eventually) resulted in an offer, I surprised myself slightly by accepting without hesitation.

I had previously known almost nothing about the LU School of Chemistry, and, when invited for interview, a hasty perusal of its publicity material was required to conceal my previous ignorance. More importantly, the impressions I formed of possible future colleagues, from people met briefly inside and outside the formal interview (not including Doug), were generally favourable. The lectureship offer was most welcome, not least because no other prospect beckoned. As I was approaching my twenty-sixth birthday, time was passing, and this could well be my last opportunity to pursue my preferred career. The 'bird in the hand' was seized with alacrity.

Uncertain about my prospects of success during the formal lectureship interview, I took a chance and talked about my strong interest in environmental science. Since then, pollution protection has become much more fashionable; it has become a *bandwagon*. However, at that time, I was concerned that it might appear to the interviewing board that I was making an insincere attempt to exploit an unconventional theme or even blind them with science. These reservations appeared well-founded when the chairman, Professor McTaggart, responded by questioning me closely to find out whether my interest was genuine. He put on the pressure by asking, 'Can you persuade the board that you have more than a superficial interest in this subject?'

While obviously attracting the attention of those interviewing me, my case was far from made, and I had to convince my audience that these genuine research intentions merited their support. I explained, 'My curriculum vitae lists the research I have completed. My already published research articles show, I believe, that I have identified successfully some serious consequences of discharging certain pollutants into the environment. I can provide greater detail if you wish. I will also add that I have written two articles for our local newspaper on problems that resulted from the discharge of farm waste into a river near my home.'

'Newspaper articles?' The note of surprise, even query, in the chairman's voice conveyed no reassurance. 'Have you copies here?'

'I'm sorry.' Apologies may defer a nemesis at times of crisis. 'In my application, I thought only to list refereed articles in respected academic journals...'

'Yes, yes, but... are your newspaper articles available here, now?'

'I don't know. Excuse me for a moment, please.' I rummaged through my briefcase, which I had only brought into the interview because I had forgotten to leave it outside. 'Yes, here's one.'

After passing the questioning to another board member, the chairman took the page and started to read it. However, my full attention had to be redirected to the new line of questioning about my (very positive) views on the considerable importance of laboratory experiments in science teaching.

Later, the chairman regained his initiative with a formality that indicated the interview was approaching its end (to my relief). He stated, 'You understand that we recommend appointments only on evidence of demonstrated research excellence. This is normally based only on high-quality publications in refereed journals. You have several such articles to your credit. However, these days, we scientists also have to explain our work to our paymasters: the general public. Communication is also essential in teaching; after all, we are considering you for an appointment entitled *lecturer*. In this newspaper article, you have shown your ability to communicate with the public on a controversial topic in its scientific context, apparently with some success. We cannot discuss with you the reasons for our decisions, but your referees' reports, your interview now, and all other relevant factors are carefully appraised before we make recommendations to the senate about candidates brought to our notice. For my own interest, and I stress this is a *personal* interest, I'd like to read any other popular articles you've published. Perhaps you'll send me copies, please? Yes?' He glanced around at his colleagues. 'Any other questions? No...?' Thank you, Dr Green.'

My interview was over.

Immediately after returning home, I fulfilled the request and sent copies of my several articles in local newspapers to Professor McTaggart, director, School of Chemistry. Later, I received a formal letter from the provost that offered me an appointment as a lecturer in chemistry at LU for a probationary period of two consecutive years, at the end of which I could apply for a permanent post. The letter stated that I would carry out 'such duties as were specified by the chemistry professors'. I had no idea whether my environmental interests or less-academic writings had contributed to my success. However, now that I was here, my intentions – as stated at the interview – must be honoured. Research into environment and/or pollution problems would be central to my work at LU. Hitherto, my research had always been overseen by more senior colleagues, inevitably concerning topics of *their* choosing. Now, as a lecturer, I would be no longer be a subordinate, but I could start substantive research on any topic that interested me. Freedom at last; was I to swim or to sink? Time alone would tell.

○

My only previous, brief, visit here had been for the interview. While I had gained vague impressions of LU and of Linkirk, the inevitable preoccupation on facing the ritual confrontation had dominated that occasion. Time had raced by, leaving only indistinct memories of faces and places, with few details now remaining. By the time I met Doug, I was here to stay – it was my home for the foreseeable future – so I needed to organise a new life urgently. I was all too conscious of being inadequately prepared to make the decisions necessary to resolve the numerous prospective problems. Domestic arrangements, including finding a place to live, would have to be worked out before the fast-approaching start of term. Pressure to complete work in Weald University before leaving Sussex had prevented a hoped-for holiday in Scotland, and the long vacation had slipped past without a break.

The attractive option just then would have been a leisurely exploration of Linkirk and the Scottish Borders, which is that swathe of countryside extending south from Edinburgh to the border with England. Reluctantly, I had to defer this pleasure; the teaching term would start all too soon and before that, well, there were so many things to do. My first priority was to find the School of Chemistry to report my arrival here, if anyone was interested. There, someone might tell me what, if anything, I was obliged to do next. My luggage, deposited somewhere with a porter earlier, needed to be relocated, retrieved and transferred to my booked temporary accommodation, wherever that might be.

My trusty LU guidebook told me that the School of Chemistry was in Bond College (Sir Percy Bond had been a generous university benefactor). Happily, though I had not noticed earlier, this was where I had left my luggage on arrival by taxi. A notice in the entrance hall informed me that Bond College Complex housed the schools of agriculture, chemistry, French, psychology and Scottish studies, and a sub-department of law. Evidently, the planners saw merit in the mixing of practitioners of different disciplines. Irrelevantly, I supposed that the psychologists had been brought here to address whatever 'complex' was troubling Bond College. I also wondered whether it was by design or serendipity that the chemists were housed in the college labelled by terms so relevant to my subject: 'bond' and 'complex'!

The School of Chemistry was on Levels 9 to 12 (how could this be within a building of only four or five floors?), and the office (for all enquiries) was on Level 10. Guided by a helpful porter, I found Dr Charlotte Fanshawe's room, which was labelled 'Chemistry Office: Please Enter'. On accepting the invitation, I found myself in a room that was overcrowded with an excess of uniformly drab furniture. Around the walls stood, in aligned ranks, metal cupboards and filing cabinets of diverse military-camouflage shades, with open doors revealing shelves (over)loaded with bulky files, distended envelopes and piles of paper. A large desk, also burdened with stationery, filled the room's centre. On it was a vase containing one outstandingly beautiful, yellow rose; the flash of colour contrasted with the drab surroundings. It appeared that nobody was present.

'May I help you?' queried a middle-aged woman who appeared from behind, or perhaps even from under, the desk, where she had apparently been working; she was clutching a thick wad of papers. The offer of help appeared to be an involuntary response to my arrival, but her harassed look was undoubtedly genuine.

'I'm Bill Green, the new lecturer. I did plan to arrive tomorrow, but things changed... so now I'm here. Should I see Dr Fanshawe?' I asked.

A warm smile replaced the harassed look. 'Welcome to LU. I'm June, June Hunter, the school secretary. We're rather busy, with term starting soon. Things get a bit out of hand.' Her despair showed all too clearly as she surveyed her chaotic domain. 'I suppose it'll all work out... somehow. It usually does. But... no. Dr Fanshawe is at a meeting now and won't be back here tonight. You could see her tomorrow. Meanwhile, I've some papers for you... if I can find them...' Her search was successful eventually, and I was handed a large, overfilled envelope.

'May I ask a silly question?'

'Yes...' June sounded doubtful.

'How is this *Level 10*? It's only the second floor.'

'Oh! That's easy! All floors, or *levels*, throughout the campus are numbered upwards from the Porters' Lodge on Mains Road, which is Level 1. Because of the hill, we come out at Level 10. It's quite simple! I was told the first provost thought up the idea.'

'We all have our claims to fame. I suppose it's logical, if not particularly obvious or useful. University bosses sometimes have odd ideas.'

'You'll get used to it... you'll probably not notice it again, now you know the truth.'

'Thanks. I'll not stop your paperchase.' Immediately, her smile returned to an expression of concern.

I left the office. Once back in the corridor, I decided to explore the School of Chemistry. A locked door allowed me only to peer through a window into a teaching laboratory. The benches were covered with sets of experimental equipment, presumably to be cleaned and checked before term. Further along, the door of a large lecture theatre was open, so I entered and went behind the front bench, anticipating that I would be here soon, lecturing undergraduates. The image was unconvincing, however, as I stood in front of rows of deserted seats in the silent, cool and empty room. I viewed, with concern, a rather complicated control panel on the front bench. A switch pressed at random started closing the window curtains. I cancelled and reversed this. The next switch produced a dim light, and yet another lit the front bench. The scene could be set for a theatrical performance, which was one possible description of teaching lectures. I had just extinguished all lights when someone entered the room.

'Who's there?' It was the school director, appearing suddenly as if propelled by an external force. He was a tall, moderately heavy man, with a reddened face that could be the result of too-good living or the effort of carrying several well-filled files that (I later noticed) was an almost invariable burden during his frequent movements across the campus. On arrival, his expression was of vague disapproval, but this changed to puzzlement when he saw me; obviously, he was trying to work out who I was.

'Good afternoon, Professor McTaggart. It's Bill Green. I'm looking at the lecture theatre. The equipment here is unfamiliar. Sorry... I hope...' I began.

'Oh. It's you... er... Green. Just arrived, have you? Welcome! Yes, it's not a bad idea to explore the lie of the land. I just wondered who...? Well, you'll have to excuse me. I'm on my way to a meeting. We agreed to meet tomorrow? Yes? See you then. Bye!'

'Bye!' My echo was probably not noticed, but the prof's remark made sense when I opened the bulky envelope, recently acquired from June, to find (along with a mass of other papers) a hand-scribbled invitation from the prof to have a chat with him tomorrow. The other papers included a lecture timetable, requiring urgent study so that I could prepare my contributions to the teaching programme, starting in about four weeks. The outline content of these lectures had already been discussed and agreed by post but, up to then, had remained a non-immediate obligation, vaguely and conveniently deferrable into the future. My arrival had changed this to the necessity to prepare for my duties starting right then; lecture writing must be my top priority. Perversely, arriving in this unfamiliar and distant place, after a busy summer, had instilled a holiday mood insidiously, and a wish to indulge in a relaxed period of exploration and to settle in slowly. It was impossible; lethargy must be banished, and my chosen career commenced – immediately!

There is no time like the present! The library was open, I found a small study cubicle, and I scanned the timetable to confirm duties and dates. With textbooks to hand, I began writing my first lecture on chemical kinetics. An important term in this subject, 'activation energy', expressed my necessity neatly: what *energy* I could muster must be directed towards *activating* myself.

Later, in the small bed of my temporary accommodation, which was a guestroom in a university residence, I reminisced about my impressions of this significant day in my new career. It had been an early start to catch the plane north, but the taxi from Edinburgh Airport to LU, although expensive, had been a worthwhile investment in comfort. During the afternoon, I achieved something positive by drafting the first of my lectures. That was good! The other obligation was to think about research. I was not quite ready for that yet, but the time would come – and soon. The thought was wearying, and so, rather than worrying about future challenges, I fell into a deep and dreamless sleep.

Chapter 2

First Sunday in September

HAMPER

a. To prevent or obstruct an action

b. Container of delectable foodstuffs

'Do come to our home for dinner this Sunday evening at about 7.00pm. Regards, Angus and Elizabeth.' The handwritten note, with the address and a sketch map, had confirmed a verbal invitation. I expressed myself as 'Pleased to accept', both in writing and verbally, and was now looking forward to a pleasant evening. While living in the LU residence had some advantages, including few domestic chores, the prospect of a social evening, and perhaps meeting friendly people, was more than welcome.

Last week, my first Scottish Sabbath had proved to be a lonely experience. Never having been a regular churchgoer, I was disinclined to risk exposing my ignorance of religious practices 'in congregation', so I took a solitary walk around Linkirk, and spent the prolonged remainder of the day writing lectures. Hence, this kind invitation from the McTaggarts, on only my second Sunday here, offered some respite from the seemingly endless treadmill of preparing for my new job.

My 'interview suit', after attention from dry cleaners, was pressed into service as my only chance of appearing presentable. Its dark blue went well with my best, indeed only, smart tie of red Italian silk decorated with lilies, which are the emblem of Florence. Continuing the Italian theme, I selected a good Chianti wine, as an appropriate offering to Angus for his kind hospitality. I had not yet presumed to use this familiar form of address to Professor McTaggart; the title 'Prof' had, thus far, seemed safer. Two bunches of flowers, 'Bonnie Jeans', were combined to present to Angus's wife, Elizabeth, whom I had not yet met. I wrapped this colourful gift in matching flowery paper. Reluctantly, I decided that a taxi was a dispensable luxury. Finding the carrying of flowers through Linkirk vaguely unsettling, I held them unobtrusively, inverted beside my leg, while descending the largely deserted LU campus into town.

My hosts' address was easily found, with the grand house being a more-than-adequate expression of Prof's successful career. The stone dwelling, of the size and style favoured by Victorian mill owners, presumably had been built for one of the formerly prosperous barons of the then largely defunct local woollen industry. I mounted the steps and pressed the doorbell, impressed by its gleaming brass surround.

'Ah. Good evening, Bill. Welcome to our humble home. Do come in,' said McTaggart.

'Good evening, er... Prof. Thank you for your kind invitation,' I responded.

While I placed the flowers and wine on a large hall table, Prof hung my coat on a hanger before ushering me into the spacious and luxuriously furnished salon. Its creature comforts included a large coal fire, stoked to maximum heat output and burning expensively in the grate. Before gaining more than the slightest impression of this opulent display of affluence, I was approached by a lady who could be described (kindly) as having generous proportions and gracious demeanour. Mrs Prof, who was almost as tall as her husband, certainly carried excess weight, but moved with agility and grace. The retention of her good figure might be due to country sports, such as golf and riding, but, alternatively, her presentation could be to the credit and artifice of a skilled dressmaker. I was conscious of a vague billowing of blue silk as she wafted towards me.

'Welcome. I'm Elizabeth. You must be Dr Green. May I call you William?' she asked. (My nod seemed adequate.) 'Angus has told me all about you. It's so kind of you to join our little dinner party. Other friends will arrive soon. Please find yourself a seat and warm yourself. The evenings do get cool at this time of year, don't you think?'

Elizabeth (should I use this name when talking to her?) exuded self-confidence. She undoubtedly came from a 'good family', which had been wealthy over several generations and still maintained their accustomed dominant position in society. Her privileged education had, rather obviously, included excellent and exclusive ladies' academies. I could think of no adequate response to the warmth of her welcome. (What, for example, could Angus have told her about me?) I took the safe option: 'Good evening, Mrs McTaggart. Thank you for your kind invitation.'

Prof mentioned the flowers and brought them in. Somehow, the freshness of the blooms, which had seemed so attractive and colourful in the shop, had visibly shrunk in the grandeur of these surroundings.

'Oh… how beautiful. It's very kind of you. I am *so* fond of "Bonnie Jeans". I must put them in water at once,' declared Elizabeth.

The sound of the doorbell resulted in both my hosts withdrawing, leaving me alone for a few moments to contemplate these impressive surroundings, furnished in the style of a late Victorian withdrawing room. Clearly, off duty, Prof enjoyed the benefits of an earlier affluent lifestyle, if not entirely due to his own successful career, then perhaps from his wife's wealth. Two large, comfortable and well-used sofas, together with several grand, high-backed armchairs, epitomised the luxury of this large, overheated room. The harmonising shades of vaguely autumnal colours expressed Elizabeth's good taste, while still retaining a homely atmosphere.

Several large, slightly dark paintings represented quintessentially Scottish scenes; they were works of highly respected and now undoubtedly collectable artists. The two that held my attention were portraits of rugged and fierce-looking men, presumably ancestors, wearing kilts and bearing swords that they appeared to be ready, even keen, to deploy with potentially devastating effect. A real sword, displayed on the wall, was remarkably similar to one depicted in the painting beside it. Before I could complete my inspection of these unfamiliar-but-fascinating artefacts and decorations, the door opened to admit a short, dark girl, followed by a slightly taller man. Prof introduced me to Walter Thompson and his friend Jennifer Logan.

I already knew that Walter was a chemistry colleague, but we had not yet met, due to his absence at a conference and on university visits. I had been looking forward very much to meeting him, as it offered the welcome prospect of making a friend. I knew Walter had been appointed last year, so I hoped to succeed in finding common ground and shared interests with the only other lecturer of about my age in the school. The absence of any smile of greeting and, indeed, no acknowledgement of my existence of any kind was a distinctly unpromising start. His appearance could only be described as 'average' and – apart from an unusually serious, even withdrawn, demeanour – he seemed to have few distinguishing features. I guessed he was a year or two older than me, perhaps twenty-eight; he was clean-shaven, with short, black hair; he wore no glasses; and he was conventionally dressed in a blazer and a college tie. He was a person who would not stand out in a crowd.

I discovered quickly that my attempts to start a conversation were of little or no interest to Walter, who maintained an appearance of bored indifference. When we were all seated, and everyone had chosen from the several sherries on offer, I addressed him directly. 'Was the conference interesting? Where was it?'

There was no immediate response. Assuming that my questions had not been heard, I was about to repeat them when Walter condescended to give me a disconcerting glance and the distinctly discouraging reply, 'Obviously, it was *interesting*, otherwise I should not have gone.' There was another pause. 'It was at an exclusive conference centre in California. It's new. I doubt you'd have heard of it.'

Any prospect of a friendly chat was disappearing rapidly; evidently, Walter's social skills did not extend to small talk or even include good manners. His attitude signalled a clear disinclination to communicate, with all responses apparently addressed to the floor rather than to me. Discomfited, I tried again. 'Did you present a paper?'

Again came a pause. 'Yes… *obviously*.' He then gave the unusually long scientific title of his presentation, which was of such obscurity that no one outside a small group of specialists could possibly be expected to know what (if anything) it was about. Jargon can be, and is, used to conceal meanings effectively from the uninitiated, and, as clearly intended now, ended successfully my attempts to talk with him about anything at all.

Walter, noticing that Prof had finished stoking the fire, took his opportunity, saying, 'Angus, Werner Ostwald asked me if you'd give a plenary lecture at their autumn meeting in Stuttgart next year. In mid-September, I think.'

'That's a bit difficult… No, I'll be in the States at that polymer meeting,' Prof responded.

The ensuing conversation between Angus and Walter excluded me from what rapidly became a private discussion. I was sitting too far from Jennifer, the only other person in the room, to talk to her. Like her 'friend' Walter, she showed no inclination to talk to anyone, appearing bored and perhaps even wanting *not* to indulge in social chit-chat. So, excluded from the present company, I resumed my examination of the paintings and ornaments. Perhaps it had not been a great idea to accept this invitation.

A few moments later, this depressing situation ended as suddenly and as unexpectedly as it had started. Elizabeth returned and loudly interrupted Walter in mid-sentence. 'Now you men must *not* talk shop. We ladies are excluded, and we cannot have that!' She had returned from the kitchen presumably, but was no longer alone. Beside her was a tall, slim girl in her mid-twenties, with shoulder-length, wavy, auburn hair, and who was wearing a loose-but-fashionable trouser suit of pale green.

I looked at the newcomer with a surge of pleasure and undivided attention. Never ever had I experienced such a spontaneous feeling of complete certainty that this was a delightful person. My unprecedented reaction to her appearance was more profound than I had ever known previously, surprising even myself. The phrase 'love at first sight' passed through my aroused feelings. The reason for such an immediate appeal was not explained easily (or able to be analysed just then). Perhaps it was the vivacity clearly evident in her bright face: her greenish eyes were alive constantly, showing interest and pleasure in everything around her. She had such a lovely smile, which was bestowed equally on everyone in turn; I fastened onto it and it held my attention more intensely than I would have thought possible. This feeling of an 'attractive force' was like nothing I had ever known previously, and it distinctly disturbed me. The evening had definitely taken a turn for the better. I also noted, automatically but with interest, that she wore no ring and was unescorted; perhaps this was evidence that she remained a free spirit. I detached my stare from this almost-hypnotic centre of interest only with conscious effort.

The newcomer was Beth Wilkinson. 'My full name is Elizabeth, but my friends call me Beth,' she explained. She was introduced as the daughter of the McTaggarts' close friends, who had also been invited to this evening gathering. However, her mother, who was on holiday in Cornwall with her father, had suffered a fall, fracturing her hip. The hospital there had advised them to defer returning home until the medical staff judged the invalid sufficiently recovered to travel. This unfortunate accident and other family news were reviewed, much of which was of as little interest to me as the earlier esoteric chemistry. However, while Beth talked, I could take a legitimate interest in what she said, without the rudeness of appearing to stare.

When these topics had run their course, she moved to an occasional chair beside Walter, who – I gathered – she already knew, and they started talking together! Dismayed by this, I wondered why such a lively and attractive person should choose to sit beside the colleague whom I had found so withdrawn and boorish. Thinking about it, I wondered why this was of any interest to me whatsoever.

Elizabeth, the consummate hostess, allowed Beth to finish her sherry before announcing dinner: 'I think we might eat now.' She added that apologies just had been received from John and Alison Bland, who also were unable to join us this evening. An unexpected crisis involving a parent had demanded their immediate support, and so our party was much smaller than planned. To me she added as an aside, 'I'm sorry that you'll not meet John socially.'

John Bland, another chemistry professor, was my immediate superior. I could hardly claim to know him, though we had met briefly, during and after my interview.

'Angus, the fire, please?' she asked, but he was already placing a substantial fire-screen around it.

The dining room complemented what Elizabeth described as the 'withdrawing room', but here the paintings depicted game birds of species that had, undoubtedly, appeared on this dining table fairly frequently. The *Stag by the Lake* above the fireplace could also be seen as equally and similarly relevant.

Elizabeth took charge, directing the meal with control and finesse that would have been the envy of many a celebrated maestro conducting a full orchestra performing a major musical work. Places were allocated around the faultlessly presented table: each with a white linen napkin, two wineglasses and a tumbler for iced water. We took our seats, with our hosts at the table ends and guests between, spaced rather widely due to our diminished numbers. My modest offering of 'Bonnie Jeans', by then miraculously revived apparently (how was that achieved?), were in a vase between candleholders that were surely sterling silver. My gift was mentioned.

'Angus, after I'd presented our paper, I was asked—' began Walter.

He was interrupted by Elizabeth with a firmness and confidence that I could only admire, though – surprisingly – I even felt a modicum of sympathy for Walter. The sharp intrusion could only have been carried off by someone absolutely certain of the justice of her cause and long accustomed to deference from 'other ranks'.

'No, Walter; no!' she declared, 'You have all week to discuss your academic acrobatics and your chemical conundrums. Now I'm asking you to be courteous to our guests and observe the social niceties of civilised conversation that can include everyone. You men would talk shop endlessly, given half a chance.'

'Half chances' were obviously not on tonight's menu.

A distinctly surly look appeared on Walter's face: the scowl to which he had treated me earlier. It seemed highly unlikely that he would participate in any alternative conversational topic, so Angus filled the vacuum skilfully. 'Bill, I noticed you brought a Chianti wine to us this evening. Thank you. Does wine interest you?'

'As you know, I worked in Florence University briefly. It's almost impossible to live in Italy without learning about wines. I didn't need too much encouragement,' I explained.

'How interesting. Do you speak Italian?' queried Elizabeth, supporting her husband.

'Italians are kind at helping foreigners speak their language, and they encouraged my poor efforts. I found that I could communicate, at a basic level, without too much trouble. Before going there, I took some evening classes.'

'Chianti is south of Florence, isn't it?' Elizabeth asked.

'Yes, you're right. Have you been there?' I was interested.

'Angus and I had one short holiday in Italy. We drove through several wine-growing regions – it's almost inevitable, I know – but I think we included Chianti. I remember little except the excessive heat and humidity. It was too hot, being July or August.'

'Perhaps we might open the bottle you have so thoughtfully brought, if anyone would like to taste it,' suggested the Prof, who then fetched the wine and drew the cork.

I glanced at Walter, across the table, and saw little to suggest that he had any interest.

As the drink was poured, I explained my choice of wine: 'I was pleased to find this particular vintage in Linkirk, because it was one of the most palatable that some of us enjoyed when we visited Greve, the capital of Chianti, one September. There is an "official tasting" of one of the local vintages, Black Cockerel, which is uncorked only after it has matured for two years. At this wine festival, you buy a wine glass for a token sum and then tour the many stalls in the town square, which is actually triangular. Each vintner gives you several wines to taste, but, after a few, I found it difficult to recall tastes and to maintain discrimination. It was a convivial evening. Happily, one of our party was teetotal, unlike many Italians, and our sober driver returned us safely to Florence.'

The Chianti wine, served to accompany the excellent steak, was pronounced most palatable, and conversation languished while the food was given the attention it so richly deserved. The atmosphere relaxed somewhat when second helpings of meat, rich gravy, crisp roast potatoes and vegetables were offered – and accepted.

Conversation ranged widely across varied topics, though chemistry and university politics remained taboo. Recent changes to Linkirk's traffic regulations were criticised. The consensus was that these had little merit, serving only to confuse the unfortunate motorists. Jennifer expressed her strong views, mainly because 'her' road had inexplicably become one-way. (I think this was the only time she spoke.) The range of dresses offered by a new fashion boutique in High Street was discussed, almost exclusively by Elizabeth, who was unhappy about the limited choices available for a woman with a 'fuller figure'. Beth, with no such problem, said little. I found the limitation on conversational topics distinctly unusual for a group of academics, where shop is usually the principal, even only, subject for discussion. Angus was certainly a dominant personality in LU, but, here at home, a different hierarchical pecking order ruled. Walter contributed virtually nothing, opening his mouth only to satisfy his large appetite and drink the quality wines that were dispensed generously by Angus.

The choice of sweets was either tiramisu or tropical-fruit salad with plum brandy. Elizabeth cajoled, 'Please try both.' She said that the former was in honour of my visit. 'I've never made it before, and I hope my amateur effort is acceptable.'

I tried my generous serving. 'Yes, it's excellent. I've never tasted better in Italy.'

The complement, sincerely meant, was echoed around the table. Strictly, my comment was not an untruth, but only because I had never previously tasted this confection in Italy or elsewhere. Its flavour appealed to my sweet tooth. I added, 'The Italian name, tiramisu, means "pick me up". The ingredients are regarded as a restorative and are intended to provide energy; sugar, coffee, some alcohol and eggs, I think.'

Beth mentioned she had visited an exhibition of paintings recently, which were by a young local artist, of Italian ancestry, who had now achieved a 'one woman show' in a reputable Edinburgh gallery. 'I admired her landscape paintings in the gallery; you know, the one that used to be in Cross Street. Dad bought one there.'

Both McTaggarts agreed that her pictures were interesting, but it remained unsaid that nothing painted during the last century or so was likely to grace the walls of their home.

Beth persisted. 'I found her new style... really garish... and disappointing. Through half-closed eyes, I could discern vague patterns... but I'd never buy one, even if I could afford the prices she's asking now, which I certainly can't.'

Our hosts expressed a lack of interest in abstract painting, saying, 'We just don't understand it.' Instead, they recalled art galleries visited abroad: 'Including Florence's Uffizi Gallery, after we'd been to Chianti.' The inconvenient necessity to queue for entry there apparently rated equally, or more memorably, than the masterpieces on display.

'Perhaps I should mention an amusing comment heard in the Uffizi Gallery.' Belatedly, I wondered if this story would be appropriate, but, having committed myself, I had to continue. 'I don't usually eavesdrop on conversations between strangers, but on reaching *The Holy Family*, the famous portrayal by Michelangelo, two Americans were already admiring it. One turned to the other and, after glancing at his guidebook, said with genuine admiration, "Gee, that guy Cinquecento sure could paint!"'

The laughter round the table seemed genuine enough.

'I don't understand. Is this some kind of anti-American joke? Who's this Sisken-whatever?' Walter, apparently angry, had broken his silence unexpectedly. From his heightened colour and the belligerent look he threw across the table, it was clear that the wine had done nothing to mellow his feelings towards me.

My forebodings had been justified. This story had not been appropriate in the present company, and his question still required an answer. '"*Cinquecento*" translates as "sixteenth century". Michelangelo is an artist who most visitors to the world-renowned Uffizi Gallery might be expected to recognise, if they had sufficient interest go there. I didn't intend to be anti-anyone; people of all nations can show ignorance.'

'Then why stress that they were *American?*'

'No stress was intended. They *were* American, as I think I made clear. I'm sorry if the story offended you. That was not my intention, I assure you.'

'Walter has nothing to be offended about.' Elizabeth had taken the initiative and closed the topic firmly. 'Now, if I can't persuade anyone to have some more…? Perhaps we might go next door to drink our coffee in comfort.'

I let the others return and approached my hostess. 'I'm sorry if my story—'

'No, no. Don't worry. Walter has these moods. He's angry because I refused to let him start some science monologue that would exclude everyone and everything else. His irritation was, I assure you, directed at me. Your story was an excuse for him to remind us all of his self-importance. His real problem is that he suffers badly from a lack of self-confidence, and I'm afraid it's getting worse…' After a short pause, she continued, 'It's probably not for me to say this, but I'll give you a hint. His feelings of inferiority could well make him a difficult colleague for you. He doesn't know you and probably resents your appointment here. He could be difficult to work with. But don't quote me; I've said nothing.' She grinned, looking suddenly like a mischievous twelve-year-old. 'Go and join the others. I'll bring the coffee through directly.'

An offer to help was waved aside. Elizabeth was smiling as she left, but the possibility of enjoying my coffee had receded rapidly.

Our hostess's temporary absence was being exploited by Walter, who was bringing Angus up to date with news of his travels. I sat near Beth who, either by chance or choice, was outside the 'conference conclave', so it was natural that we should chat together. Again, I felt as if I was in strong magnetic field (or something of the kind); attractive forces that centred on my neighbour seemingly grew in intensity when I came closer to her. My appreciation of the good fortune that allowed me to enjoy her undivided attention had the perverse effect of making me tongue-tied in my attempts to avoid putting a foot wrong. While I was trying to reduce the feeling of high blood pressure (and unmix my anatomical metaphors), *she* did most of the talking. My wish to appear calm (if only outwardly), while thinking up suitable and sensible things to say, persisted throughout our conversation together.

I learned, with some pleasure, that she had been mildly amused by Walter's recent discomfiture. She had known him for many years, but only as a friend of her brother. This was followed by the news that she had returned home to Linkirk only recently, to teach in a local primary school after a spell of similar work in London.

She explained, 'It didn't suit me. I was delighted to get back home.' Her father, the manager of a local bank, had supported her 'unfortunate London debacle' (her words), which 'had cost a fortune'.

In turn, I told her that my job interview had been my first ever visit to Linkirk, indeed to Scotland, and that, so far, I had found the town to be a pleasant place to live. Coming from distant Sussex, I looked forward to exploring the local countryside and seeing how the Scottish Borders scenery differed from the south of England. My rather broad hint that I would appreciate her advice on which parts of Tweeddale merited visiting was left unanswered. Just as I was about to suggest tactfully that we could meet sometime soon so that she could advise me about local beauty spots and attractions, the ritual of dispensing coffee commenced. Our chat was effectively terminated at that critical point to help ourselves to cream or milk, and sugar (demerara).

Meanwhile, Prof was dispensing liqueurs, prompting my selection discreetly from the several single malt whiskies on offer. My eventual choice (effectively his!) turned out to be the fiercest drink I had ever imbibed. After the first, admittedly generous, sip, it took me several moments to recover my equanimity. When my aural affliction had abated and my ability to sense external stimuli had been partially restored, I heard Angus outlining his plans to visit the 'ancestral home' (perhaps Elizabeth's?) soon. This would be a welcome diversion to provide much-needed relaxation, before he faced 'the rigors of term'.

I felt a strong twinge of envy, being reminded painfully of my own commitments and the amount of work I had to complete during the short time before I also would experience the rigors of my first term. Mine would undoubtedly be much greater, but I had no possibility of making any such excursion.

Elizabeth continued the theme by telling us about the health problems besetting her elderly relatives, which required a family get-together to resolve.

By then, I was struggling to finish the whisky. I decided reluctantly that it was impracticable to dispose of the remaining fiery drink privately by decanting it into a nearby pot containing a tropical-looking plant, as the action might be noticed. At the same time, I was trying to maintain an appearance of interest in what was being said, though the firewater had made it impossible for me to take part in the conversation.

Suddenly, Beth exclaimed, 'Goodness. Is it that time already? I don't want to break up the party, but I've got an early start tomorrow and must go. Thank you, Elizabeth. It was a wonderful meal and great company! I've enjoyed the evening immensely. Thank you, Angus. Good night, all. Bye for now.'

The remaining three of us expressed a similar appreciation and also prepared to depart. Walter, it appeared, had once again restarted his private discussions with Angus. I gave my own thanks, principally to Elizabeth, while delaying my exit sufficiently to allow Beth to leave, presumably in her own car. I had no wish either to appear to be seeking a lift or to have to refuse any offer of transport that she might feel obliged to make. Walter, as I anticipated correctly, did not deign to notice my existence. In my present state of emotional overload, to say nothing about that last drink, it was preferable to walk the short distance back to the campus alone. This might aid digestion, and, with luck, give my head a chance to clear.

○

Retracing my earlier path through the then almost deserted streets and ascending the LU campus hill, I recalled the sharply conflicting emotions that had been aroused during this interesting, and generally pleasant, evening. The strengths and contrasts of my responses to these new acquaintances disturbed me profoundly.

On the one hand, I hardly could bear to allow myself think of Beth, so strong were my feelings of attraction. Indeed, it was difficult – 'impossible' was a more realistic description – to put her out of my mind. I *did* want to see her again: Yes, yes and yes again! But how and why might such a meeting ever take place? More importantly, how would *she* feel about it? I had no idea. Realistically, it was unlikely that our paths would ever cross again, so that, however painful to me, our brief but wonderfully pleasurable (for me) encounter was already history. No doubt, in time, my strong (magnetic?) feelings of attraction to her would fade.

The situation with Walter offered an unpleasant contrast in all respects. The professional relationship that bound us together (though now it seemed more like something we would have to endure together) was in an entirely different category. Due to working in the same school, inevitably, we would come into regular or even frequent contact. His (marginal) seniority and intentional hostility, if sustained, would be hard to bear, even allowing for Elizabeth's private comments. What could I do about it? Possibly very little or, more realistically, probably nothing. To simply endure it was not a welcome prospect.

Altogether, the evening had provoked unexpectedly disparate, even desperate, and certainly disturbing thoughts. This was particularly distressing just then when I needed a clear and untroubled mind to work myself into my new job. How I could and should proceed required immediate and serious consideration. But not tonight.

Chapter 3

FIRST MONDAY OF SEPTEMBER

CONVERSE

a. Communicate by talking

b. An alternative viewpoint; contrariety

I WAS NOW AN *OFFICIAL* STAFF MEMBER OF THE LU SCHOOL OF Chemistry; *my* name had appeared on the door of *my* academic office, which now bore the label 'Dr William GREEN, Lecturer in Chemistry'. With the first positive step of my career achieved, I was now perched (perhaps precariously) on the lowest rung of the 'academic ladder'. Previously, as a fellow at Weald University, a handwritten label on a shared room had epitomised impermanence. At LU, I had every opportunity to start worthwhile research, which is essential to academic advancement, though my abilities still had to be proven.

I viewed my, admittedly basic, accommodation with a touch of proprietorial pride, though blank walls and empty bookcases maintained the ambience of a still untenanted office. The room was bright, with walls repainted recently in magnolia, reflecting sunshine from the large window facing south across the pleasing Scottish Borders hills. I briefly surveyed this agreeable panorama from my large desk, sitting on the least uncomfortable of the three upholstered-but-unyielding and already-well-used seats, all wooden, worn and wobbly. Additional stackable chairs, also far from new, formed an untidy pile in one corner. These were presumably for student tutorials, using the principle that 'designed discomfort does discourage dozing'. The standard furniture issued to LU lecturers could be described (kindly) as utilitarian. The depressing-grey filing cabinet remained empty. The chore of distributing my recently arrived books and papers was deferred until I could find the necessary energy. Later would do! A nagging headache persisted, presumably resulting from that last strong whisky that Prof had 'recommended' after dinner last evening. That day, my thought processes were definitely the worse for wear, or perhaps whisky.

The only new item in my office was a computer, which I switched on to review emails. Numerous messages were deleted without conscious thought, including offers of unrequired/unrequested products, cash loans, and prizes I'd apparently 'already won!' (how?) were positively unwelcome. The few real messages brought pleasure; there were two from former colleagues now in distant places, summarising their news and good wishes, but replies could wait.

Without conscious intent, I found and opened my favourite electronic card game, provided (free!) as an indispensable service, or attraction/distraction, by the computer manufacturer. In principle, I regard such frivolity as excessively time-wasting, but, in practice, I have to confess that my disapproval had become more theoretical recently. Too often I used such games to procrastinate, deferring the effort necessary to start serious work. I liked to regard myself as an adept, or mild addict, winning most contests against the machine, after repeated practice with this favourite electronic challenge. This morning, however, my skills were at a low ebb; three failed games yielded the machine's pseudo-apology of 'Sorry! You have lost.' I turned off the computer following this unwelcome confirmation that my mental processes today were not in good form.

On a 'thank you' card from the campus shop, I wrote 'It is my pleasure to express sincere appreciation for your welcome and a wonderful dinner in your lovely and comfortable home' and addressed it to Mrs Elizabeth McTaggart. After rereading, it seemed appropriate to add 'I was privileged to be invited and enjoyed the occasion immensely.' The too-short note had become too long, even effusive. After further contemplation, I decided that, in my slightly fragile state, this was the best I could currently manage. Only then did I notice, with surprise, that the flowers featured on the card were 'Bonnie Jeans'. Without further consideration of whether or not this was suitable, which was a mental feat beyond my ability at that point, I sealed the blue envelope to post.

This task naturally prompted pleasurable daydreams about the happy moments of last evening. Not for the first time that day, Beth's image appeared unbidden in my mind's eye. My depression lifted somewhat on recalling the many memorable aspects of that all-too-fleeting encounter. I decided that, of all the girls of my acquaintance, Beth was – by a large margin – the most attractive and charming I had ever met. But optimistic musings and hopes that the contact might be repeated were rudely dispelled by the more realistic view that I would probably never see her again.

Unwilling to contemplate this unwelcome prospect, I reviewed the attitudes of my colleagues off duty. The spontaneous hostility shown by Walter Thompson had been an unwelcome shock, and if this attitude was maintained at work, it could make my life here difficult, or worse. I preferred not to dwell on this unpleasant possibility just then. Equally worrying was the ambiguous behaviour shown by Angus. When his wife was present, he behaved as the ideal, welcoming host, but he had rather obviously transferred his full attention to Walter as soon as she withdrew.

While trying to work out how these attitudes could affect my future, the telephone rang. After a brief indecision as to whether, in my present fragile state, it might be better to leave it unanswered, I decided that a response would be politic. Later, an explanation for ignoring the call might be difficult to fabricate.

'Hello,' I said on picking up the receiver.

'John Bland here,' he confirmed.

'Good morning, Professor.'

'I wondered if you're going to the coffee room soon?'

Presumably this was a question, not a statement. 'Yes. Any time now.'

'I think we should have a short meeting. Will you come to my room now?'

After agreeing, I thought about the possible reasons for this hastily convened meeting. Prof was my immediate superior, within the supremely hierarchical structure that is university governance. For me, the most pressing reason for a discussion with my boss was an overdue, then urgent, overall review of my teaching duties. Apart from lectures, my other teaching duties – including laboratory supervisions and tutorials – remained incompletely decided. The timetable for undergraduate courses, received only after my arrival, included few details, and the Staff Handbook gave little more.

I found it inexplicable that, so far, my training had included no formal instruction in educational theory or techniques, despite my appointment as a *lecturer* (as stated on the door!). In about two weeks, I was contracted to teach students – lecturing and in laboratories – on diverse aspects of my specialist subject. How should I manage this? No detailed guidance about contents of *my* courses had been given by the professors, who were 'in charge of and responsible for all teaching' (according to the Staff Handbook). So, during the short time before term started, apparently, I alone would have to decide what to include in my courses. This considerable challenge taxed my woefully limited experience. I had already worked out that the only possible way to cope was to (re-)present the contents of the lectures I had attended at the same stages of my own undergraduate studies. (It was possible, even highly likely, that this material had already undergone similar recycling by my teachers, from even earlier courses.) I now appreciated that the quite arbitrary decision to retain all my lecture notes (which were only readable by me!) had been of much greater value than I could have anticipated. Recycling (perhaps again) these notes that had enabled me to graduate with a good degree was, undoubtedly, the safest policy or, more realistically, the only way to get by during this first year. Next year, assuming I was still here, the situation could be reviewed from a more mature perspective – hopefully!

Nevertheless, as a *lecturer*, I felt obliged to rework my second-hand notes, upgrading the content, particularly where I had experienced difficulties myself. To teach, I had to understand *everything* I was presenting and not omit those areas of ignorance that I had managed to conceal from the examiners. There was, however, no certainty that I possessed the skills required to transform my older notes into stimulating new lectures. Perhaps 'beginner's keenness' might enable me to present my subject in a form that would engage undergraduate interest. Time would soon reveal if such youthful enthusiasm would be acceptable to and comprehendible by my audiences.

This absence of appropriate training was worrying, and it overlaid my limited, positive self-concept with negative forebodings. Such doubts must be concealed when I faced my classes, where my attention-holding abilities would be tested rigorously very soon. My unpreparedness for some impending duties was uppermost in my mind when going to this impromptu meeting with my boss. I had no idea how these worries might be alleviated, but hoped Prof might be able to disperse some concerns, at this late stage, though I was far from optimistic that this prospect was realistic...

○

A short time later, I went to his office, as requested. His door label was 'Professor John Bland, Professor of Physical Chemistry, and Secretary'. The anonymous secretary was Miss Ruth Cameron, a spinster in her mid-fifties, who oversaw the administrative duties of our sub-department. She was courteous and efficient, though overworked and over-impressed by Prof, whom she rated almost as highly as he did himself.

'Do go in, Dr Green. Prof's expecting you,' she offered.

I did as I was bid. His room was exactly twice the size of mine: Professors occupied two units of accommodation space. His desk was also larger and his chairs (all with arms) were more comfortable and less worn than mine. A standard-issue LU computer was on a side table, the screen turned to the wall, suggesting it was rarely or, more probably, never used. Several filing cabinets, of different-but-unmatching military-camouflage shades, were distributed around the walls. Prof's bookcases were superior due to being fronted with glass doors and well filled. Otherwise, our rooms were remarkably similar, with magnolia walls and a southerly outlook.

John Bland sat at his desk; he was a bespectacled, rotund or indeed overweight man of medium height and aged about sixty. He was quite bald and pink; his overall appearance strongly resembled a recently and well-washed baby. I wondered if his roseate colouring was evidence of an unhealthy heart condition. (Later, I noticed that the pink hue darkened perceptibly towards a dangerously dark shade of red when he became agitated.) He appeared to be smiling now, though it was difficult to be sure.

'Come in… er… Bill. Do sit down. Have you had coffee?' he asked.

'Good morning, Prof. No, I've not yet had coffee,' I confirmed.

'We might go along later… together, but… now, we've a meeting to have.'

'Yes. But, first, may I ask about your parents? We were sorry you weren't at the McTaggarts' last night. We were told your parents are not in good health.' It sounded stilted, even to me, though my concern was sincere.

'McTaggarts? Yes. Er… the health of my parents? It's not good at all. Old age has its problems that are not easily resolved. Progress is being made. We – that is, my wife and I – hope we can do something… Last evening was pleasant?'

'Yes. Very pleasant.'

Conversation lapsed. After a long interval of silence, I felt obliged to take some initiative, if only to express a positive interest in our meeting. 'I've written lectures for the A11 course and started on the B14 set.'

'What's that? I thought you'd come to talk about your research programme,' Bland stated.

I was at once disorientated, though similar experiences of being wrong-footed were all too familiar. On numerous previous occasions, I had encountered comparable non-sequiturs in conversations with senior academic colleagues, often long-serving Professors. Now my problem was to work out what my 'Boss' expected, by attempting to guess the probable course of his reasoning and what he wanted from me. Apparently, I should have anticipated, without any proffered clues, Prof's (arbitrary) agenda for this unexpected meeting. The puzzled look on Prof's face suggested genuine surprise at my perversity, rather than any deliberate attempt by him to discomfort a junior. I tried again; surely he would recognise my priorities. 'It's urgent that I prepare for my teaching. Soon, when my lecture notes are written, I can concentrate on research.' I should have foreseen the futility of this approach.

'I suppose that's one way of looking at it.' His tone and look implied that such a view must be regarded as unusual, if not downright eccentric. His response continued as though he were enlightening an immature person who was totally unfamiliar with the workings of universities, or even a small child having difficulties with a simple idea. His 'helpful' and patronising homily, delivered to dispel my ignorance, sounded as if it had been lifted verbatim from the Staff Handbook: 'As an LU lecturer, you are expected to carry out original research. It can, of course, be on a topic of your own choosing. Anything you publish in reputable journals may be helpful in advancing your personal career when we review your status in the school, later this year. We will then decide whether we can offer you a position as a member of our *permanent* staff. Later, research achievements are important, if and when you may be considered for promotion. My advice to you is to start *good* research as soon as possible.'

This gratuitous statement of the obvious, unnecessarily stressing my vulnerable position, angered me. My response, starting, 'You pompous, patronising bastard...' remained suppressed, but only through heroic efforts of self-control. Despite the headache, which was still there, I somehow managed a calm and reasonable tone. 'I've got several projects in prospect, as mentioned at my interview [John Bland had been on the board]. I'll start on those as soon as I can. You mentioned that you might find me a research student. Is this still likely?' I had been keen to ask this question, but had delayed because hope, however tenuous, was preferable to a final negative answer.

'Could be. Could be,' he replied.

These words were meaningless, with neither tone nor facial expression adding any clues. Was it 'No,' meant kindly? Or was he hinting that a research student might somehow be 'found' to work with me? Uncertainty remained unresolved by a change of subject.

'Here's another prospect you might like to consider.' He handed me a visiting card. 'These people made enquiries, mentioning they *might* sponsor a research project. If you're interested, contact that name. I'll leave you to make contact, but tell me of any progress.'

'Do you know what they want done?' I enquired.

'Not exactly, but probably to clean up waste and environmental pollution. Talk to that man; his name's on the card. Telephone him to discuss it with him. Now, you mentioned coffee.'

The point of this last comment was unclear. Meetings with this man differed in form and content from sane conversations with normal people in that they lacked essential coherence of structure and content. I believed it not unreasonable to expect that *professors* should be appointed for their excellent communication skills. People with that hubristic title should be capable of expressing viewpoints clearly, perhaps not always concisely, but what they say should be recognisably logical. Up to then, I had seen little evidence that my current 'Boss' possessed the clarity of thought that might reasonably be expected of academics. However, it seemed that our meeting had achieved its intended purpose, at least for one of us.

'Thank you, Prof. You've been most helpful,' I concluded, and with that I left the room. Aware of having uttered a palpable falsehood, I had seen no other way of ending our meeting. One thing was now quite clear to me: maintaining reasonable career prospects in LU was going to require tact by the bucketful.

Once back in the corridor, I decided I could go to indulge in the long-anticipated coffee, possibly complemented by a relaxing and social chat with colleagues. The decision being made, I walked to the coffee room, where I helped myself to the only beverage available: warm water indifferently flavoured with instant granules. The nasty taste they left in my mouth joined others left over from the meeting.

Being attracted by his friendly wave, I sat beside Doug Montgomery, whom I had not seen since my arrival, when he had welcomed me to LU with his unorthodox opinions on university life. He appeared slightly uneasy, though his greeting was friendly: 'Hello, er... Bill. How's life treating you? All's well, I hope?'

I assured him, 'Although I'm busy, things are going as well as can be expected. I'm settling in... slowly. I'm finding getting started here requires a lot of effort.'

After a slight pause, he stated, 'I think I owe you an apology.' Doug noticed my surprise. 'Oh, yes. I hope you'll excuse me. My welcome to you was not as warm as it should've been. My critical views on academic life were hardly a suitable topic to bore you with when you'd just arrived here all keen, bright-eyed and bushy-tailed. I'm sorry if my introduction to LU lacked good taste.'

'Not at all. What you did say – at least, what I remember of it – intrigued me. I'd be interested to hear it all again... sometime soon. Certainly, I took no offence.'

'It's kind of you to say so. Things've been rather difficult for me recently, though that's no excuse. I'm just back from a few days with my parents, and I feel more like my normal self. I'm sorry for my less than welcoming... welcome. Tell me, may I do anything to help you get started here?'

'Perhaps you'll help resolve something that's puzzling me. I've just had a *meeting* with John Bland. I haven't a clue what it was all about.'

'You're not the first. He got top marks in the obfuscation paper when he graduated. How he ever became a prof, I'll never understand. What do you want to know?'

'Why he felt it so important to tell me *again* that I *must* start research.'

'Which you happened to know already. Right?'

'Exactly. The fact that I've done almost nothing in that direction since I got here is a nagging worry. I believe that my first priority is lecture preparation, and I still think it's most urgent. I'm finding too many things that must be done immediately and wonder if I'll ever cope.'

'Just listen to your Uncle Doug. "Let not the bastards thee dismay," which is a traditional, old Scottish proverb that I've just made it up. Everyone has self-doubt when starting. You're not the first. But, realistically, it's up to you, and you alone, to survive these trials and tribulations as best you can. Do you want me to go on?'

'Please do. I need reassurance.'

'I don't usually do *reassurance*. I'll only mention, *not offer*, advice that helped me in a similar situation, ages ago. A colleague, now sadly no longer with us, told me to make sure that I always set and stuck to my own agenda. Unrequested advice usually has little value and, mostly, none at all. People who simplify your problems probably... no, I should say *almost certainly*... don't understand just why you find a particular situation difficult. If they did, then they might properly appreciate your problem. So, free advice is often just that: *free* of value and therefore *worthless*. Don't let offered simple solutions fluster you, because these can only upset your own better judgement and ability to cope. You do as *you* think fit; after all, it's you that must face the consequences. Make your own mistakes, not those given freely by unqualified advisers… and that includes me.'

After a brief pause, he continued, 'Let me tell you a silly story about John Bland. You know he has a reputation for stinginess? Don't expect him to buy you a pint or even a half. Anyway, after returning from a conference in some inflation-ridden country, he *gave* a colleague a pile of paper currency. Amazed by this sudden and unexpected generosity, Jack counted his gift, only to find that its value was a grand total of 13p!'

Doug's support was welcome, and my spirits revived sufficiently to ask, 'Prof gave me this card and suggested, I think, that I should ring this person. He said he might sponsor me to do some research. Is this worth pursuing?'

Doug read the card. 'Industrial dirty washing. Yes, I… we all know this name. Up to now, he's had no takers, as far as I've heard. Not for his want of trying.'

'What do you mean? Industrial dirty washing? Prof did mention rubbish.'

'Rubbish. That's rich from him. I won't make the obvious riposte. Why don't we meet for lunch? I'll discuss it with you then. That is, if I haven't bored you enough already. OK? See you later.'

I disposed of the then cold coffee and returned to my office, where I thought about the advice from both Prof and Doug. I felt my life was becoming too complicated to manage. Finding time to plan, becoming more efficient and establishing priorities seemed to have got beyond my ability to cope. The headache had now faded sufficiently for me to continue lecture preparations (taking Doug's advice to pursue my own agenda).

◎

The university's Staff Club dining room was busy, though Doug and I managed to find a table to ourselves. The battered fish with chips on offer was hot and crispy, contrasting with the mushy peas.

'It reminds me of Yorkshire,' Doug said, before asking, 'Have you been asked to Angus's for dinner yet?'

'Yes, last evening. It was quite an occasion. I enjoyed it, with one exception...'

'That whisky? Yes? It's something of a challenge for the uninitiated. It requires a government health warning. It shouldn't be offered to the innocent.'

'Is everyone invited?'

'Usually, yes. Elizabeth likes to meet the recruits. If you're accepted, you'll be asked again; others languish for years in the wilderness. I've not been there recently.'

'May I ask a difficult question? I don't know whether I've done something wrong, but I've got no one else to talk to.'

'Ask away, though difficult questions are usually difficult to answer.'

'Walter Thompson was there, and I found him exceptionally brusque and unfriendly.'

'Nothing new there. Walter is singularly lacking in all the social graces, as you've obviously noticed already. He's insecure. He was exceptionally lucky to get the lecturer job last year. Maybe I'm wrong, and perhaps I shouldn't tell you this, but there's a rumour he might soon be promoted to a readership. The idea was probably started by our Walter himself. He's cultivated Angus assiduously, and that's where the real patronage lies. It's far too early for him to expect promotion, but he lives in hope. He probably thinks your appointment is using up money that could have benefitted him, so now he feels resentful and he enjoys that. Don't let him rile you.'

'But... I'm hardly to blame for being appointed.'

'Agreed. But who knows what logic, if any, governs the irreproachable decisions made by our Facilitation Centre? The fact is that you're here now. For the moment, perhaps you should minimise all contact with Walter, while his present mood lasts. Be as pleasant as you can manage, but don't overdo it. As for me, I'd prefer to keep my distance from him, but without making it too... too obvious.'

'Apropos of our earlier conversation, should I pursue the contact Prof gave me?'

'I really don't know. It's one of those conundrums where only you can judge what's best for you… and live with the consequences. Honestly, I can't offer any useful advice.' After a short pause, Doug asked hesitantly, 'Bill, would you be interested in sharing a flat or, should I say, apartment?'

This totally unexpected offer was received gratefully. In the next few days, I had to agree either to stay in the expensive university residence for the complete term or to move out very soon. My preference was to live off-campus, though – because of my preoccupation with lecture writing – I had not yet found any suitable accommodation. Now, it seemed that this problems might, with luck, have been solved without effort. 'The quick answer is…' My voice tailed off.

Doug noticed my sudden change of expression from spontaneous enthusiasm to concern, wariness and perhaps even alarm. 'No. No. No. I'm not making any proposal… or proposition. There's no hidden agenda. You can take the offer at face value.'

'You had me worried for a second. But… yes. Yes, I am very interested.'

'As I said, I've had problems recently. The wife and I may soon part and go our own ways. It was a poorly kept secret that I was playing away from home, and Gwen found out. She's of the unforgiving type, as I well knew, but, to be fair, she's got right on her side. I still hope that we might repair the damage, for the sake of the kids, if nothing else. But it's best to move out now, and so I've rented a small flat. Originally, I'd planned to share with Jack Roberts, but I learned today that he's off back to Cardiff. He's got a role as chair and is now a prof, the lucky so-and-so. So there's a vacancy, and it could be mutually beneficial for us to share costs, if you'd consider it. Are you interested?'

'Interested? Yes, but first I'd like to view the property. I'll make my decision quickly, OK?'

'It's only just off the campus. The main house was extended with a granny flat, but apparently Granny died before she could move in and her loss is my gain. We'd each have a bedroom and share the sitting room. If, for any reason, it doesn't work out, then we lose very little, a couple of months' rent each, and we're free go our separate ways. I should warn you that I hope Gwen and I can reconcile our differences and get together again, but I'm not optimistic. Interested?'

'Provisionally, yes... but I can't commit myself just now.'

'We can view it together this afternoon... at, say, around 3.00pm. I want to get away early today, but that'd let us see the place in daylight.'

○

The apartment, near the LU campus on the edge of Linkirk, was all that I could reasonably expect. The rooms were small but adequately furnished in a slightly dated style. Having its own front door was a distinct bonus. Although I asked for time to sleep on my decision, I already knew that my mind was made up – positively. It was unlikely that anything better, or even its equal, would become available locally, with the new academic year starting so soon.

Afterwards, I decided that a walk in the fresh air would be welcome, to allow me to plan work priorities and, at the same time, explore Linkirk. I crossed High Street and went on to The Green beside the river, Meggett Water, enjoying what warmth remained in the afternoon sunshine. Preoccupied with my own problems, I was surprised to hear my name being called, and I looked around to see Beth's smiling face. The pleasure, felt so intensely in her company last evening, surged again. My greeting expressed my happiness most inadequately: 'This *is* an unexpected pleasure!'

'Hello. I'm pleased to meet you, too. I'm off home... from school... it's across that bridge. I prefer to walk after all day in the classroom,' she elaborated.

This opportunity could not be missed. 'Would you join me for a cup of tea?' The suspense lasted only seconds, though it was felt most keenly, before my wish was granted.

'Thank you. I can't stay too long, mind, but... yes, I'd like that.'

Back on High Street, the garish fluorescent lights of a modern eatery, its walls covered with menus and pictures of massive portions of garishly coloured food, was passed without a second glance from Beth. She led the way to The Cosy Kettle (how can a kettle be 'cosy'?), which was decorated with chintz curtains and white tablecloths, but had no plastic in sight. Beth had old-fashioned tastes apparently. The friendly waitress, in a black dress and white apron, greeted my companion by name. Afternoon tea, including sandwiches and tray bakes, soon appeared on our table.

Due to enjoying Beth's company so intensely, I found it difficult to start a conversation. Given a free choice, I would have opted to savour the moment, preferably in companionable silence, but good manners dictated that *something* must be said. However, small talk – which was never my forte with the ladies, even on a good day – can be fraught with pitfalls. So, figuring it was better to be trite than trivial, I tried, 'Good day at school?'

'Yes, yes. I'm one of those lucky people who enjoy their work,' Beth answered.

Her account of what appeared to be a very ordinary day did not quite hold my full attention. The unexpected pleasure of enjoying Beth's company at close quarters was all that I desired for this golden moment; her activities in the classroom remained secondary. I noticed that, in the light from the nearby table lamp, her eyes were a grey-green hue. Her company was everything I could wish for just now (and more!), so I paid insufficient attention to her words. Floating on my comfortable cloud, I was suddenly conscious of having missed her question, hearing only, 'Don't you agree?'

'Mmm, I suppose so.'

But had I correctly caught a positive intimation in her voice? Happily, it seemed that I had, because Beth moved on to say, 'Did you enjoy last evening?'

'Oh yes, very much. The McTaggarts are most hospitable. That meal was excellent.'

Once back on safer ground, my attention was not allowed to waver again.

'Walter was in a difficult mood,' said Beth pensively.

I could strongly agree with this sentiment, but, unable to anticipate where the conversation might lead, judged it best not to express my extremely positive opinions about Walter's 'hostile attitudes'. Nevertheless, some, *any*, safe and preferably neutral response was needed. 'I didn't meet him until yesterday. We both work in chemistry.'

'Yes. Yes, I know. Elizabeth must have told me. I've known him a long time. He comes from a village called Bothyglen, out Glasgow way, but he went to school in Linkirk. He was in the same class as my brother, Stewart. Sometimes he came to our house, but that all ended when Stewart left home to work in Aberdeen.'

'Inevitably, he and I will meet at work. Perhaps we can get over last evening's bad start and begin again. I found him difficult to talk to.'

'Yes. He can be withdrawn, I know. Heavens, is that the time? Sorry, I must fly.'

Opportunities are to be grasped, and the auguries thus far had been favourable, so, I took my chance with fate once more. 'May we meet again?' (My 'Please!' remained unsaid.)

'Of course. That is, I mean, if you'd like to.'

'I'd love to. How can I contact you?'

A piece of paper was found and a phone number written on it. 'That's my home number. Will you let me pay, please?' she asked.

However, I had already picked up the docket. 'It was my invitation, so it's my treat. Bye for now.'

'Many thanks for the tea. Bye!'

There was a brief flurry of coat fastening, scarf tying and handbag finding, and Beth was gone.

The brightness had gone out of the day when I left The Cosy Kettle, but something of the cosiness remained as I returned, very slowly, to mundanity.

Chapter 4

Third Sunday in September

CONTENT	
	a. What is inside a container
	b. Experience of satisfaction or pleasure

THREE WEEKS LATER, DOUG AND I WERE FINISHING A LEISURELY Sunday breakfast, which was one of our infrequent meals together. The shared-accommodation arrangement was working out remarkably well, with both of us using the flat only as a base while otherwise living quite independent lives. The initial meeting with our prospective landlords had gone well, enabling us to rent the apartment with the minimum of formality. I judged, perhaps optimistically, that my budget would probably cover living costs, but any hope of owning a car had receded.

Doug had moved in first and, as senior tenant, exercised his prerogative by taking the slightly larger bedroom. I accepted this as reasonable and moved in easily because so few of my belongings had been unpacked. We settled into a routine rapidly, including a late start at weekends, which – according to Doug – enabled 'two growing lads' to enjoy a 'proper Scottish breakfast'. We ignored politically correct dietary guidance, by not limiting menus to a limp lettuce leaf or two, but indulging ourselves with cholesterol-congested calories. Right then, the table was littered with the remains of a generous brunch.

I had just enjoyed my first taste of black pudding, brought by Doug 'from home'. He fried it skilfully on a hot pan then, at the apposite second, turned them with a flick of the wrist. Finally, over cups of strong tea, 'to aid digestion, as every chemist knows', we were both pleasantly relaxed, or as Doug expressed it (again ignoring political nicety) 'I'm at peace with all men and even some *weemen*.'

'Bill, I'll be out most of today. I'm visiting an aged aunt, and staying for tea is obligatory. I won't be back until 8.00pm, or later. See you whenever...'

'Right, Doug. See you.'

My own plans were to spend the morning putting my office into some kind of order. But my eagerly anticipated treat was that Beth had responded favourably to my suggestion that, weather permitting, we might walk beside the river to Meggettglen Castle. My expressed wish to visit this famous ancient monument was a transparent excuse to spend the afternoon with her; I could think of no more pleasant company.

◉

After I had left the flat, I bought a sandwich for lunch in Linkirk, where the shop owner offered friendly greetings with the hope that sunny periods would appear – if the forecasters were correct. The town was less busy than on a weekday, though many smartly dressed people were about this Sunday morning, many to attend religious services. A steady stream were entering the First Presbyterian Church, which was built of dark-reddish stone and dominated one end of the town. This imposing building, with its tall bell tower that broadcasting a sonorous summons, faced Main Street across a small roundabout. The number and sizes of cars parked outside the church attested to the affluence of its congregation, who had partially obstructed the road into Linkirk from the west. Vehicles, awaiting the return of their worshipping owners, also encroached onto the pavement at this narrow junction, thus thoughtlessly denying its use to pedestrians.

Prominent among the larger cars was a large Bentley, resembling the vehicle I had noticed outside the McTaggart home. I supposed it belonged to Angus, as surely there were few vehicles of similar grandeur in Linkirk? Further along Main Street, I thought that I had glimpsed the bald head of John Bland going into one of the other, smaller churches. Clearly, religious observance was taken seriously here, prompting the thought that yet another aspect of my life required review: should I join a church?

Recently, churchgoing had not featured in my lifestyle, not from any conscious decision, but because other activities filled my day of rest adequately. Most of my friends were not, as far as I was aware, regular worshipers. On the rare occasions when we had touched upon topics sacred or profane, their views tended towards the flippant or superficial. Right then, living in this Scottish town, I wondered whether it might be worth conforming, though, paradoxically, I might achieve this most acceptably as a Dissenter. Social contacts made through a church might yield friends and encourage activities outside the university. Perhaps a colleague (Doug?) might offer objective advice. I was mindful of the need for caution here; those subscribing to religious faiths unhesitatingly favour their own observances as superior in every respect to all competing rivals. It could be difficult to obtain a reliable appraisal of the relative merits of the numerous alternative places of worship. I would have to avoid any possibility of insensitive proselytising, which would be most unwelcome and unlikely to attract me as a recruit.

It being too late to follow up these ideas today, I wandered to The Green where a few free spirits were enjoying secular relaxations. By the river, some children were watching, with squeals of delight, the frenzy of competitions between ducks scrambling to grab the crusts of bread the children were throwing. On the grass, a dog was obviously revelling in his exercise of ball-retrieving, then demanding, repeatedly and loudly, that his static owner throw it again for his pleasure. The dog's species was bouncy barking boomerang, I thought. By then, the walk and fresh air had aided the digestion of my unaccustomedly large breakfast, so, again, my thoughts turned to the priorities that beset the ambitious, young lecturer constantly. Accordingly, I returned to the almost deserted LU campus. Car parks that were overfilled on weekdays were almost empty, with just a few discarded plastic bags blowing about in the light wind.

○

Approaching my office, I was surprised when a door opened suddenly to reveal Walter. Since the evening at the McTaggarts, we had 'enjoyed' almost no contact, except distant sightings during work breaks, among groups of colleagues in the coffee room. Discussions of news during these periods of relaxation, usually had little or no substantial content, and were composed mainly of gossip or ephemeral trivia about school or university. However, on these occasions, I had no reason to revise my views that Walter positively disliked and/or resented me, was still avoiding my company, and was offering no friendly overtures. I was, therefore, profoundly taken aback when he appeared to be actually smiling at me and, even more unexpectedly, offered a civilised greeting: 'Good morning, William. Are you working on the Sabbath?'

'It's a good time to get my room into some kind of order. You're busy too?' I queried.

'Will you spare a few moments for a chat?'

This sudden change of attitude confused me, and I hesitated while deciding whether to accept this apparently proffered olive branch or to spurn it. I was all too aware that I could be being set up for some new unpleasantness. Caution dictated that all friendly overtures from Walter should be treated with the greatest prudence. Hitherto, chatting with me definitely had not featured on his agenda, and my few tentative attempts to communicate with him had been rebuffed – positively! Just possibly, he had genuinely changed his mind, opening the welcome prospect of making a fresh start towards establishing a normal relationship between colleagues. Had he accepted that I was here to stay? The only way to find out if this sudden cordiality was genuine or involved some subterfuge was to test it – cautiously.

'Yes. I'd be pleased to do that,' I confirmed, which was not true, but I was trying to appear friendly.

'William, I believe you're an expert on Italy,' he stated.

I laughed. 'I wouldn't describe myself as an expert on anything. Certainly, I can't claim expert knowledge of a topic as huge as... well... Italy.'

'But you've lived there, I think you said?' It seemed to be a question.

'Yes. I worked in Florence for some weeks, as a research student. I saw some other places. Like me, you know that students don't have much spare time or cash.'

'You did research on environmental science?'

Where was this change of subject leading? 'Yes. I was there mainly as a chemist, but we did some environmental science. The Italian fieldwork was most interesting.'

'We – that is, Angus and I – have recently started working on pollution science. It is our second subject, complementing our fundamental research. [I was puzzled by the supreme importance he invested in whatever unspecified work he was doing, but did not interrupt.] We've not yet published in our new field but have high hopes. We want to take fundamental measurements of the damage caused by acid rain. We all know about the areas of forest devastation in Central Europe, but acids released from power stations presumably also must affect mountain rocks. We want to know where we can find areas of pure limestone that are open to the weather but otherwise uncontaminated. A place remote from cities, roads and people's feet. We'll study what changes are occurring there to determine if they've been caused by acid rain.'

'Acid attacks limestone and you want a clean wilderness site for study.'

'Exactly'. Walter was more relaxed than I had ever seen him and, apparently, enjoying our conversation! He continued, 'We need rocks from a remote limestone mountain exposed to acid rain. Do you have any ideas about where there are areas of pristine chalk?'

It still was not clear where all this was leading, but it seemed safe to state the obvious. 'Why not start with the White Cliffs of Dover? They're chalk.'

Walter hesitated before deciding that he could only get an answer by disclosing his ulterior motive. 'I want to travel next summer to visit a former colleague. She's now living in Austria. Believe it or not, but I've never been to Europe. I've never even crossed the English Channel. If I can get our lords and masters to give me some cash from the LU research travel fund, I can start the environmental work and also reduce my travel costs. I'd rather you kept that reason strictly confidential.'

'Your secret's safe with me. I can think of two possible locations. One is Carrara, near Florence, or Firenze. It's famous for marble; from the time of Michelangelo onwards, his *David* was—'

'Never heard of him.'

'*David* is one of… or possibly *the* most famous sculptured stone statue in the world. I think the rock Michelangelo used came from the Apennines, somewhere near Carrara. Marble is still extracted there—'

'It sounds unsuitable. They won't allow me to climb on quarry faces that are still in use. I'd be spotted and thrown out. If they're working the rock, it'd be contaminated by explosives and dust. Also, it sounds too far from Austria. You said two places…?'

'The other possibility is the Dolomites, which are high mountains in northern Italy. You must have seen photographs of their jagged, white peaks. Vegetation doesn't grow on the almost perpendicular cliffs or steep rock faces. Getting to the best rock could be difficult, as the mountains are extremely rugged—'

'Don't worry about that. I've done some serious rock climbing of the challenging peaks on Skye and some places in the States. I think I can handle that side of things.'

'The Dolomites must be a protected conservation area. It might be difficult to get permission for experiments—'

'Again, don't worry; that's my problem. Between ourselves, I wouldn't bother too much with the legal niceties. My work'll do no real damage. I'd collect only a few small rock pieces to bring back here. My equipment would be far from the public gaze. In a large and rugged mountainous area, I can find a quiet backwater easily, or a remote valley where only a few ramblers venture. I'll work alone, well away from the tourist hordes and any environmental police, if they exist. Where is it exactly?'

'In Italy. Roughly north of Lake Garda and south from Innsbruck in Austria. Perhaps we could work together? I do have some skills in environmental science.'

'We'll see. Could be. Might do.'

These words reminded me of John Bland's vagaries, but here I interpreted their meaning as a clear and unambiguous *no!* 'I remember now, a rock climber friend stayed at a village, somewhere handy to the

Dolomites called Dobb... I forget. Dobboc... or something. He thought it was a good base. I'll find a map... I'll let you know. Dobbiaco, I think.'

'Thanks, William. That'll start me off. I'll think about it. Bye for now.'

Our contact had ended. Walter only wanted information; social niceties were of secondary, realistically *zero*, importance. He had *no* intention of normalising our relationship. His questions answered, he need waste no more of his valuable time discussing trivia with me, the interloping newcomer. As I left, I saw him go to his desk and start writing. Months later, I realised he must have recorded everything I had said because he certainly fully exploited my advice. At the time, I took his interest in my proposals as a compliment, but I know now that my sly colleague, who was capable of thinking up few original ideas himself, had tried to profit from mine.

○

Once in the corridor, I saw the portly figure of John Bland some distance away. My attention was attracted by his almost furtive demeanour as he reached above a door, found a key and used it to enter the room. Passing the still partially open door, I was surprised to see Prof seated at a table covered with complicated scientific equipment. Had I seen him going to church earlier? I decided to offer a civil greeting, rather than walking past anonymously. 'Good morning, Prof.'

Apparently, he had been too preoccupied to notice me, as he said, 'Hello! Hello! Who's that?'

'Bill Green, Prof. Good morning.'

'Oh, yes. It's you... er... Bill.' Once my identity had been fully established, he went on, 'You might wonder what I'm doing here on a Sunday morning.'

Most perceptively, he had expressed my thoughts, but it had seemed hardly tactful to betray my inquisitiveness, so my non-committal reply was politic: 'No, Prof, I'm just going to my office and happened to see you here.'

We both knew that scientific research sometimes involves routine tasks that extend into unsociable hours. However, we also knew, from personal inconvenience, that senior academics usually offload such unwelcome work onto their juniors: graduate students.

Almost talking to himself, John continued, 'It may surprise you, but I still enjoy my practical chemistry even after all these years. I've just been to church and, before lunch, I'm able to take a few measurements…' There was a pause. Though I was uncertain as to whether our exchange had ended, he resumed his soliloquy, 'This is my personal laboratory. I don't allow anyone else to work or even enter here. My *health and safety* regulations are a little relaxed, as you may notice. I keep this room for *my* research only; it's my private domain. I'm like the photographer working in a dark room. It's essential because I study how light affects chemicals.'

I already knew this because, before my interview, I had looked up the research fields of my possible future colleagues, in case such apparent interest might help my application. Hitherto, it had yielded no tangible benefit, but, at last, I could reveal some familiarity with Prof's work. 'I read your article on…'

My reward was a tedious explanation of his research, evidently still continuing in the intricate apparatus covering the table that occupied much of this room. Its construction was a tribute to the skills of the glass-blower who had fabricated a messy and certainly home-made construction of glass tubes connected by wires that were intertwined into a knotty concoction that could only be understood or used by its designer. It might, alternatively, have marketable value as a piece of modern art, perhaps as a fanciful representation – in glass, plastic and metals – of an unknown number of octopuses wrestling. I knew that such esoteric, home-made equipment was the preferred approach to experiments by some older physical chemists. Weald University had several examples of specialised apparatus that differed little from this lash-up (as described by a friend). My attention returned to Prof, who was apparently instructing himself audibly on how to perform his self-imposed task: 'Now I adjust this gas flow. A few more readings here and… Yes! There! It's a bit high… mmm. No matter; these experiments go on for weeks and must be repeated if the results…'

I awaited a suitable pause, then interjected, 'I'll wish you a good day, Prof.'

After leaving his archaic, undoubtedly hazardous, domain, I wondered how and why this 'private' laboratory was permitted to remain in use. Surely no school safety committee could sanction the continued functioning of such equipment, maintained by John Bland for his own personal amusement, even if it masqueraded as research. A special dispensation (perhaps only quasi-legal) must apply to professors, giving licence whereby *only* Prof could work here. Did he think himself immune from accidents? And what would be the consequences for the school if he suffered serious injury? His exposure to danger in this *private* laboratory far exceeded anything that would be tolerated in any other workplace I had ever encountered. Most disturbingly, there were several large and heavy metal cylinders, apparently free standing, storing gases for experiments, without the usual and essential rigid support. I pondered the conundrum posed by these obvious dangers, which, realistically, were none of my business. I could not prevent my seniors (and presumably my 'betters') risking their own safety, particularly if such perils offered no threats to anyone else.

◎

Once in my office, I rearranged the furniture to my liking, placed books on shelves and filed papers. Unresolved was the problem of whether I could easily find *any* particular item when seeking it later. With these tasks completed, I went to the deserted coffee room, where I brewed tea and ate a lonely sandwich.

Next, I returned to my office, where I found pen and paper, and as a dutiful, only son wrote to my widowed mother. I had suffered real guilt when accepting this job, which was so distant from my native Sussex, and thereby leaving her very much on her own. Until then, I had lived mainly in the family home. It was only after much heart-searching that I accepted the job here as the sole opportunity of entering my preferred career. I still wondered if this had been my best choice or, indeed, if there was a right choice and what (definitely second-choice) employment prospects might be found nearer home. However, I still had to establish myself here, though perhaps confronting this considerable challenge was a principal reason for my accepting the LU lectureship.

Two years ago, my father had been tragically killed in a motorway accident, which was an unexpected bereavement because he was a skilled and careful driver. The crash had occurred during foggy, wet conditions, and the exact causes of the multiple pile-up were never determined fully. The shock and loss to my mother were incalculable. She opted to remain in the house where she had lived throughout her married life, then prematurely curtailed. Ever since that horrible day, she had kept herself fully, even compulsively, occupied in her job as a teacher in a school for children with special educational needs. Her commitment amounted to a vocation, and she unstintingly spent much of her leisure time preparing 'special lessons for special children'. For Mother, each and every pupil was special. Gardening was her relaxation. More recently, she had started an Open University study, a history of the Renaissance, soon after visiting me in Florence. I wondered if I had inadvertently introduced yet another activity into her already overfilled lifestyle.

Since I had come to Scotland, it seemed that my mother believed her sole offspring had voluntarily separated himself from civilisation to be friendless in some far-distant place. As with many individuals from the Home Counties, we knew little about those tracts of land that stretch northwards from Watford towards frozen Arctic wastes. In attempting to allay her concerns, I had suggested that she might spend her short half-term break, in late October, braving the unknown by coming to Linkirk to see the place for herself. I wondered, perhaps a little unkindly, if such a visit might initiate another subject for her to study, perhaps Scottish history, of which there seemed to be an abundant supply. These introspective thoughts led me to suppose that I must have inherited her work ethic, as I was often pursuing several projects concurrently. For my foreseeable future, things would have to remain this way.

'Bookish' is the term that most satisfactorily describes our family talent. Mother's great commitment is to teach reading and writing to youngsters, who are often disinterested initially, by encouraging them to appreciate fully the benefits and joys of literacy. My father, a journalist on a local paper, was strongly motivated to increase the interest of dull news stories by exploiting lively prose to engage readers' attention. He was a *wordsmith* who took his work seriously and also motivated me to increase my word capacity by using the dictionary and thesaurus. My initial attempts to introduce flowery language into school essays had sometimes provoked hilarity from teachers and class alike – while embarrassing me. But I had persisted, always remembering Father's advice: 'No matter what you do in life, communication is *always* important. There is no finer tool for expressing yourself than the English language. Use it well, and you'll do well.'

My letter completed, I recalled the recent discussion with Walter, which triggered a disturbing train of thought. Remembering Angus's focus on my environmental interests during the interview, I was wondering if this had motivated his new collaboration with Thompson. Just at that time, increasing interest in pollution and the environment were becoming the topical research subject. It seemed possible that my 'popular articles' had brought the potential of working in this field to Prof's attention, making it a bandwagon to surmount (fashionably). Thompson, of course, was not present at the interview, and the aspect that worried me was that he, *not me*, by then appeared to be the preferred collaborator. Perhaps, after I had completed some worthwhile work in this field, bridges could be built between us all. Nevertheless, it was not a comforting situation: it was yet another problem to confront.

However, the prospect of meeting Beth beckoned; banishing these distasteful thoughts temporarily, I set off happily. However, when passing John Bland's personal laboratory door, then closed, I was seized with an uncharacteristic inquisitiveness. Later, and much later, I had ample reason to wonder what had prompted this nosy action and its complicated, unpredictable and, eventually, tragic consequences. After a quick check that nobody was about to witness my guilty action, I reached to the ledge above the door. Despite the expectation, I was surprised to find a key that, on testing, opened the door to Prof's private sanctuary. It was a small moment of triumph. I had penetrated at least one secret of this community that seemed reluctant to admit outsiders as full members. After relocking the door, I returned the key precisely, remembering its location, if a need-to-know should ever arise. I recall no particular feeling of foreboding.

When I reached the end of Main Street, I circumnavigated the roundabout easily, which was clear of the clutter of churchgoers' vehicles by then, and continued across Meggett Bridge while happily anticipating meeting Beth. The sun seemed to me to be particularly bright, and sparkling reflections from the river cheered my mood. The ducks were now foraging for themselves, with no young crust-throwers about. Just before our agreed meeting time, the eagerly anticipated event took place: Beth appeared. On a first date, you cannot be *absolutely* sure! Dressed smartly in a short, green coat with contrasting brown slacks, she was a sight for sore eyes (mine) as she walked purposely towards me. Lurking pessimistic thoughts disappeared.

Our greetings were somewhat stilted. Shaking hands seemed too formal, and I preferred not to risk an embrace. Our compromise was a self-conscious wave, followed by mutual reassurances that all was well. My query about Beth's family brought a similar response. Never at ease when starting a conversation, I asked the rather obvious question, 'What would you like to do?'

'I thought you wanted to walk the riverside path to the old castle?' she enquired.

'Yes. I'd enjoy that, but only if you'd like that too.'

'I've done some homework. I read the guidebook and brought it with me, so we'll both learn some history. I thought you wanted that.'

Decisiveness was in order. 'Yes, let's go!' I declared.

The slight strangeness of our meeting relaxed naturally when we set off companionably, beside the sparkling waters, towards Meggettglen Castle, which was a listed monument.

Beth explained (slightly betraying attempts to avoid a schoolmarm image) that this had been the former seat of the Scott family. As the local laird's fortified base against outside attack, it also enabled him to control his local loyal, though sometimes restive, subjects. The oldest parts of the castle dated from the fourteenth century, being built after wars that had gained Scotland some independence from England, negotiated by Robert the Bruce and William Wallace. This interested me, having always lived in peaceful Sussex, which no foreign invaders had penetrated since the arrival of my namesake, who was better known as William the Conqueror. Somehow, history in Scotland seemed more tangible and immediate, with references to English invaders slightly offending my Anglo-Saxon origins and sympathies. It crossed my mind that Beth might be trying to tell me something: did she regard me as a modern successor to the historical marauding foe? After all, we were in the Scottish Borders region, recalling the former serious divisions.

This brief discussion of history, emphasising our cultural differences, brought back unintentionally the slight sense of strangeness and brittleness I had felt earlier when we met. We walked in a less-companionable silence for a while. To recapture the joy of previous encounters, I asked Beth how she had felt about her time in London. Following our discussions about former Scottish/English conflicts, this might have been an unpromising topic, but the diversion worked.

She explained, 'I don't regret being away for a while. Probably, it was the best thing I could've done. I'd almost never been away from home, not for any length of time. I didn't go to boarding school, to college or anywhere except on holidays with my parents.'

'Why London?' I questioned.

'I've had several holidays there, and I thought it a wonderful place. I particularly enjoyed the time there two years ago when we – that is, my parents and I – stayed for a fortnight. There were theatres and concerts; we don't get much drama or music in Linkirk. We also saw the sights: Hampton Court, the River Thames, Buckingham Palace and St Paul's Cathedral. I wanted to go for longer and see everything.'

'So you went.'

'About this time last year. I had no job and knew that none was likely in any local school. A friend from our training college here told me that they needed a teacher in the school where she was teaching in London. I jumped at the chance, applied and was appointed. I shared a flat with her and two other girls, who were both Londoners.'

'What was so bad about that?'

'It was nothing terrible, just that it was totally different from the tourists' London I'd seen and liked. I spent a lot of time preparing lessons. Travel between work and our flat also took lots of time and cash. That flat, in endless drab suburbs, wasn't a home, and that depressed me. I missed the country. I couldn't afford the rent, travel, etc. out of my salary. You only realise how lucky you are whenever what you value most has gone.

I stuck it out for a couple of terms and went home at every opportunity. Daddy was an absolute dear, he subsidised me without question, and, at the end of it all, I was welcomed back like the prodigal daughter. I'm truly glad to be home. I learned a lot by going away, and I won't leave again in a hurry. Now, with a job that I enjoy, the future is much rosier. But Linkirk is also changing.'

'You think so? How?'

'Oh, yes. Several friends also left around the time I went south. LU is expanding, and many more strangers are appearing here than when I was young.'

'Another invasion of the English, like me.'

'No, I meant that, recently, people have been coming here from many other countries. I suppose that's the advance of the multicultural society. I see it in the children at school. It's interesting and inevitable, but getting used to all the changes takes time.'

From outside, Meggettglen Castle was a forbidding-looking, battlemented fortress, built of rough lumps of dark rock and extending several floors upwards. Its strategic location had been selected carefully, being at the narrowest part of the river valley, where slopes on both sides were particularly steep. The peaceful scene, including Meggett Water running gently over the rocks, could be contrasted imaginatively with whatever battles had been fought here during less peaceful times.

I purchased tickets and was given a leaflet telling us about the interesting features of this largely intact but dank and forbidding edifice. Particularly noticeable was the coldness and lack of amenities in this defensive home, though it obviously had been occupied for long periods, to judge from the deep depressions worn into the hard stone steps. The lower floors, dating back some seven centuries, included a prison of unimaginable discomfort and a well for water. There were also living quarters, by then unfurnished. The 'more recent' (seventeenth century) upper floors offered only marginally greater comfort. Finally, walking out onto the battlemented top floor, we both appreciated the warm sunshine and bright panoramic vistas across the Scottish Borders region, which contrasted greatly with the interior of this cold, dark habitation.

We descended the staircase with care; gallantly, I elected to go first as a soft landing for Beth, should she trip.

Once we had left the castle and were back on the riverside path, Beth stated, 'I've told you Beth's story. Now I'll hear about Bill.'

'I'm just a simple sort of guy,' I explained.

'Come off it! That's not true. You're either being modest or coy. You're hiding an interesting personality or hiding secrets you don't want me to know.'

'Far from it. I've lived a very ordinary life with little excitement. I understood your comments about your life in London because I'm having difficulties in fitting in here. At times, I wonder just how things will work out for me eventually.'

'In Linkirk? Surely, with your lectureship, you've a really bright future?'

'With luck, yes! I'm pleased to have been appointed here. But, when I arrived, I knew nobody. Life here is different in all kinds of subtle ways from everything I've ever known. I'll take time to adjust. Certainly, it's too early to judge how my future might develop, but I'm trying to be optimistic and hoping I'll make a success of it.'

'But surely you know what you want…?'

'I have little experience of lecturing, teaching generally… or planning my own research. There are many tough tasks. There's so much to do that I hardly know where to start.'

'You'll come through. I know you will!'

Although Beth hardly knew me, her unexpected expression of confidence, stated so sincerely, gave me a warm glow. I responded, 'Thank you. I can only do my best.' It was hardly an adequate reply.

'Good. So none of your family will be coming to join you?'

'No. Following my father's premature, accidental death, there's only my mother, who's well settled in her Sussex home. Like you, she's a teacher, who's long been in a job that she's very good at, enjoys and is committed to. I'm sure that she wouldn't move away easily, even if I wanted her to come here, which I can't even consider yet. After all, my own future is far from secure; my appointment here is temporary, and will be reviewed after only one or two years.' I felt that our relationship had moved to the point where I could indulge in a few confidences. 'I've no wife, no fiancée and have never been engaged. A free spirit, that's me. Recently, I did have a girlfriend for a while. We went out together a few times but weren't ever particularly close. After I told her I was coming north, she seemed to lose all interest, and we simply drifted apart. I don't know why I'm telling you all this, but I wouldn't have asked you out if there was someone else.'

'Thank you. In the same situation, I wouldn't have accepted your invitation. So now we both know where we stand.'

On reaching Main Street, I thought the auguries boded well, so I told her, 'Beth, Doug is away visiting some relative, so would you like to come and see our apartment? We could cook a meal, always assuming that we can buy the necessities. What do you say?'

'I was going to church, but I'm tempted… If do I come, I can't stay long.'

'Message received and understood. So you'll come?'

Because so few shops were open in Linkirk on a Sunday afternoon, our meal was tolerable rather than good. It was a case of 'Congenial company is a choice condiment that camouflages catastrophe when consuming comestibles'. A glass of white wine served to tenderise our slightly tough chicken. After eating and at Beth's insistence, domestic chores were completed rapidly and companionably: I washed and she dried the plates. We then sat on the sagging settee to watch TV; it was a programme showing experts valuing antiques for their owners.

I slid my arm along the top cushion of our shared seat, but, before reaching Beth's shoulder, she rose to adjust the TV's sound level. I could not decide whether her move was coincidental or evasive. A little later, a repeated attempt was again outmanoeuvred by Beth getting up.

She said, 'I really must go. I did say I couldn't stay long. School starts early, and I find it hard to arrive on time.'

I was unable to persuade her to stay any longer, but all was not lost: we had agreed to meet again, soon. I walked her most of the way home. At the corner of the street where she lived, I was pleasantly surprised by the sudden and brief contact of her lips on my cheek, slightly below my right eye. Though with poor aim and one-sided, this peck might be regarded as our first kiss, but it went a long way towards offsetting my earlier feelings when we were on the settee that my overtures were unwelcome. Then I was alone: she had disappeared rapidly around the corner.

◎

Doug was home before me.

'Been entertaining, have you? Who's the lucky lady?' he asked.

'How did you know it was a lady?' I responded.

'For a start, most men I know wouldn't have left a wine bottle half full.'

We soon remedied this omission. Doug also happened to have another, unopened, bottle in his room.

He explained, 'My venerable relation, whom I've just visited, is teetotal. Emergency rations for afterwards are essential.'

Chapter 5

PITCH	a.	Express an opinion forcefully
	b.	Oily, tarry, black material

THE TEACHING TERM HAD STARTED. WEEKDAY BREAKFASTS WERE now hurried affairs with staff strictly observing punctual starts for 9.00am lectures. While students might drift in later, and a minority did, it was unthinkable for a lecturer to arrive late. However, on Thursday, both Doug and I began our teaching at 10.00am, allowing us a less frenetic start. Our preferred weekday breakfast was a 'healthy option', and, just then, fuelled by muesli and toast, we were enjoying the luxury of second cups of tea.

I broke the companionable silence: 'If you feel like talking and answering a question…?'

'I'm always pleased to share my prejudices, Bill. You should know that by now,' answered Doug.

'Some time ago, you described the research that John Bland talked about as…'

'"Industrial dirty washing." Oh yes! I remember. I'm always happy to discuss such topics; in fact, so happy that you must stop me when I start boring you.'

'I accept that deciding whether or not to become an "industrial laundrette" is down to me, but some background would be helpful... about what I should do.'

'We all start off with noble principles. Nobel Prizes beckon. When we start research, each one of us hopes to make momentous discoveries and earth-shattering insights that will change the course of science forever. But... there are difficulties. The wheel was invented a while ago. Penicillin was found fortuitously by Fleming. So, what's left to be discovered by the rest of us mere mortals?' Doug poured more of the cool, by then almost black, tea. 'Well, tea that doesn't stew is one. Such observations could point to brilliant breakthroughs, truly benefitting mankind.'

'It's hardly a sure-fire topic for a research council grant.'

'Agreed, but you must apply for every grant available. It impresses our bosses if we doggedly pursue government money, though the chance of success is low and even declining. But if you have a really excellent idea, have a go! Collaborations with colleagues and/or Europeans are good. Try to interest the Italians you know.'

'I've thought about that. But... thanks for mentioning it.'

'Realistically, you must get other, junior researchers working with you, for *you*, on *your* ideas and in *your* laboratory, as I've said before. Industrial cash can be a good start. It's never easy to find financial support, as you'll find out. *Un*fortunately, research earnings do nothing to improve your personal cash flow.'

'After we talked, I rang John Bland's contact and spoke to a friendly sounding Dr Albert Miller. He suggested we meet for lunch today, at somewhere called The Meggettglen Inn, to talk about pollution clean-up.'

'How appropriate! A *meal* from Miller! But don't let him *grind* you down. Remember, there's *no* such thing as a *free* lunch. More of Doug's Scottish wisdom is this: friendliness must be distinguished from plausibility and *vice versa*.'

'How do I decide?'

'It's very difficult. Only you can judge, or guess, what's best for you. If the work seems genuinely scientifically interesting *and* you really believe you have something worthwhile to offer, then it may repay your gamble of investing time and effort. If not, then decline, opt out and reject the bait. Always remember that things may not be quite as they seem. My accumulated wisdom is probably biased, but it's from personal, often unhappy, experiences. Certainly, I've been at this game far longer than you, so learn from my mistakes... if you can. Our colleagues may offer different advice; mine is just one hard-earned opinion about this type of research.'

Tea was drunk.

'Just talking about the problems helps. I must straighten out my thoughts before this meeting... if you don't mind?' I asked.

'Not at all. Let me ramble on.' Doug toasted more bread. 'So much for my attempts to lose weight.' His tone became more serious. 'These days, many large businesses have their own research laboratories; at least, that's what they call them. They're good for the firm's image. Sometimes, "Laboratory" is even included in the firm's title, highlighting their scientific credentials or (with me being cynical) scientific plausibility. But their in-house experts and expertise are always harnessed to pull only in the directions that the firm's managers believe will make them money. When that's achieved, or when the outlook looks bleak or expensive, the financial plug is pulled and their scientific priorities change. Pharmaceutical firms, for example, make new drugs. The very few successful medicines appear on the market, and all others are scrapped forever, immediately after a serious snag is found.'

'I've a friend in industry who complained that, whenever he thought he was advancing science, his project was changed. He gave up research and now manages a manufacturing plant. But, he's paid much more than me.'

'Exactly. He suppresses frustrated scientific ambitions with luxury. But now I'm reaching the bit that should interest you. It's inevitable that, occasionally, large firms come up against problems outside their experience or that might interfere with their commercial programmes. An attractive, sometimes cheap, alternative is to fill a knowledge gap or solve some minor difficulty by employing a university.'

'Why should we be interested? Surely such projects are trivial?'

'Not necessarily. Let me be quite clear about this. Much of the industrial research sponsored in universities is of the highest order and is truly excellent. I really mean that. Such collaborations cover many different types; indeed, each and every one is unique. An important commercial objective may fall within the scope some academic's field of expertise, so that he may be genuinely keen to, and capable of, contributing. Novel queries from industry can also stimulate novel thinking. We academics are supposed to live in ivory towers, but a shove from the big, bad commercial world can do us good by shaking our complacency. The priority for us academics is to be sure that any research we undertake has genuine scientific merit. This may be difficult for you to judge when you talk with Mr Miller. Why, for example, has John Bland shown no interest? Is the work impossible? Is industry simply looking for cheap labour to solve a trivial difficulty? You'll have to decide whether this particular project offers you some worthwhile scientific challenges.'

'Understood. Research problems vary from challenging to trivial and the scientifically pointless. So, if this one appears unpromising, do I reject it?'

'It's not quite that easy. It's sometimes politic to accept industrial money to show that universities contribute to the wealth of our nation. After all, ultimately, our wages come from taxes. In practice, academics accept some business contracts even if the science may be superficial.'

'But surely there must be something in it for us?'

'We get the satisfaction of a job well done, but benefits can be difficult to quantify. Research-contract cash always goes directly to university administration, which appropriates a chunk of it into its own coffers, for the privilege of 'managing' our money for us. They call this 'overheads'. They don't say much about it, not usually even a 'Thanks,' for finance that they played no part in either finding or earning. They don't have to solve the research problem either: it's their free lunch. They just enforce their rules, which were invented and imposed by our Facilitation Centre, to be obeyed by the rest of us. Most of the remaining cash – 'overhead discounted', if you like – pays for a researcher, whom you'll have to find, supervise, train and make sure he/she solves the paymaster's problems. They may get a research degree from the work, some even get a job with the sponsor. If you've played your cards skilfully, your laboratory can end up with some useful equipment bought by the firm, which you might get to keep on permanent loan. Also, the sponsor may allow you to publish a scientific report in a learned journal, which can help you to get promotion. Then we all bask in the kudos of knowing that we're moving the boundaries of knowledge ever onwards, outwards and upwards.'

'Isn't that a rather one-sided view?'

'Of course, of course. I've said my opinions tend to be cynical, recalling my own experiences, which often have been less than successful… Also, remember that if you understand and apply the rules of the game, you needn't be exploited. Indeed, if you're astute enough, you can often do yourself a bit of good along the way.'

'I wish I'd more time to think through the implications.'

'You've got all the time you need. Talk research with industry, whenever possible. Ask every relevant question you can think of, but don't necessarily accept all answers at face value. Today's meeting could be a useful career step. You might actually get a research contract because it seems that some real cash is on offer, which is not always the case. However, if it is, find a student and agree to supervise their research.'

'It's as easy as that?'

'It can be. Also, ensure your sponsors are supplied regularly with learned-sounding reports, *always* including something *new* positively relating to the problem they're paying for. You benefit by getting a student who can be 'encouraged', under your supervision, to include some novel experiments outside the contract. With care, such 'moonlighting research' can be of greater interest to you and your student, than the contracted work. Sponsored programmes can be mundane or sometimes downright boring. You might brighten a post-graduate's tedious life by introducing him/her to some novel 'good ideas', thus (off the record) pursuing your own research agenda.'

'So someone else pays me to work on my own projects?'

'Unknowingly, yes! But keep it to yourselves. Don't be too greedy. By careful planning, you and the student might succeed in publishing joint articles reporting research completed during such "borrowed" time. A long list of such papers appearing in reputable scientific journals is generally accepted as incontrovertible evidence of your academic brilliance and is *the* essential requirement for promotion. The more, the better, it seems, in the publication-numbers game where excellence is sometimes secondary. It always amuses me that scientific reports, written in a strictly conformist and stilted style, are referred to as "literature". Imaginative and lively writing is positively and actively discouraged by the editors of our scientific journals. I wonder what, if anything, they read for their personal relaxation.'

'So, how much does teaching count in the race for promotion?'

'Not much… if anything! That's the view of this ageing teacher, but it would be denied loudly and vehemently by any and all of our profs. They're not always so excellent themselves at their professing (terrible pun, I know). I'm sure that most of the time and personal effort expended by most academics, here and in similar places elsewhere, is directed primarily at furthering their own research interests. It seems that a long list of published papers is the passport to academic advancement.'

'So, I must make up my own mind. OK! I don't know whether your comments make that easier or more difficult. Perhaps we'll talk again, later?'

'No problem. You already know very well that my answers always tend towards *nonconformist* viewpoints. After all I've said, it's only fair to add a "career health warning". You could ask (but are much too polite) why, if I know so much about the "system", I didn't get a chair with the much-prized title of "professor"? It's simple! I'm too outspoken! My views aren't accepted by everyone, but that's never stopped me sharing them around. Alternative and novel ideas are mostly unpopular with the university establishment, particularly concerning that elusive concept of research. (I know that this is a contradiction in terms!) But I still believe that there's some truth in what I say. A lack of tact is certainly a disqualification for promotion here, as I think our "friend" Walter has learned very early in his career. He could go far, if he can keep up his fawning approach to authority, to Angus in particular. As for me, I'm too old to learn a new job. I've got a secure position here and can remain in a pleasant environment, vegetating comfortably. My views are summarised by this local and ancient saying (which I've just thought up): my academic life remains tolerable, but only if I don't take the bastards at their own inflated valuations.'

'So I decide for myself about the possible benefits of industrial sponsorship?'

'Exactly. And on that poignant note I'll say, "Enjoy your day." I must go now and maintain the carefully cultivated illusion that I still work in LU.'

'Just now, enjoying my day seems unlikely. I'll tell you later how I get on.'

'Do just that!'

○

As I got off the bus, the driver pointed out, 'That's t'Meggyglen. Not many arrives 'ere by bus. 'Njoy yourself.'

After the departure of the bus with its chatty driver, I saw the lunchtime popularity of this hostelry. The large car park was well filled with large, 'expense-account' vehicles. Certainly, few of The Meggettglen Inn's many patrons arrived by public transport. Perhaps I should have come by taxi?

The large, yellow building was modern, but designed to recall the rural architecture of an earlier age. This pseudo-venerable appearance was echoed by the large, illuminated sign with a fanciful view of the eponymous glen. Coloured lights traced the outline of the eaves; being lit in daylight, these gave a slightly tawdry air to the place, but were probably effective in attracting notice from passing motorists. My feeling was that – whether the food was good, bad or indifferent – prices would be high.

On entering the large, busy foyer to find reception, I heard, 'Dr Green?' I turned to meet the tall, thin man in his mid-fifties who had addressed me. His hair was grey, cut short and of similar colour to his suit, which appeared to me to have been the work of a costly tailor. Though smart, it was no longer new. Inappropriately, I thought his appearance was not unlike many successful academics. (Why should this surprise me?) 'Yes, that's me. Mr Miller?'

'That's me! Pleased to meet you. Do call me Albert; I prefer it to Bert,' he replied.

'I'm Bill, but how did you know me?'

'I saw you arriving when I was parking my car.' Albert accompanied this with a warm smile, which I accepted as a sympathetic appreciation of the chronic financial shortages that beset most young academics. His disarming charm made me feel at ease immediately, though I also remembered Doug's hints about the illusory nature of free lunches. His face was transformed frequently by a bright smile, though I was to find disconcerting the stare of concentrated attention that appeared during serious conversations.

Albert took the initiative. 'I've taken the liberty of reserving a table. If we go in now, we can get to know one another and perhaps talk shop over lunch. The steak here is good, and it's our treat. What'll you drink?'

Inexperience in business situations counselled caution, so I chose orange juice to avoid any possible loss of concentration after wine. Albert made the same choice.

The meal ordered, my host lost no time in starting to talk about the reasons for our meeting, outlining his main responsibilities in his firm.

After our steaks arrived, he said, 'I've told you a little about me, and we'll get to the main points of our discussion later. Meanwhile, let us relax and enjoy the food. Give me your impressions of Scotland. I guess that, like me, you come from southern England?'

Conversation flowed easily and naturally, touching on a wide range of topics, while we gave the steak the serious attention it merited. I enjoyed the feeling of satisfying satiation after an 'excellent but not over-large' meal. I hoped that this indulgence would not result in afternoon drowsiness. We both declined the tempting range of sweets, preferring the reviving powers of coffee.

When Albert's small talk ended with a question, I was so taken aback by its unexpected form that it took me a moment to think up a suitable reply.

'The real reason for contacting you is, frankly, to ask if you'll help us launder some of our dirty washing?' he'd asked.

The query so closely echoed Doug's disparaging appraisal of such projects that my thought processes were temporarily confused. Presumably, this was unintended by Albert, so I played for time, stating, 'I'd have to know much, much more about your dirty washing before reaching for soap and a scrubbing brush.'

'That's perfectly reasonable. We, that is, my firm, are all too well aware that we have a difficult pollution problem to resolve and don't want anyone to disappear in a cloud of suds. I could outline it in these pleasant surroundings, but you might understand it better if you see the problem *in situ*. Could you visit our factory sometime soon?'

There seemed little point in pretending I had numerous unmissable engagements or that LU could only function with my constant presence. I responded, 'I've arranged my duties to leave this afternoon completely free. I could go now, or we can agree another time.'

'Good. Now also suits me, so I suggest we go straight there. But, first, I must ask you to sign a confidentiality agreement. This is usual and normal practice. Because of the commercial sensitivity of what I'm going to show you, we require you to agree not to disclose any of the information given to you to anyone else. Perhaps you'll not be altogether surprised [Albert's smile appeared] that I happen to have an agreement form... here. You'd better read it before saying or signing anything.'

I scanned through the few pages of legal terminology, noticing that both form and content were superficially similar (if not identical) to an agreement I'd signed before a previous factory visit. The confidentiality requirements were stated clearly and seemed to cover exactly what Albert had said. Because this was the only way forward, I signed after minimal hesitation, wondering whether this had been the wise decision.

Albert gave me a copy. 'So, we go to our factory now?'

○

Ten minutes later, we were in his large, grey BMW on our way to Glasgow. Albert was a good driver and kept within speed limits, sometimes to the discomfiture of other motorists.

He declared, 'Bill, I know you've got expertise in environmental matters [I wondered how he knew], but perhaps I'll outline our story in my own rather-elementary way. I don't want to patronise you, but simple explanations can be best in the long run.'

I thanked him for his candour and sat back, in comfort, to listen.

He continued, 'Our chemical factory, where we are going now, is near Glasgow and we have manufactured there for decades. Three years ago, another firm, a former rival, decided to relocate and – to our surprise – they offered us their site adjoining ours, for purchase. We looked at their run-down factory area and were amazed – 'shocked' is a better word, at the level of pollution they intended to leave. It includes several large pits full of some oily chemical waste, which is partially buried. Now we have to dispose of it, and that's what I want to talk to you about, but only after you've seen it.'

We drove on in silence, before Albert continued, 'I'd like to stress that our firm has always tried to be environmentally responsible. Now we're all too conscious of the many unknown hazards posed by the cesspit of iniquity adjoining our site. This mess of pollutants could damage us in all sorts of ways – it could leak into our ground or contaminate our products – and it is now our problem, though not made by us.' There was a short silence while we passed a slow tractor and trailer. 'Our board was badly split on what to do. Some directors believed that we shouldn't touch anything so frightful, even with a long bargepole; we should *always* make polluters clear up their own messes. Others, including our then chairman, focussed on the considerable commercial value and industrial potential of the site. The inputs and skills of some directors, who are focussed primarily on finances, argued that our interests would best be served by acquiring the land, because, eventually, the pollution could be remedied cost-effectively. Part of the area might be sold on for housing. I'm not at all convinced that this is realistic. Our chairman argued that, planned carefully, most things can be achieved at a reasonable price, and we should be able to rehabilitate the site and still make a profit.'

Albert negotiated a busy roundabout, ignoring the horn of an impatient driver who, his overtaking thwarted, was now broadcasting his wish to exceed the speed limit. Ignoring the traffic, I was wondering privately what, if anything, I might be capable of contributing towards resolving the incredibly difficult pollution problem unfolding.

He carried on, 'After negotiations with our former neighbour, we bought the site. Pollution regulations were less severe then than now. I don't know whether we got an asset or an albatross around our necks, but it still remains a financial gamble. Uncertainties about rehabilitation costs had made valuation of the factory virtually impossible. It cost the traditional peppercorn amount and our obligation to rehabilitate the site. So, now we own it, but we've yet to see who got the best bargain! Changed pollution attitudes have increased our clean-up costs. Perhaps our former leader was more optimistic than realistic. But... he can no longer plan the necessary remediation because he died last year. To paraphrase Shakespeare (*Julius Caesar*, was it?), the evil that men do lives after them, the good is oft interred with their bones. So let it be with our late, revered chairman... only that can't be so.'

'Why not?' I asked.

'He was cremated.' This remark was not flippant. Evidently, Albert felt the late chairman had managed to evade responsibility for his decisions, almost improperly and without prospect of redress. He went on, 'We've expansion plans that need more factory space, and now have to reclaim *our own* land before we can use it.'

'I don't know if or how I can help. I do have a genuine interest in environmental science, but no particular expertise or experience in cleaning up noxious factory waste. I must stress I'm *not* a specialist in this field. Frankly, I should say here and now that I believe you may be wasting your time, perhaps also mine, by showing me the problem. You need expertise that I just don't have. There must be firms specialising in this sort of work. They'll know much, much more than I do.'

'Yes, and they're expensive. We're not expecting you to perform miracles. Before calling in the specialists, we want someone to tell us what kinds of chemical waste and what types of pollution we're dealing with. We've our own scientists, but they're fairly fully occupied with our business targets. [Doug's comments came to mind.] We just hope you might be able to do some rather basic tests that will give us a better idea of exactly what types of hazardous substances you can find on our site. Later, with an open mind and using whatever information you've given us, we'll decide for ourselves what the next step is. Think about it while I drive through our factory, to show you our manufacturing base.' Albert was obviously a loyal employee.

The red-and-white pole barring the firm's entrance was raised by a uniformed security guard, and Albert was waved through without formality.

'If you don't mind, I'll take you directly to the polluted areas and we'll see as much as possible before daylight fades,' he explained.

We entered a typical chemical factory landscape of utilitarian buildings. Red-brick walls were built within external steel frameworks, giving everything a highly functional appearance. Metal chimneys discharged white clouds of steam. Numerous containers of diverse shapes, sizes and colours filled roadside storage areas where forklift trucks bustled about, moving items between manufacturing plants. A mildly acrid odour, faintly reminiscent of petroleum, pervaded the atmosphere. Road markings defined storage sites and large notices, mostly in red, identified 'Assembly Points', 'Fire Hydrants', 'Water' and open areas 'For Emergency Use Only'. The high standards of maintenance and tidiness impressed me: this was an efficient factory, which was safeguarding employees' welfare.

Albert stopped at a gate in a high, red-brick wall, which was the factory boundary, and waited until a security guard opened heavy gates that were bolted securely and locked. Beyond this barrier, the abandoned, deserted industrial site contrasted sharply with the efficient activity within the well-maintained factory we had just left. The architectural styles were similar, but, without maintenance, the buildings had deteriorated seriously, with some apparently approaching imminent collapse. Vegetation grew out of walls, roofs and brickwork crumbled, notices were faded, and former roadways sprouted plant growth. On open ground, no plant life grew, perhaps evidence of polluted soil.

We moved on slowly, carefully avoiding the many potholes and other hazards, including loose bricks, broken bottles and lumps of discarded metal scattered on the disused roadways.

Albert explained, 'Security is an ever-increasing problem for us. We do our best to discourage intruders, who sneak in to enjoy – if that's the word – their addictions, hidden from the world. We've had incursions by hard drug users and, equally worrying, youngsters intent on glue-sniffing. It's a constant battle because of the other dangers these trespassers don't know about, though perhaps the real problem is that they've already lost their sense of self-preservation. The possibility of collapsing masonry is serious. Worse, we have no idea what hazards are posed by the poisonous sumps of noxious chemical waste.'

The car stopped beside one of Albert's 'goo-filled sumps': a large depression containing an oily, tar-like, black material that exuded a smell recalling, but stronger than, that noticeable during road resurfacing.

He continued, 'We know that plastics were once manufactured here. We believe that, prior to the recent rise in environmental concern, all their chemical waste was simply dumped into these pits. There are six pools like this across the site. We have to find out just how dangerous this black goo is and how it can be removed. After we've established what's in it, even only approximately, then we hope that we can decide on ways to deal with it safely.'

'This goo is the 'dirty washing' that you hope I might analyse?' I queried.

'That's as good a description as any. Yes. Certainly, it's an open-ended problem. We could invest a great deal of time and money in finding out exactly what's in this waste. On the other hand, if you could give us an partial-but-realistic analysis, we might start deciding how best to start the clean-up.'

Albert found a metal bar and, holding the 'clean' end, prodded the black surface of a tarry pool. A surface skin was pushed down, before rupturing to release a thick oily liquid with a petrol-like smell. Surface stirring was difficult; the liquid stuck to the rod, which Albert dropped, leaving it for later use.

I watched with interest, remaining shocked that such a vast quantity of uncharacterised waste had just been dumped. 'I'll have to think about all this. I'm not sure that my talents are sufficient to help you and that's not just me being modest. You'd make a contract with LU?'

'We can do that. We've got two contracts running with Professor Bland currently. He surprised me by declining this particular problem.'

'He mentioned it to me, but didn't explain why he wasn't interested. I tried to question him, but he was rather vague.'

Albert glanced at me knowingly, with an almost mischievous grin, but – wisely and tactfully – did not comment.

○

We returned to Albert's office in the administration building, where, after coffee, Albert asked his secretary arrange a taxi to take me back to Linkirk. He stated, 'It's our treat. It'll be far quicker and more comfortable than going by bus.'

I thanked him, ending our discussion with, 'I think I've got some idea of what you want from me. Give me time to consider all I've seen here and do some library work, and I'll contact you again in a few days. May I also talk to John Bland, if I get any bright ideas? Has he signed a confidentiality agreement?'

'Oh, yes. John Bland has seen everything I've shown you and you can talk freely about it to him. I think he's already done some work on the goo for us. Possibly, that discouraged him. We'll give you fresh samples, and you can see what you can find out. Contact us when you're ready.'

The thought that John Bland had opted out of this project made me feel I was being presumptuous even to try. But, by not having committed myself, I still had plenty of time to withdraw gracefully.

○

With the afternoon's work completed, I relaxed in the taxi home, which was an unaccustomed luxury. The driver apparently preferred not to chat, so I reviewed my impressions of the derelict factory, including the 'goo pits', trying to work out just what, if anything, I might usefully be capable of doing next.

When I reached the flat, I found that Doug was already home.

He asked immediately, 'How did things go?'.

'I could adjust very readily to the benefits of industry,' I confirmed. 'The taxi home only reinforced my wish to have a car. As for the industrial pollution… what a mess! It's more like a labour of Hercules than a "project for Bill"!'

'So you told them, "No! No! No! Not at any price!"?'

'Not really. I rather surprised myself by agreeing to think about it. If I could actually achieve something, it might give me some insights into industrial research. I said I'd talk to John Bland first.'

'Good luck with that endeavour! But let me make a prediction: any talk you have with our John will, I'm convinced, only waste your time. Now sit down and forget today's problems. Relax and have a glass of beer to wash away all lingering tastes of dust, chemicals and all those noxious fumes you've been breathing.'

Chapter 6

First Friday in October

STUNT	a. Retard development or growth
	b. Unusual, entertaining event

ARRIVING FOR WORK THE FOLLOWING MORNING, JUST WHEN JOHN Bland had left his car, I mentioned yesterday's factory visit: 'Prof, have you a spare moment, please?'

'Yes… Yes, of course,' he confirmed.

We exchanged banalities about the weather while going to his office, but, once inside, Prof seemed to become aware of my presence suddenly, saying, with apparent surprise, 'You wanted to see me?'

'Yes, please. I want to discuss my contact with Dr Miller,' I said.

'Albert Miller? We're doing research for him. He's a good man.'

'I visited the factory yesterday, and he showed me the polluted areas.'

'What of it?'

'You told me to keep you informed about my contacts with him.'

'Did I? Well, if you say so.'

Not for the first time, I had to decide whether anything was likely to be gained by persisting after so *unpromising* a start. 'I hoped you might offer some advice.'

'Of course! Your appointment here requires you to carry out original research...'

I was treated to yet another verbatim repetition of the sermon that Prof had already given me – too many times. Already word-perfect on the text, I did my best to remain calm, even suppressing several tempting rejoinders. Remembering Doug's prediction that seeking Prof's advice would only waste time, I ended the pointless conversation as tactfully as possible: 'Thank you, Prof. Good morning.'

○

After having collected my notes, I arrived in good time for my 9.00am lecture. This was my first contact with this subsidiary class of some sixty students, who had opted to take first-year chemistry only, before continuing to graduate in a different main subject. It seemed unlikely that this group would be responsive to my words of wisdom, with many being content to scrape the necessary chemistry pass with minimum effort.

Early arrivals were reading newspapers or clustered in groups, chatting quietly. Most had gravitated to the back seats of the lecture theatre. Apart from a few keen individuals in the second row, my audience apparently preferred to maintain the maximum distance from their lecturer. Many were wearing the colourful gold-and-platinum sporting colours of LU, represented by yellow-and-white shirts emblazoned with 'LU'. The reason, I supposed, was a competition, enigmatically described as the Traditional Annual Cylinder Race (aka the Cylinder Race), which was scheduled for that afternoon. Publicity promoting this unique sporting occasion had appeared around the campus recently. I hoped to watch and enjoy this unusual event, but first I had a class to teach; sporting pleasures were for later.

My audience increased slowly as others arrived unhurriedly. At 9.05am, a quick count showed that only thirty-two of the sixty-two names on my list were present.

Nevertheless, I decided to start: 'Good morning. Even if we're not all here yet, I'll start now. I'm Dr Green. My ten lectures will cover...'

Latecomers continued to appear, increasing the class. Some slipped unobtrusively and quietly into the already-crowded back rows. Others caused minor disturbances by pushing past colleagues to join friends, to exchange mumbled greetings and conversations that had to be completed before sparing any attention to hear the lecture, which was their ostensible reason for being here. I was interested to notice, after lecturing at Weald University, that similar attitudes and behaviours were shown by students in both places. Any overt display of interest in the subject you were reading, which might be witnessed by your peers, must be avoided!

By then, the noise of background chatter had risen above my comfort zone, so I resorted to one of my few available sanctions. I reduced the audibility of my delivery progressively, which had the desired effect: the majority of the class, wishing to hear what I was saying, somehow discouraged the persistent mumblings of the less considerate minority. When audience noise level had diminished, I reverted to normal volume, ending a minute early.

◉

I went to the coffee room, where – after a quick cup of coffee – I had no time to relax. Walter was present, also taking a break, but, on the single occasion that our glances met, he appeared as cold and distant as ever – or was I becoming paranoid? There was no sign of a thaw in his overt antipathy. However, with a laboratory class to supervise, I had no time to reflect on this. It was much more important to fulfil my obligations by safeguarding the health and safety of my class while developing their experimental skills. During practical classes, early in the academic year, the demonstrators of these skills – laboratory teachers – tend to be worked to maximum capacity. Students seem to have forgotten any practical expertise learned in previous years; their self-confidence, skills and even willingness to attempt experiments seem to evaporate during the long vacation. The situation is not helped by laboratory equipment demonstrating its perverse abilities not to function at all or to malfunction, and sometimes bits go missing.

As a newcomer, I was unfamiliar with the specific problems found in the practical exercises favoured here and, importantly, where replacement equipment was stored. My morning was alternatively frustrating, due to experiments going wrong, and occasionally rewarding, when a persistent difficulty was overcome. Confidence can conceal ignorance, and a welcome reluctance by students to take any initiative usually enabled me to bluff my way through. Harry, the technician, an unsung hero of science teaching, often quietly resolved and cured questions puzzling both teachers and taught alike. Nevertheless, by the end of the class, I was quite weary, but relieved that my first, presumably most testing, session had passed without obvious disaster. It was a taxing, but not bad, morning's work. Some students had even managed to complete a first experiment. I looked forward to the Cylinder Race, after which I intended to try to think up a first response to Albert about the pollution problems seen yesterday.

These thoughts were interrupted rudely when, on returning to my office, I was passing Walter's room. His door opened abruptly and my name was called, indeed shouted, unnecessarily loudly: 'Green!'

How *could* he know I was there just then?

'That's me.' I turned to confront Walter, whose red face was contorted with rage. I could think of no reason for such obvious wrath. Adopting flippancy to defuse an impending confrontation, I affected an upper-crust accent: 'Ah, Thompson, old man. What ails thee? Why the formality?'

Walter's scowl remained as we moved into his room and he closed the door. He almost growled, 'I think we have something to discuss.'

'Not to my knowledge, Thompson; you'd better explain yourself.' As I advanced, he retreated, as if fearing physical attack. Abandoning my affected accent and staring at him, eye to eye, I said loudly, 'Incidentally, and for future reference, I don't like being yelled at in the corridor. I've no idea why you're behaving in this peculiar manner. If you've something to say to me, say it! I'll try to understand. Just now, you should calm down. You look so excited that you might, with any luck, do yourself some permanent damage. In the meantime, I'm listening.'

'You visited that Glasgow factory yesterday!' It sounded like an accusation.

'So?'

'I was deciding whether or not to take on that work.'

'So?'

'I've been here longer than you. I'm senior. That research was offered to me *first!*'

'So, we all await the Great Thompson making up his great mind. Great! There's one great problem! I don't accept that you're that great! Your aggressive pose solves nothing. Prof asked me if I was interested. I was and I still am.' Still undecided, this had to be my best opening gambit. I could not, and must never, concede ground.

'I've plans to—'

'Stop posing as the injured innocent. It's unconvincing, and you're only playacting. You may be able to fool yourself, but you're certainly not fooling me.'

'You try to steal my project and then pretend—'

Now I was really angry. 'Don't take that line! If you're accusing me of *stealing* I'll take you to whatever ethics committee we have here to muzzle bullies like you.'

Walter's eyes bulged, and he seemed to find difficulty in expressing himself. 'You come here… take over work from those of us who've—'

'Bullshit! When you disentangle your hormones and calm down a lot, then we *might* talk, but not right now. Your act, and that's all it is, is unconvincing and bores me. Now, I'm going to make a written record of your outburst, before I forget the gist. Then, if I've any, *any*, more nonsense from you, I *will* make a formal and serious complaint. I don't know how to do it, but be assured I'll find the way. For now, I'll accept an apology for your nasty outburst, and expect better manners in future.' I executed a mocking bow and waited for a reply. When none was given, I continued, 'I award no Oscars for your performance. Try to be more convincing in future.' Privately, I was pleased to see the now genuine anger on Walter's face. Evidently, as I had guessed, this act was only a charade. I left without further comment, but could not resist slamming the door. Nevertheless, as my adrenalin level returned to normal, I had to face the unwelcome fact that my actions had probably made me a real enemy in the school. This achievement did not augur well for my future.

Lunch was less grand than yesterday's steak, but, just then, I was in no mood to savour culinary delights. I ate alone because I knew so few regulars in this dining room, but the solitude did allow me time to review recent developments.

My teaching duties were proceeding satisfactorily, as far as I could judge. It can be difficult for a lecturer to know if all his pearls of wisdom are being understood, much less fully appreciated, by undergraduate classes. I had been informed officially, in writing, that 'at unpredictable intervals during lecture terms' questionnaires would be distributed to my students to record their appraisals of 'aspects of your teaching'. The Facilitation Centre oversaw these surveys, including the collection and analysis of responses (removing any temptation for lectures to 'lose' critical comments). Later, as dictated by the Staff Handbook, the survey results would be 'communicated to the Professors and the Lecturer concerned' (listed in that order). Wryly, I thought, there was no reciprocal arrangement whereby staff could comment on student shortcomings: lax timekeeping, talking during lectures, dropped pens that must be retrieved with discomfort to others, etc. Nevertheless, my feeling remained that behaviour in LU classes differed little from the aspiring scientists taught in Weald University.

The really worrying, even *sinister*, incident had been my clash with Thompson. His unexpected aggressive outburst would not succeed in discouraging my research application to Albert. But he had exacerbated the bad feeling between us considerably. Why was he so aggressive? I remained convinced that his outburst was entirely spurious and a performance intended to intimidate me, the newcomer here.

I recalled comments by a former colleague, a self-styled amateur psychologist, about a mutual acquaintance who intermittently exhibited disproportionate aggression during confrontations. This 'expert' exemplified such outbursts as 'mad-dog syndrome'. A sudden, large, even extreme, escalation of tension during acrimonious debate can be used, on occasion, to achieve dominance, thus 'winning' the argument regardless of the relative merits of any or all relevant facts. Moreover, the threat of unpredictable overreaction, once applied successfully, can be held in reserve for use again to deter further opposition. On reflection, I decided that my instinct to point out the artificiality of Walter's anger had taken the edge off the effectiveness of his threat, this time. Nevertheless, the incident had been most unpleasant. In future, my dealings with Walter, during any shared duties, would pose further problems, which would just have to be dealt with pragmatically as and when any occurred.

I also recalled (with some surprise) that, during our heated exchange, I had told Walter of my intention to bid for Albert's pollution research contract. This might have scored me a debating point, but it was a decision that still had to be thought through thoroughly. Now I must decide whether I really meant what I had said and if I should bid seriously against Walter. In any normal relationship, we could have explored possible compromises, most probably a joint collaboration, but the confrontation had ruled this out. Now, if I withdrew entirely, for whatever reasons, it would appear to Walter that he had intimidated me successfully, which set an unacceptable precedent for the future. When the 'mad dog' wins, he can and will try again. I also supposed Walter would be unlikely to withdraw, thereby losing face. However, I did not remember him stating a positive intention to make a bid. Nevertheless, if he did proceed, this would lead to an interesting situation whereby Albert would have to adjudicate between who would succeed in a direct competition. Rival researchers often have to bid competitively for limited funds, but the distinguishing feature here was the severe underlying tension between us, about which Albert knew nothing.

Having considered this dilemma over lunch, I decided that, to retain my self-confidence (which had never been abundant) and establish my position in the school, I must do everything possible to secure this research contract. I also preferred that our colleagues knew nothing about that recent quarrel. Walter's attempt to discourage me had resulted in exactly the outcome he had opposed! This afternoon, I would contact Albert to confirm my interest. I wondered if we had any other competitors?

○

A noisy, cheerful crowd of supporters in front of Bond College awaited the start of the Cylinder Race. For the occasion, the steep main road through the centre of LU, The Spine, had been temporarily closed to traffic. On the carriageway, I counted six of the heavy, unwieldy metal cylinders used to transport oxygen and other gases around laboratories and hospitals. Each one was mounted on an improvised set of wheels; two crude carts were obviously home-made and the robust trolleys used to move these ponderous gas containers had been adapted for others. Each displayed prominently an LU college name, and was attended by a group of four burly students, with their muscular physiques identifying them as rugby players or weightlifters. All wore the LU sporting colours, which had appeared in my lecture, and were indulging in warm-up routines, encouraged by partisan groups of vociferous fans.

On the kerb, I found myself beside a young lady whose forebears had come from a Far Eastern country, though her accent was local. She was shouting encouragement to a competitor, who was also oriental, in a less-than-ladylike manner.

Such a knowledgeable spectator seemed pleased to tell me about the race: 'That tall boy is my brother, Li, who's now in the second year. The blue tape shows he's from Bond College. The race is won by the college team who get their cylinder most quickly from here to the provost's office.'

'Why?' I queried.

'It's tradition. It happens at the start of every teaching year. Intercollegiate rivalry for glory. Sport is celebrated.' She noticed my increasing puzzlement. 'Winners' names are immortalised on a list in every college. Every competitor enjoys a free dinner tonight in LU's Great Hall and hears the provost's speech.'

'The notices said the race is unique. What's so special about it?'

'It helps new students, freshers, to become part of LU and to take pride in their college. That's why it's held now, just after they come here. It's just a bit of harmless fun. The provost, the big boss himself over there, will start the race.'

'But who had the bright idea of pushing heavy cylinders uphill to the Facilitation Centre from here? And why? It looks dangerous. Those metal tubes are heavy; I once tried to lift one. If it fell or slipped, it could cause severe injury or worse.'

'You don't know the story?'

I shook my head.

She explained, 'It was the year LU was started. The first provost, Dr McClintock, was a medical doctor by training and he had a *very important visitor* [VIV] in Biggar House. This VIV took ill suddenly and the provost, from his doctor's training, I suppose, decided that oxygen was needed urgently to revive him. He called his secretary, the porter and other people to get oxygen to the patient *fast*. All the emergency phone calls resulted in several oxygen cylinders arriving from different parts of the campus: science, engineering, technology and I don't know where else... and an ambulance, I think. The cylinders were hauled up The Spine by staff responding to this call for help from the boss that could not be disregarded. The first one to arrive was from chemistry. That's why the Cylinder Race starts here.'

'Did the visitor survive?'

'Oh, yes. I don't know if any oxygen was used. But, later, after fully recovering, he was told about what became known as the First Cylinder Race. He was so impressed that he suggested it should be an annual affair. It's said he presented the winner's cup and still pays for the evening dinner. Look, they're about to start.'

The provost, whom I recognised from my interview and successor to the original medical diagnostician, came forwards and waved a gold-and-platinum banner. Retreating rapidly, he dodged the rush of a tight bunch of competitors jostling for advantage. Huge initial efforts were made to accelerate the cylinders up the gentler initial hill to gain maximum momentum before tackling the later, steeper upward slopes. As in all sports, tactics were essential for success. Two teams collided, but recovered rapidly, being anxious not to concede the slightest advantage to their rivals. Happily, nobody appeared to be injured or needing treatment by the strategically located first-aid stewards. The athletes, if they could be so described, turned the first corner rapidly, after much jockeying for the favourable inside lane, and disappeared onward and upward. From where we were, we could not see who won. I thanked my charming, now excited informant who ran off, keen to know the outcome. I returned to work at a more dignified pace.

This unique LU tradition had certainly amused me as an inoffensive, though certainly hazardous, form of entertainment, obviously giving pleasure to many. Perhaps it really did foster community spirit. The will to win was obvious among the competitors, who appeared to risk – perhaps not life – but the possibility of serious damage to limbs for little real reward. Although most sports involve injuries or accidents, racing with unwieldy, heavy cylinders seemed to me to be particularly fraught with danger. Such a cumbersome object might even be lethal – should it fall on someone – or, alternatively, become effectively unstoppable if set free on this hill unintentionally. I wondered if the LU safety committee had made a hazard assessment of the event and whether anyone had ever suffered injury. It was not my problem, but my safety-conscious imagination visualised the risks all too vividly.

I was unsurprised not to see Walter enjoying this sporting spectacle. The good-natured competition between high-spirited students contrasted disturbingly with my recent, acrimonious war of words with my hostile colleague. It still rankled. I saw no way to defuse this situation that I neither sought nor understood. In former ages, such differences could be resolved by physical confrontation, but the duelling era had long past. Now, serious disagreements could persist and fester, and the only sanction available, litigation, was prohibitively expensive and outcomes unpredictable.

○

The fairly empty corridors in Bond College contrasted with the usual bustle during teaching terms. Presumably, the students were now either celebrating 'our' victory in the Cylinder Race or, alternatively, devising fanciful explanations for 'our' inexplicable defeat. I would, no doubt, learn the outcome later. Just then, I needed to answer my ringing phone. My caller was a Mr Smith, who was representing a contractor specialising in road repairs, who asked if Dr Green would spare a few minutes of his valuable time, please.

Dr Green would, being curious to know the reason for this unexpected call.

'I believe Dr Miller has shown you the tarmac pits in their factory,' Mr Smith maintained.

'It's not tarmac.' I checked myself. Having signed Albert's confidentiality agreement, I must exercise extreme caution in dealing with this stranger, who had already shocked me by his knowledge of my movements yesterday! Uncertain about how to proceed, I resorted to ignorance: 'I've no idea what you're talking about.'

'Let me explain. My firm is entering the road-resurfacing business—'

'But you just said that you specialised in roads…'

'No matter. Please hear me out. I want to outline an attractive business opportunity for you. It could be mutually beneficial. You need say nothing to breach your confidentiality agreement, but we both know there's a large amount of tarmac in the factory you visited yesterday. [How much did this man know about me? How and why had he found out about my movements? I never learned!] 'That tarmac is commercially valuable. Also, we both know that Dr Miller and his firm want to get rid of it as a pollution hazard. I'm prepared to take it all; it's the easy option for them. It's a cost-free solution to their problem. We can usefully use that tarmac to resurface roads. A final disposal that ends the matter. Everyone's happy.'

'So why are you ringing me? I don't know anything about any tar.'

'But you could advise Dr Miller that this is his best option to solve his difficulty. You'd do a few tests for us, pass on the advice and we'll pay you well.'

'I cannot help. You've been misinformed. I am unwilling and unqualified to advise whether or not any tar you claim to know of is suitable for roads.'

'We would respect your judgement. Your skills as a scientist—'

'I suggest you talk with Dr Miller. I'm sorry, but I must go now. Goodbye.' I hoped terminating the call would emphasise my decision to remain uninvolved.

I tried to work out what was going on. Someone knew I had discussed the tar with Albert. Who? And how? Now, for material reward, I was being asked (or perhaps bribed) to represent the commercial interests of a firm about whom I knew nothing but who had been sufficiently bold to contact me directly. Who was this Mr Smith? Was that his real name? What kind of reputation had his firm? There were far too many disturbing imponderables. They wanted to acquire the tar for free, presumably expecting to make a handsome profit by using it for road resurfacing. I knew very little about tars and their suitability, or otherwise, for road surfacing or any other use. If I were foolish enough to become involved with this proposal and anything went wrong, it would be me, in the guise of an expert adviser, who would end up in massive trouble. 'The hazardous goo', as Albert called it, probably contained enough toxic material to cause a major pollution incident. Worse, if it contained carcinogens, this would pose an additional threat to everyone handling it. Moreover, unsuitable tar could melt on a hot day, causing traffic accidents. I must, *must*, not get involved.

Perhaps I should visit the library to learn something about the chemistry of tars. A superficial familiarity with the subject's jargon might help me deflect future unwelcome queries. On making that decision, I left my office.

In the corridor, I met Prof. McTaggart bearing his inevitable bundle of folders. 'Afternoon, Bill. Have you got a few moments? Would you come to my room just now?'

I would, so we both walked to his office.

When seated, he continued, 'How're things going for you? I meant to ask before now, but what with the new term and this malfunction of the finance computer…'

It was interesting that he also had his problems, but I preferred to skip details, having more than sufficient preoccupations of my own.

'I'm fine, thank you. I've started teaching. I lectured to 1.1.5 this morning and demonstrated in the 2.1.1 laboratory class. I'm just starting to think about research,' I responded.

'Yes. It takes a while to get yourself established.'

It was a relief to be spared the John Bland 'research homily'. 'May I ask you a question?'

He nodded in agreement.

'I met Dr Albert Miller yesterday, who took me to a factory near Glasgow. Do you know about their tar-pollution problem?'

Another nod from him.

'Today, Walter told me that he is interested in it also. I wondered if there is some understanding that he has priority to take the work?'

'No. It's entirely up to Albert to negotiate with either or both of you, and to decide who'll be funded for what... or not. You make your best case. May the best man win! We'll talk again later, but keep me informed about how things are going generally.'

The impression I gained was that my professorial bosses were not exerting themselves unduly to smooth the paths of new recruits **struggling** to establish themselves in their school.

'One thing more, if I may? I had a phone call from a Mr Smith...'

'Oh? My advice is to keep him firmly at arm's length. I wonder if his name really is Smith? It's almost too good to be true. Always be cautious and keep the university well away from all dealings with him. We're not sure about his credentials. He could be perfectly genuine, but his ability to pop up unexpectedly arouses suspicions.'

'I'm glad to know I did the right thing. I claimed to know nothing about tar.'

'That's the best policy.'

I did not add that this accurately expressed my own ignorance.

○

My library visit was less than productive. The only conclusion, after searching the few books mentioning tar, was that, realistically, I had found nothing useful.

Next, I wrote to Albert. My expression of appreciation for his hospitality was politic. I thanked him for his clear introduction to a research problem that interested me, but I could offer no scientific proposals at this stage. However, if he supplied me with tar samples, I could start preliminary tests to try to find out what was in it, and, naturally, I would welcome all further information he could provide. My letter was notably short on substance but strong on suggestions that, in future, I might make useful contributions towards cleaning the site. Perhaps my rapid response and positive expression of interest would compensate for the shortcomings of the content.

In planning what I should do next, the idea of contacting Beth appeared much more attractive than embarking on any of the many and pressing priorities that involved work. I indulged myself in some brief daydreaming, vividly recalling the happiest moments of our riverside walk, followed by the companionable meal together. I wanted to see her again and spend time with her – very soon.

My phone call was answered on the first ring by Beth herself, leaving me temporarily tongue-tied. I asked, rather tentatively, when we might meet again, to which she replied that she would ring back. The shortness of our exchange and the terseness of her tone left me nonplussed. Had I offended her? Was I taking too much for granted? What, oh what, was I to do if there was no return call? The pain of uncertainty was sharper than I thought possible. Was I alone and pursuing a one-sided friendship?

The computer, while giving no comfort, at least provided a temporary diversion. Conjured up by subliminal reflexes, my favourite computer card game appeared effortlessly on the screen, and my subsequent responses progressed the puzzle to a rapid and successful completion. The phone ringing dispelled instantly all satisfaction gained.

It was Beth. What a relief!

'Sorry, Bill, to cut you so short just now. You rang at a really awkward moment. Something on the stove had just caught fire,' she explained.

'Sorry about the stove.' My condolences were necessary, though I was unaware of the conflagration.

'Not to worry. You asked, I think, when we might meet. What about tonight?'

All my negative presentiments instantly evaporated and were replaced by a warm, anticipatory glow. 'Do you have anything special in mind?'

'Would you like to help me in babysitting?'

'I don't know that I've any talent for such a responsibility. Possibly, I could be instructed. What would the parents think of a babysitter without a qualification diploma?'

'I look after Irene and Babs sometimes to give Tom and Valerie an evening out. Valerie and I were in the same class at school. Come, and we'll watch TV together.'

'But how will Valerie and… er… her husband… feel about me?'

'It's no problem. I've just talked to her, that's why it took me a while to get back to you. We're welcome to watch their TV and have supper. They usually leave a tray… I suppose they feel they can't pay me.'

'If you're sure?'

And so it was arranged.

○

Going to Valerie's house, Beth's description, I passed a convenience shop and thought it might be appreciated by everyone (particularly Beth) if I thanked my unknown hostess's hospitality with flowers. This time, I bought a potted plant, hidden in a plastic bag, thereby avoiding my shyness about carrying flowers in public.

The house in question – a semi-detached, red-brick villa – was one of several identical houses in a small cul-de-sac. I could almost hear the Estate Agent describing the property as 'An ideal starter home for newly married, young couples.' The two children, both being girls, represented only the slightest departure from the ideal norm. Going in, I was introduced to Valerie transiently, in the small hall with Beth, and waved towards the lounge to meet Tom.

He asked, 'So, you're Beth's friend?'

No immediate and suitable response came to mind, so I simply replied, 'We met fairly recently.'

'Now here are the ladies. We're a little late already, so please excuse us dashing off. Come back soon, and we'll be more sociable. The girls can fix the details. Bye for now.'

Beth came into the room, radiating the warm smile that I found so special. I wondered, not for the first time, what I had done to engage the attention of so attractive a companion.

'So you're here for your first babysitting lesson?' enquired Beth.

'That, if you like, but there are other reasons,' I confirmed. These reasons were not explored because Beth had noticed the plastic bag, which, in the flurry of introductions, had been forgotten and remained suspended from my hand. 'I quite forgot. I brought your friend Valerie this plant.'

Beth appeared puzzled.

'You did say she was giving us supper. I thought… it was the least…I could do,' I stated.

'That's really nice, but you should have given it to her yourself. Why don't you write a note?'

I followed her suggestion. The plant, minus the bag (and receipt), plus an explanatory note were left on the hall table. When I returned, Beth was seated on a comfortable (but single) armchair, which was evidently her customary place here, where she seemed very much at home. I sat on the matching sofa.

'Tell me everything you've been doing since I saw you last,' she directed.

It was difficult to answer adequately, despite my pleasure from her interest. Tar chemistry – however enthralling to, well, tar chemists – was well outside the range of social chit-chat suitable for a cosy soirée with so attractive a companion. For quite different reasons, my recent exchanges with Walter were unlikely to impress and might contain unknown pitfalls. Risky topics both when I wanted to hold Beth's attention. With a flash of inspiration, I remembered a safer, neutral topic. 'I watched the Cylinder Race today. It was quite an event, though it looks dangerous, with men rushing uphill pushing heavy lumps of metal. I was pleased nobody got injured. But I've not yet heard who won.'

Beth found the local evening paper, which reported Carlisle College as the victor; Bond College only managed third place. My slight feelings of regret hinted at an unsuspected loyalty.

Now it was my turn: 'I'm just as interested to hear all your news.'

Beth said that a visit from a school inspector that afternoon had been rather stressful. Talking about it seemed to relax her slight tension.

'Shall we watch TV? There's a programme I sometimes follow,' she offered.

The programme fancifully portrayed events in the busy accident-and-emergency department of an imaginary hospital. Having seen a few previous episodes, I hoped fervently that the location was entirely fictional and that I would never, in distress, find myself subject to such chaotic and dramatic emergency treatment. The storyline primarily concerned conflicts involving the personalities, romances and private lives of the main characters – doctors, nurses and policemen – while they patched up their often bloody patients. Despite such continuing, acrimonious and personal vendettas, the protagonists nevertheless managed medical miracles. Neatly fitting between their quarrelsome interactions, they delivered highly successful treatments, curing patients suffering acutely from a variety of (usually) life-threatening conditions. Several patients were restored to vigorous health, exuding excessive gratitude to their saviours when leaving hospital to resume their 'normal' lives. Significantly, not one of them died. The programme had already started when we began watching, but the storyline did not require detailed knowledge of previous events, and none of the disputes between the principal characters were resolved in this instalment. Viewers were invited to look forward to the tempting sequel next week. I did not mention the ease with which I could resist the temptation of this particular sugar-coated medical pill.

However, a much more pleasant, and less-resistible, temptation fully attracted my immediate interest when Beth, after turning off the TV, sat down beside me on the sofa. I was conscious of the warmth of her arm beside mine and detected the faint flower-like fragrance of her perfume. Companionable silence was preferred to talk and, just then, I could think of nothing worth saying. Reviewing the recent TV offering was a definite non-starter. Instead, I moved my arm, slowly and gently, until it encircled her shoulder. I noticed no detectable resistance and might have felt a slight movement closer, or was my imagination working overtime? Her head came to rest on my shoulder; this time, she undoubtedly had initiated the contact. Gently, I turned my face, to find her mouth gratifyingly close. The separation closed slowly by mutual consent and for the first glorious time our lips met. It was a deeply satisfying kiss. Time was temporarily suspended; later, neither of us remembered whether it was short or long. We disengaged; the only sound being my, 'Wheeeeew.'

I stroked her neck, just above her collar, and wished fervently that this moment could last forever. All extraneous thoughts disappeared in a true meeting of emotions.

This was confirmed by Beth: 'That was very good. Would that such golden seconds could last forever and never end. I won't ask where you learned to kiss, but you learned well.'

'It was you who inspired me,' I replied. Without conscious intent, my hand began to move itself downwards, when interruption occurred in the form of a faint wail from upstairs. Reality had returned.

Beth was away at once and shortly afterwards the crying ceased. She returned with a supper tray bearing refreshments that were generous and tasty. The situation had transformed seamlessly from the warmth of our amorous contact into the cosy glow of comfortable domesticity.

'I know it's early, but Valerie and Tom will be back soon. They never stay out late. We don't want to be caught in a compromising situation, do we?' she asked.

'No,' I agreed reluctantly, but, given a free choice, this would not have been my considered opinion. I would have been only too pleased to risk compromising situations with Beth any time. But, with hopes of future temptations, just then was not the best time to press this viewpoint.

When Tom and Valerie returned, Beth mentioned the small problem of the crying child. We were told that the dinner party had been very pleasant. Beth mentioned that the TV had not been particularly good, which was an appraisal I could support. Thanks were exchanged for babysitting, supper and the plant. We made our goodbyes and left.

On walking Beth home, I was more than pleased to agree to meet again soon. She asked whether we should 'say goodnight' at the end of her road, rather than outside her home. Here, we had the privacy to enjoy real kisses and relive some of the ardour savoured earlier.

Afterwards, while walking home alone, I reflected on the progress of events. My friendship with Beth had blossomed more quickly and more happily than I could ever have imagined. I only hoped that she felt similarly about our rapidly ripening relationship. There seemed to be good grounds for optimism.

Chapter 7

BOUND

a. Constrained, thereby limiting freedom

b. Direction in which we are progressing

ALTHOUGH CHRISTENED SIMON STARR, OUR CHEMISTRY laboratory superintendent was informally known as 'The Tsar'. He accepted this honorary, if slightly irreverent, title without complaint, as recognition of his (often self-proclaimed) invaluable contributions to the school's research excellence. Responsibility for maintaining the most sophisticated, delicate technical equipment in Bond College was his heavy burden, which was felt most keenly. Anyone working within his 'Tsardom', alias the Instrument Laboratory, could not escape the implication that Mr Starr regarded all equipment in his care as prized, personal possessions worthy of his jealous protection. He delighted in the efficient functioning of all 'his' instruments, often giving the impression he would much prefer that researchers did not upset the smooth running of his domain by actually *using* any of the school's apparatus. Many an undergraduate had smarted under the force of his imaginative verbal condemnations of shortcomings in their laboratory skills or, worse, for the unforgivable crime of attempting an inappropriate experiment. It was not unknown for experienced, even senior, staff to strategically withdraw after 'equipment failures' rather than admit working with the delicate instrument that had unexpectedly and unaccountably 'developed a malfunction'. Not that it could have been their fault, of course.

The Tsar, whom I had met only briefly, was not in the Instrument Laboratory when I went tactfully to seek guidance about which of 'his' instruments I might use. I supposed he was currently away repairing some delicate machine that was temporarily 'bollocksed'. He had used this colourful term, which was unacceptable in polite society, to describe to me an incident in which his precious equipment had been damaged during careless use by 'some ham-fisted crap-shoveller'. Such unskilled workers could include, by implication, anyone from the newest, rawest chemistry recruit to the Provost himself (who probably knew nothing about the Tsar and his Tsardom). School technical staff, all nominally supervised by Mr Starr, generally preferred to avoid risking his displeasure by contriving to work elsewhere, whenever possible. It is not only senior academics who build personal empires.

I found real pleasure in surveying the extensive range of quality equipment available, with every instrument maintained meticulously and ready for use. Among these scientific goodies, I was delighted to find a versatile instrument that had been most productive during my previous research at Weald University. Better still, this differential scanning calorimetry (DSC) apparatus was a newer and more sophisticated model than the one I had already used. The instruction manual suggested it was the most advanced apparatus available. It was a promising omen for a research project I intended to start as soon as possible (even John Bland might approve?).

My detailed inspection of the equipment coincided with Walter's arrival. Surprisingly, he talked to me normally, as if last week's confrontation had never taken place. Once again, his unpredictability confused me, perhaps intentionally. His irrational mood swings confounded my hopes of ever establishing a normal relationship with him.

He stated, 'William, you're welcome to admire, from afar, my latest toy. My persistent lobbying has given me the chance to start work on...

You mustn't even think about laying one finger on it. This is my *fiefdom*, and this instrument is to be used *exclusively* for my research.'

Taken aback, I did not try to conceal my anger: '*Fiefdom?* I was told that everything here is for everyone's use.' I gestured, including the whole room.

'Then I'm afraid you've been misinformed. This particular item is for *my* exclusive use. It's off limits, so don't even think about touching it.'

While our discussion superficially resembled an almost-normal conversation between colleagues, for me, it further ratcheted up the tension between us. Effortlessly, Walter managed to disadvantage me *every* time we met. I was growing increasingly confused as to how I could and should respond to him. Having clung to the hope that we might move towards a mutually acceptable *modus operandi*, this morning's conversation had *again* rudely dispelled this aspiration. His claim that the equipment I most wanted to use was off limits to *me*, was an unpleasant rebuff. But could he commandeer school equipment for his sole use? What other arbitrary restrictions might he contrive to curtail my work? Unprofitably, I *again* decided that I must minimise contact with this man and distance myself, taking nothing for granted. More problems appeared inevitable after Albert gave his decision about the tar-pollution contract, which I still awaited with apprehension.

'I thought everything here is available to—' I began.

'No!' Walter started tinkering with '*his*' equipment. His withdrawal ended our conversation more eloquently than words; I was wiped out from his attention.

There seemed little point in exploring the Instrument Laboratory further until I could know which apparatus was available, so I returned to my office. Waiting outside it was a young man, whom I did not recognise.

'Hello. May I help you?' I asked.

'Mr Starr sent me t'help in your lab. I've come. I'm Roger Masters,' the young man responded.

Roger was in his early twenties, tall and thin, and his long, somewhat blotched face and inexpertly cut, darkish hair (had he done this to himself?) gave him an unkempt appearance. This visual impression of dishevelment was accentuated by that day's shave, which, being kind, had been only partially successful. Several cuts on his face suggested an incomplete mastery of the razor, auguring poorly for his technical ability to handle scientific equipment. His distinctly off-white coat was overdue for laundering, being conspicuously grubby, besides being too short for his long frame and ending above his knees. He appeared, throughout our brief acquaintance, to be chronically depressed. I never decided whether this was resignation from living in an unforgiving world, due to poor health or perhaps both. It occurred to me (rather unkindly) that The Tsar's motivation in allocating me this help might have been his understandable wish to distance Roger from other more demanding duties.

We went into the laboratory adjoining my office, which was a workspace vacated on the retirement of a former staff member, who it was said (or, more accurately, gossiped) had abandoned chemistry for good. Exactly whose *good* was unspecified, but to *me*, his ungrateful legatee, this 'abandonment' was wholly *bad*. My absentee benefactor had bequeathed me a collection of superannuated, by then totally useless, junk research equipment. This included an extended tangle of glass tubing, wires, plastic, etc. that superficially resembled the equipment in John Bland's personal laboratory. More worryingly, there remained very many chemical-containing bottles, most unlabelled and many showing evidence of long-term degradation or even decay. Both anonymity and age posed unknown hazards to anyone attempting their disposal, thereby risking pollution or even personal injury. Nevertheless, before I could start my research, I had been made responsible for clearing away all these nasty, dangerous and redundant remnants of abandoned, long-forgotten projects. When I complained mildly that this task was unreasonable, John Bland had 'compromised' (only under his definition of that word) by offering me help, apparently in the form of Roger. To my intense irritation (which I only just suppressed), he had not missed the opportunity to restate, yet again, his homily about my urgent need to start research. The fact that this was being obstructed perversely by the university's inability to ensure that former staff disposed of their own messes was not mentioned. Looking at my technical assistant, Roger, as he visibly recoiled from the task facing us, I wondered if it would be easier for everyone if I worked alone, thereby releasing my 'helper' for other duties.

I had already noticed that Roger walked with an unusual gait: he seemed to be keeping his knees as far apart as possible. Intermittent expressions of pain flitted across his face. I asked him what was wrong.

'I fell orf me moto'bike in Main Street yesterday. Comin' t'work, I were. Scraped my legs on t'road. Walkin's painful too. The lorry stopped in time.'

'Should you be here at all?' I suppressed a vivid mental picture of the horrific accident scene, with a stationary lorry only inches away from the prostrate and helpless motorcyclist. Instead, I seized on the chance of ridding myself of my assistant without hurting his feelings. 'Wouldn't you be better off at home, resting your leg?'

'Me mam won't hear nothin' of 't. I've 'ad too much time orf, she says. She don't want me round t'house no more.' It seemed a not unreasonable ambition.

'OK. Then we'd better make a start.'

Dividing the work between us posed safety problems. One task was breaking – into small, disposable fragments – the extended tangle of glass tubing built onto its frame. This unwieldy and by then purposeless lash-up would be consigned to waste bins as small bits. I showed Roger carefully how to crack glass tubing safely, using a file and a hot, molten-glass rod, despite his protests.

'I done all that afore. No problems,' he declared.

Hoping this was true, and with his memory refreshed, I risked letting him start on this part of our clean-up.

'If you've any – *any* – doubts at all, ask me *before* you try anything dangerous. Please take care!' I exclaimed.

I preferred to face the challenges and dangers of disposing of the redundant chemicals, some of which were hazardous, myself. The problems – though admittedly on a much smaller scale – were, in principle, similar to those posed by the disposal of Albert's tar. Chemical waste is often potentially dangerous/polluting, whether it arises from the commercial manufacture of products for profitable sale in price-sensitive markets or from research striving to advance science. The man in the street, the eager purchaser of the latest technological wonders, takes little interest in how these goodies are obtained, being more concerned with how they can enhance the comfort and status of our increasingly artificial lifestyles. It is only when things go wrong in the factory or disposal site, exposing the public to real or imagined pollution risks, that local scares develop into protests. The demand then is that the dangerous waste, generated for the consumers''benefit', should be got rid of elsewhere, anywhere, always providing that it is far, far away from the consumers themselves.

While undertaking my unwelcome chore, I idly contrasted Albert's motivation for chemical clean-up with mine. His firm was volunteering to decontaminate polluted industrial land, in the expectation that this 'altruistic' investment might yield a profit eventually. In contrast, I had been allocated a laboratory on the condition that if I cleaned it up, I could use it. I had been coerced into clearing up my predecessor's leavings before I could start the research I was constantly urged to start *at once*.

These thoughts naturally led me on to think about the wider problems of waste disposal. Environmental protection is all too often an unprofitable 'investment opportunity', as our commercial institutions know too well, despite the fundamental truth that all life requires unpolluted space in which to thrive. A clean, natural environment is not prized (as much as it is merited) as a priceless legacy, bequeathed to us by our forbearers and to be held in our trust to be passed on again *in its pristine state* to future generations. Like so many human activities, this essential inheritance is neither recognised adequately nor valued meaningfully by our monetary systems. In an ideal world, every polluter would be made to pay for the clean-up: the most cost-efficient option is usually the treatment of each threat at its source. But the world is not always ideal. In our industrial society, manufacturers in competitive markets strive towards reaching the lowest price at any hidden cost. Despite 'green claims', there is a reluctance to invest in meeting the ever-more-stringent pollution controls. After a factory closure and the 'disappearance' of its owners, any contamination on the abandoned industrial site must be cleaned up by someone. Rarely, a firm like Albert's seizes a clean-up opportunity for exploitation. More usually, the problem devolves to local government, with the costs passed onto reluctant taxpayers, presumably including the consumers who (too cheaply!) bought the goods responsible for the original pollution, closing the circle. A society that minimises investment in waste treatment should be mindful that most of us contribute in throwaway cultures.

While musing on these hitherto unresolved problems of modern society, I set aside all unlabelled containers as potentially dangerous, for later individual appraisal. Working systematically, I semi-cleared several well-laden shelves quite quickly and then turned to monitor Roger's progress. What horror! Just then, he was pushing a glass tube from a rubber sleeve in which it was stuck.

I waved while shouting a warning: 'Stop! That's dangerous! Don't push that glass—'

It was too late! There was the sharp crack of snapping glass, a yelp of pain and a flow of blood from Roger's hand.

Together, we washed what appeared to be a superficial cut, but it continued to bleed.

'Me mam says I'm accident prone,' he stated sheepishly.

I was beginning to feel increasing sympathy for Roger's 'mam', but was more concerned about his injury.

'Go to the Medical Centre, now! Now! No argument! Let them see this cut. Later, after the staff meeting, come back to tell me what they said. Say at 4.00pm? OK?'

I found an accident report form and filled in my version of events, particularly mentioning my warnings to the *injured party* about the dangers of handling glass, before he started work. I described the action taken as 'Cut bandaged. Roger Masters sent to the Medical Centre.' It was all I could do for now.

○

The first staff meeting of term was scheduled for 2.00pm. I was looking forward to this formal occasion with great interest, as I was keen to learn how the school was managed. Arriving a little early, I found most of my colleagues were already seated around the long table in the School of Chemistry boardroom. I was pleased to be able to recognise almost everyone present by sight, if not yet all by name. Those present seemed to be already occupying their usual places. I worked this out because staff who taught within the several distinctive sub-disciplines of chemistry tended to sit together, forming identifiable groups (perhaps pressure groups?). Accordingly, I took one of the few unoccupied seats with the group of physical chemists, beside Doug and near the end of the table furthest from the meeting's chair. The agenda had been circulated. Being keen to participate fully, I had a notebook to record anything of interest and note future commitments that might involve me.

I noticed that the woman sitting on my other side, Dr Wong, had arranged neatly two piles of paper together on the table. She was obviously checking a printer's proof against her typed manuscript; presumably it was a research article soon to be published. Even before the meeting started, she was comparing the texts carefully, line by line, as two rulers, one on each page, were moved gradually downwards. At intervals, she made corrections to the proof. Clearly not everyone present intended to devote their (her) undivided attention to the transaction of school business.

While I could not be absolutely sure, it appeared that other papers arranged carefully in front of several other colleagues similarly (and partially) hid alternative interests that took precedence over meeting formalities. One appeared to be writing a letter. Another had a hardly concealed scientific journal, which he was obviously reading. Someone else had what looked suspiciously like a crossword puzzle, partially hidden among other papers, and a pencil in his hand. These colleagues appeared to have found ways of pursuing more important or, for the crossword-puzzle man, more diverting activities. Nevertheless, they could, no doubt, follow the progress of the business, participating if and when necessary. I remembered the advice of a teacher friend, who had impressed on me the necessity of always attending formal meetings, if only to oppose the allocation of unpopular duties that can most conveniently be delegated to an absentee, who was not present to object in person.

Prof. McTaggart bustled in, exactly on schedule and clutching his inevitable burden of folders under one arm. He was talking to Dr Charlotte Fanshawe, the school administrator, no doubt about topics listed for immanent discussion by the staff. He took the chair at the table head, with Charlotte, acting as secretary, beside him. After some paper shuffling, he rapped the table to bring the meeting to order.

'We've got a lot to discuss. We should make a start,' he stated, and he rearranged more papers. 'First, it's my pleasure to welcome Dr William Green to LU. We hope that you'll prosper here and look forward to your contributions to the work of the school.'

'Thank you, Prof. I'm pleased to be here,' I responded.

'Agenda item one, apologies from…' He went on to list the apologies in question. 'Agenda item two. The minutes of the last meeting have been circulated. Any changes?'

Inevitably, there was a pedant present, who had actually read the minutes, who said, 'Sorry, Chairman, but "accommodation" is spelled incorrectly on page two. There is a split infinitive on page two, line fourteen. Two commas are required on page four, line seven.'

'Thank you, Professor Bland for keeping us right, as always,' said the chairman. There was a just perceptible hint of irritation. 'Are these corrected?'

Charlotte nodded and the chairman, while signing the large book she had handed to him, remembered to ask, a little late, 'Is it your wish that I sign these minutes as a correct record?'

The audible murmur evidently expressed accord, rather than acclamation.

Angus McTaggart, the veteran chairman of countless meetings, guided our deliberations through the agenda items rapidly. He allowed the expression of opinions, but terminated quickly any argument that strayed from the point at issue. Agreements were reached by consensus, with few disagreements. The smooth functioning of the school had been worked out over many years, by cooperation between colleagues, most of whom accepted the common interest of maintaining the established status quo. This arrangement allowed maximum freedom to pursue research interests, some of which I could see were continuing uninterrupted during the meeting (though a *crossword* was hardly classifiable as *research*).

After the first few agenda items, I found my attention wandering. A few brief debates continued older and apparently long-running but minor differences of opinion, such as details of the contents of courses taught. It seemed to me that these esoteric debates resulted in little or, usually, no action. The academic futures of a few individual students, who had failed critical examinations, were discussed, and the decisions taken then were communicated to student advisers. Doug, who contributed the details, took note of each decision. Later, the colleague reading the technical journal temporarily interrupted his studies to request additional laboratory space. This was refused. However, after renewed pleas from the claimant, a 'final' decision was deferred to the next meeting. Diverse points of dissatisfaction were aired, though the resulting discussions produced no resolutions identifiable to me. The meeting appeared to consist of ritual exchanges of views, but yielded few, if any, tangible results, much less any significant actions. Perhaps this periodic opportunity to air grievances, real or imagined, was a routine, necessary rite undertaken to maintain the smooth running of the school. The occasion seemed to provide a safety valve rather than a forum for erudite academic debate. I had to conclude that the occasion was much less interesting than I had anticipated; indeed, most of the business was distinctly boring.

Only three items held any personal interest. The first, the only time that voices were raised and emotions shown, was a heated debate about our priorities in the list of new equipment that *might* be purchased for the Instrument Laboratory this year. The Facilitation Centre had not yet revealed how much money would be made available to us. Consequently, achieving a high priority on this list was important in improving the chance that a proposer would get the new equipment he/she sought. No consensus could be reached, so a subcommittee was set up to make recommendations.

I thought it timely to speak: 'May I, as a new boy here, ask about the availability of equipment in the Instrument Laboratory to staff, please?'

Prof. McTaggart was surprised. 'Everything there is equally available to all of us.'

'So there are no fiefdoms?' I noticed Walter, just across the table from me, sit upright suddenly with a wary look on his face.

'There aren't any... er... *fiefdoms*... as you choose to call them. Has anyone said anything different? If so, you've been misinformed,' Prof confirmed. The matter was closed.

I moved my right hand behind my left forearm and privately displayed to Walter two extended fingers in the V-sign, a well-known expression of derision. Walter's head jerked back just perceptibly, confirming my signal was understood, though he affected close attention to the next agenda item.

The second item of unexpected interest came with the school inspection report by the Health and Safety Team, who recorded sixteen breaches of agreed laboratory practices, itemised on a tabled list. Almost all had since been rectified. The one serious unresolved item was that the team had been unable to gain access to a room that I recognised, with surprise, as Prof's private laboratory. I thought it unlikely that this domain could ever pass *any* safety inspection.

John Bland explained, 'That was once my laboratory. I know that some equipment still remains there, which was used by Dr Lesnikovich when he was here. I asked him to remove it when he left, but I'm not sure he did. I ask the indulgence of the meeting to see what can be done to comply with the request.'

I was shocked; this was not just being frugal with the facts, it was more like a deliberate lie. Prof's weekend visits to the school were apparently made to evade compliance with current regulations, enabling him to continue working with antediluvian equipment. Later, this apparatus would be abandoned, bequeathed as an unwelcome legacy to whomsoever was unlucky enough to inherit the laboratory. I felt sincere sympathy for the unknown successor.

The last item of interest provided me with a tantalising challenge. In discussions of research priorities, several colleagues mentioned interests in environmental-science topics, though the individual programmes outlined were in different areas across this vast subject. Nevertheless, I discerned a common-but-unstated anti-pollution theme in several of the projects mentioned as topics for future applications to seek research support. It was obviously unacceptable for a newcomer, a beginner like me, to point out to more senior staff these common features of their ideas, so I decided reluctantly to remain silent for now. However, this appeared to be promising and fertile ground that just might be ripe for later cultivation. I would consider whether I might take some initiative, but only after careful appraisal.

Leaving, after the meeting, I passed close to the chairman, who was sorting through his papers, which were by then strewn untidily across the table. I heard John Bland angrily say, 'This afternoon you interrupted me *three* times!'

Angus McTaggart looked at him with puzzlement. 'I can only remember *twice*.'

A chairman's devastating response! This revealing comment confirmed my suspicion that a distinct tension existed between these two men.

○

Roger awaited me in my laboratory (to be!). His hand, bandaged professionally, was in a white supporting sling that contrasted with his greyish overall. I asked him how he had got on.

'Two stitches, I 'ad. It weren't nice,' he stated.

'No. I imagine not. Did you show them the accident report?' I questioned.

'Yes. And… I took it to the Fas… Fa'litation Centre.'

'Why? Doesn't Dr Fanshawe deal with it?'

'Dunno abaht that. What I thought were that I'm due compensation. Industrial injury, this's.' The bandaged hand was raised for inspection.

'Industrial injury? Compensation…? What did they say?'

'They said I 'ad to 'ave a solicitor, lawyer or someone, and make some case.' He made it sound a most unreasonable request.

'Show me the form. You've not mentioned here that I told you *not* to push the glass. Don't you remember? What are you going to do now?'

'Nothin'. Lawyers and suchlike cost. I only wanted £50 to get a new… second-hand TV. If I've got to pay people, they'll get more out of it than me.'

'Go and tell *all* this to Mr Starr. Thank you for your help. That's all for now.'

After his departure, I surveyed the partially cleared room. While deciding what to do next, the phone rang, and, on hearing Mr Smith's voice, I regretted answering it.

'Dr Green. How're you? I'll come to the point directly. When we last talked, we discussed the tar Mr Miller wants to dispose of. I think we agreed that the best use for it would be to surface roads and that my firm could help you with that,' he declared.

'No! No, Mr Smith! You're quite wrong. I *distinctly* remember saying that if you know of some tar and if you want to do business with Mr Miller, it has nothing – *nothing whatsoever* – to do with me.'

'But we agreed you'd be our scientific adviser or consultant, if you prefer…'

'No. We decided nothing of the sort. You know that as well as I do. It's not a good idea. I'm not a tar specialist. I couldn't, shouldn't, can't and won't agree to give you *any* advice, professional, environmental or scientific.'

'This is your chance to do the environment a favour. You'd get paid too…'

'I doubt it, and, *no*, I'm not – *not* – interested. I know nothing about any tar you mention. Discuss your ideas with Mr Miller. Goodbye!'

The cheek of the man. Unbelievable. My thoughts remained unspoken. *I can only hope that ends the matter.* I dragged my attention back to the urgent necessity to clear 'my' laboratory, but, before I could restart this chore, the phone rang again. I hesitated. Could it be Mr Smith *again*? No, this time it was Albert.

He explained, 'Your research proposal has reached us. We've had a preliminary look at it. I don't want to raise your expectations at this stage, and we'll need to discuss details, but – without making promises – I hope we'll be able reach an agreement. To be frank, some of your costs seem a bit high; did John Bland advise you there? On second thoughts, don't answer that.'

I let out a short laugh, while I recalled Prof's advice (which, for once, had been acceptable): 'Ask for double what you need.' I replied, 'Thanks for responding so quickly. I appreciate your call and particularly what you've just said.' Even if it was a definite 'maybe'. 'What's next?'

'We'll meet soon. Perhaps here, at the factory. Afterwards, if we've agreed the details, we'll make a formal contract with LU. Anything else?'

'One rather odd thing, which is a little worrying. Do you know a Mr Smith?'

'Been bothering you, has he?'

'You could say that, yes. I've told him clearly that I don't know anything about any tar. Then he assumed that I'm qualified to advise you to give it to his firm.'

'What did you say to him?'

'I said I won't get involved. It's no business of mine. Albert, I want you to know I'm not, and have no intention of, acting as his agent. First, I'm simply not qualified to express opinions on tar. Second, I don't know if your tar is suitable for roads or if it's an environmental hazard. It could, for all I know, cause pollution if it's used as or in tarmac. Finally, I've no wish to be Mr Smith's consultant. I don't like his methods, his ringing me and… er… to be blunt, I don't trust him.'

'Understood. That's what I'd expect you to say. I'll ring Smith to tell him unambiguously that our tar is not available… to him, that is.'

We ended the call, and no sooner had the handset been replaced, than it rang yet again. But this was quite different: it was Beth.

'Can you talk for a few minutes?' she queried.

'Yes. Yes.' I was always delighted to talk… for as long as she wished. It was my real pleasure. My laboratory refurbishment, on reflection, was not *that* urgent.

'I hope you won't mind if I say this.'

I braced myself for possibly unwelcome developments.

'We've been meeting quite a bit recently. Now, I think it might be a good idea for you to meet my parents,' she stated.

My apprehension disappeared, replaced by this welcome indication that our friendship might be becoming *really* serious. 'That would give me real pleasure. But how do they feel about it?'

'I should say that it's Mother's idea. She suggested you might like to come here for dinner next Sunday evening.'

It was time to meet her parents! That was an interesting development. I wondered if Beth felt that our relationship was becoming sufficiently serious to think about our long-term future, or were her parents simply seeking reassurances about their daughter's new friend? Surely Beth was of an age to select her own friends? Alternatively, was she herself keen to see how I related to her nearest and dearest: her family? Either way, the evening could to be a testing, even uncomfortable, occasion for us all, particularly if there was the faintest implication that I was a possible future son-in-law. No, I must set aside such thoughts and limit planning to the immediate future.

Up to then, Beth's company had always been most congenial and relaxed, giving me untold pleasure. The probability was that, like her, her parents would be similarly friendly and easy to get along with. However, the knowledge that her mother had suggested the invitation was more difficult to assess. Meanwhile, I had to decide whether or not to accept. On balance, I preferred that the meeting took place sooner rather than later, though there was another uncertainty.

'How do you feel about it?' she asked.

'It must happen sometime,' I concluded.

That was a revealing comment, which found a welcome echo in my own high hopes for continuing our relationship. Her reply was quite positive: 'I'd like you to come. Will you do that?'

'Yes, thank you. I'd love to accept your, or your mother's, kind invitation.'

So it was agreed.

By then, it was clear that little more was likely to be achieved at work that day. This final decision had used up the last of my energy; it had been a taxing day. I could not start another mundane, trivial task – such as chemistry. Laboratory clean-ups and injured technicians would have to await my pleasure.

I left for home before the phone could ring again.

Chapter 8

CULTIVATE	
	a. Tending plants; gardening or farming
	b. Build friendships, nurture relationships

WHILE I WALKED THROUGH THE OLDER STREETS OF LINKIRK, THE morning was sunny and dry. John Bland's sketch map, to guide me to his home, was both explicit and neat; I easily found my way. This contrasted sharply with the convoluted manner in which he presented me with this unexpected invitation. Never a master of verbal communication, Prof had been unusually tentative in seeking help with a project, which I only slowly identified as a simple request to work with him in his garden this Saturday morning.

In the coffee room the previous afternoon, Prof had, unusually, sat down opposite me and, without preamble, asked, 'Do you play sport on Saturday?'

Taken aback, I (at once and correctly) recognised this as an unskilful attempt to be subtle; he was moving, unsubtly and indirectly, towards some as yet unrevealed goal. My instinct was to avoid replying until I knew exactly what he wanted. This strategy did not encourage easy communication, so I was vague: 'No. I've not had time for sport, yet.'

An unstructured discussion followed, touching on the merits of sport in keeping fit and the health benefits of vigorous exercise. I remained mystified by Prof's hidden motives for his sudden interest in my plans for the morrow. Sport had never featured in our previous conversations, and Prof's overweight figure suggested he was not, and probably never had been, athletic.

Eventually, clues about his reasons for embarking on our conversational mystery tour emerged, but only after he asked directly, 'Am I right in thinking, Bill, that you're free tomorrow?'

I suppressed various barbed ripostes that had entered my mind unbidden, querying why my leisure pursuits might interest him. Finally, curiosity overcame my instinctively defensive stance, and I admitted there were no engagements. One reason, unstated, was that Beth would be in Edinburgh all day, visiting her sister to celebrate the birthday of her only niece.

'I'd like to make a deal with you… which you're… er… free to turn down.'

Caution returned, replacing curiosity. What kind of deal? Would my career be forever blighted if I declined the deal? I said, 'Perhaps you'd explain a bit more.'

Prof looked puzzled, as if he found my request as unreasonable. Nevertheless, he responded, accepting reluctantly that junior staff have to be mildly humoured sometimes, 'In my… our… garden, I've an apple tree. It's old, diseased and now gives little fruit. My wife wants to reorganise that… place…' Finally, the deal that emerged was that if I helped to dispose of this aged, unproductive and condemned apple tree, I would be reward with lunch at the Bland home.

It was difficult to decide how to respond to this proffered deal. Never having felled a tree, I had no idea how much effort or skill was required. Moreover, the culinary delights of a Bland household lunch were an equally unknown quantity, though Doug had mentioned something about Prof's meanness. Nevertheless, without clinching criteria, I decided to gamble and accept. Time spent in healthy outdoor activity might well be as interesting and as beneficial as anything else I might do. (Clearing that laboratory was one unattractive alternative.) I was advised to wear older clothes for our gardening activities, that would be starting at about 10.00am. These simple instructions were later emphasised by repetition, as Prof visited my room as he was going home.

○

On the day in question, I was wearing the least stained of my older trousers and the large, blue pullover, or Guernsey as my mother called it, that she had knitted during a brief phase of her interest in the craft, which she said was, 'to use up that wool'. This garment was at least one, perhaps three, sizes too large, and so my garb was, I hoped, suitable for tree felling.

At 9.45am, on nearing my destination, I saw a young man walking purposefully in the same direction. He seemed familiar, but I did not know his name. 'Aren't you in chemistry?' I asked him.

'Yes. And you, I think, are the new man here?' He had a pronounced Germanic accent. 'I am Hans Gutmann, I do vork under supervisor of *Herr Professor Doktor* Bland. I am student of him. Now I go to cut one *Apfel* tree for Prof.'

'So we will work together,' I added, relieved to notice that Hans was fit and strong, auguring well for the unknown challenges posed by our forthcoming task.

His informal garb included a black-and-red striped shirt in the distinctive livery of some football club. Although the large '25' on his back seemed to exceed the number of players in a team, I did not explore this mystery further.

'You also? This vill make better. One other student tell me, last year Prof ask him to paint house of glass...'

'Greenhouse,' I interposed.

'Yes! Greenhause. He break glass; three piece of glasses he breaks. Now, *Herr Professor Doktor* not ask him now, not today. More glass get broke! Ha!'

'According to my map, we've arrived.'

We were outside a three-storey end house of a red-brick terrace that had been built for relatively affluent families, perhaps during the late Victorian era. However, this formerly high-status residential area had since deteriorated appreciably from its original grandeur. While some houses were still well maintained, many others had been neglected, to varying extents. This latter group tended to have multiple bell pushes with name cards beside the front door, indicating conversions to rented flats or bedsit rooms. Such older, larger houses with large rooms were now all too ripe for conversion into high-density but short-term occupation, housing more transitory inhabitants. Some landlords obviously had minimised their investments in property upkeep. It was easy to predict which trend would ultimately prevail, with the proximity of LU maintaining a strong local demand for budget student housing. This economic reality could ultimately determine the future character of the district.

Number thirteen Elgin Terrace gave the impression of having remained undecided between these trends, though the single bell indicated single ownership. This end house, which was larger than its neighbours, also had a relatively large garden at the side. It showed few signs of deterioration apart from an urgent need for repainting the woodwork. In the garden, a start had been made towards improving its appearance. A trug – containing uprooted native plants, or weeds to gardeners – was surrounded by scattered tools. Some desiccated bulbs lay on a plastic sheet, presumably awaiting bedding into the then weed-free, prepared soil. To enter, Hans had to lift the gate off its hinges, after which we ascended the stone steps to the front door.

At 10.03am I pressed the bell, without audible response. Just before repeating the summons, a bolt was withdrawn and the door opened to reveal a large, worried-looking woman of untidy appearance. Her long, mousy-coloured hair was held together by a large, red, plastic clip, in an ineffectual attempt to form a bun. She was dressed *informally* in a large, blue pullover, resembling mine, and a long, loose, black skirt – clothes that emphasised her ample girth.

Through gold-rimmed glasses, she appeared both surprised and concerned to see visitors. Without addressing us, she called down the entrance hall, 'Darling, your friends are here.'

'Darling' turned out to be John Bland, who shared his wife's air of detachment by appearing equally bewildered about what action might now be required of him. His hesitation resolved itself as he introduced us to, 'My dear wife, Alison,' before we descended into the basement kitchen. 'It is, after all, an informal occasion,' he explained.

This old-fashioned, well-lived-in room contained a large, black, iron stove, with an oven, and also a huge sink of a type no longer in vogue. I was reminded vividly of the basement working kitchen in a National Trust property I had once visited. My feeling was that I had just entered a living museum that recalled how people lived in former times. Evidently, the house had not been modernised during the century or so since it had been built. The presence of electric light came almost as a surprise. In keeping with its antiquated ambience, the room was warm, comfortable and filled with tantalising aromas, including coffee. This was already prepared: hot and ready to pour. We sat on old but remarkably comfortable wooden chairs matching the central farmhouse table, and savoured the freshly brewed beverage. Warm, home-made and very palatable biscuits, just out of the oven, were most acceptable.

After a silence, John told us, 'This house belonged to Alison's parents, who lived here happily for fifty years. Unfortunately, they've recently become infirm and need care, so are unable to remain any longer in their old home. So Ally and I are now by ourselves, even if it's a bit large for just the two of us.' John Bland said this with genuine sadness and no hint of irony. 'It's old-fashioned and difficult to maintain. There's so much we could do. But where would we start? Anyway, we like it as it is.'

No response was possible because, with high-pitched cries of joy, two small children burst in through the back door. Both threw themselves on John and Ally, bubbling with enthusiasm to tell their news and show off their latest artistic creations. The looks of happiness and close interest in the children from both fond grandparents were immediate and genuine. I was amazed by the close likenesses of grandfather and grandson, who was then sitting on John's knee and nibbling the biscuit that John had been eating. The child's round head – with short, blond hair – was smaller, but his facial features closely replicated those of his grandfather. The similarities extended to their shiny, pink skin, appearing as if it had been well washed recently, as after a hot bath. Also both wore loose clothes, including blue, oversized pullovers.

The animation that lit up Grandpa's face markedly contrasted with the vague, puzzled and/or worried expressions that characterised him when in LU. I now recognised John Bland as a family man, who was happy in his home, but worried in his workplace.

Addressing me now, his voice took on a new strength and confidence. 'This is Jonathan. He's five. He's mad about painting and, like Grandma, he'll be a talented artist. Say hello, Jonathan.'

The brief, mumbled sound thrown towards me was followed by a detailed explanation, to Grandpa, of his art work.

A woman, who came in after the children, was introduced as Annabel, the children's mother. Again, strong family resemblances identified her as John and Alison's daughter. Meanwhile, the little girl on Grandma's lap, similarly revelling in undivided adult attention, was drinking milky coffee, which was really more milk than coffee. Hans and I finished our stronger beverage.

'Sorry Jonathan, Susan, but I have work to do. These nice men have come to help Grandpa,' stated John.

The boy protested mildly on being set down. I also felt a wrench on leaving so contented a scene of domestic harmony, but the deal had agreed that lunch was to be earned.

○

We workers went outside, where we viewed the condemned apple tree. It was not large, though it was certainly long past its prime: the bark of the sloping main trunk was cracked extensively, and, in places, was blackened and distorted by swellings. A few misshapen apples were visible among the leaves, which were already withering to autumnal brown.

'Ally wants to grow vegetables here. We much prefer our own fresh, home-grown food,' explained John. 'After the tree is cut down, I want to get out all the roots... if we can.'

'This is no problem. To take down tree. I have done before on farm of my father. In Germany, I do it,' confirmed Hans.

I hoped Hans's competence would match his confidence.

John had reverted to his hesitant alter ego. 'I hope so. I wonder if this job is too ambitious... for us. Er... we'll need tools. Over here.'

He then directed us to his shed. The shed housed an extensive and diverse array of tools; implements that dated from at least the era of Ally's parents, with many probably older. All were characterised by the sturdy manufacturing norms of former eras, but lacked all recent maintenance. Rust was the dominant colour. Again, I remembered the museum display of older farming tools, probably seen at the same National Trust property recalled in the Bland kitchen.

Hans hesitated momentarily, taken aback by the dilapidated state of everything. Then, overcoming his surprise, seized a large axe with such fervour that John retreated perceptibly. A whetstone was found, and our keen axe-wielder showed his skill by quickly generating a shining, highly lethal cutting edge.

John's concern increased. 'Don't you think it'd be safer to use… a saw?'

'No problem. I vork good with *Beil, Axt*. How you say? Axe?' queried Hans.

'I still think…'

But Hans went about his task with enthusiasm, even pleasure. Watched by both of us, a few accurate and efficient strokes severed the main trunk just above the roots, rapidly felling the tree. Waving us helpers aside, though we saw the need to remain beyond danger, he severed all the main branches rapidly.

'Now I cut these. Perhaps Bill also.' Hans pulled the larger segments of the dismembered tree onto a paved area where the branches were reduced rapidly to a pile of small logs. 'For vinter fire. Varm!'

Feeling I had contributed little, if anything, and noticing that John was still in his indecisive-behaviour mode, I found tools capable of extracting the roots that remained embedded firmly in the ground.

In less than an hour, the job was complete. Where the tree had been, there was by then a freshly dug area suitable for vegetable growing. The small pile of logs was in the outhouse. Hans and I were breathing heavily from our exertions, but John – after vigorous attempts to assist wherever possible, though making a tiny overall contribution – was quite out of breath. He had seriously overestimated the time required for the task: 11.30am was far too early for lunch. John appeared uncertain what to do now.

Surprisingly, the inspiration came from Hans. With a laugh, he resolved the dilemma. 'Now ve paint ze (how you call it?) *Gewaechshaus…* ze greenhause.'

Oblivious to the irony intended, John seized the shining moment. 'Oh Hans, what a good idea! I'll get paint and… er… brushes.'

Hans attempted to backtrack: 'I not so good; I not paint.'

Prof. disregarded this, and Hans ignored my whisper of, 'Break some glass to get yourself out of the greenhouse.'

I was prepared to do something, *anything, other than painting,* so I took the initiative. 'Prof, shall I dig around the cleared patch? A bigger area will then be ready for planting.' My real motivation, the difficulties of removing paint from hands, hair and even clothes, remained unstated.

'Yes. Yes, good thinking. By the way, I think… er… you should call me John. Prof is a… a bit too… too formal,' he offered.

○

An hour later, we were called in for lunch, welcomed by the appetising aroma of steak and kidney pie. Home cooking was a much appreciated treat, as we were all hungry after our efforts. The young family were gone, though I picked out Jonathan's latest creations, by then on the wall among his other paintings.

Lunch was excellent and a tribute to Alison's culinary skills (explaining, I supposed, why both of our hosts were decidedly overweight). The pie, with its crisp crust topping and ample gravy, was as good as I had ever tasted. The local beer, Real Brew (whatever that meant), complemented the traditional food. Alison pointed out that the apple pie to follow was not from the late tree: the fruit was from her brother's farm. The excellence of the meal, and the fatigue from our recent exertions and perhaps also the beer tended to discourage conversation, which was rather intermittent.

Hans told us about his family in Germany and that, after two years at LU, he would return home. He had not yet decided whether to work on the family farm or go into the chemical industry.

Alison expressed sadness about the recent, painful family decision that her parents needed nursing care and could not possibly be supported here at home. 'It's the best we could do for them, but it's some consolation that they share a large, comfortable room in the care home.'

John referred to Ally's recent painting achievements (watercolours rather than greenhouses, a distinction not made). He hoped that her 'brilliant' landscapes, captured during a recent holiday in Oban, might soon be exhibited in the LU Staff Club. Without a direct invitation, neither Hans nor I asked to see the artistic work that John proudly rated as being of the highest quality. His fulsome praise was disputed coyly by the artist.

I mentioned my wish to explore the Scottish Borders and elsewhere in Scotland but not before spring. Conversation lapsed, and we, the 'guest workers', departed soon after our good meal. Our offer to wash up had been declined politely but firmly.

After Hans had gone his own way, I found much to ponder about John's hitherto incomprehensible personality. Surprising myself, I even began to detect feelings of sympathy for a man attempting, though certainly not successfully, to reconcile two roles in his conservative, even reactionary, lifestyle. My visit had shown me that, at home, John was a contented patriarch, maintaining traditional, if now old-fashioned, values within his happy family circle. In contrast, his attempts to resist the march of progress within the university had been much less successful. His distinctly introverted behaviour at LU resulted undoubtedly from an inability to accept the many recent changes of attitudes and priorities within academia. Secrecy and guile enabled him to continue his research using antiquated methods, now unacceptable for reasons of safety, even if this involved deception and even lies, as at the staff meeting. He seemed to have given up participating actively in school activities, preferring instead to minimise contact with colleagues by obfuscation and often meaningless statements. I wondered about his effectiveness as a teacher. As a rare survivor of the genus *Proffontosaurus originalis*, he had withdrawn into himself, rather than either adjusting to the new regime or accepting retirement gracefully. I now saw that, at work, John was deeply unhappy. He continued at LU through habit and inertia, rather than enthusiasm. I almost felt sorry for him, but only *almost*...

○

Wearied by my unaccustomed physical exertions, I passed the afternoon seated and working in my office. Perhaps the expected muscle stiffening would appear tomorrow. (My subsequent resolution was to become fitter by regular exercising.) The uninterrupted time passed pleasantly, enabling me to complete several clerical chores (without even opening the computer game!). Some lecture notes benefitted from detailed revision. The safety aspects of a new laboratory experiment, to be introduced into a practical course, were appraised critically and the complementary paperwork completed. Useful background reading for a possible research project was started.

I left my office after completing the aforementioned chores and went home.

I arrived home feeling slightly less weary than just after my ample lunch. There, Doug was already preparing the steak, chips and salad that he customarily referred to as, 'weekend fuel, essential to recharging my batteries'. Having already eaten well, I contented myself with a toasted cheese sandwich followed by fresh fruit.

Doug opened another beer and conversation with, 'Well, old lad, what joy today?'

I wondered how much beer he had already drunk.

'What have you been up to?' he asked.

'John Bland asked us to help him cut down an old apple tree,' I explained.

'Mean bastard! That's cunning use of tied labour to avoid paying the proper price.'

'Nevertheless, his wife gave us an excellent lunch. It was quite a social occasion.'

'Oh. Ally the Artist. Who else was there? You did say *us*?'

'A German called Hans something. He worked very hard. In fact, he did most of the work. He's one of John's postgrad researchers.'

'I know him. He's a nice guy. It *must* be unethical to use students as casual labour. I believe there's a large brick wall in the garden of some American prof with a plaque saying: "Built in Part Fulfilment of the

Regulations of the Degree of Doctor of Philosophy of the University of *Wherever*." I forget where. Our John is not the first, last nor only exploiter of captive labour. I hope the lunch repaid your efforts.'

'It was truly very good.' I left a short silence. 'At his home, I saw a different, unexpected side of John Bland. At heart, he's a family man. He was much more relaxed than I've ever seen him at LU. He was even decisive at times!'

'Don't be taken in by the *poseur en famille*. He *is* indecisive, making him a lousy administrator. He's *paid* vastly more than he *earns*, while the rest of us try to keep the place going without help from his Professorial Leadership.'

'Maybe so, but it's interesting to see another, more human side at home.'

'He's got you brainwashed! The sooner he retires and disappears forever into the bosom of his family, the better for all of us. The trouble is that LU, in its wisdom, will replace him with a clone or, heaven forbid, someone worse, whenever he's put out to grass eventually. Now let's talk about something more pleasant while I enjoy this excellent steak.' He paused to drink some of his beer. 'What are you doing this evening?'

'After all that effort, I'm going to relax and perhaps watch TV.'

He replied with incredulity, '*What?* On *Saturday* evening? In my expert and considered opinion, *Saturday* evening TV is wall-to-wall *crap* (excuse my bluntness). Excepting, of course, the football. Aren't you coming to our new members' welcome evening at the Staff Club? Didn't you get an invitation?'

'I'm not sure. It's difficult to read, much less remember, all the circulars I get. Perhaps there was one. I forget the date.'

'Tonight, Old Son. Tonight! You must come. We'll give you for free, totally without cost, a few beers or, better still, some of our "explosive punch", expertly blended by *yours truly* or, to you, *yours sincerely*. Then having drunk *once* for free, we'll inveigle you into joining our club, with the privilege of paying into our coffers for however long you're on LU's staff. It's a good bargain for the club.'

'Am I right in guessing that you have some special interest?'

'I'm to be co-opted onto the management committee, or so the rumour goes.'

'Co-opted? Shouldn't you be elected? What happened to democracy?'

'That might happen later. For now, this is punishment or perhaps I'm accepting some responsibility, after daring to criticise our restaurant service. Last month, I wrote to complain that cost of lunch had gone up while both quality and quantities had fallen. The reward for my public-spirited action was, from the secretary's lips, "If you can do better, join our management and show us how!" So now I'm to serve my sentence. My first task, a pleasure, is to blend the wine punch to welcome new members tonight and make sure that it lives up to its name. I claim to punch above my weight. So, come and see if I succeed.'

The thought of the punch, rather than the ponderous pun, decided me. 'I'll come.'

○

A hectic half-hour spent rearranging tables and inflating balloons to decorate the walls brought a mildly festive flavour to the Staff Club's dining room. The blobs of primary colour provided more cheer than the set of drab and depressing images being exhibited right then. These had been painted by an aspiring but, for me, uninspired local artist. Despite our efforts in 'preparing for the mob' (Doug's phrase), I now felt less tired than earlier. The likely reason was that my exertions were interrupted frequently by requests to taste and to comment on the palatability of the punch that Doug was synthesising.

It was traditional, I learned, that a chemist masterminded the creation of this legendary LU unguent because it was said that, 'chemists understand alcoholic beverages best'. Doug had probably originated this self-serving claim to maintain his position, established in earlier years. To reaffirm this reputation, it was important (to him, at least) that the temperature of the punch should be exactly correct (chemistry had, unknowingly, lent a thermometer for 'confirmatory purposes'). Wine, spirits (almost empty bottles from the bar and older, unsaleable stock), spices (Doug's secret brew) and a little lemonade had to be mixed in *exactly* the correct proportions. Frequent tasting was essential, as it was the only known method of quality control. Strangely, despite the many samples tested and tasted, the level of alcoholic beverage in the huge container did not perceptibly fall, though the store of reserve bottles slowly diminished. Committee members (plus me, as Doug's 'apprentice') were now fairly relaxed, merry would be an exaggeration, when guests began to arrive.

As the proud originator of the social lubricant, 'Doctor' Doug stationed himself behind his unique punch, stating this was, 'To dispense suitable doses to the thirsty hordes.' He wore a pristine, white laboratory coat as his badge of status. Thanking me for my help, he suggested I should circulate and meet some of my new colleagues.

As I set off, I heard a loud voice calling, 'Doctor Doug! Where's your stethoscope?'

Later, there were cries of, 'Get your choc ice here! Ices! Ices! They're lovely!'

When I returned later for a refill, Doug's white coat had disappeared.

With my restricted choice of wardrobe, I had opted to wear my everyday suit, and, at that point, I felt distinctly overdressed. Indeed, in present company, the informal garb I had worn earlier for tree felling would have been more in keeping with the democratic spirit of this evening's dress code. True, a few individuals were in semi-formal, even smart, attire, but this minority tended to be older. Most people favoured loose garments, often with long hair arranged in (or naturally forming) equally loose coiffeurs. Looking around the room, I identified a few instances of possibly intentional stereotyping, with academics appearing or seeking to appear as parodies, even caricatures, of the fictional denizens of ivory-tower colleges. One such person appeared at my side just then. He was a small, elderly man with a serious expression, grey beard and purple bow tie. The bright-yellow waistcoat, new or little used, contrasted with the venerable appearance of his faded and well-worn brown sports jacket, grey flannels and brown shoes.

Peering at me through thick glasses, his opening question was unambiguous: 'Are you a new staff member?'

I confirmed that I was.

'Oh, good. The last three people I've approached said they'd been here for years. One even claimed to work in the same school as me. Do you think that's true? I don't think it could be right. I'm *sure* I'd have noticed her before. But, as you're a newcomer, finally, my quest is successful! Tell me, do you like it here?'

My answer was vague. My interlocutor made no response, showed no interest in my reply and seemed detached from our exchanges.

Soon he took his leave: 'You must excuse me; I have to find and welcome other new staff…if I can.'

It crossed my mind that John Bland variants existed.

Alone, with my glass replenished, I surveyed the scene to decide what to do next. For a while, I people-watched contentedly. Constantly shifting, ever-shuffling groups chatted together for a while before dispersing, only to regroup and initiate other animated conversations. Individuals wandered off continually to seek different and, possibly, more congenial company whenever a topic under discussion palled. For me, the evening was passing pleasantly, though I thought, with a pang of longing, the time could have spent much more enjoyably in Beth's company.

Next, I joined a group that was being addressed, almost harangued, by a tall and absolutely bald man armed with a voice that, while not loud, possessed exceptional carrying power. He was describing, to everyone within earshot, his current research project. This had some unexplained connection with a cure for alopecia that would result from the counting of hairs on the dorsal (whatever that meant) skins of gorillas. I listened to his monologue only briefly, before deciding that my capacity (and wish) to learn more about this esoteric topic had reached satiation. Suppressing a query about where he found the gorillas required, I moved on.

The next group I overheard were busy analysing the recent, numerous and serious shortcomings of the Government. Everyone present obviously regarded themselves as an informed authority on the topic, with all contributing, but nobody listening. (What's new in political debate?) This was another topic that was a joy to skip.

Moving on quickly, I regarded as deliciously missable a discussion that included a high-pitched voice proclaiming, 'what the postmodernists are missing is…' I was glad to count myself a 'postmodernist' (whoever they are) in missing it (whatever 'it' might have been). Another snatch of conversation overheard in passing was equally off-putting; indeed, it seemed destined to continue indefinitely without ever reaching a, the or any point: "So I said to her, I said, don't you say that to me. I said to her..."

I paused for a punch refill, after which I found myself near a group of convivial friends exchanging and enjoying each other's stories. There was no obligation here to seek out, or to welcome, newcomers; such diversions might, after all, disturb the tipsy fellowship of the occasion. Being long-term colleagues, exclusively male and displaced from the bar due to this party, they maintained their usual Saturday evening indulgence in gossip and relaxation, when yet another daunting academic year was just beginning.

'So there he was, standing in the rain, clad only in his underpants...' was received with loud laughter; I had just missed the point of the story.

Another raconteur took the initiative. 'Did you ever hear about Billy Anstruther, who was appointed boss here in, I think, the early eighties? No? He came and settled himself into Provost's House. His first Sunday here, he was out in his garden in well-worn clothes. He was some kind of agriculturist and was pruning roses when Geordie George hailed him over the fence. You know that Provost's House is next to that plant farm or whatever, something to do with botany?'

'Is that the Geordie George who's the trade unionist?' piped up one of his compatriots.

'Aye, that's the boy. Anyway, he shouts at Billy A, "Hi mate." When this "mate" goes over, Geordie asks him, "Do you get overtime for Sunday work?" Billy, soon to be Sir William, thinks seriously for a moment before deciding that provosts are not paid extra for weekend work and so replies, "No." Immediately, Geordie launches into an admonishing tirade, commiserating about this terrible injustice and offering him union membership to fight for his rights. Billy said he'd think about it, thanked him, wished Geordie a good morning and they parted. A week or so later Billy A visited the plant farm, or whatever, beside his home, during his inaugural inspection tour of LU. Apparently, when Geordie recognised the new provost suddenly, he disappeared from the welcoming party.'

There was more laughter.

The silence was soon filled by another raconteur. 'A story I like shows just how much academic attitudes towards students have changed. Years ago, this chemistry prof, who was something of a health freak, used his car to take student groups regularly to the sea for a swim.'

'Nowadays, that would attract serious concern. It would infringe some *health and safety directive,*' someone added.

There were assenting sounds.

Another of the group, glancing around with a knowing look, said, 'Or worse!'

There were louder assenting sounds.

Anyway, one day, when returning home, the car stopped for no apparent reason. After several unsuccessful attempts to restart, it was decided that the petrol feed tube was blocked. One brave, or foolhardy, student volunteered to suck it clear and was rewarded for this public-spirited action with a mouthful of petrol. He was in some discomfort and the prof noticed they had stopped fortuitously outside a pub. In those days, it was unthought of that a professor could buy intoxicating drink for a student. But, as a chemist, he diagnosed that alcohol would wash the petrol from the student's mouth. So, he bought a double whisky, solely for rinsing purposes and on the strict condition that *not one drop* would be swallowed. Things are a bit different now,' said the speaker, and he sipped and swallowed his drink, which appeared to be whisky.

The group readily agreed that social norms had changed considerably from those distant days. This story reminded everyone that glasses needed periodic recharging. Several approached Doug urgently, who was emptying his container, which was then tipped to dispense the remaining precious liquid.

At that point, I was feeling really weary. I had been welcomed to the club adequately and had met as many of the present LU staff as I was likely to encounter. The membership form, buried somewhere on my desk, must be relocated and completed to join officially, but that was for the future. My earlier exertions had taken their toll, and, combined with the effects of Doug's punch, the need for rest was by then overwhelming. After the social evening or, more realistically, its liquid component, I anticipated that, tomorrow, the stiffness of my limbs would very likely be complemented by headache and/or hangover, which I hoped would be mild.

Chapter 9

FIT		
	a.	Healthy; in good health
	b.	Compatible; join components together

THE DEAFENING ROARING FROM THE LARGE, RAMSHACKLE machine spreading tar on the road made my head ache. Somehow, I knew that Mr Smith was driving this loud contraption, but he seemed oblivious to the din. Walking on the sticky, tarry surface behind the moving, metallic monster was difficult: the effort pained my stiff legs. Worst of all, much of the asphalt spread was sliding downwards into the adjoining field where John Bland – still in his outsized, blue jumper – was shouting at me to start my research immediately, or sooner. Disregarding him, I tried to shovel some tarry goo back onto the carriageway, but my ineffectual contributions were continually overwhelmed by Mr Smith pouring more black fluid onto the road.

Then my duvet slid off the bed, arousing me as I fell with it, onto the floor. Slowly awakening, my vivid fantasy receded mercifully as I untangled the bedclothes. The headache, a real but unwelcome hangover from the dream, reminded me sternly that, last evening, I had imbibed more alcohol than was advisable. Aches in my legs, felt just then, were the price of yesterday's exertions in John's garden, working in an unfit state.

I needed no psychologist to interpret my dream: work worries had become so ingrained that they dominated my subconscious thoughts, even when asleep. As my brain cleared, I recalled, with surprise, that Walter had not featured in this disturbing nocturnal fantasy. Clearly, the jumbled contents of my mind were far too complicated to analyse just now, so I deferred attempts at self-psychoanalysis. That day, Sunday, the *day of rest*, I would recuperate from unwise physical exertions – and that punch!

Already being 9.00am, it was urgent that I start the day. The jobs awaiting me involved the weekly laundry, including the soiled garments beside my bed. These and the untidy room reminded me that this was *my* week to wield the vacuum cleaner and clean the flat generally. No further rest was permissible, and, reluctantly, I rose and left my room.

In the kitchen, Doug was also just emerging; I had no idea what time he had come in last night. Unsurprisingly, neither of us suggested a breakfast fry; the first urgent medicine was coffee: black, strong and hot. After this restorative, we risked more substantial nourishment, with muesli being sufficient just then.

'Did you enjoy last evening?' Doug was the first to show positive evidence of recovery.

'Yes, but I drank more of your punch than I should have,' I concluded.

'I noticed. An old hand, like me, can tell.'

We reviewed, privately, last evening's over indulgences, until Doug asked, 'So what delights are in prospect today?'

Then I remembered. 'This evening I'm invited to Beth's home, to meet her parents.' (How could I have forgotten so momentous an event, even briefly?)

'Oh! Ooooh! Things are getting serious. It's best-behaviour time. For a start, you'd better brighten yourself up a bit…'

'To make a good impression,' I finished for him. 'Yes. How'll I do that?'

'Just now, your face is as pale as a polar bear's bum. You need some colour, other than green, in your cheeks. Get some fresh air into you. Get out! Walk!'

'Look at the weather. The forecast's poor: cold wind and rain later.'

'Medicine's no good if it tastes good.' More coffee was imbibed to aid recovery. Doug went on, 'Last evening, someone told me about a walking group she's involved in. She wanted me to join. No chance! She said they're going out today. But where…? Yes! It's at 2.00pm at The Office… You know, that pub out on Edinburgh Road? Maybe you should join them? I believe that name allows customers getting home late to tell their wives that they were detained in The Office.'

○

By 2.00pm, with almost all domestic duties completed, I felt appreciably more like myself, though the weather showed no similar improvement. The rain was steady, if not heavy – yet. Perhaps the fresh air might restore both equanimity and normal flesh-colour to my cheeks. After leaving the bus at The Office pub, I joined a group of about ten people, all suitably attired for wet-weather walking, in 'sensible' outdoor clothes and hiking boots. My own preparations for a wet Scottish Sunday, a plastic mac and light walking shoes, were less adequate.

I approached a short man of military bearing who appeared, by virtue of his official-looking clipboard, to be in charge. His waterproof garments enveloped him entirely, except for a small area of face, in which the only distinguishing features visible were a white moustache and light-blue eyes that met mine in a severe and penetrating no-nonsense stare.

'Name?' he barked. It sounded more like a military command than a welcome.

'You don't know me. I wondered if I might join your group? For today, that is,' I answered.

'Nevertheless, I need your name.' After listing me on his clipboard, he unbent sufficiently to introduce himself: 'I am Major Arthur Wilson. Most people call me Arthur. We are in the process of starting the Linkirk Environmental and Rambling Club. Today, I'm the walk leader, and we welcome everyone who wants to join our rambles. We're pleased to meet you. [This was good to know, even if not obvious.] I must ask you for £2, our walk fee. If you want us to post out our programme to you, that'll be a further £5, please.'

Five minutes later, and £7 poorer, I was part of the group and Arthur (though he was usually addressed as Major, which he seemed to prefer) formally welcomed everybody. His description of our intended route meant little, but the gestures suggested that we would go up one valley, cross a hill and descend the next valley to return here in about two hours. A short talk of environmental interest would be given by someone he described as, 'one of our members; a lecturer from the LU School of Biology' (and, therefore, a colleague; perhaps she who had mentioned this ramble to Doug).

At that point, with steady watery discouragement from above, I wondered whether my health could possibly benefit from Dr Doug's prescribed exercise. However, after a slight hesitation, I resolved that – having come so far and paid the fee – I would participate. We all followed Major/Arthur along an unmade, muddy, uphill track, down which flowed a steady stream, replenished continually from above. Social contact between well-cocooned fellow walkers was effectively impossible, so my companions remained anonymous, each isolated within his/her personal wrapping. Walking in single file, on the slightly drier centre of the track, further discouraged conversational overtures. With only a minimum of face visible, it was difficult to distinguish individuals. Residual lassitude from my uncomfortable start this morning further disinclined me from attempting small talk with these strangers, characterised mainly by their varied head gear: hood, tam-o'-shanter and, for one man, a black beret.

We passed some open fields, tenanted by wet sheep nibbling dripping grass, then went onwards through a deciduous wood. Most of the fallen leaves were already on our path, with the remaining canopy giving almost no shelter. We soon reached cross-tracks. Without hesitation, our leader continued straight across, to be challenged by the black-beret man, who strongly advocated the path to the right. I heard little of the exchange, which was resolved by Arthur, being unpersuaded, decisively continuing in his preferred direction with the military manner of the marching major maintaining his mission.

Further on, we stopped beside a small, open area in the woodland, where several large trees had fallen with some now in advanced stages of decay.

Major was delighted introduce Dr Karen Reed, from the LU School of Botany, who he stated, 'had been persuaded to say a few words on the environment, particularly about woodland ecology.'

A woman in her forties stepped forwards towards a large fallen tree. She pushed back her hood, and told us in a clear and confident voice, 'I'll be brief in this weather. My remarks are addressed to anyone interested in our environment and, in particular, *biodiversity*. This word is used occasionally by politicians. I have my own views about whether or not they understand fully what it means, but it sounds impressive and knowledgeable. Without giving my two-hour lecture on the topic, we can find in this decayed tree one small aspect of biodiversity. Here, not obviously, dead trees are helping conservation by harbouring our indigenous flora and fauna.

'Until recently, many forestry managers, charged with woodland care, had adopted the policy that wooded areas should be cleared of fallen trees and tidied according to human views on orderliness. They simply removed, allegedly on our behalf, anything we might view as "unsightly rubbish". However, conservationists are now aware that this is unnatural and damages our environment by reducing biodiversity. [A view she was obviously advocating.] Various beetles – creepy-crawlies – play an essential role in the decay of wood and bark. These specialist inhabitants of healthy forests contribute to natural woodland cycles by breaking down dead timber. What we humans might regard as rubbish is recycled naturally, though by minute insect workers who need *much* longer times to "tidy up" than a man with a machine. Now it's being realised that some of these insects and beetles, usually invisible to us in their hidden niches, are becoming rare, because their habitats are being destroyed so thoughtlessly and needlessly. To remove the threats facing these valuable creatures, we only need to allow woodlands to regenerate themselves naturally, as throughout ages past. When trees degrade naturally, with timber remaining where it falls, these specialist woodland beasties use decaying wood as food sources and thrive, thereby playing their proper role in the life, death and *regeneration* of forests. Such insects are an indispensable part of healthy woodland fauna; these unfamiliar and unseen but essential creatures form part of the *diversity* of life around us. That is *biodiversity*; let's protect it! As with so many environmental features, the situation must be understood and encouraged to flourish, if our countryside is to retain its long-term health. Thank you for your attention.'

This succinct account of a topical problem was applauded warmly. The muffled clapping of gloves helped restore circulation to cold hands, and the dead trees were left to their slow, if largely invisible, decay. We continued on our walk and, soon, we reached the cross-tracks where our route had been disputed earlier. This confirmed conclusively, if rather publicly, that Major's confident guidance had been wrong. Without comment, Arthur turned along the path previously indicated, while the black-beret man maintained a dignified silence more eloquent than criticism. We arrived at The Office pub (which was closed), somewhat later than predicted.

The party dispersed rapidly, being reluctant to linger in the continuing rain. Once I reached the bus stop, I was surprised when a car stopped to offer me a lift. I accepted gratefully, finding that my benefactress was Dr Reed, who offered, 'Call me Karen'.

While returning to Linkirk, I told her truthfully that I had enjoyed her talk. We confirmed that we were indeed colleagues at LU and discussed our very different interests in environmental science.

Later, Karen said, 'One of my jobs is to list LU staff prepared to visit local schools to talk to sixth forms on scientific topics. May I add your name? It's a good thing to do.' For whom or why this was 'good' was not explained.

Grateful for her kind lift home, I agreed.

'That's fixed then; I'll send on details,' she confirmed as I got out of her car.

Later, I realised that yet another open-ended commitment had been accepted without any knowledge of how much time and effort it required. This, on top of the endless things to do already in my in tray! Just then, getting started at LU was all I could manage. My offer must be withdrawn, or at least deferred, until my lectures were written, research started and all 1,001 obligations were fitted together into my 'efficient' new work programme, *which was yet to be devised*. Surely, I could organise my life *better* than this?

○

After a prolonged hot shower and wearing my one, indeed only, presentable (interview) suit yet again, I felt somewhat refreshed. The mirror showed some colour in my cheeks, though it could be the glow induced by hot water. The stiffness had gone from my muscles; apparently, Dr Doug's prescription had worked. But how would I fare this evening? The joyful prospect of being in Beth's company was lessened by uncertainty, never having experienced the 'pleasure' of meeting *formally* the parents of a girlfriend. I was distinctly apprehensive.

Advice from my father, long ago, after a school friend had invited me to supper, was to show appreciation to the lady of the house by giving her a small gift to recognise her kind hospitality. His support had extended to helping me select the gift, which I still remembered to be pink carnations. This time, being anxious to do the right thing, I had purchased the same flowers, but, for this special occasion, they were a much larger bunch. On that earlier visit, I had been distinctly discomfited when carrying flowers in the street, because a boy – a stranger about my own age – had cried out, 'Sissy'. That memory still rankled, though on this wet evening there was nobody about to notice or care! For Beth's father, I bought the same Chianti wine that had been appreciated by the McTaggarts (or so they said). What if the Wilkinsons were abstainers? Remembering that Beth had taken wine on the evening we had first met, I hoped that the wine would be acceptable. Not wishing to exclude Beth, an African violet completed my offerings.

Carrying these fragile gifts to the Wilkinson's home, through wet and windy streets, was not easy. It was a relief to reach the corner where Beth and I had previous parted, with gifts intact, but then I continued onward along her road. 'Roseville' was well named, with the house set above an upward-sloping garden, which had many rose bushes, behind the substantial stone wall of the footpath. The detached villa itself was quite large and built of white-painted material set in a black timber frame. Ten steep stone steps led up to the front door, which I reached without damaging my burden. The house was positioned to give fine views across grassy Linkirk Greenside and to the weir across Meggett Water beyond. Reflected streetlights twinkled on the fast-flowing river, which was still in flood.

It was time to take my own plunge: a firm press on the bell produced a distant ring, followed remarkably rapidly by the appearance of a smiling Beth. A welcoming sweep of her hand invited me in. I freed my hands quickly by depositing my gifts on a hall table, during which time I was delighted to receive a quick peck on the cheek. This reassuring token salute confirmed amply the warmth of her welcome.

I had a brief impression of her (which, for me, was knee-weakening) smart appearance, with a mauve jumper of some fluffy, woollen material matching a lilac skirt, and set off by some strings of what appeared to be real pearls. Her appearance was very attractive.

Then, I was ushered rapidly towards a lighted room. The dreaded moment, anticipated with much apprehension, had arrived!

'This is my mother… and my dad…' stated Beth.

Introductions were performed somewhat formally, before we all sat down, giving the appearance of relaxation that I certainly did not feel. It took me a while to regain sufficient equanimity to begin getting to know Beth's nearest and dearest. My top priority had to be to give a good initial impression, while my preferred focus of interest had to remain temporarily outside my attention.

Mother, referred to later as 'Mumsy', was a small, petite person and ladylike in every respect. 'Old-fashioned' was the most fitting description that came to mind, though I would have found it difficult to explain just what that meant. Her kindly, often serious face appeared to be an older, though less-frequently smiling, version of Beth. These similarities of appearance I found both attractive and indefinably disturbing.

'I'm very pleased to meet you, William,' she said; her gentle voice was soprano and speech precise, almost pedantic.

Her grey hair was abundant, giving her head the appearance of being relatively large, in contrast with her slight build, which was emphasised by the narrow waist of her blue dress. She wore a single brooch, a gold horseshoe with a red stone, and I wondered if the expensive-looking pearls that suited Beth so well were hers. Mother tended to be quiet, speaking mainly when addressed directly and showing little curiosity, evidently content to listen to rather than lead the conversation. She often deferred to her husband, though reproved him on occasion, as when he asked me questions that she regarded as too personal. It was possible that she possessed the stronger character, but chose to let her husband believe that he was the dominant partner. Later, she said that she worked in a charity shop to raise money for cancer research; it seemed a most fitting occupation for such a demure and serious lady.

Beth's father, Dad, was tall, somewhat overweight and walked with a slight stoop. Like his wife, his expression was often serious; this was an impression emphasised by his glasses, which had wide, dark rims. Indeed, this appearance might have been cultivated to express his serious and thoughtful personality, traits worthy of the manager of a large local bank, which Beth had mentioned was his occupation. In contrast with his wife, and consistent with his sober demeanour, his voice was deep, with the musical inflection of the western Highlands. Although not obvious on first acquaintance, I later discovered he had a highly developed sense of humour and an extensive fund of jokes, not all of which were suitable for mixed company. An accomplished raconteur, he found pleasure in telling amusing and very occasionally rude stories. Unlike the womenfolk, he had dressed comfortably for the evening, not recognising whatever significance that they might or might not attach to the occasion. His clothes were a statement that, for him, Sunday evening was an off-duty time of relaxation. As a gesture of formality, he wore a tie that matched his dark-brown cardigan. This outer garment had seen prolonged previous service, having been used sufficiently long to now be 'comfortable'. Unlike the perhaps new and fashionable shoes worn by the ladies, Mr Wilkinson relaxed in well-worn-in carpet slippers. While I could be absolutely certain that none of the apparel worn by either Beth or Mumsy had come from the charity shop, the same was not necessarily true of Dad.

My determination to be on my best behaviour, as Beth's 'friend', inhibited my ability to relax in this comfortable sitting room, which registered only as a blurred outline impression. Table lamps gave a warm, low light that was insufficient to reveal details of the wall pictures, which appeared to be black-and-white etchings. The coal fire was a luxury, and particularly welcome after my earlier damp outing and the cold, wet streets outside. There was no sofa: instead, individual easy chairs of various styles and colours were informally distributed to best receive the fire's warmth. I found myself (by chance or by design) sitting between Beth's parents.

'Would you like a sherry, Mr… er… Mr Green?' enquired Dad.

'Oh, Dad… I told you he's *doctor*.' Beth sounded pained.

'Bill. Please call me Bill. Sherry would be… welcome. Thank you,' I replied.

Sherry was poured, Beth went to see to things in the kitchen, and Dad asked the rather obvious question: 'How're you settling into the university, Bill?'

'Well, thank you. It's our busy time of year, and there seem to be too many things to do… all at once… I hardly know where to start,' I responded.

'How do you like it here… after the south?' questioned Beth's mother.

'I've always lived in Sussex, except for a few weeks in Italy. But I've liked what I've seen here so far. I hope to see more, but that will probably not be before the spring.'

Remembering that my hosts' absence from the McTaggart's dinner party had been due to Mrs Wilkinson suffering a holiday accident, I asked her how her recovery was proceeding.

She assured me that it was going as well as could be expected, but I did notice that she still walked with a pronounced limp.

Conversation was stilted, as between strangers; I shared Mr W's lack of inclination or ability to make small talk. I also had the nagging feeling of having met Dad already, but could recall neither when nor where. It was not at LU. Then, remembering the bank that he managed, I realised I was talking to my financial mentor, who could, if so inclined, know my penury to the nearest penny. This knowledge did not help my self-confidence. He seemed not to have recognised me, or perhaps bankers are adept at hiding their ability to know or to assess accurately the worldly wealth of strangers. His informal dress had changed his appearance considerably from the smart, besuited businessman to whom I had talked briefly when opening my account. It was a relief to us all, Mumsy had said little, when Beth came in.

'We can eat now,' she stated.

The meal was traditional: generous and tasty helpings of roast pork; potatoes, roast and boiled; with carrots and sprouts. The apple sauce was home-made and, while its maker was not identified, the implication was that it had been made by Beth.

Mr W, who seemed to regard it as his prerogative, carved the joint, as a necessary but mildly boring chore. He showed little skill and his wife prompted him to, 'Get on with it, before the meal goes cold.'

The Soave wine (Italian, perhaps Beth's choice) was pleasant, if not memorable.

To avoid continuing the earlier conversational doldrums, I asked Beth if she had enjoyed the visit to Edinburgh yesterday. It turned out that all three of my hosts had spent the time with their family: Meta (presumably Beth's sister), Roger and their only offspring, Anna. The antics of the two-year-old birthday girl were recounted with all the interest and enthusiasm of happy grandparents revelling in the wonder of the new generation. Everything was accepted as boding well for their future happiness. Hints were made about having another newcomer before too long, but it was not clear whether this was expected or simply hoped for. Without siblings myself, I was pleased for their joy and, to my surprise, Mumsy suggested that Beth and I might visit Meta and her family sometime soon. I agreed with this great idea.

From Edinburgh, it was natural to move on to Aberdeen, where Beth's brother, Stewart – the eldest of the three siblings – worked in the oil industry, though the details of his work were not mentioned. His parents were deeply disturbed by his personal situation; he was apparently in crisis. He was unmarried, but, recently, had undergone a serious row with his partner who had walked out of their joint home. The tone of the discussion assumed tacitly that I would strongly disapprove of this unacceptable behaviour. The partnership had been short, the family never having met the young *lady* (was *lady* being stressed?). I wondered if any of this could be construed as relating to my friendship with Beth.

(A question that we had not addressed seriously as yet was were my intentions honourable, in an old-fashioned, conventional sense.) Giving the impression of being tactful, Mr W now nudged the conversation gently in a new direction, which, however, I found most unwelcome.

'I believe you know Walter Thompson,' declared Dad.

'Yes, indeed. We both work at LU in the School of Chemistry. Our offices are in the same corridor.' I tried to sound interested and positive, but hoped to avoid detailing our precise relationship.

'He was in Stewart's class at primary school. The boys were quite friendly then, and he sometimes came to our home. We lived in a different place then. They played for the same football team: Stewart was goalie and Walter was centre forward; the *striker*, I think he called himself. [He seemed proud of his command of sporting jargon.] So they practised (or is it trained?) in our back garden.'

'And we had to stand in the cold to watch their games and their cup ties... whatever that means,' Mrs W was not going to be outdone. 'He'd a nasty temper, that Walter. I remember him being sent off home for hitting one of the opposing team. Is that what they mean by "striker"?'

We agreed that the word could be ambiguous.

Mr W continued the theme, 'He got on well enough with Stewart, who was the taller and stronger of the two. I don't remember them scrapping with each other, as lads do. But, once, when Walter was angered by some little boy, he and Stewart tied him to a tree in our garden with our clothesline. I sent Walter home and ended their training for some time.'

'He didn't upset me, or Meta, in our play.' This unexpected comment was from Beth.

Dad was quick to reply, 'Boys of that age don't deign to notice the existence of small girls. He'd have made a point of ignoring you.' This caused a slight hiatus, filled when he turned to me and said, 'How's he getting on at the university?'

It was impossible for me to give a natural, unbiased reply to this innocent question, while keeping to my 'make a good first impression' policy. A preferred answer might have been, 'He has remained a miserable, aggressive, bad-tempered sod and is still an objectionable bastard whenever he can get away with it.' However, strong language aside, tact must be maintained. I actually replied, 'We have different specialities and work in our different ways in, I hope, the best interests of the school.' Stilted, trite and platitudinous, it was but the best I could manage, even if it bent veracity well beyond breaking point.

'Is he senior to you?' asked Mr W, who was reproved by Mrs W for such an intrusive question.

'Don't worry, it's not a problem. We're both lecturers at the university career grade. He might claim to be senior to me, but only because he was appointed last year,' I confirmed.

For reasons that I came to appreciate only slowly, Mr W seemed reluctant to abandon this topic. Perhaps, despite my best intentions, I had betrayed my dislike of Walter and it could be that Dad shared this sentiment. He was also probably finding it difficult to understand, and to accept, the considerable success evidently being enjoyed by then by Walter in his LU career. Apparently, this contrasted sharply with his son's achievements, a comparison that could only bring anguish to a father. If I had interpreted his earlier comments correctly, which were admittedly short on detail, Stewart had problems in obtaining work, even in jobs that were neither skilled nor well paid.

To my discomfort, Walter remained the focus of Mr W's attention: 'He got into lots of trouble at school. We worried at one stage if he might be a bad influence on Stewart. But then the Thompsons moved away and the matter resolved itself.'

There was a short pause. I did not want to betray my intense dislike of Walter by making an awkward change of subject, so the topic continued.

Mr W explained, 'Just before Walter left that school, a story about him caused quite a stir at the time. A teacher kept him in school late, as punishment for some misdemeanour. The next day, that teacher – who'd recently filled up his car with petrol – was stranded going home when his petrol ran out. It was generally accepted, though I don't remember if it was ever proven, that Walter had siphoned petrol from the tank knowing the teacher lived a long way away across a moor. It was his revenge! A nasty business.'

I was dismayed that Walter, though absent, was capable of intruding into this social occasion, managing still to exert his malign and unwelcome influence. I had heard more than enough about him, but, before I could move towards a new subject (anything), Beth expressed her view, which – not for the first time – was sympathetic to Walter. Thinking kindly of people is a trait I normally admire, if sometimes only in theory, but (as every scientist knows) theories can have limits and exceptions. Moreover, sympathy is wasted on some people, and, for me, Walter was a prime example. I heard her words, and, for once, was mutely unable to agree.

'Walter's from a dysfunctional family,' she clarified. 'He had a disturbed childhood. His parents were unhappy together – contemplating divorce, I think – and, when they separated for a time, he was fostered by social services. He's more to be pitied than blamed. He may be difficult to get on with, and he might have a temper – at one time he certainly did – but he's settled down at last and he deserves his chance. He seems to be doing very well.'

I disagreed profoundly (the fabled unchanging pattern of *spots on leopards* came to mind), but her pause was my chance to turn to a more congenial topic: 'May I congratulate and thank the cook or cooks for a really excellent meal? I don't know who was the culinary supremo, but I enjoyed it more than I can say.'

'Beth was the supremo, as you call it, this evening,' confirmed Mr W.

'Mumsy taught me, and… I do enjoy cooking.' Beth was being coy.

Now we were finishing our sweet – *pudding*, as my mother would have said. It had been tiramisu (*Again!* Maybe I should regard it as a Scottish delicacy? Perhaps 'tira*macsu*'? This was another thought that remained unsaid!).

Beth now admitted she had difficulty in finding a recipe and had bought a cookery book for this sole entry. Possibly, though not mentioned, she was competing with Elizabeth McTaggart's offering, by then over a month ago.

Mumsy's praise was less supportive than I expected. 'I'm not much of a judge of foreign food, but it's very nice.'

Dad, with more conservative tastes in culinary (and probably numerous other) matters, had opted for fresh-fruit salad and described 'the Italian concoction' as, 'a plaster'. I later learned that his use of this term was not necessarily pejorative. He used it to describe any dish that was not recognisable instantly as traditional Scottish fare. So, it fell to me alone to pronounce the sweet excellent, and say truthfully that it was the best I'd ever tasted (the only competition being from Elizabeth McT!). I hoped that my lone positive judgement was sufficient, while avoiding the effusiveness that might have offended Beth after her kindness in preparing, for my enjoyment, this unfamiliar sweet.

My offer to help clear away was declined, so we moved back in front of the by then poked, restoked and blazing coal fire to enjoy coffee. There was no 'special' whisky! Replete and relaxed, conversation had at last moved on to more acceptable topics. I could now relax, noticing that this was a comfortable room, with a well-lived-in appearance, somewhat reminiscent of Mr W's off-duty apparel.

He asked, 'What did you do today, with all that rain?' He ignored his wife's disapproving glare, at his nosiness.

I gave a brief account of my earlier ramble, which surprised him.

'Out in *all that rain?*' he questioned.

I said that everyone participating had completed the route.

My mention of the environmental talk raised no interest, so that was abandoned quickly. Instead, I said that, after a week spent mainly indoors, today's outing had refreshed me, even though it had been particularly cool and damp. I did not feel the need to mention why my health had been in such a fragile state when setting off. Again, I was being stingy with the facts, as I had been several times that evening, but I was trying to avoid any direct untruths.

'That reminds me of a ghost story. Do you want to hear it?' asked Mr W.

I nodded with a sceptical smile, implying that I regarded such tales as fiction instinctively.

'Oh Daaaad… You've told that story—' began Beth.

'Yes, daughter, but I think your friend here, Dr… Bill, does not believe such tales, and he hasn't heard this one yet,' interjected Mr W. He turned to me and said, 'Whether or not you believe me is up to you, but I assure you that the story is true.'

'I'll listen with pleasure. I've heard a few ghost yarns, but I've yet to believe one,' I confirmed.

I was handed a generous tot of (normal!) whisky, with no water. It was assumed I would participate in this civilised, male custom; the ladies preferred liqueurs.

Dad began, 'Our hero, we'll call him Mac, was a keen hiker who preferred walking alone at his own paces and in his own places in the remote Highlands. During one of his longer walks, bad weather closed in, with fog and rain disorientating him so that he lost his way totally. Eventually, the tired Mac became seriously worried and night had fallen long before he finally reached a road. He'd no idea where he was, but he followed the road, knowing it would bring him to habitation, sooner or later. I should say all this took place long ago, when traffic was lighter, but he still had a reasonable chance of a lift. Sure enough, later, he heard the sound of a car, growing louder as he approached the top of a steep rise before he stood back to thumb a lift. Because the car didn't stop at once, Mac assumed the driver had noticed him only at the last moment. Nevertheless, when it did stop, he ran to it gratefully, opened the door and collapsed into the passenger seat, pulling in his knapsack as the vehicle started down the other side of the rise at once. He turned and stated, "That was a bit quick off the mark..." Mac was reduced to silence, experiencing emotions close to terror, because... the driving seat was *empty*! He was quite alone in the car!'

There was a most dramatic pause. The well-told story had engaged my interest. Drinks were sipped.

Mr W went on, 'Our tired hero, his mind confused, watched as the car accelerated downwards towards a sharp bend in the road. Danger threatened... Would there be a car crash? And he was in the car! At the last moment, a ghostly hand reached in through the quarter-light, the small window that featured in such older cars, and pulled at the wheel. Mac had suffered enough. He opened the door and threw himself out onto the grass verge in a confusion of raincoat, knapsack, hat, etc. A while later, he got up, his mind regaining some composure slowly, and set off downhill, now safely on foot. Walking in a daze, he was absolutely convinced he had just experienced an apparition. He soon reached some level ground in front of a house where several people were talking outside.

'Cautiously, and still badly disorientated by his recent ghostly experience, he approached them, and was greeted kindly as a tired and benighted traveller. Help was offered. Gaining courage, he recounted what he now believed was a supernatural happening. One of his audience laughed suddenly and loudly. Mac was shocked by this lack of sensitivity to his plight and absence of sympathy, indeed of manners. Apologising, the man who had laughed explained that he had been the car driver and noticed no hitch-hiker. He was entirely preoccupied with his need to reach home before the petrol in an almost empty tank ran dry. At the last hill, the car had spluttered and, in desperation, he had jumped out and pushed it vigorously, just reaching the top of the ridge. As the vehicle ran downhill to the level road near his home, he'd stood on the running board. His had been the ghostly, disembodied hand that had turned the steering wheel!'

Mr W finished his whisky, satisfied by my appreciative laughter, while I thought about his story.

Then he added, 'The point is that, however improbable, there can sometimes be a rational explanation for even the weirdest of happenings.'

Beth wondered if the story was really true.

Dad said that it was sufficiently plausible to have occurred and 'Mac's friend' had assured him it was true.

The story provided a coda to the evening: conversation and hospitality had reached a natural conclusion. It was time for me to go home. I thanked my hosts warmly and said truthfully that I had thoroughly enjoyed their kind hospitality. Tactfully, Beth's parents remained in the sitting room while she saw me to the front door. Our lips met, all too briefly, but the moment could not be prolonged. We would meet again, soon.

As I went outside, I found that the rain had cleared, but, walking home, the same could not be said of the confusion of thoughts clamouring for attention in my brain. Since coming here, things that must be thought about continued to accumulate at an alarming rate, while I was finding it increasingly difficult to make decisions, to plan my future and to prioritise. Just then, keeping up to date seemed to have become unachievable. I thought, yet again, that I had probably *bitten off more than I could chew* by taking this job.

That evening had been much, much more relaxed and pleasant than expected. But just what had I expected? I had accepted already that a serious relationship was being, or perhaps by then was, established, with unusual rapidity, between Beth and me. We had met only five weeks ago, and, by accepting her parents' hospitality, I was effectively confirming that we were *an item* and going out together.

I wondered how Beth viewed her own future, possibly even a shared future together, and what she hoped for in life. Perhaps I should ask her. If anything was to come of this friendship, the worldly riches that I could contribute to our joint lifestyle would be strictly limited (as Dad undoubtedly already knew). I depended exclusively on my salary, a far from princely income, whereas Beth enjoyed a comfortable home, which I could not hope to match in the foreseeable future. It was time for us to have a heart-to-heart discussion about our future options (a comfortingly vague term).

While memories of the pleasant evening glowed in my memory, it occurred to me suddenly that, in my attempts to do the right thing and be pleasant to Mumsy and Dad, there had been virtually no contact with Beth. I should not have allowed this to happen. The persistent thought that permeated and dominated an unexpectedly high proportion of my cerebration at that time was, *I want to see Beth again and soon.* She had become the focus of my happiness, my hopes and, perhaps even of my future. I had to face the fact that, for the first time ever, I must have *fallen in love...*

Chapter 10

FIFTH FRIDAY IN OCTOBER

# REJOIN	a. Counter answer; rebuttal statement
	b. Put together again

'IN CONCLUSION, I SUGGEST STRONGLY THAT, BEFORE WE MEET next week, you read the references I've listed on the board and also the introduction to... Thank you for your attention.' This well-intentioned advice concluded my lecture to our honours-degree class, potentially our brightest and keenest students. The reading recommended would introduce the difficult content of my next lecture, making it a little easier to understand. However, glancing around, I spotted nobody noting my *pearls of wisdom* postscript. No doubt, as always, the number of alternative versions of the content of my lecture would equal the number of students present. The variable accuracies and legibility of such improvised jottings, or *lecture notes*, all too often led to later questioning, usually starting respectfully, '*Sir, you know, in your lecture, did you mean...?*' to which, all too often, my reply had to begin, '*No!*'

Having completed my lecture hour (with the four-minute overrun offsetting my start delayed by latecomers), I was left in no doubt that the top priority for my audience was a rapid departure. Presumably, they were off to the Student's Union for coffee and discussions about plans to celebrate Halloween suitably. My final advice, I guessed, was dismissed as a trivial afterthought and, anyway, came outside my allotted time.

The final moments of my lectures tended to be audibly 'applauded' by a chorus of clicks from the snap-closures of note files, a reminder that 'Ending time approacheth'. This was one feature of charades acted out by the students who chose, whenever possible, to imply disinterest in their chosen subject, which they had voluntarily come here to *read*. This early in the year, examinations appeared to be invisibly distant, months away and, just then, could safely be ignored. Undergraduates 'knew', or managed to convince themselves, that sufficient time remained to make up the necessary study and revision later. It was also well known (incorrectly) that the swatting up on notes was best left until the final weeks, days or even hours before examinations.

Right then, I was, equally, looking forward to a caffeine infusion, regarding my need as more deserving than theirs; after all, who had been doing all the talking, a stressful activity known to dry one's mouth? (This comparison disregarded the *sotto voce* background talking, subliminally impinging on my consciousness throughout the past hour.) Moreover, I had needed to start earlier, refreshing my memory of lecture content. So, my conscience clear (as usual, I hoped), I went to the coffee room.

When I arrived, I sat alone but within earshot of a group of colleagues discussing football, a conversational topic of chronic and inexhaustible interest to these fans, including Doug, but – quite definitely – not to me. Eagerly awaited fixtures were discussed with a quantity of, apparently, highly specialised knowledge that never failed to amaze me. The weekend was upon us again, and the fortunes of favoured teams were once more being subjected to critical and learned-sounding analyses before the forthcoming confrontations, which all too frequently seemed to yield unpredicted results.

I find it difficult to take seriously what my father invariably referred to, on the rare occasions when we talked about professional sport, as 'ritual confrontations between rival teams of overpaid gladiators'. We were not a 'footie family': we lived too far from the arenas where these crowd-attracting sporting contests were enacted. Father found it unrewarding to accept as significant or take interest in the antics of these absurdly over-rewarded sporting professionals, who work in a particularly successful and lucrative branch of the entertainment industry. He regarded the saddest aspect of mass support for commercial sport to be the time spent by the spectators who, he believed, could more profitably, healthily and enjoyably play the game themselves. Had the decline in our country's sporting achievements arisen directly from the proxy culture of identifying with heroes of the turf who could be described as 'the privileged kickers of balls on their fans' behalf'? Listening to my colleague's exchanges, I anticipated Monday when, no doubt, the same coffee-imbibing 'experts' would be presenting equally cogent, insightful (though more convoluted) explanations for their failures to forecast correctly the outcomes of this weekend's tribal contests. Detailed justifications would, no doubt, be explained to anyone with the time and patience to listen. It occurred to me that similar anticipatory sporting analyses, also followed by explanatory inquests, maintain buoyant newspaper sales.

No verbal participation was required from me; my posture of rapt attention implied my interest was fully engaged by the 'footie wisdom' being expounded, free, gratis and of no value. Unbeknown to my companions, my thoughts were far away from any interest in the speculative trajectories of 'bags of air', which were soon to be assaulted aggressively on manicured lawns by 'celebrities' idolised by crowds of devoted *fanatical* supporters. Of more immediate comfort was my coffee, working its revival wonders by dispersing chalk dust. But, also, I anticipated – with growing concern – my imminent interview with Angus. After considerable mental anguish, I had decided that a discussion with him would now be profitable and judged (wrongly, as it would transpire) that it held the welcome prospect of resolving one of my uncertainties.

○

Just as apprehension increases at a dentist's door, when pain from an aching tooth is said to disappear, the *case against* discussing *my idea* with Prof. McTaggart seemed suddenly stronger when I was in his secretary's room. Miss French greeted me with one unsmiling nod, as I entered by one door, and gave a second, equally impersonal nod towards the other door through which I would access the

Professorial Presence. Her minimally distracted attention returned to typing, undisturbed by my passage.

She was a formidable, severe-looking woman, who was approaching retirement, and was tall and slim, with a tight bun of dark hair and no make-up. Her clothes were sober and sensible, from the high collar of the fawn jumper with matching skirt, longer than currently fashionable, down to well-polished, plain, brown shoes. She was said to hold strong, unbending religious views and was sometimes seen in High Street distributing tracts warning of the dangers of sin. Like so many convinced believers, she did not radiate happiness or personify the joy of life, but seemed to maintain a permanently depressed view of the unfortunate state of the imperfect world in which she found herself. On the few occasions we had talked, she had always said little, as just then, and her penetrating glare implied an innate ability to detect character weaknesses. To my relief, she had never raised the subject of salvation with me, which was possibly forbidden in this workplace. Perhaps she preferred not to mix work with pleasure, or perhaps she just regarded me as a hopeless case. She was punctilious in her job: all the numerous letters emanating from the school director were presented immaculately. While Prof profited from her exemplary contributions to his correspondence, these tasks were conducted in a less than blissful atmosphere. I wondered who had masterminded her appointment: Angus in the interests of efficiency or Elizabeth to ensure her spouse's attention remained focussed on his duties at LU.

I knocked on the door and heard a distant growl, which might have been, 'Enter', so I did. Prof, businesslike in shirt sleeves with pen in hand, was reading documents.

After a glance, he said, 'Oh… Bill… Let me finish, then you'll have my full attention.'

I sat opposite him (was he sitting on *the Chair of Chemistry?*) and glanced around his office. A side table was covered with piles of worn and slightly battered files, resembling in size and appearance the burdens that invariably accompanied him on his frequent peregrinations around the campus. Why did he not use a briefcase? Reserve battalions of similar files were visible through the glass doors of bookcases beyond. These 'encumbrances of the busy man' were readily available for future LU meetings across his wide spheres of influence. A senior professor, who is also an effective administrator, must anticipate all eventualities, including surprise questions; essential background information must always be readily to hand. Remembering the Scout motto, 'Be prepared', I wondered if he had been a Scout in his youth.

On the walls were framed graduation diplomas and prize certificates, apparently academic achievements that were perhaps analogous to the aggressive ancestors portrayed in his paintings at home. These documents charted the roots from which he had sprung, testifying to the firm foundations of his present eminence in LU. Interestingly, there was a picture of a youthful Elizabeth, in mortarboard and gown, which was a graduation photograph showing she also had achieved scholarly distinction. The positioning seemed to imply that she and Prof had graduated to a 'degree of marriage'.

This room, across the building from mine, looked north towards Biggar House. Prof's desk faced the Facilitation Centre, where he spent a significant part of each working week: his duties as LU vice principal extended beyond chemistry to include much wider academic responsibilities. I thought (though not seriously) that this office might have been selected to allow signals to summon him to emergencies at 'The Big House'. On his desk were two phones (though why was a mystery, as how could he use *both*?), but no computer. Presumably, the redoubtable Miss French managed all secretarial tasks and research colleagues were all well-endowed with electronic aids. This was the School of Chemistry's executive boardroom: *decisions* were made here, *actions* elsewhere.

After reading the document in question, Prof's signature was added to the typescript, then it was tossed into the out tray (with no corrections required). Prof turned to me and asked, 'How're things going?'

'Very well, thank you, Prof.' It was unlikely that my concerns would be welcome.

'I think we might move on from "Prof". In these democratic days, I'm Angus, just as you're Bill. Now, to business. How far have you got with Albert Miller in discussing tar disposal?'

'Yes... Angus... thank you. Regarding the tar, agreement for me to start preliminary work has been reached verbally. Written confirmation and samples will follow.'

'Good! I hope that all goes well. Keep me informed. Is that why you're here or is there something else?'

'Yes. There's another matter I want to raise. I don't know if this is the right time. I've only been here a short while... As a new boy... I'm not sure'

'We'll never know unless you come to the point. There's no use beating about the bush.'

It was time to express myself clearly and forcefully; I took a deep breath and plunged in, 'I noticed at the staff meeting that several interesting research projects concerned with environmental protection and/or pollution reduction are being proposed. However, potentially valuable connections *between* them were not considered. As you know, this subject interests me and... I wondered if we might form, in chemistry, an environmental-research group, to bring together everyone working in these fields and related topics. The coordination of our combined efforts could benefit all the staff who are interested.'

Prof, now Angus, gazed towards Biggar House, without speaking. My concerns about the temerity of my proposal returned in force; his silence did not help.

'Maybe it's too early for me... as a junior... who's not been here long. I don't know,' I continued.

After a pause, he stated, 'Yes. There may be merit in what I *think* you're saying. There is strong competition for limited research funds, and we must all adopt every profitable strategy, work together to get grants, etc. So, how do you plan to promote it?'

'Me? I... er... don't know. I thought you...?'

'Me? [It was almost an echo!] No! Not *me*, it's *your* idea, man! I'll be direct with you, but I *will not* direct you. You won't thank me now, but, just possibly, you might do so sometime in the future. We'll see. [I guessed this was a favourite response, and often deployed previously.] Universities are competitive places, and if you want to get on, you – *you, Bill Green* – must take on your own initiatives and you *may* be successful. I think you've the germ of a useful idea here, but it must be developed in *much more* detail.

Write a case. List who's doing what. Work out a plan, with costs. Say what *you* think needs doing, and how, who, what, why, which, where and when. Get a summary proposal onto paper and only then come back to me. I do encourage you to proceed, but *all* initial efforts must be yours, if anything useful is to be achieved. You'll have to be forceful, assertive and imaginative. Good luck!'

'Thank you… Angus. I appreciate—'

'You may not thank me when you realise how much work this may involve. Now, away and get started; you've no time to waste.'

The interview had ended, though its outcome was far from clear. I might have been given a little lukewarm encouragement, but it seemed more likely that I had unwittingly and unwisely transgressed some procedural imperatives. Worryingly, the thrust of Angus's response was disconcertingly familiar; it echoed John Bland's 'start research soon' homily. I was left wondering if I should have asked additional questions, but the unilateral termination of discussion had given me no opportunity. As I left, Miss French gave me her usual indecipherable 'knowing look', which left me uncertain about what, if anything, she might or might not know about me.

I mumbled, 'Good noon,' noticing it was that exact time.

○

Once back in my office, I thought about that first conversation I'd had with Doug, in the Staff Club after my arrival here. I recalled his freely offered advice that, 'Ideas for research are not too difficult to come by. There are plenty of bright people in the university to think them up. The trick is to exploit every opportunity, even the ideas of others, to further one's own interests.' What Angus had just said resonated uncomfortably with this view of survival in the academic jungle, and, by approaching him with an undeveloped idea, I had wasted his time – and mine. Without a clear programme, I was implicitly expecting him to support my initiative, do some of the work and contribute to its development. I should have anticipated his unwillingness to lead a project requiring considerable effort, which was not necessarily in his interests but could become his problem if the plan failed. So, quite reasonably, he had bounced my proposal back to me to undertake all the groundwork! Later, if *my* idea failed, I (not him) would be at fault and, presumably, suffer any consequences.

Another question was that if my plan succeeded, who would benefit? It was unanswerable, but one possible *unwelcome* outcome was that the main beneficiaries might not include me, even though I had initiated the original idea. However, having proposed the concept to Angus, I was now committed and obliged to advance it. He who hesitates goes nowhere, and if my concept was to germinate, I now must plan and act decisively. These were fine sentiments, but could I establish a school group involving colleagues who might be less than enthusiastic? Participants could include Walter Thompson and John Bland. Could I, or indeed anyone, work with them?

Yet again, there was serious thinking to do. Perhaps next I should discuss with Doug how best to progress. Just outlining my ideas to him might help me to identify priorities, and I need not necessarily accept any of his always-generous advice. While wonderfully willing to waffle about the wicked ways of the world, he himself apparently had abandoned all attempts at achieving academic advancement.

However, planning these grandiose academic schemes must be deferred. My mother was flying to Edinburgh this afternoon during her mid-term break, on her first visit to Scotland. Before that, I must collect a hire car. What time did the bus leave?

◎

At the airport, I signed for the car, but left its collection until after the arrival of the London flight. It was now expected at 5.15pm, having been delayed for 'operational reasons'. (*We* feel no obligation to give *you*, the customer, any explanation!) The wait was long enough to be mildly boring but too short to do anything useful. So, to fill the time, I bought a mean little notebook, at a far-from-mean (airport) price, to list my preliminary ideas as to how I could form an environmental-research group at LU. Strangely, I work easily in public places, effectively isolating myself from the distractions of the bustle and background noises. Sometimes, such sessions – being solitary in public – have proved more productive than time spent alone in the privacy and quiet of my office. Here, I also had to ignore my numb posterior, discomforted by the hard seats provided, possibly designed to discourage their use. The period of enforced wait passed while I compiled a dauntingly long list of things to do to further *my idea*.

In due course, I went to arrivals, by then reviewing my immediate plans, all too conscious that this could be a difficult weekend for both Mother and me. During recent years, while I lived at home with her, we had been fairly close, both continuing to feel keenly the untimely death of my father. Then, my decision to move here had brought major changes to both our lives, and I was anxious to know how she was faring on her own. Feeling some guilt, I intended that this rare excursion should be as enjoyable as possible for her. Aware of my limitations as a guide, having hardly ventured beyond Linkirk, I thought we might explore Edinburgh or the local countryside together.

At that point, my maturing relationship with Beth required me to face the considerable problem of introducing them. Would Mother understand how important this had become for me? My emotional life had been transformed totally since Beth and I had found one another, meeting most days and spending our leisure time together. After that first and pleasant Sunday evening in her home, further visits had been less formal. We had talked or watched TV, and usually enjoyed a bite of supper. It was early days yet, but I found huge satisfaction in our relationship. However, despite my good intentions, we had not yet faced the possibility of long-term commitment. My feelings about my/our futures remained unclear, even to me. Beth's parents seemed relaxed about our friendship, but they had each other. In contrast, my mother was alone and distant, so how would she view my ripening friendship with Beth?

I recalled clearly my personal anxiety before meeting Beth's parents, which, happily, had been followed by the further, more relaxed visits. However, Beth, awaiting the complementary encounter, was surely experiencing a similar foreboding. Her stable family background contrasted sharply with my mother's solitary, undoubtedly lonely lifestyle, within our smaller family circle. The Wilkinsons were mutually supportive, though, admittedly, Stewart was – at best – 'semi-detached'.

I would be mightily relieved when Mother's visit was over. With an irreconcilable mixture of filial pleasure, in anticipation of being with her again after our separation, and sharply felt conscience about the stress, even unhappiness, that I was probably but unintentionally causing her, I awaited her appearance impatiently. I had decided that, for better or worse, Beth should be invited join us for dinner tomorrow evening. Given my feelings for her, Mother's visit could not be allowed to pass without bringing together the two ladies in my life. My fervent hope was that the meeting would pass off pleasantly, though I had discussed no aspect of my conundrum with either of them. Nevertheless, I understood only too well the conflicts of loyalties within the relationships and fully appreciated Mother's point of view. She was bound to feel uncomfortable because this meeting was on unfamiliar ground. She would see Beth as a threat, a rival competing for the affections of her only son and an incentive for me to remain hereabouts. For my part, I had elected to come to this distant place, as my flight from the nest, but could plan no long-term future while on a short-term contract. However, knowing their personalities and appreciating their different points of view, I was optimistic enough to hope that their meeting would pass off pleasantly.

Watching passengers emerge, I suffered a brief but horrible surge of despair, thinking that she had not come. My delay in recognition was due to the unfamiliar, heavy, brown overcoat (perhaps new) that she was wearing, possibly bought to combat the cold northern winter. The joy of seeing her face was tempered by my concern that she looked older and stressed. Perhaps this was from her dread of flying, which I had suggested thoughtlessly as the easiest way to travel. I watched her briefly while she looked around, alone, lost and uncertain. When our eyes met in recognition, genuine pleasure lit her face, banishing the tense look. Seconds later, we embraced warmly.

The greeting gave both of us genuine joy; the moment was prolonged as long as possible by mutual consent. There followed the usual obligatory comments about the journey ('Flying is not my favourite. The delay was irritating. Though it was not too bad, I suppose,' she said), and then about me ('I'm starting to settle in. The job is going well. You'll see it all soon,' I told her). I took her suitcase and we left arrivals.

Mother talked more or less continuously, enjoying sharing all her news. Having been alone, this opportunity to update me on the important events in her life was not to be missed. She was maintaining the continuity of our close relationship by filing the gaps since my defection. There were updates on pupils, some of whom I recalled, and activities of colleagues, whose names were still vaguely familiar. For my part, I found it all remote and of less interest than formerly. Feeling slightly guilty, I gave monosyllabic responses when I sensed that, more from tone of voice than content, a reply was needed.

After locating the car, my immediate concerns included the difficulties of driving an unfamiliar car through a strange city after dark in rush-hour traffic. Although a fairly experienced driver, I had experienced little recent practice, and navigation required all my concentration. After two circuits of at least one, possibly two, roundabouts, we finally left the airport and joined the dense traffic on the busy Edinburgh ring road.

After a pause between stories and news, I turned to our immediate plans. 'We could have a meal in Edinburgh or wait until we get to Linkirk, which'll take an hour or so. I don't know Edinburgh. I've never been into the city. We'd just have to find ourselves somewhere to eat. That shouldn't be too difficult. What do you think?'

'Willikins. [This was a pet name; I cringed. Although it expressed endearment, for me it was well past its sell-by date.] I'm hungry. I had only an early light lunch,' she admonished.

'At the next junction, we'll go into Edinburgh and find a restaurant.'

'Good, I'll leave the decision to you. I was telling you about Jane Holden…'

Night driving through unfamiliar city streets on a busy Friday evening was a challenge, and I stopped responding coherently to the continuing flow of news about people I hardly knew. First, we passed prosperous suburbs, with large houses fronted by gardens. Later, the buildings of dark stone became higher and crowded closer to the street, confining me to negotiate narrow chasms bounded by dimly perceived forbidding cliffs on both sides. Eventually, in a shopping area, I noticed an open restaurant, together with a parking space from which, *luckily*, someone was leaving, and, with real relief, I brought the car to a kerbside halt.

The restaurant was acceptable, and we both enjoyed the 'plate of the day': beef, Yorkshire pudding and seasonal veg.

Mother apparently had recounted all her news from home and turned her attention to me. 'I'm not sure you're eating properly. You look pale. You've lost weight?'

My reply was non-committal. I had weighed myself in the Wilkinson's cloakroom recently. I had lost five pounds.

She continued, 'Tell me, are you enjoying being here? Do you really like Scotland?'

'It's far too early to answer those questions yet.'

It seemed pointless to try to explain my difficulties in settling in or the many problems in starting work. Mother was neither a scientist nor a graduate; in the past, discussions about lecturing or research had been unsatisfactory for both of us. The 'tar problem' could be of no possible interest. I could almost hear her non-committal, even dismissive, comment, perhaps, 'I'm sure it's all very interesting, Willikins.' I was even less keen to talk about Beth, though the subject was bound to come up, but not just yet – later. My best policy was to be positive about my new life, concentrating on neutral subjects while avoiding topics with emotional overtones. However, we were both aware that these were present as a subtext. My day-to-day tasks just then absorbed all available energy, and if forced, I *might* have to review possible career changes, but only if things were to go seriously wrong. My overriding wish was to hold onto, tenaciously, my happy relationship with Beth, but shyness, defensiveness and even wariness made me keep those thoughts to myself; they were *not for discussion – not just then.*

I explained, 'I've seen so little of Scotland that I don't know whether I like it here… yet. I'll see how things go and face the future later, when I have to.' I paused. 'The university's in a nice situation, as you'll soon see for yourself. It's built onto the side of a hill… [I developed this theme.] I'm very lucky to be able to share a flat with a colleague. You won't meet Doug because he's away with his wife. They're trying to resolve marriage problems. [I did not mention that Doug was, as he put it, 'Going to the Highlands with Gwen to see if we can sort out this mess. I'm not optimistic though; it's a separate-rooms job, and I'm paying.'] So we'll have the flat to ourselves. [I had carefully cleaned and tidied it.] You'll have his room. Tomorrow, I'll show you the LU campus and Linkirk. I'm told it's a fairly typical Scottish Borders town.'

'That'll be nice. I'm looking forward to it,' she confirmed.

I wondered if that were true.

○

After our meal, returning to the Edinburgh ring road was not easy; several times, I lost my way. Despite the break, I felt distinctly drowsy after the busy day and substantial meal. I wondered, not for the first time, if whomsoever decides the content and positioning of road signs takes advice from strangers, brought to the district to test the comprehensibility of their efforts. Around here, this seemed unlikely. Eventually, more by good luck than good road labelling, we found ourselves heading to Linkirk. On the bus earlier, I had enjoyed the open Scottish Borders panoramas, but there was little to see after dark.

Without anything to interest her, Mother mentioned the need for some redecoration of 'our home', adding significantly, 'You can help when you're home at Christmas.' This had not been discussed, let alone decided. Nevertheless, I agreed with this plan. I was relieved to reach Linkirk.

Little interest was shown in the flat; Mother's home-making instinct was indulged by repositioning the cushions and placing the chairs symmetrically around the table. Later, small efforts to tidy and rearrange would, no doubt, continue.

'Yes. It's very nice...' was her non-committal verdict, after the few rooms had been seen.

It was hardly an expression of enthusiasm, but I did not say that the flat suited me fine. This could not upset Doug who – without effort, thought or even noticing any of the changes – would restore the ambience of comfortable disorder within minutes, even seconds, of his return.

After a hot-water bottle, carried north carefully to maintain civilised standards of comfort, had been filled and placed in her bed (to air it properly, she claimed), we sat down to share a glass of wine in celebration of our reunion. We talked about our plans for the next two days: seeing the town and meeting my friends (I thought of Beth, but did not mention her name). I learned a little more about the progress of school friends, who were doing well in their careers. The unspoken implication (or was I unduly sensitive?) being that *one* (that is, *me*) does not have to come to places *this distant* to prosper in one's chosen profession. I forbore from saying that, for me, I *did* have to come here to find the job I wanted above all others. Nevertheless, it remained to be seen whether I could make a success of it. Both being tired by our long, stressful day and anticipating a busy morrow, we retired early.

Chapter 11

First Monday in November

# DEFER	a. Put off from today what can be done tomorrow b. Make concessions; relinquish the initiative

MONDAY STARTED EARLY, AS WE LEFT LINKIRK AT AROUND 7.00AM, to avoid a last-minute rush; we had, instead, a first-minute rush of breakfasting and packing. The roads were quiet and the rounded, green Scottish Borders hills appeared at their best in the early light. I was keen, indeed anxious, to know if Mother had enjoyed her all-too-brief visit, but was reluctant to ask directly. Her silence contrasted with the flood of news on arrival, so I hurried on, anticipating delays nearer Edinburgh.

Thinking back, I decided that our companionable weekend together had brought some enjoyment for both of us. She had seen my new home and a tiny part of Scotland. Inevitably, my focus was mainly on memories of the encounter of greatest personal importance: the meal with Beth on Saturday evening. This occasion had passed pleasantly enough, as far as my antenna, tuned to maximum sensitivity, could detect. I recalled nothing untoward that had disturbed the superficial serenity of the soirée. Although each of us must have felt quite differently about the significance of the occasion, it had been a slightly formal, though unexceptional meeting.

By chance, we had met Beth on High Street before reaching our rendezvous, 'Linkirk's Best Restaurant' (which was owned by a Mr Best). Having to make introductions in darkness, away from a street lamp, meant I could not appraise their first impressions on their meeting. By the time we reached the restaurant, which was also dimly lit, the two teachers had already found common ground in talking about their schools. Aware of the similar tendency for academics to talk shop, I decided, on reflection, that this was most likely to have arisen from an unspoken agreement to keep to 'safe topics' during this first encounter; its possible significance for all our futures would be avoided.

In the restaurant, coats were taken, our table found and drinks selected.

When seated, Beth asked all the correct questions: 'Did you have a good journey, Mrs Green?'; 'It's not the best time to visit Scotland, with these short days, is it?'; 'What are your first impressions of Linkirk?'; etc.

Mother's replies were positive: 'Despite the initial delay, the journey was comfortable, thank you'; 'Linkirk seems a pleasant town'; etc. Though I noticed that she stopped well short of being effusive.

With our orders taken, conversation returned to the questionable benefits of some proposed changes to the methods of teaching young children to read. Their comparisons of the merits of alternative classroom practices soon became too technical for me. Next, the failings, limitations and even duplicities of two headmasters were laid bare in detail that would have shocked them, if they could have eavesdropped on these impromptu appraisals by their loyal staff. The shortcomings of two education boards were compared critically. Of concern also were the unreasonable demands of remote administrators, who were inexplicably motivated to frustrate the well-intentioned efforts of hard-working teachers in Sussex and Linkirk. Surprisingly, these resentments seemed not to include the Government, which also imposes its expertise onto educational methods.

Although, being a *lecturer*, I might have counted myself a teacher, my views on imparting knowledge to pupils keen to learn or otherwise was considered unworthy of attention by my fellow diners. I said almost nothing, enjoying both the meal and these slightly competitive exchanges, which – to my surprise – were remarkably evenly matched. Mother had longer experience of teaching, but almost all of it in one school near home. In contrast, Beth had worked in London before her present post. I gained the impression that they had gradually developed a mutual respect, if only as teachers. The shared common ground enabled potentially controversial subjects to be avoided. However, teaching, as a conversational topic, was finally exhausted and, after our sweets arrived, it was replaced seamlessly by ladies fashions. Here, I was even less qualified to contribute and so hid my male ignorance by my continuing silence.

Replete, after our generous and tasty meal, conversation slowed. Having made few comments while we ate, I now had to become more sociable.

'We thought of going into Edinburgh tomorrow,' I stated. Realising my tactlessness immediately, I found it difficult to retract. There was a just perceptible pause, before I attempted to rephrase my invitation to be all-inclusive, as intended. 'We'd both be delighted if you came, Beth. Perhaps you'd show us the sights?' I would welcome her company, but was I also speaking for Mother? I did not know, but thought not.

Betraying no indication of having noticed my initial blunder, Beth laughed. 'Thank you, but I've agreed to take my parents to Edinburgh also. Dad prefers I drive in town. We're visiting Anna and her family. Mum and Dad like to visit regularly. And, I'd guessed you'd probably want take your Mum out somewhere tomorrow. Go out and enjoy your day together.'

When leaving the restaurant there was a slight hiatus, while we decided how to complete the evening.

'Beth, come with us to the flat for a liqueur. Afterwards, I'll see you home,' I offered.

However, it was adjudged to be too late, so we walked the small extra distance to pass near Beth's home. Leave-taking was similarly awkward. We all expressed our pleasure from the evening together and the hope to repeat it before too long.

I could think of nothing further to say, other than: 'See you soon, Beth,' after which Mother and I returned to the flat.

Talking about schools had reminded Mother of other news, which had been omitted from earlier bulletins, and these were now related. Feeling fatigued, I did not listen carefully, but the comments that penetrated my reverie were, 'I'd think she's a good and committed teacher. She seems a nice girl.' So I had to be content with this appraisal, which fell far short of my own feelings about Beth.

As we drove on to Edinburgh, I decided that the evening with Beth had been about as successful as could reasonably be expected, though defining just what I had expected was necessarily rather vague. My hope was still that the two ladies in my life would respect, even like, one another, but this was not something that I could influence easily. Perhaps my motivation for introducing them expressed my hope that Beth and I were moving towards a long-term relationship, complementing the contact made by my visit to her home. Also, having mentioned Beth in letters to Mother, it was appropriate that they should meet.

The evening together had enabled me to see how they got on, perhaps even giving me clues about how my relationship with Beth might develop. I vaguely recalled my father saying, 'Men marry women like their mothers.' I had not known Grandma Green, who died before I was born, so could not judge the merit of this comment. However, after our meal, I thought Mother and Beth possessed real similarities of character. Perhaps Dad was right. But, for me, our present friendship was more than pleasant: I was enjoying every moment of it. She had brought this unexpected, sudden burst of sunshine into my life, which I treasured and would not readily relinquish. We had, after all, met only recently; there was no urgency, as yet, to think about the longer term.

Obviously, any shared future depended on my prospects improving. My current workload, in getting started at LU, made it pointless to even think about a next career step. Such planning could only become worthwhile *after* I had established myself in a permanent lectureship somewhere. That achieved, I might be able to offer Beth security, but realising such daydreams would depend on her wishes and, inevitably, also her patience. Meanwhile, her company was a joy that I could not risk losing, providing oases of happiness in the daily grind of keeping ahead of my seemingly endless academic duties.

Nevertheless, my growing amity with Beth was distancing me from Mother, further stressing our close relationship, which was already strained by my coming here. If I settled in Linkirk permanently, she would be very isolated and facing a lonely future because I was sure that she would not move to Scotland. I had no ideas about how to be fair within this triangle, though perhaps the most significant changes had already been made. Such indecision! However, all thoughts of my future, with or without Beth, were premature, as I was not sure of what I myself wanted or was capable of achieving yet. Just then, returning home, Mother also chose not to raise the topic, perhaps hoping it would, in time, go away. Her silence could be expressing her concern about my growing independence, about her own future or both. Either way, I felt guilty that my actions were causing her pain. Was I being selfish? Realistically, probably!

In daylight, driving the Edinburgh Bypass was easier than our earlier journey, but, with lane closures, dense traffic slowed our progress.

Perhaps it was the road signs that prompted Mother to recall yesterday's outing. 'Edinburgh is a dark city. I expected it to be less drab.'

I pointed out that the day had been overcast.

'All that dark stone depresses me. It's not a warm place. I was interested to see it this once, but I'd not hurry back.' Thus, the attractions of Scotland's capital were dismissed.

I did not mention my hope that she might return in the brighter spring.

Arriving at the airport in good time, Christmas was mentioned again.

'It's only eight weeks, Willikins,' she reminded.

I cringed.

During the festive season, particularly after Father died, Mother enjoyed the then infrequent contacts with our few relations, some of whom visited us at this time of year. It seemed that our holiday programme had already been planned in detail, and my participation taken for granted. The unstated implication remained that my sojourn in Linkirk was, should or might be only temporary. Because I had not planned ahead, I could offer no alternative programme. I could not reject all her hopes and plans during these, our last moments together, when we were unlikely to meet again before the vacation. I could not abandon her to a solitary Christmas and New Year, so I confirmed, 'Of course I'll be home after term ends.' Nevertheless, I wondered if Mother's house was still my home, though perhaps it would remain so while she lived there. After she flew south, I would miss her. I had enjoyed her companionship over the weekend, even feeling some nostalgia for the life I had left so recently. Decisions about the future would remain difficult.

I returned the hire car, regretting this loss of convenience and the comfort of having my own transport. I must review my finances to decide if and when I could buy a car, without risking financial disaster. Could I ask Beth's father for an overdraft? Would he view such an investment as the mismanagement of my finances? Most importantly, would he sanction a loan? Would my cash flow problems ease next term? Do used cars' prices rise in the spring? All had the same answer: 'I don't know.'

Relinquishing the car keys was a wrench. Much more so was the farewell, which was brief by mutual consent, at the departure gate.

○

Back at LU, a tall, dark man was standing outside my office, apparently awaiting me. His face was familiar; did I know him from the coffee room?

'Dr Green?' he asked.

On my nod, he came into my room and said, 'I Samir Mahomed. Prof. Bland has said I to speak you.'

'Yes. It's my pleasure! But, first, you'll have to tell me what we speak about.'

'He say that I to do research with you. I to work with you.'

'Me?' This was an unexpected, even extraordinary, proposal. I was so taken aback that it took me a few moments to respond: 'Who do you work for now?'

'Prof. Bland. I do Doctor of Philosophy in LU. He supervise research of me.'

He was increasingly incomprehensible. 'Please help me understand what you're saying. You've started a PhD with Prof. Bland and he's told you to change and work with me? Is this true?' Seated, I looked at my visitor with increased interest. Samir nodded, smiling at my obvious incredulity. Being from Egypt, he spoke fair English, but conversation was made difficult by a stutter that embarrassed him. At over six feet tall, he was thin and dressed informally in an open-necked shirt, despite the coolish day. His glasses did not conceal the intelligent and attentive look in his eyes.

While taking in his appearance, my mind worked overtime. Good research students are highly prized and eagerly sought by academic staff, to contribute towards advancing their pet research projects. Any promising graduate could choose between the best opportunities offered by staff, each keen to expand their research group: great efforts are always made to attract the most talented scientists. I had once overheard Doug comparing our school unfavourably, at examination results' time, with the rutting season on a Scottish moor. Hopeful staff, in the role of stags, attempt to round up as many graduating students as possible, the hinds, to be recruited into their herds/groups, colourfully described by Doug as their harems.

He stated, 'The difference is that, in LU higher, research degrees and scientific articles are gestated, while, on the moors, fawns are born. So we are a natural, self-perpetuating and evolving species: *Homo academicus*. It's Darwinism in action!'

The suggestion that I should take over the supervision of Samir – *after* he had started research with John Bland – was an exceptional, even weird, situation. Good researchers are not lightly let go by their supervisors, so I felt the need to proceed with extreme caution. Reasons for a change of supervisor could be that the student had been difficult in some way: he/she could be uncooperative, disruptive or antagonistic towards colleagues, or even to Prof himself. Other possibilities were a lack of research talent, being inept or clumsy in the laboratory, or having training so inadequate that he/she was incapable of carrying out instructions. I found most of these reasons difficult to identify with this softly spoken and apparently reasonable man. However, interviews are not always the most reliable method of character appraisal, so I had to handle this unusual situation with tact. Rejecting John's invitation to supervise him could jeopardise my future chances of acquiring students. Seizing the moment – thereby gaining a dissatisfied or otherwise unsatisfactory colleague, while appearing to benefit from John Bland's loss – might equally probably lead on to later problems. As always, I could not predict how Prof might react to any of the few responses available, but there was a distinct element of gambling in deciding between the choices apparently on offer.

'It's almost unheard of for a student to change supervisor. Also, if you start a new project now, it will take you longer overall to complete your PhD. Alternatively, if you decide to work with me, we'd start our research together. I have no other students working with me... yet. I arrived here only this term. Whose idea was it for you to transfer from Prof. Bland to me?' I asked.

'I-I do wish it. W-w-work of Prof. Bland is boring. I not learn to do research, chemistry or anything. I do no w-work, except calculate numbers from graph by computer. One year almost, I do nothing else. I not learn chemistry.'

'So you said you wanted to work for me?' It sounded unlikely, even as I said it.

He smiled. 'No, not quite w-which you say. I learn nothing and w-w-was bored. More students from my country, Egypt, do PhD in university in south England. They d-do interesting research, not as me!' He paused.

'Which university?'

'W-W-Weald University, in somewhere... I forget name.'

'Sussex. I know it well! I worked there recently, before coming here. Go on.'

'I write to good friend, Ebeid, he from my Egypt university, to ask if to work in... Weald is good?'

I nodded.

'He talk to supervisor. The supervisor write to Prof. Bland to ask reference of me. But, I not ask friend of me to do this. The letter annoy Prof. Bland.'

I could understand that this must have inflicted a severe shock on John's pride. Learning that a student, apparently working contentedly under his direction, had applied to move elsewhere would upset most academics profoundly. Mohamed was clearly embarrassed by this story and stuttering badly.

'I'll have to speak to Prof. Bland. Before that, we'll try to decide whether you really want to work with me. I don't want you to change your mind later because my research is just as boring as Prof's. Tell me, apart from his research project, would you like to stay on at LU, if we can find something that interests you?'

'Yes. LU is OK for me. I have f-f-friends here.'

'Let's talk about possible research topics. Later, you can decide if you want to do the work I suggest. But do you mind if I talk to Prof. Bland about you?'

He smiled. 'I think I not favourite student of Prof. Bland. OK, it b-better you talk with him. Is easier for me to stay... live here. There are some Egypt men in one LU house, they are friends of me, now. I not need go to... Weald.'

I was beginning to feel hopeful that Samir was an able student and my heaven-sent opportunity to start real research. (*Thank you, John! I can now take your advice!* I thought.) Although unprepared, I outlined an environmental project that I hoped would interest him. His questions were intelligent and he challenged me on the details, as I pieced together a programme. His stutter receded as I engaged his interest, which was an optimistic sign.

With our discussion completed, I declared, 'We'll meet again after you've thought about what I've said, and, please, read this article. If these ideas interest you, then we can begin as soon as Prof. Bland agrees. If you aren't keen, let me know, and that'll close the matter. I'll keep Prof. Bland up to date. Is there anything else you want to ask?'

'Should I talk with other staff here?' he queried.

'You must decide what's best for you. Sorry, I'm the last person to advise on that.' That was unbiased, perhaps, but I did add, 'Even so, I hope you'll decide to work with me.'

'Thank you, sir.'

It was a reassuring reply.

After Samir left, I rang John and asked to see him.

'Yes. It happens I'm free now,' he replied.

I went to his office. Once there, I came straight to the point: 'I've just talked to your student, Samir—'

'Yes. Yes. It's a frightfully embarrassing situation for me.' He lapsed into a silence – a reverie of self-pity lasting so long that I began to wonder if he had forgotten my presence. He said at last, 'It seems he doesn't like the research I gave him. I got a letter from some place asking for a reference, saying he intended to work there. That wasn't a happy experience for me. It's never happened before. He didn't even tell me he'd applied!'

'He told me he'd only made tentative enquiries...'

'Yes. Yes. He said the same to me, but I don't know...'

My position was difficult to defend. 'He came to see me, and I don't find this easy either. I'm not trying to poach one of your students. I'd never spoken to him until—'

'No. No. It's not your fault, I'm sure.' He sounded less than totally convinced. 'The problem is that if he leaves, it'll harm the school. It'd look as if we can't teach our students. If we can persuade him to stay, it'd be an internal matter and not look so bad.'

This was an interesting viewpoint, which had not occurred to me. I responded, 'Just now, he did say he might stay... er... I outlined one possible research idea.'

'When we appointed you... er... Bill, I said we might find you student. Then, hearing Mohamed wanted to go, I thought of you.'

Deferring consideration of the unwelcome implications in the obscure logic of this argument, I said, 'Thank you. I appreciate your support. Without wishing to pry into your... difficulties, may I ask your opinion of his abilities?'

'I have no complaints about his work. He's not very imaginative. He's rather... uncommunicative. He is... was... a satisfactory student. He works long hours, though it's the value of what's done that's more important than time spent.'

Though short on specifics, this was as good a reference as I could expect. That Samir appeared unimaginative could easily have resulted from his disinterest in the work he had been given, and I wondered *unkindly* if this was due to John's less-than-inspiring leadership. The clear statement that he was a satisfactory student confirmed, I decided, that nastiness or serious problems were not the reasons for this proposed change. Good! I left John's office more optimistic than on entering! Right then, I needed to persuade Samir that he wanted to work with me.

○

Back in my office – following the early tension and, later, the surprise of the day – I found it difficult to resume *work*. Because my efforts were frustrated by my mind's obsession with re-reviewing the weekend's events, that chronic concern resurfaced: would I *ever* succeed in organising myself *efficiently* in LU? Was the task beyond me? Why were there always *too many* things to do *right then*?

Resolutely, I kept the computer *off*, to work usefully rather than indulge my perhaps mild addiction. Instead, I attempted, ultimately unprofitably, to prioritise my things to do, thereby wasting the time that would otherwise have been squandered on computer-game challenges.

I reviewed an incomplete research application, which was seeking finance for environmental research, knowing that – in my present lethargic state – this was likely to be only be half-hearted. The more active half of my heart was preoccupied with Beth, with me not having seen her since Saturday, and, to make it worse, no date had been arranged for any next meeting. This distracted me from formulating the compelling case capable of convincing the research council that they should fund my application with large infusions of cash. Again, getting back to my priorities, I decided that my top concern was to restore contact with Beth, after our less-than-satisfactory parting on Saturday. Successful grant applications are only written when personal tensions are relaxed.

The unfinished jottings joined some other, similarly incomplete, drafts in the filing cabinet, which I would put into impeccable order – later. Closing the file drawer, which had been labelled in a rare moment of optimism as 'Projects in Progress', hid the chaos within. It recalled the alternative filing system favoured by a former colleague, who possessed even more filled files than Angus, which was quite an achievement!

(There were no filing cabinets in this colleague's overstuffed office. Piles of bulging files covered every horizontal surface: shelves, desks, chairs, windowsills, parts of the floor, etc. On the spine of each file was a content statement, starting simply with 'Bumf', then 'More Bumf' and 'Even More Bumf', followed by every conceivable combination of diverse and relevant adjectives, but always the same final noun. Yet, whenever he required a document, unerringly, he pulled out the correct file. His mental filing system was more efficient than most conventional indices.)

Unable to maintain concentration, I was not going to achieve anything useful this afternoon and so I went into town to engineer a 'chance' encounter with Beth. My hopes were realised when, from Main Street, I saw her on the bridge coming home from school. When we met, her smile was brief and reserved.

'I thought you're snowed under with work!' she declared; her tone was disapproving and the greeting lacked its customary warmth.

'I hoped we might have tea together,' I explained.

Glancing at her watch, she replied, 'I can't stay long. But... oh, all right.'

We proceeded to The Cosy Kettle. While waiting to order, Beth's expression remained serious, so I asked directly, 'Perhaps you'll tell me what's the matter. Am I in the doghouse?'

'Are you? Why should you be?'

'You seem a bit... distant. Is it something that I've done... or not done?'

'To be frank, you seemed... different... and rather remote on Saturday.'

'Being equally frank, I found it hard to divide my time fairly between you and Mother. I'm sorry if this was a problem. I think Mother felt... the same. I'd not seen her for some time. She's not happy that I'm working so far away from her.'

Our alternative viewpoints were explored in detail before I managed to explain my problem and had accepted that she was not being unreasonable. After apologising for any lapses of manners, it seemed that our differences were patched up, at least just for that time. This was a warning for the future: sensibilities are upset all too easily. The stiffness melted slowly, and things appeared to be returning to normal.

'I enjoyed the time spent with your mother. She's a very committed teacher. Perhaps I shouldn't judge, but I think she's a good one,' confirmed Beth.

'Interestingly, she said much the same about you,' I offered. 'It sounds like a "mutual admiration" society; I'm not sure I approve.'

We laughed.

'I felt we didn't see much of you during her visit,' I stated.

Beth's face became serious. 'You're very fond of your mother?'

'Yes. Our family is very… few in number. My coming here leaves her very much alone. So I was, I suppose, trying to make up to her… after leaving her… by herself.'

'The fact that you've found a girlfriend so soon makes things more difficult?'

'That wasn't mentioned. But, *yes*, I'm sure you're right.'

'So what do you want to do? Do you want us to go on seeing each other?'

This was the one thing that I was absolutely certain about and wanted to continue, if at all possible. 'Yes! Yes! And, yes, again, though I can speak only for myself. If you want it otherwise, then I'll obviously have to accept your decision. But, if you're at all keen that we go on… as before, then I'd like us to remain… friends.' I tried to avoid betraying any note of pleading, which I knew would not help our relationship.

'I feel the same way. We haven't been together long; it's still early days. Yes, Bill, let's go on being friends. I'd like that.'

It was music to my ears and banished my tears.

We left The Cosy Kettle and went to the corner near her home. The light was fading and few people were about. After glancing around, she took me into her arms and kissed me firmly on the lips. The sudden and unexpected contact brought me great pleasure and a slight taste of lemon from her cake.

'Perhaps that'll give you just a little reassurance that I'm still interested. Very interested! See you soon!' And, with that, she was gone.

As I walked away, the spring in my step was back as I went along Main Street.

When I reached home, Doug's car was outside our flat; he was back from his Halloween attempt at reconciliation with Gwen. I had met her only once, when she called to see Doug. She had seemed friendly, but – although I offered tea while she awaited Doug's return – she did not stay. Being an attractive person of short stature and slim build, she left the impression of compensating for her small size with great strength of character.

As I entered the sitting room, it was obvious that the weekend had resolved nothing for my friend.

'Come in, Bill. Join me in drowning my sorrows. Have a drink,' he offered.

On the table were two wine bottles; surprisingly, both were open, together with a half-empty/full bottle of whisky. I poured myself a red wine and sat down to hear his news, though it was easily guessed.

'I gather things didn't work out,' I said.

'You're correct... right. Oh... yes.' He had drunk enough alcohol to blur his speech.

'Tell me about the weekend.' It might help ease his mind, though I doubted it.

'It wasn't a success. Nothing was resolved. I'd hoped for some sort of reapp... reapp... you know what... I mean?'

'Rapprochement?'

'Might work. But... no. Certainly not. Unforgiving woman, my dear ex-wife. You're stuck with me here, sharing the flat. You'll not... be rid of me that easily.'

He was past the stage of making much sense. The prospect of a binge-drinking session was unwelcome, and I was not going to encourage him. I stated, 'You rest here, and I'll make supper.'

Anticipating just this situation, I already had assembled in the kitchen all the wherewithal necessary to prepare our usual substantial meal of steak, chips and peas. So I set aside my almost-untouched wine and started to cook the dinner that, on previous occasions, had always proved acceptable to Doug.

In unusual silence, providing evidence of his inner capitulation, Doug ate hungrily, without – I was pleased to see – imbibing much more alcohol. The food seemed to sober him somewhat and encourage confidentiality.

'The weekend was an expensive waste of time. The expense, you know, was all mine,' he explained.

'You don't need to tell me this,' I replied.

'You're a good listener, Bill. You're helping me get it off my chest, now I've nobody else to tell my troubles to. Am I boring you?'

'No, not at all.' Though, to be truthful, I was not in the mood to listen to details of his marriage breakdown. That day's difference with Beth was disquieting evidence of a fragility in my own fledgling relationship.

Contemplating Doug's pain, from stresses appearing so long into his married life, was something that I preferred to not engage in, particularly now. Nevertheless, I felt obliged to offer what succour I could, being mindful of his obvious distress on realising that it was now extremely unlikely that he could ever restore his formerly happy rapport with Gwen. I did feel sorry for him, even if – as he so freely admitted – it was all his own fault. What could I learn from his mistakes? I would like to believe (despite Doug's very human fallibility) that I was far too fond of Beth to stray from the straight and narrow path – ever. Also, I wanted to be optimistic that any relationship I might enter into with Beth would remain strong enough to outlast minor differences: today's events were a step in that direction. Most life-long commitments presumably start with the participants being starry-eyed, but are not necessarily maintained that way indefinitely.

Chapter 12

SECOND SATURDAY IN NOVEMBER

BLOW	a.	Windy conditions; gust of strong wind
	b.	Reversal of fortune; damaging occurrence

'WELL, WHAT DO YOU THINK OF OUR SCOTTISH COUNTRYSIDE?'
Beth looked up briefly, while driving carefully along this narrow road,
winding through a broad valley between low, rounded hills. Having
headed southwest from Linkirk, we were beside a small river: Yarrow
Water, from the map. Few other cars were about; the only life visible
were the sheep, as white dots scattered across the landscape. Somehow
these resilient vegetarians managed to subsist on the ubiquitous
greenish vegetation that once had been grass during the brief summer.
The panorama was unfamiliar, with few habitations and muted colours
contrasting with the populous, more colourful and intensively farmed
land of my native Sussex. I still thought of England as home and, with
a nostalgic twinge, recalled that the border was not far across those hills
to our left...

I interrupted my reverie to reply enthusiastically, 'Interesting. It's very
different from our Sussex countryside, but it's all immensely enjoyable,

thanks to you. I'm still concerned that your parents might be missing their car today.'

'Their car, this car, is also *equally* my car. We decided that this venerable vehicle is all we need. We don't use it much, except to visit family,' she confirmed.

'But perhaps your parents might've wanted it today?'

'No, not today. Mum is hosting afternoon tea for the Ladies' Guild of the church and Dad has his crosswords.'

'Crosswords? What's he cross about?' I must have sounded puzzled.

'Crossword *puzzles*. For newspapers. He makes them up. It's his hobby, and he's paid for them. Someone has to do it, you know. They don't set themselves.' The school teacher in Beth's character or training surfaced briefly. 'Setting crosswords requires great skill, I'll have you know, William Green.'

'Yes, miss. Will you keep me in after school, please, miss?'

'Not today. Just see it doesn't happen again.'

My response of, 'That's a pity. I'll try harder next time,' was ignored as we continued in companionable silence.

To our left, an expanse of slate-grey water appeared, stretching towards some low, dark hills, matching the overcast sky above.

'That's St Mary's Lough. It's not at its best. It's more picturesque in sunshine. Rain's coming and it's windy too; look at those waves. Shall I stop?' asked Beth.

'Yes, a leg stretch would be good,' I confirmed.

She pulled over, and we got out.

I noticed an inn beyond the grassy knoll where we parked. 'Who or what was, er... *Tibbie Shiels*...? Is that right?'

Beth stated, 'I don't know who he or she was, but this place is quite famous. Robert Louis Stephenson was supposed to like this place, or so Mr Day, our English teacher, said.'

The rain began in earnest, and the wind was chilling, so we returned to the car and moved on.

'Why are we going to Moffat?' I enquired.

'No particular reason,' she said, 'You said a trip out would be welcome after a bad week. If you'd said *toowwn* [said with an exaggerated English accent], I suppose you'd have meant Edinburgh. Because you said country, I thought of Moffat as it's not too far, and we'll get lunch there. OK?'

I nodded.

'Later, if it clears up, we might have a walk, as I've been in all week too! Incidentally, you didn't say why your week was so *terrible*.'

'Terrible is too strong a word. It was bad, but not *all* bad. It's just that the constant effort of trying to do *all* the things expected of me is sometimes discouraging. Lectures, tutorials and applying for research money. It seems endless… There're loads of laboratory reports to mark. The pressures of starting this job tire me out. There's more to being a lecturer than I expected. Sometimes I wonder if I've chosen the right career.' I had not intended to reveal these innermost feelings of self-doubt, which surfaced intermittently, but – being relaxed and encouraged by her interest – I found it easy to share my most personal worries: 'The first term is probably the worst. Soon I'll get my second wind and, refreshed by our day out, return to normal. Ready to carry on…'

With a qualm of conscience, I remembered Beth had also mentioned having a bad week, so it was not a good time for me to parade my unresolved predicaments. 'You said you'd experienced problems at school. Would it help to share them?'

Her face was tense, from driving in heavy rain. Without wanting to distract her attention, I genuinely wanted to know what had upset her and offer whatever comfort a sympathetic ear might provide. It might also be helpful to know about the types of situation that upset her to anticipate possible stresses in our relationship. If this was falling in love, I was a willing participant.

Beth's expression relaxed slightly. 'Like you, my week had its moments. There was a minor-but-unpleasant incident in the playground on… Tuesday. Yes, my duty day. A child in my class, Tony, fell rather heavily, though I didn't actually see him fall. He told me Jock McLean had knocked him over. Now, I am certain I'd seen Jock on the other side of the playground at that time, apparently teasing two younger children. I remembered it particularly because I was about to intervene. Jock's a mildly aggressive child, even a bully if he can get away with it. He'd caused trouble with Tony before. I told Tony he might have been mistaken and hoped that ended the matter.'

'But it didn't?' I asked.

Beth's face betrayed her continuing tension. 'No. Tony told his parents I'd called him a liar, which I hadn't. His parents went to the headmaster, and I was asked to explain myself. Jock was questioned, and there was a meeting between everyone concerned, with Jock as a reluctant witness. However, before this, Tony admitted to his mother that he had tripped on an untied bootlace, and the complaint was withdrawn. Apparently, Tony simply wanted to get back at Jock. It was all very trivial, time-wasting and unnecessary… but, for me, upsetting.'

My inclination was to express admiration for anyone who continued to teach such children voluntarily. However, this was hardly a tactful commiseration to offer Beth, to whom teaching was a vocation or even a privilege. Instead, I pointed out that, in the potentially nasty situation, truth had prevailed. True to her principles, she had down-faced the lie and probably discomfited the bully. This seemed to have been the right answer, from the approving smile.

'We're at an interesting part of the road,' she stated.

After crossing a high ridge, we descended a steep slope beside a rugged, rocky gorge, down which a small stream cascaded. Further on, this glen entered a wider valley bounded by steep, grassy mountainsides with much higher hills on both sides. We came to a worn patch of muddy ground, a roadside park for cars, into which – slightly to my surprise – Beth drove and stopped. I then noticed the spectacular waterfall in front of us. Within a narrow cleft in the cliff-like mountainside, there was a most impressive display of cascading, white water: a small river descended precipitously in one almost-unbroken drop from the high ground above to the valley floor.

Beth said, 'It's the Grey Mare's Tail Waterfall.'

(To interrupt my story, I might mention here that – during this, my first visit to this valley, which much later became my desperate refuge – I experienced no premonition whatsoever of the terrible and anxious time to come. At that point, I was happy, pleased to be alive and enjoying every moment in this Area of Outstanding Natural Beauty.)

Although it was still wet and windy, we left the car briefly to look more closely at this spectacular cascade in full flood. As we walked along a rough path, I offered Beth some shelter by putting my arm around her shoulder. My gesture was rewarded by a sudden kiss on the lips, and, whatever the weather was doing, I had the welcome confirmation that, emotionally, the wind was blowing favourably in my direction.

We did not venture far and, once back in the car, I asked, 'Do we return home this way?'

'Probably. It's the most direct road, though there are others. Why?' questioned Beth.

'If the weather has improved when we're going back, how'd you like to walk up a bit of that path over there? It seems to go up beside the waterfall.'

'I did climb it once, years ago. It goes up to a lake, high in the hills. But… yes.'

Continuing along the narrow and constantly curving road, beside the same swift stream, we could see only the lower grassy slopes of the steep-sided valley: cloud obscured the hilltops.

'Do you mind driving?' I asked, aware of the care necessary on this unfenced road, after Beth braked sharply to allow sheep to wander in front of us.

'Not at all. I quite like driving,' she replied. 'In any case, our insurance only covers Dad and me. I think you'd be in trouble if you drove and things went wrong.'

Near the valley end, the road plunged into a dark pinewood.

'I may be imagining things, but was that a *peacock* on a gatepost? Or am I hallucinating?' I enquired.

'I think I saw peacocks hereabouts, years ago. But, no, I didn't spot one just now.' Beth was less surprised, but the question remained unresolved.

More torturous curves, matched by vertical undulations, were negotiated before the narrow road became level to enter the small town of Moffat. At first glance, the main street appeared to be exceptionally wide, with the shops and hotels on its opposite sides unusually far apart. Then I worked out that there were two parallel streets separated by car parking areas. This tourist-friendly plan encouraged visitors to leave their vehicles, followed by their cash (of course), in the strategically located, but perhaps misnamed, gift shops nearby. But few visitors were here today.

Prominent in the town centre was the statue of a large sheep, apparently a ram, on a stone plinth. This contrasted interestingly with the more usual effigies of bygone local landowners or memorials to their unfortunate tenants who, in wars, had died fulfilling patriotic obligations. Instead, *Ram Rampant* represented and recognised a real revenue-raising resource for rural residents, which provided fleeces and mutton. We had seen already the latest generation of these hardy, woolly quadrupeds, still populating the inhospitable surrounding uplands. I recalled a remark made by a friend, observing a congregation dispersing after a church service: 'When they say "We, like sheep…" what they really mean is "with mint sauce and two veg".' I decided it would be unwise to repeat this just now, as Beth might not appreciate such ironic humour.

Instead, I said, 'Beth, after our excursion, would you do me the honour of visiting my residence, for us to partake of dinner together? Do, please, say aye. Doug said he'll be out. I've already bought the wherewithal, and if you'll take pot luck, I promise it's not lamb or ram. I would welcome the expert advice of a skilled cook, if she's in the mood… There's also Shiraz wine, to accompany the steak…'

'How formal you've suddenly become! Your kind and generous invitation, my dear sir, is fully understood. What you're saying is that if I come to your residence, I may cook your supper. But, who'll wash up? Or is that my extra treat?' she asked.

'How well you understand me and penetrate my carefully hidden plans. But it's not quite that bad. The potatoes are already peeled, the carrots are diced and the wine is near the radiator. Also, I promise faithfully to wash up.'

Beth smiled.

So I added, 'Assuming you'll dry the dishes and put them away.'

Our plans made, we ran through the rain to the nearest hostelry and ordered a light lunch. Although the bar was almost empty, service was slow, giving us ample time to peruse a local guidebook that had been left on our table. Sitting side-by-side, closer than strictly necessary, was companionable. An unexpected brush of Beth's lips across my cheek brought disproportionate pleasure. Then, my cheeks coloured on noticing a disapproving glare from another customer, an obese woman whose scowl seemed a permanent fixture. Her husband – a small, thin man with a hunted look – said nothing during all our time there. I supposed they had never, even briefly, experienced the happiness I was revelling in. It seemed unlikely; not everyone is as fortunate as us.

Beth opened the guidebook to see the local attractions. We learned that the Star Hotel, Moffat, with its seventeenth-century brick façade, was the United Kingdom's slimmest free-standing hotel, being only twenty feet wide, information unlikely to be of much use. For no good reason, I was more interested by a valley, north of here, called The Devil's Beef Tub, because of its former use by rustlers, known locally as 'reivers', to hide cattle stolen in raids.

Lunch was disappointing. The 'traditional Scottish broth' could be better described as 'over-boiled, watery cabbage of unknown provenance'. The ham in the sandwich had no flavour and a rubbery texture. The coffee, though almost black, somehow managed to be tasteless. Beth declined alcohol, saying, 'I'm driving,' and I followed suit. We could look forward to an evening meal that would make up for this poor offering. The disinterested waiter gave the impression of overwork, for no reason apparent in this off-season, near-deserted hotel. I paid without comment (or gratuity) vowing never again to enter this poor hostelry.

Once back in the car, Beth set off purposefully without mentioning any intended destination. We ascended a winding hill, past the town graveyard, before she explained, 'I want to see The Devil's Beef Tub, then you can tell me all about it.'

'I can tell you… what? I've never been here before,' I declared.

'But you're the scientist. You know all about the environment.'

I could think of no answer other than a long lecture on what I think science is about. A different approach was needed: 'Did you do science at school?' Strangely, I had never asked her that question before.

'Yes, of course, but I was never any good at it. Our teacher, Miss Wellington, was hopeless at explaining things. We called her "The Old Boot".'

'Well, now that you're a teacher, you can understand how hurtful that might be.'

I wondered if this was too blunt, but, from her concerned look, I saw I had given her pause for thought. Pursuit of this theme was, however, deflected deftly. She stopped at a slight bend in the road on the exposed hilltop we had reached; it was an unsuitable place to park, but traffic was light. The wind was particularly gusty with squally blasts of rain, so, in raincoats, we crossed the road to look into the secluded valley beyond.

Beth asked, 'Do you think that's the deep valley where stolen cattle were hidden?'

I agreed that this was probable and cattle rustling here had been a well-established way of life, long before the Wild West was invented.

Beth's response was rapid: 'I guess it has *Wayned* since those days.'

I affected not to notice the pun. 'So how did that big valley, that gap in the mountains, get there, Mr Environmentalist?'

'If you'd listened to Miss Wellington, you might have learned.'

'She didn't teach us about rocks. You're putting me off because you don't want to admit that you don't know either.'

There was more than a grain of truth in this, but not wanting to admit ignorance, I began, 'This 'ere is a classic example of glacial erosion. When the climate was much colder, tens of thousands of years ago, winter snows didn't melt completely in summers but accumulated into great fields of ice or huge glaciers that, eventually, grew to be hundreds of feet thick. During the Ice Age, here was like the Arctic is now. For thousands of years, ice moved slowly across the rock, scratching away the surface, like sandpaper, to gouge out these big holes in time. The rock is hard, but the continual grating of ice containing grit and stones wears it away slowly. After these cold times, the climate warmed slowly, with the glaciers melting over many centuries, and the bits of rock in the ice fell out to form the small hills of sand and stones, called moraines, that you saw down in the valley. I don't know why this deep valley was dug here, either the rock was soft or perhaps two moving glaciers met. Is that enough?'

'How long is it since the glaciers went?'

'I think the last glaciers in Britain melted over 10,000 years ago. The tops of all these hills around us were rounded – 'sand-glaciered', if you like – by moving ice.'

'Wow, 10,000 years. That's a long, long time.'

'Not by geological standards. It's just the blink of a geological eye. I don't know the ages the rocks under our feet, but I'd guess… oh, maybe some hundreds of millions of years. They were here a long time, ages, before the ice came.'

'*Millions* of years? Are you sure?'

A sharper, wetter squall sent us running back to the car, and geological epochs were forgotten in our haste to reach shelter. With poor visibility from drifting patches of low cloud, we urgently needed to find a safer parking place. After we had driven off, around the bend, Beth found a suitable, flattish area, near piles of road stone. We stopped close behind another car that was already parked in this informal lay-by. When the mist blew away, I was pleased to recognise a venerable veteran of the road: a Morris Minor. It had been maintained in meticulous condition, except for one obvious and unfortunate disability: the offside rear tyre was flat.

I explained, 'My father had a car exactly like that. He said they were among the most reliable cars ever made. He only sold his when the garage couldn't get spares. That one must belong to a keen enthusiast.'

When the squall had blown away and the rain had reduced, visibility improved slightly. We saw the single occupant of the car, a man, get out and, although without a raincoat, stand looking despondently at his problem.

I joined him and said, 'Good afternoon.'

My voice startled him; he visibly jumped and replied, 'I didn't hear you… in this wind.'

'Your car's in lovely order; there aren't many of these about now. My father had one; it was dark blue. He had to sell it, as there were no spare parts. It must be hard to keep it on the road.'

'Yes. This car has been of great interest since I retired.'

My original impression had been of a middle-aged man of average height with darkish hair. But then I saw that he was greying and older than my first estimate. His eyes met mine, and I was treated to a long contemplative stare before his serious expression dissolved into an unexpectedly warm smile. I must have passed some kind of test because his hand was extended suddenly.

He said, 'Dickey Richards. Dickey's not my real name, which is Brian, but everyone calls me Dickey.'

His depressed look vanished and his predicament was forgotten briefly while I introduced myself. But, glancing back at his flat rear wheel, his look of concern returned. He explained, 'I'm in real trouble. This is my second flat tyre today. I'm not superstitious; I think it's the thirteenth, though not a Friday, but it's a bad day… a bad day. I must have driven over nails or something. I've been unwise – foolish – to pass several garages carrying a useless spare wheel. Now I must decide what to do next.'

While speaking, he unlocked his car boot, which had a hinged door that opened upwards. This he rested loose against the back window. My father had warned me *never* to leave this door on his car unsecured in this dangerous position, from which it could easily fall, injuring anyone who was hit as it fell. Such sensible advice, offered during my early years and justified with reasons, had impressed on me that a vivid imagination is the best form of self-preservation, and superior to health and safety rules.

My new acquaintance bent forwards for some undisclosed purpose, into the luggage space, which contained numerous items that my father would have described collectively as *junk*. Just then, to my horror, a gust of wind caught the unsecured, upstanding door, which trembled briefly before accelerating downwards. In my mind's eye, I all too clearly visualised the sharp door edge slamming down onto Dickey's unprotected head. Serious injury, probably short of decapitation, seemed a real prospect as I lunged forwards, and managed to catch and hold the door before it could crack down on Dickey's vulnerable scalp. A sharp rap on my fingers was the immediate reward for my intervention, just as Beth appeared at my elbow.

'Well done, Bill,' she declared.

I fastened the door in its properly secured position with the metal rod, and inspected my hand, which was bruised rather than cut.

Dickey, unperturbed, continued his search in the boot and mumbled, in an offhand manner, 'I always forget to fasten that door. One day it'll be the death of me.' How right he was, and today could well have been that day.

He had not noticed Beth's arrival, but, without hesitation, she made her presence forcefully felt, without introduction: 'You silly old man! You're lucky to be alive. You could've had your block knocked off. And it would've been your own damn silly fault. Perhaps you deserved it. But, think of others, like us. We'd have had to clear up the mess. All thanks to your stupidity.'

This was the first time I had ever seen Beth fully roused, and it was a revelation. There is a view that people with auburn hair can express their wrath more vehemently than most – an opinion that I could now endorse. Indeed, during those few moments, I thought that I had never seen Beth looking so beautiful or so animated. I was amazed by the power of her delivery and thankful for not being the target of her wrath. Dickey's face was an interesting mix of fear for his safety and amazement at the unexpected appearance of this virago on what, until then, had been a deserted road with only bad weather and a flat tyre to contend with. I thought irrelevantly that he probably felt the harshness of an Ice Age appearing rapidly in the form of Beth.

Dickey was reduced to speechlessness; Beth was out of breath and of words, though possibly only temporarily; and I was taken aback by the local tempest that had erupted suddenly into our pleasant, romantic excursion. Nursing my bruised hand, I took Beth's elbow and led her back to her car, gently but firmly.

I told her, 'Everything you said is true. [It was indisputable.] I couldn't have expressed myself better. [I doubted I could have done so well.] I don't dispute a word. [Truly, I would not have dared.] But what do we do now?' I was attempting to test the wind strength and speed before offering opinions.

Her reply should have shocked me: 'Let the silly old sod stew in his own juice.'

'Now that's not very kind.'

'I don't feel very kind.'

Was there just a hint of dispersal of the storm? Perhaps this was the time to abandon caution, but should I take my chance? I did: 'Now that's not the Beth that I know and love.'

For a long moment, I could not read the look in her eyes, which were apparently focussed somewhere infinitely distant behind my head. Meanwhile, my mind adjusted, while simultaneously repelling, to the pessimistic possibility that my spontaneous expression of affection might have been ill-timed. Slowly, her face crumpled into what at first seemed to presage tears, but then transformed miraculously into a smile as her look focussed on me briefly. Suddenly, I was seized and my lips were crushed against hers with a literally breath-taking ferocity that was likely to cause worse bruising than that already suffered by my still-throbbing fingers. The kiss subsided slowly, becoming a normal embrace that disentangled in slow motion as our bodies resolved themselves back into separate individuals.

'Repeat, *exactly*, what you just said,' she demanded.

'It was something like… the Beth that I know and I love,' I attempted.

'Do you mean it? *Really* mean it?'

'I'd not planned to say it just now, but, yes, I've been thinking that way for some time.' Though not intended, this seemed defensive. I continued, 'Since we're having this frank chat, do you feel the same way? Or am I taking things too much for granted?'

'I'm delighted by what you said. And, yes, *yes*, I do feel the same way about you.'

'Go on, say it properly. The three little words.'

'*I love you.*'

The kiss that followed was less passionate than the previous one (it had to be!), but was still truly warm and affectionate.

We both became aware that rain was now falling heavily, if unnoticed, on our ardour. We sheltered in the car, still in a daze but distinctly wet and quite oblivious to our watery discomfort. It was only when we were sitting together, each reviewing in our own ways the momentous events of the last few minutes, that I remembered Mr Richards and his fortuitous role in bringing us closer together. Not being visible, he must have returned to his car. I wondered what he might be thinking about the couple who had appeared so unexpectedly and acted so strangely. Sooner or later, this still-unresolved situation had to be resolved, and then was as good a time as any to face it.

'Correct me if I'm wrong, but do I remember, long ago, a motorist in trouble?' I questioned.

'That silly man, with no sense of self-preservation? That idiot… Is he in trouble?' she responded.

'Yes, he's in a real pickle! How do you feel about lifebelts? Figuratively speaking.'

Beth's face, always expressive, was a picture. I imagined her thoughts, perhaps including, 'A lifebelt might help to bang sense into his thick head'; 'He can stew in his own juice'; 'Why should we bother?'; and 'He might remember all that I said'. Soon, to my relief, her feelings of compassion and kindness slowly became dominant.

'What's his problem?' asked Beth.

I outlined the impossibility of driving a car with *two* unusable wheels.

'I suppose we must offer help. What can we do?' she queried.

First, we had to re-establish contact, which was delayed until the next dry spell. Dickey introduced himself to Beth formally, with extreme wariness, as if expecting a rapid resumption of hostilities, while offering me a look of sympathy for my friend's volatility. However, a more cordial relationship developed as we discussed what would, could, should, might and ought to be done next.

'But I mustn't upset your day. You've got better things to do than bail out the mess this silly old buffer got himself into,' Dickey said.

Beth took the initiative. 'We'd planned a scenic drive, but now it's become pointless with this rain. We may just as well go home. But, first, we're going to help you. I suggest we take the two flat tyres down to Moffat and enquire where they can be repaired. It might be difficult to find a garage open on Saturday afternoon.'

Dickey was reluctant to leave his vehicle, arguing that vintage cars are valuable and attractive to thieves. I pointed out that the missing wheel would make it difficult to move quickly, and we would return soon. Beth added that a person alone might not deter a determined thief; memories of past cattle rustling hereabouts may have prompted this pessimistic idea. The wary look reappeared briefly on Dickey's face. Then, agreeing Beth's plan was the least worst option, we detached the unusable wheel, took the other from the boot, with care this time, and returned to Moffat.

After enquiries at a filling station, we found a private house outside the town, recognised easily by the breakdown van parked outside. The man who answered our knock was unsurprised by our request and agreed, for a fairly steep fee, to arrange the necessary repairs. He would get the wheels repaired and later see Mr Richards safely on his way. I asked Dickey if he had sufficient cash, but he thanked me and assured us that all would be well. He also thanked Beth, though he still remained wary. Knowing that everything possible had been done, we bade him farewell and parted.

Dickey's problems had taken so long to resolve that we stopped to eat at a roadside inn. Our earlier plans were abandoned, as we had to get home and change damp clothing.

'An odd person, Dickey,' I said, as we came into Linkirk. 'He didn't even give us a proper thank you for getting him out of that mess. We don't know who he is, and we'll never hear of him or from him again.'

Later, my forecast was shown to be very, very far from accurate, though my character assessment may have been nearer the truth.

Chapter 13

SECOND SUNDAY IN NOVEMBER

SCALE

a. Basis for comparisons of relative sizes

b. Challenging climb to the highest pinnacles

I WOKE RELUCTANTLY ON SUNDAY. MEMORIES OF A DREAM involving lost cattle trying to find distant pastures from an icy valley faded only slowly. But why had these ideas of the night, connected with yesterday's events, persisted in my subconscious? And why were they accompanied by mild unease? Yesterday had changed my fortunes for the better unexpectedly: Beth and I had now formed a long-term relationship. My slightly unhappy dream was replaced by joyful memories of those precious moments on a wet and windswept road. The bright and happy prospect to cherish was that both of us had agreed on committing ourselves to our joint bond.

Sunday, on which I had no urgent need to rise immediately, allowed my then relaxed mind to indulge itself (and me) in the most pleasant of daydreams. Subconscious images of the night were replaced by fleeting and indistinct images of a wedding – white, of course – in an unfamiliar church. Later, Beth and I were suddenly in Italy, on the Ponte Vecchio in

Florence, admiring her new diamond-and-garnet ring, which I had just bought in a jewellery shop on The Old Bridge. Recently, my appointment to the Permanent Staff of LU had been confirmed, so – after our honeymoon – there would be the 'joys' of house hunting. Wish fulfilment is an indulgence, and, in my unaccustomed relaxed state, I noticed that these musings lacked any sensual content. Right then, that was a step too far and quite beyond my present conception. Companionable activities could later be realised together and might be devalued by anticipation. Or was I being uncharacteristically superstitious? I thought, *Don't even think that way now, the very thought might prevent it ever coming to pass.*

Fancy is pleasant, but realism soon returns. During yesterday's moment of intense candour, we had expressed our love for each other and having both said it out loud, our commitment had been shared. Realistically, I could offer her little as a penurious lecturer with only a short contract. Next year, I could even be jobless in a depressed labour market. There was also the disturbing thought that her father could know, exactly, my tiny bank credit and income, at the minimum of the lecturer scale.

I made breakfast, which – by Doug's custom (he was away at his parents) – was porridge, tea and toast with marmalade (made by Doug's mother to a Scottish recipe with whisky). I had not yet tried Doug's suggested addition to the porridge of a tot of whisky. I indulged myself by returning to bed with a loaded tray for a leisurely breakfast; it was only 8.00am on a cold winter day. The music centre played Schumann's First and Third Symphonies, providing a suitable background sound for reminiscences by matching my then cheerful mood. It was a good time for introspective reflections.

But was I being wildly optimistic by indulging myself in smug, self-serving speculations? How would *she* feel today, tomorrow and next week? I supposed that other young romantics suffer similar mood swings, and periods of indecision to protect easily bruised feelings and attempts to reconcile realism with optimism. Dispassionately, I could say that, as a potential swain, I was inexperienced and truly a virgin, which was unusual among my peers, for whom partner-type relationships often started young. It was never like that for me. My unattached state was not due to lack of opportunity. Growing up in Burgess Heath, I had known many girls of a similar age, as neighbours, at school and at the youth club. However, hitherto I had formed few close relationships. Indeed, at least one of my youthful, budding friendships was probably a casualty of my jealousy. Just then, buoyed up with new optimism, it was timely to review those early experiences, so as to learn any useful lessons that could help me avoid past pitfalls.

At around sixteen, I went out occasionally with Alice, usually to the cinema, where if the film was sufficiently romantic, we tried a few caresses, insofar as these were practicable in seats designed to discourage, even prevent, amorous activities. Afterwards, there was the odd peck on the cheek outside her home, always furtive and brief in case someone might see. Why anyone should have the slightest interest in our amateur and unconvincing imitations of the passions seen on the screen, we never considered. Our romance was strictly at arm's length; Alice would tolerate *no* hanky-panky! How long this might have lasted, I cannot guess, but it was already withering through boredom when it ended abruptly. By chance, our car had stopped in traffic when I saw her going into the cinema with Sam Wilks, from my class at school. She was laughing at something he had said, and I felt a pang of jealousy at her real pleasure; she had never laughed so uninhibitedly at my jokes. We never went out again; our paths diverged naturally with little regret from me. Later, I heard she had married a bookie; certainly, the odds on a comfortable life were better than she could have expected from this aspiring academic.

During my first year at university, I went around with Debbie; we were studying the same scientific subjects. Because her surname was Gourlay and laboratory space was allocated alphabetically, the system meant we usually worked on adjoining benches. This proximity extended to lectures and also to coffee breaks. Being quiet, unassuming and always ready to talk through our study problems made her a congenial colleague. Our scientific discussions certainly benefitted both of us, and I probably gained the most due to her great skill in recording our lecture contents in detailed, *legible* notes.

Being of short stature, favouring dark clothes that matched her short, black hair, and rarely using make-up, Debbie presented a rather prosaic appearance. Her two enlivening features were a bright smile and a sense of humour. Normally serious, even remote, the twinkle that appeared in her dark eyes when she was happy totally transformed her face. She always enjoyed a joke; I never needed to explain the point of a story to her. Despite our common ground, our friendship never extended beyond our studies, apart from on very few social evenings.

I once took her to an orchestral concert, at great expense, only to learn later that it was not her taste in music. Occasionally, I visited the house she shared with other girls and felt distinctly uncomfortable as the only male, even though they (rather obviously) tried to make me feel at home. These social contacts ceased, by mutual consent, after she became friendly with a woman of strongly masculine appearance. After that first year, I heard that Debbie had transferred to a psychology degree, leaving me with unanswered questions and I preferred not to probe in detail.

These short friendships, while inflicting no serious pain, nevertheless reduced my self-confidence and discouraged further attempts to seek female company. That year, our chemistry class was mainly male, and, after Debbie's defection, I made no overtures to any of the remaining girls. Science is a time-demanding discipline, and I preferred to focus my efforts on gaining a good degree, which was an ambition I finally realised.

Studying for a research degree also requires dedication, and, again, if pursued diligently, leaves little time for dalliance. I remained chaste, indulging in no romancing. However, during my final post-graduate year, I worked in the same laboratory as Rosa, a German girl on a student-exchange scheme' that was to 'Foster friendship between our nations', according to a poster above her workspace. Nevertheless, I thought Rosa was not an ideal ambassadress for her country, being quintessentially Teutonic and seemingly ill at ease at being abroad. I was not alone in thinking this because, once, when our group was relaxing over our coffee, someone referred to her as a 'professional foreigner', and a gust of laughter endorsed his diagnosis. Though only about twenty-six, she was overweight and had the most withdrawn personality I have ever known. It may be unfair to attach national stereotypes to individuals, but, for me, she personified the incipient *Hausfrau*. She made, though maybe I flatter myself, overtures that might have been friendship, but these coincided with my final, intense effort to finish the experiments necessary to complete my thesis. Her interest embarrassed me. The situation, which I possibly imagined, was resolved when I applied for the LU job. Her apparent interest evaporated, as the proverbial Scotch mist before the sun, to my secret relief.

As the curriculum vitae of an intended suitor, this was an abysmal career achievement so far. Based on three romantic 'outings', my form (expressed, as for a racehorse) might be described as 'bucked', 'chucked' and 'ducked'. (It still was inappropriate to refer to the fourth consonant: I was not a 'prickocious' youth.) But, happily, the usual path towards life-long partnership with a fellow human being still does not require a list of qualifications, plus references (which are indispensable in academic applications). Assessments of suitability in the pair-bonding stakes tend to be based exclusively on the whims, fancies and intuitions of the participants; indeed, the very absence of too much experience is generally (at least, in theory!) regarded as desirable. So, I conformed to the nominally preferred state; really, I could still describe myself as *extra virgin* (like good grade olive oil). I did not pursue the thought that no alternative to this purity standard appears on labels of this commodity, though the past participle of a verb describing such a state of impurity came to mind: not *lapsed virgin*!

Thoughts of comestibles reminded me that I had invited Beth to a special supper that evening, after yesterday's late start home and slow journey due to the bad weather. Beth, unused to long drives, was tiring when we came to a pub, and I had persuaded her to stop, arguing that a meal (my treat) would revive her. The bar was busy, and the food, slow to arrive, was indifferent, trying rather than justifying our patience.

'Please come to the flat tomorrow and see if I can do better.' I was testing my luck.

'It was to be a joint venture, as I remember. We'd cook together,' she confirmed.

'No offer of expertise refused.' Mindful of my limited cooking skills, I preferred that these were not to be tested too rigorously.

'Dad and Mum like to attend the Remembrance Service in our church tomorrow, and I always go too.' This was said without any suggestion that I should join them, which relieved me of a possibly difficult decision.

Instead, she offered, 'Let's go for a walk after lunch, weather permitting. I'll meet you at Town Bridge at 2.00pm.'

'Could we walk up that path beside the Grey Mare's Tail Waterfall?'

Her reply was vague: 'We'll see.'

I had disliked this phrase since childhood. My mother used these words habitually as a synonym for no, thereby avoiding the negative. I almost invariably appealed against such arbitrary decisions.

Indulging in daydreams had to end, as I needed to tackle my usual weekend chores in addition to preparing for my *special* supper guest. As I worked, I heard the distant sounds of a band, recalling church parades in my youth. This was one of the few Sundays when, at Father's wish, we attended a local church, *to remember* two uncles killed on active service in World War II. This prompted a review of my lapsed religious observances and what I did or, more importantly, what I did not believe. Certainties repeatedly expressed by a fervent Sunday school teacher had never convinced me sufficiently to adopt her unquestioned faith. Up to then, I had totally failed to reconcile the comforts and promises offered by the organised religions with the many harsh and arbitrary realities of the real world. I was also unable to accept that there was sufficiently reliable evidence available to sustain the untestable claims made by the diverse faiths. This appraisal of religious practices had only started when I realised that Beth attended church regularly and, unlike me, seemed to be a conventional, unquestioning believer. Because I had never joined any congregation, and without having a spontaneous interest in spiritual matters, I felt no need to add an additional complication to my already busy life. For me, churchgoing had never served a positive purpose, so I saw no reason to start now. Besides, which of the many varied churches should I join, and why? It would take a life's work to decide between them; the majority of people seem to remain in the faith into which they are born, which is the simplest decision! When and if ever Beth raised the subject, I would be vague and respond as best I could. Another unresolved problem would be shelved!

After my scrupulous completion of domestic chores, to this week's highest standards, I graded some laboratory reports. Though hard to admit, there was a distinct possibility that – in my present relaxed mood, anticipating this afternoon's company — some marks awarded might have been marginally more generous than the content fully merited. In mitigation, I would argue that the grading of students' scripts is not a precise science: occasional generosity might even encourage greater efforts and achievement.

○

At Town Bridge, ten minutes early for our 2.00pm date, I was delighted to see the then familiar car parked nearby. Our greetings were warm, though I thought Beth showed a tiny hint of shyness, perhaps because neither of us quite knew how the other really felt after yesterday's spontaneous declarations of affection. When in the car, we set off at once.

'You wanted to go to the Grey Mare's Tail Waterfall, if I'm correct,' said Beth.

This was unexpected: 'We'll see' could mean 'Yes!' Her desire to please was welcome, but it was important not to disregard her preferences.

'Only if you want to. It's just an idea. If you've a better one, I'll happily go along,' I offered.

'No, I'd like to. The only problem is the weather. Did you hear a forecast?'

'Not exactly. The radio was on, but I didn't pay much attention. I think it's to be bad, though perhaps not around here. But… those clouds in front are very black.'

'Let's press on and decide after we get there.'

So we lapsed into companionable silence, while — it seemed to me — Beth drove slightly faster than yesterday.

When we reached our destination, there were only two other cars parked in the area below the waterfall, and no one else about. The sky was still overcast and very dark in places, but we decided that, having come here, we might as well start our walk. Cocooned in jumpers and covered by rainwear, we set off up the steep footpath, while enjoying the spectacle on our left. A huge cascade of white water fell almost vertically, with the stream swollen by recent rain. We progressed upwards with effort, both unfit from a recent lack of exercise, and we soon became breathless.

Pausing, Beth asked about the geology, as she had yesterday, 'I looked at a guide book this morning… [Puff. Puff.] It said this is a hanging valley. What's that?'

Glad of an excuse to rest, I said, 'The long, deep, U-shaped valley behind us – a… glen, I suppose you'd call it here – was carved out during the Ice Age by a glacier flowing for thousands of years. Our path here leads us up the side of that glen to a high plateau, which catches the rain now that the permanent ice is gone. This rainwater forms little streams and each is carving its own small valley slowly into the rock. These are geologically very young valleys, not having had time to cut deep, so the water falls, I suppose, some 200 feet down into the main valley. The smaller, young valley "hangs" above the major, old one below… I think we, or I, were unwise to start this walk.' The sudden change of subject followed my noticing that dense cloud had obscured the high ground above us and a rainstorm, even a cloudburst, had arrived.

Deluges of large, cold raindrops fell from the dark, scudding clouds. Walking had become distinctly hazardous in the accompanying vigorous squalls of wind. Our downward progress was slowed by the muddy, slippery surface of the path, which was already a minor stream. Supporting each other, we gingerly descended the track we had ascended so easily and so recently. Taking care, we managed to avoid slipping into or getting blown off the treacherous, precipitous drop to our right. Our waterproofs gave some protection, but, nevertheless, when we reached the car, we were both soaked and cold. Beth was visibly shivering. With water pouring off my outer garments, and my jumper and shirt sodden in places, I was reluctant to get into her car.

Beth, similarly drenched, showed no such hesitation, throwing herself into the driving seat with obvious relief, shouting, 'Don't stand about. Get in!'

I accepted her invitation gladly.

We sat watching the downpour, though we were unable to see much beyond the rain-lashed windows, while our breathing and pulse rates slowed towards normal. The rain remained heavy, and strong gusts of wind rocked the car.

'It wasn't a good idea to walk today,' I declared.

Beth smiled at my understatement.

'Now what happens? Is it safe to drive?' I queried.

'First, we get the heater going. Then… it's straight home,' Beth suggested.

We set off. With reduced visibility, driving was not easy in the continuing downpour. At times, the wipers could hardly cope and, soon, fading light added to the difficulties. When the car had heated up sufficiently, we stopped to remove our wettest outer layers so that the circulating hot air warmed and dried us.

'We'll need hot baths after this. So much for my invitation to a leisurely dinner at my flat,' I grumbled.

'You're doing it again!' Beth's serious expression showed genuine grievance.

'I don't understand.'

'You ask a girl to dinner, *if she helps you cook it.* That's bad enough. Last evening, *you* cancelled it. Then the excuse was the lateness of the hour.'

My, 'Well, it was,' simply did not register.

She continued, 'Now we get a bit damp and, *again, you* withdraw the invitation. I think *you* don't want me to come to dinner.'

'What I don't want is that you get a chill, pneumonia or something dire, because you've kindly humoured me by going on this ill-fated walk. I'm only thinking of you. I don't want you ill…' My confused brain had finally picked up the message that she was gently mocking me. But how could the situation be resolved? 'Will you go home, bathe, change, whatever… and then come to the flat?'

'No. No! *No!*'

This time, I really was lost for words.

There was silence while she challenged me with a long, unblinking stare. 'You've got a bath in your flat, right? What's wrong with me using it while you cook the meal? I'll remind you that, originally, you promised to be the chef. Then you can bathe, always assuming you want to, and if I've left any hot water. While you're thawing out, I'll enjoy the sumptuous banquet that you'll have prepared during my luxurious soak. Does hat resolve your problems, Mister, Doctor, Sir?'

This alternative programme appeared acceptable, though I still felt that other possible complications remained unconsidered. 'Will your parents worry or …?'

'They're out at a friends' and won't be back until late; that is, after 10.30pm. They don't know I've got drenched, and they've no reason to know, much less to worry. I'm beginning to think, yet again, that you're trying to renege on our date.'

'I surrender. I'll cook the meal. You *will* be pampered. But only so far… I should warn you that I've no bath salts or fizzy bubbles.'

'I'll get by! What's for dinner? I'm beginning to feel peckish.'

'Steak, roast potatoes, carrots and peas. My real culinary achievement is the sweet… lemon meringue pie.'

'You've been busy. I suppose I'll have to start thinking about forgiving you.'

'Thank you, kind lady, but it might be safer to wait and see if you survive my *kitchenical* skills. A chemist friend once said that cooking is only a branch of chemistry. My mother holds a different view: "If you can read a cookery book, then you can cook." There's probably some truth in both views. It may not be widely known, but the laboratory skills learned in a chemist's training are often useful in the kitchen. I suppose cooks prefer to preserve their mystique, so that the secrets of how raw ingredients are transformed into gourmet delights appear more like art forms than science. The "kitchen magic" of a master chef must never be confused with the smelly and incomprehensible activities carried out in laboratories by white-coated scientists. Nevertheless, in this age of oven-ready, convenience meals, science is steadily probing the mysteries of cookery chemistry.'

'Lecture over?'

'Sorry. Yes, my lecture is definitely over. Just tell me to shut up whenever I start. In future, I'll try not to project prolix presentations of piddling philosophy on you.'

'Oh, it's not quite that bad. Indeed, some was *quite* interesting.' The comment might have been complementary had there been less stress on '*quite*'.

Still in our damp outer garments, we were pleased to reach the warm flat. Happily, I had left on the heating, making my home feel cosy and comfortable, in a well-worn way, after this morning's efforts. As agreed, Beth took over my bedroom, and I ran the bath, before shutting the living-room door fairly loudly, tactfully signalling, 'I'm now out of your way.' It was time to start work on what I fervently hoped would be the most successful meal I had ever cooked (which still did not claim much). The problem was to know when to start grilling the steaks ('The best we have, sir,' the butcher had assured me), re-roasting the frozen (but pre-roasted) potatoes and boiling vegetables. While setting the table, I paused to open the wine, which, of course, had to be tasted to be sure that its quality matched the occasion.

Just then Beth reappeared; she was a vision in red. My heart jumped, and skipped a beat or several, causing temporary arrhythmia. She had donned my red tracksuit, wrapped her auburn hair up in a turban fashioned from the red towel, and was wearing my maroon dressing gown. Her face, rosy-cheeked and illuminated by a bright smile, positively glowed. The effect was overwhelming and released a sudden flood of hormones into my all-too-receptive brain, making it difficult to maintain any semblance of composure. The informality of her attire resulted in an uncomfortably powerful surge of desire that I suppressed only by titanic self-control, leaving me distinctly weak at the knees(among other places). By an extreme effort, I quenched my first inclination, which was to sweep her off her feet and carry her towards the bedroom. Conflicting emotions continued to fight for supremacy, but natural impulses were suppressed rigorously, and the wine, still in my mouth, was swallowed entirely untasted.

'So, drinking alone, are we? You didn't even ask a friend to find a glass… and, talking about finding things, I borrowed some garments. I hope you don't mind. Now you go and make yourself comfortable. [This seemed unachievable, at least in the short-term.] I'll take over here and finish important jobs like emptying the wine bottle.'

Still in inner turmoil, I ventured, 'I tasted the wine to see if it's OK.'

'Well, what like is it?'

'I don't know.'

'Then that's one job you can delegate to me. Why don't you go and change… or something? You look as if you've lost the use of your limbs.' How right she was!

Before shutting the door, again rather loudly, I saw her reading the wine bottle label. I could ask her opinion, whenever I got back, always assuming that – in this debilitated state – I did not disappear down the plughole with the bath water.

The bath was reviving, and I luxuriated in the warm water during the first moments of pure self-indulgence, taking the time to allow recent emotional overloads to correct themselves – well, partially. This was starting satisfactorily, when – to my shock and horror – the light went out. I sat up, transfixed and dripping, wondering what to do next. The slight scuffling sound was puzzling; it seemed nearby, but what next? It seemed that a foot was being placed delicately in the bath; doubt and uncertainty disappeared in an instant. I was going to have company in the tub! What a novel experience! I could only utter one gasping word, 'Beth'.

'Why? Who else are you expecting? Or do you entertain all your friends here?' she responded.

It soon became clear that there is not overmuch room for two people in one bath, even this large one. Thoughts of discomfort did not register as we made the best of the available space and drained some water before it cascaded onto the floor. Surprise was replaced by the rapid reversal of my recently subsiding feelings of desire, as I ran a hand over her shoulder, soaping the soft skin. This was apparently acceptable, and soon it was being reciprocated by my co-bather. Lips also came together, evidently of their own volition, in long and tender contact. Still not wishing to push my luck, or take acquiescence for granted, I slowly ran my hand down the smooth skin of her back. Confirmation that we both were enjoying the contact was evident when her hand followed a similar track down my spine, which was a novel and unexpectedly pleasant feeling that excited renewed hormonal turmoil. I was finding it increasingly difficult to judge just how far Beth was prepared to go, despite my very definite ideas on the subject. With strong self-control, I could, just then, enjoy the moment and revel in the closest proximity of her very touchable, though unseen body. I could lie there forever, in this consummate (almost) companionship.

With awkward movements, Beth sat up. 'The water's cooling, and, my leg's going to sleep...'

'So that's what's meant by sleeping together,' I responded.

'Seriously, we ought to get up...'

'Heavens, what about the food? It'll be fried to a frazzle. The house will be burned down.' I tried to hasten my exit from the slippery bath, which was not easy in darkness and with limited space available for two soapy, slippery bodies.

'Not to worry. I thought we might be preoccupied for a while, so I turned it down.'

'Genius! You think of everything. This "wash instead of walk" was a great idea.'

Towelling off together was almost as pleasurable as the bathing. It proved unnecessary to turn on the light, while we both made sure that we were thoroughly dry, which was an activity enjoyably prolonged by essential interruptions to share kisses. Again, all good things reach a natural conclusion, so what next? I, for one, was no longer in control.

Beth broke the non-monastic silence, 'Do you want to eat... or...?'

'Or... definitely or...' My reply was adequate. Without words, but expectations aroused, we made our way to the bedroom, where – to my surprise – the electric blanket was already warmed. No light was required to find our way together, to bed, and on and on to mutual satiation, all passions spent.

By then, we really had fully expressed our emotions towards each other during the 'all-too-brief but intense' experience of exquisite, tender togetherness. I had embraced more bliss in those moments than on any other occasion I could recall. At that time, each of us nurtured our own personal thoughts about the experience and the bond that had been strengthened between us immeasurably, as we relaxed comfortably together. The close encounter required no words, and perhaps we both relived the wonderful happiness that we had shared so naturally, so easily and so recently. There was also the thought – or hope, at least for me – that the future might bring repetition.

The meal was welcome when we sat down to eat eventually, and, although the steak had become a little overdone, hunger is the best relish. Neither of us could be in a critical mood, basking in the continued glow of shared joy, and very little wine was drunk; intoxication can take different forms. Only the impression of contentment remains; I remember few details about the quality of the meal. But I do recall that my, admittedly mediocre, attempt at making a lemon meringue pie was pronounced palatable, and so our appetites were assuaged. Uncleared, the unwashed dishes remained on the table, while we sat close, companionably and relaxed together on the sofa. Conversation was not necessary, much less TV, just the occasional sip of coffee to complete our repast, which had been exceptionally memorable for the auspiciousness of the occasion, rather than its gastronomic qualities.

Later, inevitably, Beth broke the spell. 'I really must drag myself away, much as I'd like to stay and indulge in domesticity. That's not possible tonight, I'm afraid.'

I saw her to the car. We treated ourselves to a few moments of renewed lip-contact, and I wished her goodnight.

She replied, 'I think we've had that already.'

It was good that she felt that way; it was a sentiment I accepted unreservedly. We parted with promises to meet again very soon.

Resolving to rise early – to clear the table, the kitchen, the bathroom and the bedroom, and to put everything back in order before Doug's immanent return – I cleaned my teeth (the rest of me having been so recently bathed). On turning in, I disregarded the crumpled state of the bed, but revelled in the still detectable faint trace of her perfume. Snugly warm, my thoughts recalled the course of the day, how the accident of our soaking had so naturally and spontaneously progressed to our coming together. Thinking back, I saw that my role was as the willing participant who had responded so enthusiastically to Beth's wonderful initiative. The clinching fact was that she had thoughtfully supplied the necessary protection – a gift that I had not regarded as unusual in the heat of the moment. This confirmation that the she was so willing a partner was particularly comforting. Before falling into a restful and dreamless sleep, I remember realising that my *extra virgin* status had gone forever.

Chapter 14

THIRD FRIDAY IN NOVEMBER

RELATE	
	a. Narrate a story
	b. Reach a sympathetic understanding

'SIR, YOU SAID YOU'D GIVE US THE VACATION-TASK QUESTIONS soon,' said Alastair McBain, the spokesman for this tutorial group, who had the appearance of a refugee from a recent disaster that had resulted in the devastation of his clothes. His ragged trousers were torn open across both knees, and the 'formerly multicoloured but by then drab' woolly sweater appeared to have been pulled repeatedly through a thorny hedge. Despite this dishevelled display, described kindly as 'casual' but more realistically seen as contrived, he was scrupulously clean. An otherwise exceptionally intelligent and diligent student, his use of 'sir' typified his genuinely courteous manners, though they were then betraying apprehension.

I glanced around the other five (more conformist) undergraduates in my honours tutorial. Their tense expressions showed that, while reluctant to pose this question themselves, all were anxious for my answer. My dilemma was whether or not to admit that I had completely forgotten this obligation, not yet having thought up any essay questions.

This structured-revision task had to be completed during the Christmas vacation and was important in contributing marks towards the final examinations. Recalling a situation that had arisen when I was in a similar tutorial group, not so long ago, I decided to play for time by saying, 'Why don't you choose your own tasks? Everyone should set their own essay question and then answer it.'

It was illuminating to see the expressions of shock and horror appearing immediately on all six faces. There was a short silence while the implications of what I had said were considered with, perhaps justifiable, concern. Almost invariably, students are wary of unfamiliar situations and show surprisingly conservative (with a small 'c') attitudes. My novel proposal had, therefore, to be deflected, if humanly possible, because the consequences of setting one's own exercise could not be predicted and might even be disadvantageous. The familiar, even if it was difficult, was always to be preferred and any essay title I set could later be challenged as 'unfair', 'too hard', etc.

'But, sir, aren't you supposed to set our essays?' asked Alastair.

'I'm here to teach you science, to instruct you in problem solving and to hone your skills in tackling challenges. Isn't that so?'

No responses were forthcoming; inconsistencies in my logic and faults in my arguments were being sought furiously.

'Am I not making life easier for you? Think up your own essay question and then answer it; what could be better? Are you afraid that the question you'll set for yourself will be easier than mine or that it will be harder?' I gave them time for thought.

There was still no response.

I continued, 'Seriously, if you genuinely try, just this once, to make up your own question, it will show you how to appraise *all* your examination questions more critically. That can only be a good thing.' With that, I could see eyes glazing over and surreptitious glances at watches hinting at the closing of communication lines.

I made a last effort: 'Essay titles are like examination questions: they don't set themselves. Although you mightn't believe me, it's just as hard, maybe harder, to set a good question, as it is to write a good answer. So I'm examined before you are.'

The knowing grins showed I was not being believed.

'I'll compromise. Think it over, and if possible, make up your own title. Because it's difficult, I'll be generous to everyone who genuinely sets their own task. I'll discuss each idea with you individually in the lab on Monday. Anyone using their own title will not suffer by doing so. Is that fair?' I concluded. Were there nods of agreement or only grudging acquiescence? 'Until next week then; here, at the same time.'

There was the usual chair-scraping departure, while untidy sheaves of notes were stuffed into already overfilled, obviously weighty bags. I do not understand why students make such considerable physical efforts to carry such heavy burdens about the campus. It seemed that every possession that might conceivably be required, plus bottles of water, had always to be close to hand.

With my tutees gone, I restacked the battered tutorial chairs, while thanking that, on balance, I had not handled my lapse over the forgotten essay questions well. The original fault was undoubtedly mine, and it must not happen again; I pinned a reminder of the Monday obligation on my board. I could not think up essay titles just now, as I had another commitment that I anticipated with little enthusiasm.

Two days previously, I had answered the phone to a cheerful voice asking, 'Is that Dr Green?'

'Hello. Yes! Dr Green here,' I confirmed.

'This is Brian Richards.'

I hesitated, the name was vaguely familiar, but why?

He tried again. 'Dickey Richards! You rescued me and my car on Saturday. Don't you remember? It had two flat tyres.'

The memory now returned, and I was annoyed that these semi-forgotten events should intrude into my work. On my desk was yet another incomplete application, already faltering, seeking research finance. My original idea had seemed simple and straightforward, but describing the science succinctly, on paper, had (as ever!) run suddenly into unforeseen difficulties. Dickey's phone call was, therefore, unwelcome, as it was disrupting my already-tenuous train of thought. I wished I had not answered it, but, having done so, I must at least be civil: 'Yes, I remember. Is all well now? Is the car fixed?'

All was indeed well. Profuse, if belated, thanks were given for what he called 'Your kind help to a stranded motorist.' Prolonged apologies were also offered for the unexplained delay in expressing this gratitude.

In turn, I thanked him for his thoughtful phone call, regarding it as closing the incident finally. For me, the necessity to impose order on my seemingly self-destructing research proposal was my first priority, but Dickey was not so easily dismissed.

'I rather wanted to ask a favour,' he declared.

My heart sank. What now?

He continued, 'Or possibly two favours. [*Twice as bad!*] First, would it be a terrible imposition to ask if you'd show me round the School of Chemistry at LU?'

Yes, for me it would indeed be a terrible imposition, and another unnecessary and unwelcome intrusion into my work time, but I could not say so. Public support for academic institutions makes it necessary, politic and polite for me to spend, say, an hour, giving the briefest of tours. There is not much to be seen in chemistry laboratories that could possibly interest the average person or the non-specialist, but if he was so keen, then perhaps I could manage a quick visit. I stated, 'Yes, if you like. I could tell you a little about what we're doing here. [Was this a bit patronising? Probably!] You mentioned a second... thing?'

'We'd very much like to invite you and your fiancée – Bet, is that her name?'

'Beth. Beth. But, no, we're not engaged. She's not actually my fiancée.'

'My wife Emma and I hope that you and your... er... friend would do us the honour of coming to our home for dinner sometime very soon. We want to thank you properly for all your kindnesses. It was only after I got home that I realised your prompt action had saved me from serious... injury. Emma was shocked to hear that the car door had almost slammed down on my head. She was... er... as disturbed as your Bet... Beth, was. But do, do please come, and both of you. It would give us the greatest pleasure. Though I say it myself, Emma is a very good cook.'

While this unexpected invitation was obviously sincere and generously offered, I received it with mixed feelings. There was real pleasure at being invited to dinner with Beth, as a couple, which recognised and cemented our relationship. On the other hand, after the door-descending incident, Beth had been 'very direct' with Dickey, and I thought she might be wary about renewing his acquaintance after such an unpromising start. However, later and to my surprise, when I mentioned the invitation, she was positively enthusiastic. So, it was arranged that Dickey would come that day, for a quick tour of LU School of Chemistry, before we met Beth (She stated, 'I must change after school, before I could think of going out.'). He would then drive us to his home.

○

My visitor arrived at Bond College on time. Dickey was more smartly dressed than on our last encounter, in navy-blue blazer and grey trousers with a sharp crease. His greetings were warm and were followed at once by renewed expressions profuse thanks for all the help we had so generously given to a stranded, helpless motorist.

'You extracted me from a mess of my own making,' he confirmed.

I responded appropriately: 'I'm glad we could assist... If we'd found ourselves in a similar situation...'

Showing my self-invited guest around my workplace posed problems. So far, Dickey had said nothing about why he wanted to visit and had never expressed any interest in science. I could not assume he would understand the equipment I could show him or how I might explain the reasons for our research projects. To the untutored eye, one laboratory probably appears much like another. It is much more straightforward when fellow scientists come to visit, because information can be exchanged through common interests, current fashions and chemical jargon. But, to the casual visitor, research objectives are not easily made clear without giving so much background detail that explanations become bogged down in a morass of side issues. Without access to apparatus that might appear spectacular or interesting to the non-specialist, I felt at a disadvantage, which was not helped by Dickey's unknown motivation. It was possible that he was some kind of scientist, though why would he not openly say so? My exploratory questions had yielded only evasive answers, increasing my bewilderment, so that I felt we were engaging in a game of verbal ping-pong:

Q. 'Have you studied chemistry?' *A.* 'Yes, at A level and so on, but that was long ago.'

Q. 'Does science interest you?' *A.* 'A bit. I've forgotten most of it now.'

Q. 'Is there anything in particular that you'd like to see?' *A.* 'Anything you think would interest a visitor.'

Q. 'Did you teach?' *A.* 'Umm... yes, For a while.'

(The score was *love/four* to Dickey.)

It was not so much his answers as his tone that discouraged further probing. I was convinced he knew much more science than he was admitting, but could not explain all his evasion. Short of demanding a justification for his wish to come to LU, I saw no way to penetrate his impenetrable reserve. Flummoxed and unsympathetic, I had to accept his replies at face value.

One way to start, avoiding technicalities, was to offer refreshment. 'How'd you like start with a cuppa?' I asked. 'School tea? It's hardly a gourmet experience, but it might give you a flavour of the school.' My pun was unintentional.

'I'd like that very much,' he confirmed.

Such ready acceptance surprised me. We adjourned to the coffee room. The tea was almost tasteless, as ever, but – surprisingly – some chocolate biscuits remained, which was unusual on a Friday. Teatime was busy, and Dickey looked around the room with interest.

He caught the eye of a colleague and asked quietly, 'Who's that by the window?'

'Dr Reid. Joe, I think. Do you know him?' I enquired.

'I've probably seen him in town.'

(My 'ping-pong' score was now down to *love/five*.)

Joe came across, and a short, completely pointless exchange occurred. Clearly, both men had met, but neither remembered when or where, and – for some unfathomable reason – neither was prepared to admit this. Nevertheless, honour seemed satisfied by the brief exchange of friendly greetings. This supported my supposition that Dickey had at some point been an academic, perhaps a scientist. Nevertheless, his behaviour remained baffling, even bizarre.

It seemed inappropriate to attempt explanations of the intricacies of chemical research to someone so vague about his knowledge and interests, so I decided to show our teaching facilities first, as possibly being more appealing to a probable non-scientist.

I took him to the large lecture theatre, where his response was polite rather than receptive: 'Very nice. How many are in your honours year?'

I answered that easily: 'Forty-two.'

Next, from an open door, we watched activities in a well-filled undergraduate laboratory, where white-coated and safety-bespectacled students were hard at work in the last practical class of the week.

'Safety issues have increased recently,' he maintained.

I agreed.

To my surprise, Dickey showed some interest in the Instrument Laboratory, though he still avoided any overt display of enthusiasm or admitting specific knowledge. I remained nonplussed and tried, but failed, to describe the work I hoped to do on the new DSC apparatus.

His response was evasive: 'That's very interesting, but technical.'

When I said I would use it to study pollution reduction, he asked, 'Can scientists stop global warming?'

I explained, 'Scientists may have theories that can explain changing climates, but it's really up to politicians to deal with the consequences. We may find ways to reduce pollution from burning coal and oil more efficiently, but... there are no simple answers.'

'If, as an environmentalist, you could choose a research project, what would it be?'

'When we burn coal, it gives us acid rain. Just now, I'm applying for money to fund research into how we might reduce the amounts of acid released from power stations.'

'So, scientists *can* solve climate change?'

'Far from it. I've an idea that, I hope, might reduce atmospheric pollution... a bit.' I could think of no good reason for this quiz. If he was interested in the much-debated-but-far-from-resolved questions of environmental pollution and protection, he, Dickey, could read both sides of the arguments in newspapers, books, etc. and reach his own conclusions without my help.

It seemed unprofitable to embark on such a complicated, open-ended topic here and just then, so I changed the subject: 'I think an important part of our job here is to make scientific knowledge available to undergraduates

– the rising generation we teach. Our hope is that these students absorb lots of information and can later produce intelligible answers to our testing examination questions. Those who qualify can then embark, well informed, on their chosen career; some remaining scientists and others will move into other careers. Briefly, that's one of our challenges here.

'Our other job is research, and, sometimes, we succeed in advancing science… a little. We publish our completed research articles in science journals, which are read mainly by other specialists like ourselves. Our conclusions are available to anyone interested, though this is not very effective in telling the wider public about our work… and why we do it. All this new knowledge is available for use by industry, by politicians or by anyone. But we can't ensure that even our best ideas are noticed. We can tell society what we think might be done to counteract the problems that we all create, such as pollution. Then politicians become involved… I really prefer not to discuss all this, just now. I'm sorry about the lecture; since coming here, I'm finding I'm pontificating. That's not good. I'd be pleased to discuss such challenging problems, but at some other time, please, with advance notice.'

'We *will* continue this conversation later,' Dickey said with emphasis.

No reply seemed to be expected and the visit appeared to have been completed naturally. We went out to find his car and to collect Beth before our convivial evening of 'dinner and conversation' at Dickey's home. Later, we would go home by taxi, so that everyone could enjoy the 'interesting wines' promised with the meal. It was a welcome prospect.

In the car park, I did not see the expected Morris Minor. Instead, I pointed out a vintage Rolls Royce and said, 'Seems some notable is visiting the provost.'

'No! *I'm* that notable! That's my other car. I'm not using the Morris today.'

Lost for a reply, I followed him to his immaculate, black vehicle, which – like the Morris – was maintained scrupulously.

'I've wanted one of these since I was a small boy. When I had a bit of luck recently, I realised that ambition,' Dickey explained.

'A bit of luck? You must have won the National Lottery [the Lottery]!' I cried.

209

◎

It was dark when, having met Beth, we reached Dickey's home in a village some distance outside Linkirk. The house stood on high ground, well above the road, and, rapidly, we ascended a steep, tarmac drive between flowerbeds and lawns before driving straight into a large garage and stopping beside the familiar Morris Minor. Walking to the front door, we saw a river — presumably Meggett Water, upstream from Linkirk — still in spate after the recent rains. Light from distant, yellow street lamps twinkled on the water cascading over the rocky riverbed.

Dickey certainly enjoyed the better things in life. His detached house, built of light-coloured stone, was not large, though it was certainly exclusive, elegant and expensive. The slopes of the south-facing garden were placed to catch all available sunshine and give vistas across the open countryside to the distant Scottish Borders uplands. That night, a cold wind discouraged lingering, and we were pleased to go into the warm home.

The feeling of comfort was complemented by the warm welcome of Emma, our hostess, who fussed us into the living room, where a log fire blazed. She was a plump, jolly woman with a ready and disarmingly relaxed smile. Her appearance was distinctly 'formerly fashionable', with a single plait of dark hair wound around the top of her head and her plain, dark-blue dress, which was unrelieved except by a silver brooch.

'Do, do come in. You're both most welcome. It's not often these days that we have the pleasure of younger guests. Do make yourselves comfortable,' Emma declared.

Beth was invited to sit beside her on an ample, luxurious sofa.

Emma continued, 'Dickey [we both noticed that Emma used this nickname] told me his version of the incident on the road, but I want to hear it from you, my dear.' She was addressing Beth, with the implication being that, woman-to-woman, Beth would reveal the truth, the whole truth and nothing but the truth.

I excused myself, to wash my hands literally, as I needed to remove the chalk remaining from my tutorial. I overheard Beth starting to relate the events of last Saturday in exquisite detail. When Dickey directed me upstairs to the bathroom, I passed a large bookcase, overfilled with what appeared to be 'academic' tomes. Completing my ablutions quickly, I tiptoed back along the landing to the books. Unaccustomed to clandestine sleuthing, I nonetheless felt justified in exploiting this opportunity to penetrate the inexplicable cloak of secrecy adopted my host. I was not altogether surprised to find the bookcase was filled mainly with chemistry texts. What disconcerted me most were the three copies of *Chemistry and Pollution* by B. B. Richards. I had used this authoritative reference work during my own research!

I suppressed, but only with great difficulty, the urge to rush downstairs brandishing a copy of Dickey's book, to ask its author what the blue blazes he thought he was playing at? I wondered what Mother's *Little Book of Polite Victorian Etiquette* would have advised, 'When a guest discovers that his host is being duplicitous, deceitful and downright double-dealing'. Nevertheless, there was satisfaction in confirming that my instincts had been correct, thoroughly vindicating my amateur detective work. So, accepting Dickey's behaviour had been distinctly eccentric, I decided that – apart from confusing me – no serious wrong had been done. More importantly, I must not upset the pleasant evening in prospect for all four of us. So, for the time being, I decided to continue playing his game, though what that game was and what rules applied remained unclear. Admittedly, my decision was influenced by the appetising aromas wafting upwards from below, reminding me that dinner time was nigh. Nevertheless, very soon, Dickey must either explain himself to me or our paths would part permanently; of that I was sure.

I closed the bathroom door firmly and rejoined the others. Beth and Emma were still exploring, in unnecessarily sanguine detail, the injuries that might result from the slamming of a car door onto the unprotected head of a silly man. Dickey dissociated himself from the grisly images emerging from his wife's imagination by offering me sherry. I almost felt sorry for him. However, all good things finish, and, eventually, the topic was played out, but only after Emma's inquest had liberally probed all Beth's observations; there was evidence of a friendship forming between these two.

Dinner was excellent. Dickey's promise of a good, home-cooked meal was generously fulfilled. He had 'invented' the marinade used for the pork, so the contents were not divulged. Again, was this his secretive nature or was I being paranoid? The fruity taste of the marinade was agreeably piquant, and reminiscent of port, with hints of plums and damsons. The vegetables had been braised in a ratatouille with red wine, which Dickey stated was 'to encourage flavour blending'. Dickey's chemical expertise extended into the kitchen. These exotics went exceptionally well with the creamy mashed potatoes.

'I can recommend this pinot grigio,' declared Dickey.

He had promised 'interesting' wines, and this one had an unusually provocative fruitiness and bouquet. On the few occasions when I had tried this wine, I had been disappointed to find it almost tasteless. However, this golden nectar was a welcome surprise, and I said so.

'It *is* rather special,' Dickey agreed. 'Last year, we visited vineyards in the Adige Valley, near Bolzano, Italy, to try their products. Now I regret taking only two cases of this and not more. It *is* good and it *has* travelled. I believe it complements the marinade.'

There was no argument there.

This mention of Italy led to a series of reminisces that dominated the conversation for a time. The Richards described, with undisguised nostalgia, spectacular roads through the Dolomite Mountains, which they encouraged us to explore. As confirmed *Italophiles*, they would have been happy to talk about nothing else all evening. Soon, I noticed that Beth had become excluded and was finding it increasingly difficult to maintain an appearance of interest. I changed the subject by asking Emma about her garden, which did interest Beth, and, thereafter, I was the silent one.

The dessert was Scottish apple pie of Emma's 'sweet-and-sour puddin'' recipe, including blackberries and loganberries, with home-made ice cream, using a recipe from the country that invented it, Italy yet again. The flavours went well with a sweet Moscato white wine, again bought directly in the vineyard. We both complemented the chef and cook, though it was unclear who had contributed which dishes in this excellent, carefully planned meal.

While finishing with English cheese and biscuits, Emma asked Beth about some technical feature of a dress she was making, in particular, problems with darts (about which I had no clue).

My flippant remark, 'The *points* of *darts* in a *dress* must cause injuries, sooner or later,' was ignored as being worthy only of an ignorant male.

The upshot was that Beth offered, 'I'll look at it, if you like. I don't know if I can help much, though.'

Later, I wondered if this withdrawal had been quite as spontaneous as it had seemed.

This gave me the prospect of clearing the air with Dickey, but I was reluctant to broach the subject of my host's unusual behaviour directly, particularly in his own home. Relaxed, in post-prandial state, I was 'At peace with all weemen and most men' (uncertain about how Dickey might react to my questions, I had inverted the genders in this phrase that my dad had occasionally used).

Happily, Dickey began, 'I must admit I've not been entirely open with you.'

'I know. I think I can guess what you're going to say.' Wine encouraged my candour.

'Go on, then!'

This unexpected response presented an inescapable challenge. 'OK. Like me, you're a scientist. Indeed, I know you're a chemist.'

Dickey nodded.

I continued, 'What I don't understand is why you were so reluctant to tell me. I should also say that, upstairs, I looked at your bookcase to confirm my hunch.'

There was a moment of silence, followed by laughter, which relieved any tension. 'Well done! You'd make a good detective. No, I've been unfair, even unreasonable.' He waved aside my interruption. 'If I try to explain, I hope you'll understand.'

'There's no need... I'm sure... you've your own good reasons...'

'First, I'd like to tell you about some problems. Afterwards, if you're willing, we might discuss together how I might be able to resolve them.' Another interruption was waved away. 'Please, hear me out, *then* you can be as direct as you like.'

'Maybe, but I'm not much good at offering advice. Indeed, I find *freely* offered advice is usually just that – free and indeed *valueless*. Self-appointed advisers usually don't understand exactly why a problem has caused the difficulty. Just now, organising my own life is more than enough for me. But I'm an attentive listener.'

'Then, if you listen, just trying to explain my situation to you might help me get some uncertainties sorted out in my own mind. We'll see.'

I nodded encouragement.

'Four years ago, I was diagnosed as having cancer. It was a devastating shock to both of us. Emma felt it and suffered quite as much as I did. We've no children and we've always been close. I was over fifty, and it seemed that the life that we'd enjoyed together was effectively over. I won't bore you with details, but I had a big operation – I remember the date well, March 31st – followed by treatments. The outcome remained doubtful for a time. I thought there was no chance I'd ever work again normally and so I gladly accepted early retirement as a reader in geochemistry at the University of Leeds-Bradford. That was easy; just then, they were encouraging redundancies. Anyway, I was totally preoccupied with my personal difficulties in returning to some kind of acceptable life. Literally, getting through one day at a time was all that mattered to me – us, I should say; Emma's strength pulled me through.'

'I'd never have guessed you'd had cancer.'

'No. Healthwise, I've done particularly well... and been exceptionally lucky. Medical science sometimes manages miracles. I'm a prime example. They treated me in time... I am, by any standard, cured, and I like to tell people about that medical success. But that's only the background to what I want to discuss. We lived in Ilkley, which is a nice enough town and convenient to work. But, after retirement, there was no reason to stay in Yorkshire. We'd moved about during my academic career and my attempts to find promotion. I never achieved the title 'professor', though it wasn't for want of trying. It was a generally successful career, with the best of it in Bristol. The move to the University of Leeds-Bradford was a mistake, but that's another story. Without family, we were free to return home. I was born in Peebles, and have cousins in Edinburgh. Emma has a few relations nearby, across the Scottish Borders. We'd kept a link here by buying a cottage near Moffat; it's called The Bothy. Anyway, after I'd recovered fully, we found the house we're in, bought it and retired here.'

'The Bothy – what's that?'

'It means something like *small dwelling*. A shack where the servants lived, often in mean circumstances. Ours is not quite that primitive; it's small but comfortable.'

'Whereabouts is it?'

'Beside the A708 road. Half-way to Moffat from the Grey Mare's Tail Waterfall.'

'So Beth and I probably saw it last weekend.'

'No, you can't see it from the road. We never cut down our beautiful trees, so it's completely hidden, unless you know exactly where the gate is.'

'A secret cottage... bothy. A hideaway and a refuge from the world.' This random comment was made lightly at the time, but I was to remember it later.

'I'd never thought of it like that. But, yes! We used it as a sort of refuge. Now, we don't need it any more. I'll sell, if ever I get round to it.'

'So... you're settled here. Chemistry is history. You're happily retired?'

'No. No. That was the *original* plan.' Dickey looked wistful. 'But now I'm bored stiff. I don't want to spend *all* my time tinkering with vintage cars, driving about the countryside and causing people trouble, people like you... I'd much prefer to return to proper work... and do some real science... again. You've *no* idea how much stronger that feeling became today and no idea of how nostalgic I found that visit. Thanks to you!'

'I'm sure Angus would talk to you. I think—'

'Thank you, but that's not quite all the story. You said earlier that perhaps I'd won the Lottery. *You were right.*'

'What? Really? I don't believe it.'

'It's true. I assure you that I'm a major Lottery winner and so I'm a rich man. The whole affair was completely out of character because I disapprove of gambling as a fool's game. The odds are ridiculous, and the chance of winning hopeless. But so, possibly, were my chances of surviving cancer. I had a weak moment, which was totally out of order. I went for my first walk out alone after the operation, to our local shop for a paper. It was a dark, black day; I was particularly low in spirits, and instead of a paper I bought a hundred Lottery tickets. I still can't explain it.' He paused. 'I filled in numbers in no particular order and went home. I didn't even tell Emma. That wasn't intentional, but I was so depressed that I went straight to bed, and my gambling spree had not even registered in my mind. Later, feeling better, to my amazement I found the tickets in my jacket pocket. They'd been broadcasting to ask a major winner in Yorkshire to come forward. After the shock of finding those tickets, I checked the numbers. It was the forty-seventh that won. In a sense, I've won two lotteries: health and wealth. Now I'm enjoying both.'

'Will you travel the world? Where'll you go?'

'We just couldn't resist spending some of the winnings. First, I bought the cars; the Rolls, a prize in itself, is a continual delight, and also the Morris Minor. Later, when I was strong enough, with medical advice, we visited Australia and South Africa. Travelling to distant places helped my recovery. But, *no*, we don't want to spend our lives looking for new places to visit. This is now home.'

'And you want to start work again? In a university?' I was almost lost for a response.

'It's what I chose to do all my working life. Recently, we've travelled, I've bought the cars of my dreams… what more could I want?'

I had no answer.

He continued, 'Because my illness could so easily have been fatal, I thought long and hard about what I could and should do with my abundant leisure time and the wealth I'm now free to enjoy. People I met in hospital, who were suffering from the same disease, died. I was fortunate to survive, and I'm now enjoying surprisingly good health. So, once cured, I thought deeply about priorities. I'm not conventionally religious, but scientists often base their decisions on the evidence available. Emma and I are financially secure; we enjoy our privileged situation by living every day to the full. After our minor spending spree, our next priority was to make a worthwhile contribution to some worthy "good causes" with some of our surplus cash… and "do some good" (horrible phrases). After much heart-searching, our joint decision was to help protect the environment. Also, I'd like to show that I, personally, can still contribute to research. So, how do I go about it?'

I was fascinated by Dickey's attitude; his opinions were both refreshing and laudable. He topped up my whisky, but I was more interested in his story than his alcohol.

He continued, 'I find it interesting that, even with all our cash, my wish is to continue doing the same things as I was paid to do all my working life. I don't know whether it's an ingrained habit or simply a total lack of imagination. Perhaps I've always been a *round* peg in a *round* hole. Perhaps I'd found my ideal career… We'll join you in a moment, dear.' This was to Emma, who had appeared briefly at the door, then he went on talking to me. 'I'm talking too much, but hear this last bit. As I'm now retired and without dependants, we want our Lottery win to work positively. You could describe it as "selfish philanthropy"; I suspect there's more of it about than is realised. Environmental protection remains a low priority for most businesses, despite assertions and spurious claims to the contrary in public-relations blurbs written professionally by so-called consultants. But, off I go again, on my hobby horse.'

'Why are you telling me all this?'

'You're a sympathetic ear. Frankly, my first need is to sort out my ideas in my own mind. Just trying to explain these problems to you now has helped me quite a bit.'

'So, what do you hope to do next?'

'First, apologise for not telling you why I wanted to visit LU School of Chemistry today. I've no adequate excuse, except that I've been undecided about approaching your prof. I wanted to see LU first, and did that this afternoon, thanks to you. That made up my mind. It's all I could hope for. Now, I've positively decided that I want to return to academia. At last, *I know* what *I want* to do. If you knew how nostalgic I felt… there… today… you'd understand. Thanks again. With my experience, and needing no salary, I hope LU might find a laboratory corner for my research. I could even support a student or two to work with me. Any ideas how and where I could start?'

'I've no doubt whatsoever that our Provost would welcome you with open arms. The university's motto is *"Plastica Omnia Vincit"*: "Plastic Vanquishes All Problems". It is an ancient academic adage… which I've just dreamed up.'

'We'd better leave it there for now. I hope we'll talk again soon, though I've done most of the talking. It's too late to go on now, but don't mention what I've said to *anyone* else… *please*. The exception is Bet… Beth, that is; ask her to keep it to herself, at least, for now. Let's join the ladies.'

Once back in front of the fire, I was content to listen to my hosts, feeling neither desire nor ability to contribute much. Having eaten well, together with receiving a surfeit of food for thought, it was easy to relax in this delightfully comfortable room. Later, Beth said that I had been unusually quiet. Dickey had outlined a technical problem with his car, but, without understanding it, nobody could suggest a solution. Emma explained a dressmaking idea to Beth, which, again, was beyond my competence. This led onto her ideas for redecorating the room we were in, which differed from what Dickey favoured. Both tried to enlist our support, but we chose to remain uninvolved.

Then it was time to order the taxi, which soon arrived. When leaving, we expressed our sincere thanks to our hosts.

Emma warmly invited us to, 'Call here to see us if you're nearby. No invitation is needed.'

Dickey added, 'In other words, *if you're passing by – don't!*' He also said positively, to me, 'We must continue our conversation *very soon*.'

Once in the taxi, I put my arm around Beth's waist, but was put off by the driver's sudden interest in his mirror.

Beth, unrelaxed, wanted to talk seriously. 'Well, what was all that about?'

'All what?' I queried.

'We were invited, *allegedly*, to thank us for helping Dickey with his car. Well, they did, and that was nice. Then, after we'd eaten, I was whisked away to talk dressmaking, while you went into a conclave with Dickey. I thought it strange. I got the impression that they'd planned to separate us, and I can't think why.'

'I felt much the same. Dickey told me his life story before outlining some future ambitions. I've no idea why he felt able to confide in me. We met only a few days ago, but he asked for both advice and help. And I've more than enough problems organising myself! Despite that, he never got round to explaining what he wants particularly. That's to come later. I wonder what he expects? He said I could tell you.'

'That's generous of him.' She paused. 'Well? Tell me what?'

'It's all far too long and complicated to start on now, always assuming I can remember the half of what he said.'

'If it's like that, I'm not sure I want to know.'

'Don't spoil a nice evening. Can we meet tomorrow and talk when my mind is clearer? Please? If it's any consolation, I'm genuinely as puzzled as you are. I really don't know what I can say, this late. Look, we're almost home. Let's get out here and walk the last bit. The fresh air'll do us both good.'

It was the rain, by then heavy, that revived me, rather than the fresh air. We did not linger. Her kiss was brief, but I looked forward to restoring normal relations tomorrow.

I agreed to try to explain what she called, 'Whatever it was that you men were discussing.'

That honest intention presupposed I was capable of clarifying whatever it was that Dickey was trying to tell me, to ask me or what? These conundrums were bothering me, and I made little progress in penetrating his motives and expectations as I walked home. Beth's unexpected interest puzzled me, but I hoped her help would enable me to disentangle some of the contents of Dickey's peroration.

Chapter 15

FOURTH SATURDAY IN NOVEMBER

| TENDER | a. Bid for contract to undertake specified work |
| | b. Soft, sensitive, affectionate feelings or relationship |

DESPITE DOUG'S DISAPPROVAL, I PREFERRED MY PORRIDGE cooked the way my father described as 'traditional brose', without saying whose tradition it was. The milk had to boil *before* adding the oats, which was a risky proceeding that all too often led to a session of stove cleaning. Milk's ability to boil over without warning, covering the cooker with a sticky mess, was a scientific mystery that I never understood. Possibly, here was a research idea for a grant application to The Scottish Brose Board? The current academic imperative of viewing all phenomena – natural or unnatural – as an opportunity to seek research funding was, by then, apparently subverting my thinking more than was reasonable or healthy.

This led me to reflect critically on the widely accepted view that research achievement can be measured by successes in the scramble for research cash. I was far from convinced by this truism. Such received wisdom is all-too-easily accepted unquestioned, and I was resisting the temptation to accept fashionable opinions without appraisal. Academic freedom should not be about the flaunting of grants won before colleagues, just as 'good' primary school pupils collect 'stars', awarded by teachers to encourage best behaviour. Education should be about learning to appreciate each situation on its merits, rather than just accepting and memorising endless facts. This explained why Doug and I differed so radically in our relationships with LU. Whereas I still had the obligation to populate my personal firmament with 'silver sparkles' (the academic analogue of stars from miss or sir), he had abandoned all pretence of 'star collecting'. With tenure, his job was secure until retirement, barring serious misdemeanour. Gently coasting through his remaining years, he was sustained by his view that comfort is more congenial than continual competition. In contrast, being a lowly probationer meant I had still to earn a secured future. Up to then, I had won no stars and, to gain promotion, must continue to feed 'star-standard' applications into the research-funding lottery.

Happily, that day I was sufficiently awake to catch the boiling milk in time, but was committing the unpardonable sin of adding *sugar* to porridge when Doug appeared.

'Salt! Salt! Words fail me,' he declared. This sounded intrinsically improbable. 'Where's the tot of whisky? We'll never make an honorary Scotsman of you.'

'Whisky is only fermented *sugar* with unknown extracts from old sherry barrels,' I retorted.

'Don't presume to hide your heathen practices under scientific irrelevancies.' He grinned. 'Morning Bill! Did you sleep well or did you fall out the wrong side of bed?'

'Morning Doug. Why are you so chirpy at this time of day?'

There was no reply.

Soon, the frying pan was sizzling the bacon, and the beguiling aroma rapidly eroded my 'healthy' decision to forego a cooked breakfast. Doug's culinary skills included the ability to produce a comprehensive fry, including black pudding. He somehow prevented the disintegration of these slices of black sausage, which remained inexplicably coherent and crispy. My poor attempts produced what he all too accurately described as 'Fried porridge!' I accepted, without admitting, this suitably described the texture, if not the taste.

Rapidly, he produced two plates, each with excessive amounts of fat, protein, calories, cholesterol and goodness knows what else besides. Disregarding the (over)statements of the 'Healthy Brigade' (Doug's label), we lads (with healthy appetites) preferred to describe our meal as tasty, nourishing, etc. fare; it all depended on viewpoint.

'There! Properly break your fast! Set you up for the day,' offered Doug.

Conversation lapsed while we did justice to our ample repast.

Later, sipping tea, Doug posed the question I was avoiding. 'Do you have any Christmas plans? It's your first break and time to recover from your busy term. Relax and enjoy yourself!'

'I've not made any plans yet. I feel obliged to go back home. If I don't, Mother'll be alone… and I'll feel badly about it. Frankly, I've not thought what's the best thing to do.'

'Beth prefers you stay here. That's the problem?'

'Nothing's been said yet. I don't know. I've been putting off discussing it.'

'But, you can enjoy the best of both cultures. Spend Christmas in England where, I believe, it's the traditional feast. Then return to Scotland for the more important celebration of Hogmanay. That way, you'll get the best of both worlds.'

'I'll think about it. What about your own plans?'

'Don't ask. What I'd like to do, I can't. I'd like to spend Christmas with my kids, so we'd be a family together, at least for that one day. Alternatively, I could have them here, if that's OK with you. But, and it's a big 'but', Gwen says she's taking Owen and Lucy to her parents in rural Wales. [He sighed.] So, possibly, I'll just stay here or perhaps go to my ageing parents, as I should. They've plenty of room, but are talking about selling their long-term home. The house is too big, too old and needs work done on it urgently. I really should spend the break with them and even help them plan their future. I'm no good at house decorating, but it'd be one way to paper over the cracks in my own life and pass the time, appearing to be normal.'

His distinctly pessimistic mood communicated itself to me. 'Christmas is supposed to be a time of *joy to all men*, but there must be loads of people who find it otherwise. I've been lucky; I've always enjoyed the break by fitting in with Mother's plans. This is the first year ever that I have even thought about what I might prefer. I'm not particularly keen to go back to Sussex. I don't know what Beth plans, but I'd prefer not to intrude on any of her family's arrangements. I've no real idea of what I'd like, other than to go cruising away from this cold and wet weather; realistically, and financially, that's out.'

We sat in silence, both contemplating our own uncertainties about the vacation and both confronting recently changed circumstances.

'Doug, do you mind if I run something past you?' I enquired.

'Only if it's nothing too athletic. And don't expect any effort from me. At least, not until my digestive system has changed down a gear or two,' he responded.

'I think you're mixing your metaphors or something.'

'Bill, you've a touching faith in my wisdom. I can't think why. My personal life is incomprehensible, even to me. I've never got far up the *academic greasy pole* because it's too easy to slip back down. They say experience is what is gained after opportunity is lost. But I'm flattered by your enduring faith in my ability to advise.'

'Talking to you helps me clarify things in my own mind. Putting into words—'

'Don't spoil it. And me thinking you're the one person who *listens* to my words of wisdom. If you see me as a dumb listening device, I really will be tempted to withhold my priceless counsel. My donnish insights have been hard won by always knowing better and faring worse than those set in "proffo-authority" over me. Perhaps my real crimes have been to highlight, too often and too obviously, glaring gaps in their own unchallengeable wisdom.'

'I sincerely do need your guidance. I'm sure you'll help me spot the most obvious pitfalls, waiting there to trap this over-optimistic beginner.'

'Well, with luck, I might just find you an alternative scenario. But I must preface all opinions that I'm unwise enough to pass on with *Doc. Doug's health warning*: "It's not usually the backseat driver who is charged with causing the accident."'

'I've never heard that saying before.'

'It's an old Scottish proverb I've just made up... So? Your problem?'

'You know I've been wondering whether we might set up a group to coordinate some of our research? If we formed a School Environmental Centre, the efforts of everyone applying for grants, finding equipment and students, etc. might be shared.'

'Yes, yes. [Doug sounded impatient.] We've already talked about this. Universities must be cost-effective, whatever that means; socially relevant, ditto; address economic goals; etc. Our masters and betters have long been bawling from that hymn sheet, though it can be difficult to know who'd benefit, except perhaps the bullshitters themselves. It'd make better sense if we put our energies into educating students *properly* in hard science rather than inventing "soft" and fashionable mishmashes of joint degrees consisting of the most easily digestible bits of this and that. Degrees that teach burger all, being designed to taste good while ignoring nutritional basics. Full of fat and hot air.' Doug burped loudly in illustration before continuing, 'Getting academics to cooperate sounds a bit optimistic... but you've talked to Angus?'

'I put it to him that we might form an environmental group...'

'*Green Chemistry* by Bill Green.'

'That's *not* my idea. I thought, as chairman, he might take the lead.'

'Oh, yes, he'll do that, all right, but I doubt he'll put much effort into starting it. Let me predict what you're going to tell me. OK?'

I nodded.

'He'd prefer not take the initiative away from a member of his staff. You thought up the idea, so it'd be best you did all the initial planning... deciding how to proceed, etc. He'd prefer not to interfere at this critical juncture so that *all the credit for success* would go to Bill. He'd help, but only from behind the scenes. Am I roughly correct?'

'Well... er... I suppose so, yes!'

'You've already noticed the two types of pitfall: the painful horns of your dilemma?' I must have shown surprise, but Doug simply raised his eyebrows and went on, 'If things go wrong, the egg will end up staining Bill's tie. Angus will say that he always doubted the wisdom of the idea, but, in these democratic days, enterprise from junior staff must be encouraged. It's a pity Green's planning did not work out as he hoped, for this or that reason. Alternatively, and here your expectations must be realistic, if things go well, our Boss-Profs will take their slice of glory to repay their indispensable roles in the obvious successes of your enterprise. Cynical? Maybe, but the world is never flat; some people always occupy the sunny and fertile ground, while others wrest a less comfortable existence in the less hospitable regions.'

'I was hoping that Angus would introduce the idea of an environmental-research group at a staff meeting and later chair a discussion to sound out interest. If the responses were positive, we might form a centre of excellence.'

'To get anywhere, *you* must be positive and *you* must convince people that this idea will work to *their* advantage. You mustn't be overconfident, mind, but you must demonstrate *your* belief in *your* idea. Also, sound out possible support, in advance. Don't be too optimistic too early, but I think you've a good idea that's maybe even capable of raising our research profile, eventually. But, why restrict it to chemistry?'

'Thank you, Doug, that is helpful. It could indeed be wider, but, would other profs agree to collaborations? Are there real contacts between the sciences? Chemistry seems to be self-sufficient. How can I reach everyone who might be interested?'

'Try writing a letter to all science directors and ask Angus to sign it?'

'Do you think he would?' I did not get the reassurance I sought.

'No idea! But what you don't ask for, you don't get.' Doug looked at the greasy plates (it was my turn for the washing-up chore) and – adopting a serious, reassuring tone – genuinely offered help: 'Perhaps, after all, I'll give you some advice. If you do decide to try to form this centre, it must be your positive decision. Make every effort to succeed, but always remember it's you who's taking the gamble. Accept the possibility and consequences of failure. Also, besides being a scientist, you must be a bit of a politician, knowing – but not showing – that your proposal may be less than welcome, if only because you've not been here long. Always keep yourself room for a tactical withdrawal, which is modern-speak for retreat.' Doug looked at his watch. 'On that discordant note, I wish you well. Now, I have the pleasure of being with my children today, and I don't want to miss a single moment of their young lives. See you!'

'Cheerio, Doug.'

But, he was gone.

After my chores, I wrote (composed, orchestrated and scored) the letter that *might* enthuse my colleagues sufficiently to attend a meeting to discuss forming a cooperative environmental-science initiative in LU. This description, devised while walking to work, seemed – when typed – far less than compelling. 'Cooperative' might bring to mind grocery shops or echo the names of organisations in former communist regimes of Eastern Europe. It was time to delete and start again.

'Centre Of Research Excellence' seemed distinctly more promising, the acronym (CORE) could be symbolised by or given a logo of an apple, representing health (based on 'an apple a day…') and green in colour, with its environmental associations. But doubts remained; the *core* is the part of the fruit that is discarded. Alternatively, the *core* contains the seeds, the plant germ, representing regeneration. It was a presentation problem to resolve later!

With the working title 'CORE', I drafted, wrote, rewrote and edited several versions of a letter publicising the inaugural meeting of CORE. Towards lunchtime, I had two versions: one too short and the other too long. My vacillation was resolved by asking Angus to sign the shorter version for circulation (happily, he agreed) and by stating that further details were available (the longer version) for everyone interested.

I rewarded myself by wasting time on that computer game, which appeared almost without conscious intent. Three cycles ran well, which I took as a good omen for the ultimate success of my morning's work. I switched it off just as the phone rang.

'Oh, so that's where you are.' It was Beth: a welcome burst of sunshine brightening the day. She expected to be busy today, but said we'd get together soon.

'Yes, you've found me out.' My inspiration had been exhausted by my literary efforts.

'You don't seem over-welcoming.'

'Not intentionally. I've just finished some difficult writing and…I didn't expect your call. How can I give the welcome you deserve and I want to give?'

'Come and visit me! We haven't seen each other all week!'

'Where are you... but... aren't you driving your parents...?'

'Dad decided to drive to these friends himself. Just now, I'm at home finishing some schoolwork. If you're free, I wondered if I could persuade you to visit a lonely—'

'Try to stop me! Is that sufficiently enthusiastic? When and where?'

'That'll do, for now. What about here, early afternoon?'

We agreed and disconnected, following suitable expressions of endearment.

○

I walked to the Wilkinson homestead via Main Street, to buy some flowers: red and white carnations. These seasonal decorations, heralding the festive season, were much evidence, but I resolutely ignored what I saw as their premature message. Nevertheless, I was reminded of my too-long-deferred obligation to reply to Mother's latest letter about our Christmas plans. The air was cool and the light fading, so I hurried on, my spirits rising when I approached the black-and-white house.

I rang the bell, which was answered with gratifying promptness.

My quick peck at Beth's cheek brought an unexpectedly sharp protest: 'Is that the best you can do? Don't I get a proper kiss from... lover boy... that was?'

'But your mother and father...?' I asked.

'Out. Out...'

In the ensuing melee, the flowers suffered, together with two pairs of lips, to repair the alleged shortcomings of my initial greeting. I hugged her in a close, warm embrace, happily responding to her enthusiasm. On parting, both of us a little overwhelmed, I heard her murmur, 'That's a wee bit better'.

'If that's the result of a few days apart... well, wheeeee. [I paused.] So, you're pleased to see me?' My reply seemed inadequate.

'I don't answer silly questions.'

By that time, we had reached the living-room sofa, and the kiss that followed was a more-than-adequate response. After its leisurely completion, a question had to be faced.

'Well? What'll we do this afternoon?' I questioned.

Just watching the emotions flitting across her face gave me real pleasure, which I indulged for a few moments, but Beth read more into my gaze than was intended.

She responded with humour: 'Sorry to disappoint you, but I've no idea when Mumsy and Dad'll be back.'

I had to concede this was a dampener, excluding certain activities and, more hopeful than expectant, I mumbled something about going to my place.

To my considerable surprise, the implied-but-unspecified activity was not vetoed – with shock – as unthinkable, but Beth, countering my optimism with realism, asked what I knew about Doug's plans. Unfortunately, I knew too little to be certain of the privacy we might welcome. He almost always watched sport on Saturday afternoons, but, that day, would it be at the field or on the TV at home? I could accept that 'abstinence makes the heart grow fonder', but, just then, 'jam tomorrow' was not being ruled out; indeed, it seemed to be ruled in. That was ggrreeaatt!

'Perhaps we could ask Dickey for a key to The Bothy?' I suggested.

'I think not.' Beth changed the subject. 'Seriously, has he contacted you again? After what you told me about his fortune and future plans, I expected him to...'

'So did I. No, I've not heard from him yet; not a word, not a dicky bird.'

'That's cockney rhyming slang, if I'm not mistaken.'

'Yes. I told you all of his story that I could remember. I expected him to contact me before now, but there's been not a word. Odd bird! I really don't know what to think.'

'Well, think about a cup of tea. While I make it, you decide what we'll do. Here's the paper; see if you can find something, somewhere we could go.'

When she returned with the tea, she asked, 'Well? What are we going to do?'

'I've found nothing. What about going out for meal?'

'Why don't we stay in and eat here?'

I said it made me feel I'd invited myself.

Beth demurred, but compromised: 'If you buy whatever you fancy, we'll make dinner together, here.'

After agreeing, I had to raise my problem. 'Beth, may we discuss the holidays? Christmas and so on...'

'Yes? I expected you to say something. You'll be going south.'

'How did you know that?' I was taken aback by her certainty.

'There you are. I'm right!' Her air of rectitude was indefinably disturbing.

'Would you come to Sussex... just for a few days?'

This time, although anticipating the answer, it was still unwelcome. 'Bill, you have to support your mother. She must resent your absence and will be alone if you don't go. I'm certain she'd prefer to have you, and you alone, without anyone else intruding.'

'You'd never intrude...'

'For this year, at least, I think we should keep to our family traditions. We haven't known each other long, and the short separation might even be good for us. I'll miss you, that I promise, but let's not rush things. I *will* look forward to you coming back, but I'm quite sure this is the best way. Believe me, I've thought about it a lot, and there's no real alternative. Trust my feminine intuition!'

I opened my mouth to reply, but was prevented by her fingers pressed on my lips. The matter was closed. The decision was not my choice, but I could just manage to accept it as reasonable. The disturbing, though inevitable, reality was that both Beth and Mother had found their relationship difficult, each conscious of their quite different situations and hopes for the future. I recalled, with unease, their slightly defensive attitudes on meeting. The absence of an invitation accounted for Beth's apprehension about her welcome there and explained her feminine intuition. I had discounted the possible alternative already, being certain that Mother would not come north. I now accepted the reality that my Christmas plans were now fixed, without any input from me. While the decision was not my choice, I had to accept the new consequences of having two ladies in my life. Next year, things would be different. (They would be, but not as I hoped for or could possibly have foreseen.)

Just then, with my difficulties so unexpectedly resolved, I tried to lighten the mood: 'I'm already looking forward to New Year. Let's enjoy our time together now.'

We left the house and, arm-in-arm, we walked to High Street, where the harbingers to the festive season of Christmas seemed less obtrusive, possibly because I could now accept its immanence. We purchased a haggis from a loquacious butcher, who offered Beth much advice (for free, as he pointed out). This was a culinary first for me with the advice (again, for free) that haggis should be enjoyed with tatties and neeps (potatoes and turnips), which he also happened to sell (not for free). This would introduce me to Scottish traditions before the feast of St Andrew next week, though this menu is more usually associated with Burns Night, which was two months away. Mince pies would be our sweet. Literally, in the same spirit, I bought a small bottle of Scotch.

Beth cooked the haggis, though it seemed fairly easy. Her businesslike approach to cooking discouraged thoughts of amorous activities, though I revelled in the shared domesticity. I prepared both potatoes and turnips, under expert direction and with care, heeding Dad's warning about sharp knives. These tasks were interrupted by a whisky tasting, to ensure the acceptability of our purchase, not that I was a competent judge. Beth tasted a massively diluted tot with a grimace of disgust and changed to red wine. After a slightly larger tot, I followed her example.

With uncanny timing, the phone rang just as the meal was being placed on the table, Beth pulled a grimace of irritation before responding to its imperious summons. Being of that select minority who can ignore a ringing phone, I shook my head, but was not noticed. Instead, I viewed our novel culinary choice, looking forward to this new-to-me evening meal despite my ample breakfast. Haggis appeared to be yet another variant on porridge, or black pudding cooked by an unskilled hand such as mine.

'That was Dad.' Beth returned, bearing the now slightly woebegone carnations. 'Thank you for the thought.'

I got another kiss; this time, a sisterly one on the cheek.

My first impression of the meal was that haggis is an acquired taste, but, already being acclimatised to porridge, I decided that I did not dislike it and agreed that it had been worth trying.

'That was Dad!' was repeated.

I nodded, assuming the call could hold no interest whatsoever for me, though I was wrong.

She explained, 'He and Mumsy are visiting the Simpsons, who live near Ayr. He said they'll stay there overnight. A controversial minister is preaching in their church there tomorrow, and they want to hear him. I also know that Rob Simpson is a connoisseur of malt whiskies, and I think Dad may have had one or two already. I'm glad he's not driving back tonight.'

It seemed politic not to respond to this news, because the thoughts that sprang into my mind certainly could be regarded as excessively opportunistic. My initial tact might yield a later dividend. My indistinct, 'Good,' was intentionally non-committal. 'I'd like a little more haggis, please. I'll try it with whisky to see how they blend. Sometime, maybe, your father might tutor me about whisky appreciation.'

So the meal progressed. Beth talked about the Simpsons, who were former neighbours and had been friends for decades. Rob had been one of Dad's colleagues in the bank. It was all most conventional; my input was minimal. We then completed the domestic chores. The dishwasher did the real work while we returned to the lounge.

Beth's, 'Want to watch TV?' was answered by my, 'No, thanks'! We sat companionably on the settee, with Beth finishing the wine while I sipped whisky, though it did not appeal to my 'foreign' tastes.

Beth's hand found its way under my elbow, and she snuggled closer, with our arms touching and her head resting on my shoulder. 'Happy?' she asked.

I agreed readily. Turning my head towards her, I found her lips close and soon we were in a tight embrace. When we sat up, to resume breathing, I found my shirt was being opened and a warm hand was massaging my chest.

'Perhaps we should continue this upstairs,' suggested Beth.

I could not disagree.

'There's just one condition. We don't keep the lights on.'

I must have shown surprise.

She explained, 'There is an old dear (a totally inappropriate courtesy title) who lives nearby and is remarkably nosy. If she suspected activity *upstairs, after dark* she might feel duty-bound to tell Mumsy.'

'But how'd she know?'

'She walks her dog. It's a repulsive, little beast of horribly tangled pedigree, but with sharp teeth, says Gordon, our postman. How anyone could keep such a miserable specimen, I don't know. Maybe it's only an excuse to nosy around; she's our local bloodhound, scenting scandals everywhere.'

It was an interesting appraisal, reminding me of Beth's forthright condemnation of Dickey on that windswept moor. Perhaps I should remember that her normally pleasant and placid personality nevertheless included the ability to express displeasure with memorable directness. However, thus far, our relationship had avoided serious cross words, and, just then, I was in no mood to reflect upon the relative worsenesses of barks and bites. While, later, I might have to think again, such thoughts were easily deferred by anticipating, with rising pleasure, the prospect of the immanent bonding of our relationship.

Our duet was a symphony of unheard sounds and cerebral sensations shared sensitively, while time flowed with a temporary tardiness and our feelings focussed on the fervour of being together in harmonious, ecstatic unity. For us *the earth did move*: smoothly, along its appointed path, tuning in with the mythical perfections of the music of the spheres, with the melodies permeating our persons and felt rather than heard. All sensory inputs were focussed inwards entirely, with each responsive to the other and giving pleasure while all inputs from beyond our immediate close embrace were blocked. How long we passed in our mutual introspection, neither knew nor cared, but – sometime later, with all passion spent – we returned slowly, satiated, to the mundane world. Shyly, each of us sought reassurances that our shared experiences were wholly pleasurable. Somehow this was communicated, and we relaxed together satisfied, and even dozed briefly, before I had to rouse myself for the effort of going home. I prized the close companionship between us and was humbled by the good fortune that had brought us together with every expectation that we would enjoy a prolonged, joint happy future. No clouds could be discerned on the horizon (as yet).

This high point in my life lives on as a treasured memory. I can recall every detail clearly. Emotions, hitherto dormant and unfelt, had been roused. I welcomed the prospect of a lifetime with Beth; even her name was music to me.

Later, after parting with tender farewells, I passed a woman ('The Old Dear'?) with an unattractive dog on a lead. Beth's description of the hound as 'a repulsive, little beast' seemed barely adequate. While both the old dear and the dog, each engaged in their own businesses, stared at me, I pointed to a council notice explicitly forbidding footpath fouling. The lack of a reply to my cheery, 'Goodnight,' did not surprise me.

Yes, altogether, it had been a good day. There was a spring in my step as, contemplating both the present and the future with huge optimism, I strode off home.

○

Classical music is the art form that I have found most capable of arousing my deepest emotions. When listening to a favourite piece, I have experienced transcendental emotions more powerful in form and intensity than can be excited by almost any other pleasurable stimulus. Following Beth's recent 'tutorials', I came to appreciate a novel overlap of feelings at my most sensitive and personal level: music generating unsuspected resonances somewhere within me. This was brought home, with pleasurable surprise, some days later on hearing Beethoven's Sixth Symphony, the *Pastoral Symphony*. My mind had become unusually relaxed and receptive, when I noticed that the glorious sounds reverberating within the private 'concert room' inside my head inspired a spontaneous and sparkling replay of a recent evening's shared joys. Since then, whenever I listen to that masterpiece, vivid images – not especially sensual – recall our evening of love. For me, this symphonic narrative traces the sequence of emotions I experienced, with the harmonic sounds recalling perceptively the most tender and deepest feelings throughout. In my private lexicon, this is now 'Beethoven's Sexth Symphony': my favourite musical work. My academic imagination helps me to trace, in the succession of mental images conjured up by its melodic stream, a somewhat different story and sequence of experiences from those associated with this work conventionally, which is said to portray 'a visit to the country'.

This musical wonderwork is Beethoven's homage to nature; although the country visited is not identified, the scenes depicted portray pastoral generality in a rural context. My preferred movement titles modify those generally accepted to alternative situations – 'Awakening of pleasurable sensations in wonderland' and 'Whispering of sweet sentiments' – instead of the 'babbling stream', when the composer was 'Beside the brook'. I associate the subsequent vigorous activities with a much more private and personal performance than the 'Joyful celebrations of country folk', but, likewise, they are completed in a climactic storm. Finally, satisfaction and satiation, with the return to normality, are wonderfully portrayed as an outpouring of 'Feelings of happiness and appreciation'. Is it the music, the memories or their associations that still stir my emotions? Perhaps all three, but, even for a scientist, beauty and pleasure do not need psychoanalysis or explanation to be enjoyed to the full.

Chapter 16

SECOND TUESDAY IN DECEMBER

PRESENT	a. Communicate information
	b. A gift
	c. The time now

SNUG IN MY HEAVIER-BUT-OLDER OVERCOAT, I WALKED TO WORK briskly up the LU campus hill. Winter had arrived; a cold wind was now blowing from higher ground, dusted white with snow. Slightly late, I hurried to be able to reread my notes before my 9.00am honours lecture on statistical mechanics (3.43, in LU jargon). This topic had baffled me at college, and I hoped that, by teaching it, I would at last fill some unfortunate gaps in my knowledge. That day's lecture concerned *entropy*, which is all about disorder, but, perversely, the topic had to be particularly well ordered to help students understand it. Yesterday had been devoted to preparing summaries for projection on screen and as notes for distribution. Consequently, every student *should* leave with a concise account of this intractable topic. All too aware of my lack of self-confidence in teaching this, I hoped my audience would be reluctant to ask questions exposing gaps in their (and *my*) knowledge. The value of reading around the subject would be stressed, but I must be prepared for questions in later tutorials.

It turned out that my forebodings had been unduly pessimistic and my preparation efforts well invested. I was surprised to find that the subject, which I had hitherto regarded as difficult, had now become comprehensible, even interesting.

I recalled a lecture given by an eminent professor who was visiting Weald University, which started, 'I've never understood this particular topic, so I'm presenting this lecture to *make* myself learn it properly. There's no better way of learning than to teach.' He then gave an excellent talk, and by then I fully understood his reasoning.

But there were other factors. Attendance was particularly low, as some students had presumably taken pre-Christmas jobs and others had simply extended their vacation. Term would end soon, and some individuals could be suffering from 'lecture saturation'. My audience was restive, indicating low levels of concentration. Anything challenging, presented just before a vacation, could be shelved for later study or even indefinitely. (Perhaps this accounted for my own difficulties with this topic.)

Relieved, even slightly smug, after delivering my lecture without embarrassment or worse, I returned to my office, accompanied by four tutorial students. They had requested the change from their usual Friday appointment so they could get home before the rush. While not convinced by this reasoning, I was, nevertheless, pleased that four out of six valued my tutoring skills sufficiently to attend. I expected questions about the lecture, but found the vacation essay was their top priority. All four had decided on their own titles and now sought reassurance about the acceptability of their choices. The two absentees, who had opted for my suggestions, were presumably less anxious about their tasks. I wondered why.

'Yes, Alastair,' I said.

McBain's ability to maintain his consistently dishevelled appearance without becoming squalid was impressive. His choice (perhaps a pose) of excessively informal attire contrasted with his precise, neat handwriting and impeccable written work. No doubt, after graduation, he would transform himself overnight from a scruffy student into a fashionable, even immaculate, man about town. As always, his polite questions were searching, initiating lively discussions in which we all participated.

Shyness, a feature of our earlier tutorials, had now gone, and I wondered if tutorial-group size could, with advantage, be reduced. I learned that my suggestion that students should decide on their own essay titles had resulted in lively arguments throughout the class, dispelling my earlier reservations. It was pleasing that, after their initial hesitation, these four had agreed to try something novel and, overcoming innate conservatism, had accepted my challenge. I was weary when they left, all apparently relaxed, expressing Seasonal Good Wishes (slightly prematurely?).

By mutual consent, the tutorial ended ten minutes early, enabling me to visit the coffee room to wash the chalky taste from my mouth and allow the stressed synapses in my brain to return to normal cerebral equilibrium. An excessively sugary confection (was it someone's birthday?) masked the insipid taste of the hot fluid available, which was nominally coffee, and rebuild my depleted energy levels. I relaxed briefly, mindful of the different and by then immanent obstacles that I faced next.

◎

The notice on the school's boardroom door stated 'Meeting in Progress. Do Not Enter'. I entered and noticed, with approval, that the coffee queue included most of those LU chemistry colleagues who had expressed an interest in the environmental initiative, together with several strangers. Angus was deep in conversation with someone I did not recognise, and John Bland hovered nearby, as if uncertain as to whether or not he was participating. Walter, drinking coffee, was sufficiently relaxed to nod to me, which I returned, but I did not return his enigmatic grin. He was talking to Albert, who had his back to me, and whose presence might or might not account for the enigmatic grin. I would soon find out. I had just lifted a cup of 'real' coffee when Dickey appeared and grasped my free hand.

His greetings were effusive: 'Thank you; thank you, Bill. I'm delighted to be here. Your help made this possible. I'm back in academia... if only visiting. It's just like old times.' He was clearly suffering a surfeit of nostalgia; the human mind can be selective in preferentially recalling only the best of times.

I avoided controversy by saying, 'I hope things work out for all of us. I wonder what, if anything, we'll achieve today?'

'Oh, I'm sure we'll achieve what you're proposing. [I wished I shared his optimism.] It was your original idea.'

I nodded.

He continued, 'It's a good one... of that I'm certain.'

Angus started formal proceedings. 'May we begin, please?' As was his right, he took his usual chair at the top of the table.

I went to the seat I had occupied previously, which was rather far down the tabular hierarchy, but he waved me up to sit near him. Walter, better briefed or more adept at proclaiming personal status, sat directly opposite me.

'This morning we meet informally to discuss a proposal that we should establish a centre of excellence in environmental studies, here in LU. This proposal has come from our newest member of chemistry staff, Dr William Green. I will ask Bill to explain his ideas in a moment. First, it's my pleasure to welcome everyone...' And so our skilled chairman launched the meeting on its intended course, his practised ability continually and smoothly moving the business ever forwards.

Including Albert and Dickey, there were six non-university visitors, presumably from industry and invited by Angus, evidence that he was supporting the project more positively than I could have hoped. There was also the less-welcome possibility that he had taken over the initiative completely.

To start, everyone was invited to introduce him/herself and explain his/her interest in attending: 'Briefly, please,' commanded Angus. 'Now, to business. While we'll be informal, I think it'd be useful to keep a record... agreed?' Our chairman took a brief mumble as assent, before continuing, 'Dr Reid, would you record a few notes for us, please?'

Joe Reid, obviously primed and already busy writing, interrupted his labours to nod agreement.

'Now, Bill, the floor is yours,' Angus stated.

I stood up, apprehensive and nervous, but as well prepared as I could manage with Doug's generous help. My proposal was intended to expand the several research programmes concerned with environmental protection and pollution prevention that had been established already, or were being planned by LU staff. By coordinating all relevant projects, both current and future, we might achieve more than by groups working individually. Preliminary ideas about ways to cooperate were outlined in papers I had already circulated. I hoped the idea was timely. I was still very much a new boy here, but I was prepared, if agreed today, to do much of the coordination work required, without infringing the academic freedom of all researchers participating. The novel feature of the proposed centre would be to establish a fund to support research agreed to be in the common interest of all industrial participants. I was brief.

'Thank you, Bill. It's an interesting idea.' While avoiding committing himself in any way, Angus firmly maintained his dominant role. 'I emphasise that this is only an exploratory discussion, and we're not seeking support… yet. Any questions?'

About an hour was spent on in-depth analyses and discussions, which I found superficial. Speakers tended to maintain a firm grasp of the obvious throughout. Points of detail were argued at the greatest length permitted by the chairman, but it was often difficult to know whether contributors were supporting or opposing the project: fence-straddling was a popular position. I was pleased that no substantial or destructive criticisms were offered, but, less happily, detected little wholehearted approval. A positive feature was that everyone remained to the session's end, though the attraction could be the gourmet lunch offered by the university. So far, so good.

The meal was in the provost's dining room in Biggar House, where catering maintained very high standards to charm visiting notables, particularly anyone regarded (or targeted) as a possible financial sponsor of university projects. The communal enjoyment of gourmet delights seems to be an acceptable ploy in purse-string-loosening exercises designed to encourage selected visitors to become involved in (i.e. pay for) our academic initiatives. Consequently, the food, beverages and surroundings here were much more sumptuous than those of the Staff Club. Angus encouraged 'the host team' to sit with our visitors (which were not collectivised as 'the visiting team'), emphasising that etiquette would not be breached by discussing environmental topics. I understood this as an implicit instruction that there would be a soft-sell for now, and the hard-sell will come later.

I was pleased to sit with Albert and Dickey, down the table from Angus, but again (perhaps coincidentally) almost opposite Walter. During the starter, smoked salmon roulade, Albert talked seriously to me while Walter listened openly, rather than fulfilling his brief by discussing research topics with his neighbours, who were strangers to me.

Albert explained, 'I'm sorry about our delay in responding to your proposal about the tar problem. Boardroom changes temporarily halted all expenditure. However, yesterday our new finance director gave me the go ahead for your work to start.' Albert tasted the roulade. 'That's excellent,' he said, but that was about the food.

I found the pause, at this critical moment, almost unbearable.

He went on, 'Now, about your ideas. We've examined your proposal carefully and decided it has merit. [My spirits rose.] But... [terrible word!]... Walter's proposal also has merit; in fact, it overlaps *substantially* with yours. [Walter smirked.] So, because, as colleagues, you can work together, we've decided to award a *joint* contract.'

Walter's triumphal smirk did nothing to soften the blow.

For me, his was the worst of all possible outcomes. I could not imagine how Walter and I could to cooperate effectively, given his chronically antagonistic attitude. Declining the offer was not an option, so I tried hard to appear pleased at the outcome. Perhaps, being optimistic, a *modus operandi* might be achievable, despite our antipathy. It was more likely, however, knowing Walter's close relationship with Angus, that I would become the junior partner and, sooner or later, be sidelined. Later, this pessimistic thought turned out to forecast future events fairly accurately.

'Thank you, Albert, for your confidence. I'm sure we'll manage a good job,' I replied.

'We'll confirm details in writing soon. Go ahead and discuss plans with Walter, and decide how you'll work together efficiently. Keep me updated with all progress,' Albert concluded.

'Thank you. I'll let you know how we'll start.' I did not refer to Walter, who, after listening throughout, was now talking to a neighbour. Assimilating this disastrous news destroyed my appetite, and, while considering my next move, I ate the starter without noticing any taste whatsoever.

'It's good to see that university catering is so much improved. It wasn't like this at Leeds-Bradford,' declared Dickey, who was enjoying the occasion with gusto and wanting me to share his pleasure.

I pointed out that teaching staff rarely entered this dining room, but he seemed unconvinced. So I told him that our provost regarded himself as a gourmet, occasionally publishing articles about culinary matters, while strictly controlling access here.

'So, it's his contribution to academic excellence,' posited Dickey.

I agreed, without saying that such self-indulgence might be of limited value to LU.

Dickey reviewed the high points of the morning session. He was convinced that the proposed centre would be a good thing, though I suspected this support might be motivated by personal, even selfish, aspirations. A revealing comment was that the initiative might enable him to restart his academic career; he even hinted about giving a few chemistry lectures. While not knowing whether such teaching would be permissible, I did not accept that a function of our centre was to provide a diversion for a retired lecturer who was bored and might be (for all that I then knew) a dilettante. The controlling factor of every centre activity (assuming it ever materialised) would be finance; the paymasters would decide which tunes every participating piper could play. However, Dickey was the richest person I had ever met, and so his cash input could be, if he so wished, instrumental in harmonising the 'music' played by our band of scientists. I then saw that my initiative could be hijacked easily by unsuspected and uncontrollable complications. I ate, rather than appreciated, the excellent lunch.

○

Short afternoon presentations by the host team outlined environmental-research ideas that might repay investigation. The unstated hope was that a guest industrialist might feel moved spontaneously to sponsor one or other of these LU programmes. Not unexpectedly, this did not happen.

My contribution, 'Reducing Acid Emissions from Power Stations', was based on a grant application that was still in preparation. This was languishing, unfinished, on my desk due to difficulties in presenting the programme convincingly. The problem was to eulogise a simple, but (I believed) potentially valuable idea, without disclosing the precise experiments that *might* reduce the acid-rain problem. I was worried that someone might appropriate, publish and thereby gain the credit for inventing *my* novel approach to pollution diminution. Maybe I was being paranoid, but I had heard reports of good research ideas being purloined. Accordingly, my talk focussed on the necessity to reduce acid rain. All the information was on the images projected, so I only had to read the captions, giving suitable verbal emphases. I concluded that the audience had received my message, judging by the two relevant questions asked.

After my spot in the limelight, I found it difficult to maintain interest throughout other colleagues' presentations. Instead, my thoughts kept wandering off to speculate on how to achieve a tolerable relationship with Walter, while remaining pessimistic that any workable joint collaboration could be established. Soon, I shut down my daydreams about imaginary and increasingly bizarre scenarios.

Suddenly, I remembered Albert saying, 'Walter's proposal overlaps substantially with yours.' The more I thought about this, the more incomprehensible it became. We had never discussed collaboration; indeed, Walter had strongly opposed my involvement in this project. How was it that his suggestions were *so* similar to mine that we were now yoked in tandem? One possibility was that he had seen a draft of my proposal to Albert, when I left it on my desk in my unlocked room or later in the secretary's in tray for typing. I thought John Bland would not have disclosed the contents of his copy, but I preferred not to speculate about the confidentiality of Angus's copy. I remained unable to dispel the suspicion that Walter had seen my application and could not, therefore, exclude the possibility that he had presented my ideas as his own. While this suspicion remained *unproven*, its plausibility would corrode the trust that underpins any successful partnership.

Reviewing this conundrum, while only partially listening to the later presentations, yielded no reassurance. I recalled Doug's comment that there are plenty of bright, young people around to think up the ideas, and you must harness their intelligence to push forward your own agenda and advancement. It seemed now that Walter was exploiting *my* ideas in exactly this way – but *how?* Our scientific interests were different, though there was the outside possibility that we could have independently thought up the same approach to resolving Albert's tar problem. I wanted very much to study Walter's proposal, to find out how closely his ideas resembled mine. Just then, I saw no way of achieving this.

During the tea break, I enjoyed a relaxing-but-totally-irrelevant chat with a visitor about his recent trip to South Africa. His wish to talk outside the agenda suggested that I was not alone in suffering presentation overload.

For the final session, I abandoned my musings about intractable problems; these must be faced, but later. More relaxed, I half-listened to the last speakers, while studying the demeanours of my colleagues. Evidently, Angus was following each lecture, fascinated by every detail, or giving this impression convincingly. John Bland was doodling, sketching faces on the agenda; unfortunately, I could not see them clearly. As at staff meetings, others appeared to be pursuing unrelated, covert activities, and, while present in body, were less than attentive in mind and spirit, rather like me.

My thoughts moved back to our earlier meeting. Although lip service had been paid to my role as initiative instigator, Angus had established himself very much as the man in charge. Clearly, as chairman, he would retain executive control firmly, directing all policy – if a centre ever materialised. This would only happen after everyone's intentions were known, including the industrial sponsors (if any), and how we might work together. Angus would also decide what contribution (if any) Dickey could make. Another of Doug's maxims came to mind: 'Whomsoever thinks up the original bright idea does not necessarily win in the scramble for academic credit.'

I then saw John Bland's latest doodle, apparently portraying Walter. (Ally was not the only artist in the family!) It then occurred to me that he might hold the school copy of Walter's application to Albert. Unfortunately, I could not ask to see this nominally confidential document.

Finally, the last and perhaps least inspiring presentation was read, almost literally. Closing the meeting, Angus thanked all the speakers for their 'thoughtful, excellent presentations' (*academic*, rather than *poetic*, license) and asked our visitors for their views on the value of the meeting. Everyone offered supportive comments, most simply echoing points already made by the chairman. The same words tended to be repeated, with minor variations, suggesting fatigue at the end of a busy day or simple statements of safe sentiments, signing off a soporific session.

Angus, still enjoying the chairman's role and still very much awake, said, 'Bill, let me have a short summary of your impressions, including what we should do next, how to proceed, etc. There's no hurry, I'll just need a couple of pages by Friday. OK?'

There was a flurry of farewells.

Albert said to me, 'I'll be in touch soon. I must fly now, literally, to Zurich this evening. See you early in the new year. Happy Christmas.'

Other visitors left with Angus.

Dickey, relaxed and enjoying reminiscing, was talking at, rather than to, Joe Reid. He was trying to identify the conference at which they had met: 'Was it Aberdeen in 1975? Rock weathering? I forget the title. Guarini gave a good talk about...'

Joe, obviously keen to go home, was being polite while sorting the few notes recorded as requested by Angus.

It seemed politic to interrupt, but I did so anyway. 'Dickey, I didn't know you were interested in rock weathering.'

Joe threw me a grateful glance and escaped.

'What are you going to do now, Bill?' Dickey asked.

'I must dump these papers in my room and do some photocopying, then I'm free. What about a bite to eat and a drink together, if that suits?'

'Great.' Dickey needed no persuasion. 'What about the Staff Club? Can we get something light? That midday meal was more than I usually... manage.'

◎

Half an hour later, in the Staff Club bar, we had ordered soup and sandwiches. More importantly, we each had a pint of Best Linkirk Beer, a delicacy I had not sampled previously. After the customary 'Cheers!', I pronounced it most palatable.

Even before the food arrived, Dickey asked if the meeting had pleased me. I said it had gone as well as could be expected, so the answer must be yes. This started a detailed appraisal of today's business, as Dickey saw it. Anticipating this possibility, I opened my notebook, to be asked immediately what I was doing.

'I need to know everyone's opinion. Your impressions will help me to plan our next priorities. Also, you'll remind me of things I've already forgotten,' I confirmed.

His curiosity satisfied, he surveyed the day's work enthusiastically. I was impressed by his almost total recall of what had been said; he had obviously fully immersed himself in the occasion. I did not mention that these notes could be used, almost verbatim, for my report to Angus, thereby saving me work. However, it required considerable effort to record intelligibly everything he recalled.

With the review completed and our beer glasses replenished, we talked about Linkirk, as seen from our different perspectives. This led back inevitably to LU and my uneasy feeling it might trigger another action replay of today's meeting. To forestall this, and sensing his relaxed mood, I challenged him about why he had concealed his scientific background earlier, when visiting the school.

His laugh was unexpected. 'That wasn't very clever. Please forgive my little deception.'

'I still don't understand why,' I pressed.

'To tell the truth, neither do I. [He paused.] Perhaps I was keeping all options open.'

This still did not make much sense and I said so.

'I told you I was thinking about trying to get back into academic work, but I'd made no decision then. I'd hoped a visit to the School of Chemistry might help make up my mind. In fact, it did! Your idea about the environmental centre was the clincher. It's right up my street. But, until I'd decided what I really wanted, I preferred to keep all my options open. Unfortunately, my responses got us both into false positions. That was my fault. Sorry! Am I forgiven? And... I should add that I did fully intend to tell all when you visited us. The trouble was that your detective work on my books penetrated my guilty secret before I got round to confessing. No, my behaviour cannot be justified... but... maybe you'll accept a sincere apology?' He laughed again.

'Of course. It's already forgotten.' I accepted this as the best response I was ever likely to get, even though his reasoning was tortuous. It seemed opportune to ask the leading question: 'If a centre is established, what research field would interest you?'

He did not reply at once. I wondered if he regarded my question as impertinent. Many researchers treasure their ideas as valuable assets and secret concepts that are *not* to be shared with *anyone, ever.* Even best friends might not be absolutely trustworthy. (To quote Doug again, 'All is fair in love, war and academic research: No confidence is ever completely safe.') A brilliant flash of inspiration, once revealed, might be purloined and all credit for that scientific advance lost by its creator, and the insight taken by a thief for later publication as his own. Priority in scientific ideas – bringing fame, kudos and (all too rarely) fortune to those credited as having blazed a trail across uncharted territory – is defended fervently: breakthroughs are jealously guarded.

Recognising that my discretion might have been unduly relaxed by the beer, I quickly added, 'Maybe I shouldn't have asked such a leading question. If I've gone too far, please consider it unsaid.' I was weary, as the day had been long and taxing.

'No, it's a perfectly reasonable question. I hesitate only because my ambition is a bit different from everyone else here. I'd like to study rock weathering.'

'Rock weathering?' My surprise was obvious, but so was his enthusiasm.

'Yes! That's not what you expected.'

I nodded assent.

'I believe that the natural formation of soil from rocks in is indisputably *the* single most important foundation of our well-being. All land-based life, plants and animals, ultimately depend on fertile soil; rock weathering underpins our very existence. Some sea life gets by with less.'

'I've never thought about this. Go on, please.'

'The fertile ground covering much of this fragile planet nurtures a vast range of plants, providing the anchor from which vegetation grows, together with essential nutrients. The diversity is enormous: think of grasslands, deserts and forests. Directly or indirectly, animals depend on soil-rooted plant life. However, the fertile ground we take for granted, which is so familiar that we hardly notice it, was formed only slowly, over very long time spans, by the effects of rain, sun, ice and the plants themselves, in disintegrating and breaking down rock... all contributing to weathering... to soil.'

'I understand that, but why do you want to study it?'

'Because we humans have already made such massive, but largely unknown, impacts on the surface of our small and, ultimately, fragile planet. Climate change is now of concern, but less is said about the many other huge injuries we inflict so mindlessly on nature. We simply don't know the extents or the consequences of the damage we've already done, and continue to perpetrate so recklessly, on the earth's sensitive skin; that is, on its outer layer of soil, which is the fertile, thin layer on which we and all the life around us depend. Forests are cleared, intensive agriculture reduces the fertility of growing zones, and the climate and countryside are modified by our economically driven actions, which lead – sooner or later – to unpredictable-but-dire consequences. We've made such huge environmental changes that we can't envisage the final outcomes of what's already been done, much less what further future damage we're all contributing to. By the time we're forced to react to all the adverse effects of past actions, it'll be too late and impossible to reverse them. I could go on... the sea...' But he stopped.

'Soil deterioration and over exploitation is obviously a serious, long-term threat to our life on earth. I've thought about pollution, but never about our overall impact on the environment. You sound pessimistic. What might you, personally, hope to achieve?'

'Frankly, I don't know. I don't think anyone knows much about how exactly rocks break down or how fast. I'd like to start finding out; at first, simply by trial and error. I can invest my own cash, time and ideas in such work, but – unlike most research these days – it's not important if results come slowly, while I'm doing it… and paying. I could be wrong, but if I'm right, the consequences could be significant.'

'You obviously feel strongly…' I was now certain that my earlier concerns, as to whether Dickey's interests were superficial, even dilettante, were quite, quite wrong.

Well into his stride, there was more from him: 'Yes. Yes. I can think of no more important research than to contribute to mankind's future security by learning as much as we can about the chemistry of the soil on which we all depend… entirely. We've *no* idea how fast this most essential of our resources is being undermined, lost and/or spoiled. Nature sustains us, but if we upset her wise, well-established ways, the checks and balances that have – up to now – generally sustained our food supplies, could deteriorate catastrophically. Once the core is infected, the apple rots quickly. I'd like to find out how natural soil forms, what steps are needed to safeguard our most precious resource and, perhaps, even show how losses can be reversed. Always assuming there is a will to respond, which seems doubtful. We refer to earth or soil by the slightly derogatory word "*dirt*", but we depend on it.'

I yawned. 'Dickey, don't think I'm bored… anything but… however, it's been a long and stressful day. That beer is soporific.'

'We'll continue another time. I've been thinking about this idea for years, literally, so I can hardly expect you to take it all in over a couple of pints. It's been great to talk about it to someone like you, who *is* capable of understanding. Also, the subject is so vast that nobody could pinch the idea. Your friend, Walter [I squirmed mentally], expressed his interest in rock weathering, when I said I'd worked on it.'

My thought was unspoken, *I'm certain he'd quickly seize any opportunity to gain funding, particularly at my expense.* I permitted myself a mild comment of surprise, while trying to appear neutral.

We finished our drinks before parting with warm expressions of hope that serious research planning together could start early in the new year. With fulsome Christmas good wishes exchanged, Dickey went to find a taxi.

I also set off home, revived by the cold air after the overheated building. Bond College was almost in darkness as I passed, which was unusual this early in the evening, but due to the end of term. My thoughts returned to the strange 'coincidence' that Walter's proposals for waste-tar disposal overlapped substantially with mine, at least in Albert's opinion. The memory of John Bland placing the key above the door of his private laboratory appeared suddenly in my mind's eye. Did I perceive a unique opportunity, perhaps a seasonal gift, if I grasped the initiative?

○

The porter was drinking tea. He said, 'Evening, sir. Working late? There's few in tonight.'

I said my visit would be brief and signed the late book, seeing only two other signatures.

The key was still above John's private door, and I noted its precise position before 'borrowing' it to enter the 'Bland Laboratory', which remained in its usual chaotic state. With great care and effort, I moved aside three heavy gas cylinders (mindful of the Cylinder Race) to gain access to two filing cabinets with locked drawers. A search of the nearby shelves located the keys that opened them; John's security system was consistent but ineffective. No labels aided my search of the top drawers, whose contents were a decade or more old. Working down led to recent material, including, to my great satisfaction, copies of the tar-project applications to Albert from me and from Walter!

The relevant papers visited the photocopier briefly, with its use recorded as an earlier time so as to leave no evidence of my late entry into John's sanctuary. All 'borrowed' files were replaced precisely, the cabinets locked and the cylinders returned to their former positions. I was sure my punctilious attention to detail had left no trace of my brief entry. During the trespass, I maintained maximum vigilance, hearing few sounds of other people about. Finally, with great relief, I replaced the door key *exactly* in its former position.

I returned to my office, where I, at last, relaxed (somewhat) to read the documents that had cost me such mental and physical effort to 'borrow'.

Albert was right. Walter's proposal bore remarkably close similarities to mine. A comparison showed many identical phrases, confirming – to me at least – that his submission had plagiarised mine. Somehow, he *must have* obtained access to my application. Perhaps he had raided John's room, just as I had, but I never established for certain how, or even if, he had seen my application. Nevertheless, I was now convinced that Walter had stolen my ideas, which was a certainty that must further poison our relationship. It was going to be virtually impossible to collaborate with a colleague whom I regarded as dishonest: I would have to be hostile and assume him to be totally untrustworthy throughout all our joint work.

My suspicions, confirmed by this evening's clandestine overtime, reinforced my resolve to defend my position vigorously. Unreservedly, I could accept Doug's maxim, 'All's fair in love, war and academic research…' Battle lines were now drawn. With Walter evidently exploiting my ideas, I might hope to benefit – equally and covertly, if necessary – from his work, if I matched his unscrupulous methods. With guile, I should be capable of profiting from this new freedom to *my* advantage, by *always* exploiting *my* ideas in *my* interest – ruthlessly.

I took the secret photocopies home to minimise the chance of anyone finding them. The porter was gone when I signed out. I felt exhausted by then, as if after carrying a heavy mental burden. I wondered if my attempts to survive in the academic jungle were worth all this effort and even whether I should go on trying. These were yet more intractable questions that needed urgent answers, but not tonight. The next day, I would face my increasingly bewildering future; that day had already brought too many indigestible and unwelcome 'mental morsels'. Meanwhile, I offered silent thanks to John for his unwitting gift of access to those confidential files…

Chapter 17

THIRD MONDAY IN MARCH

BREAK	a.	Respite; rest interval
	b.	The 'fate of the heart' when true love dies

My CHRISTMAS VACATION PASSED FAIRLY PLEASANTLY, SIMILARLY to others in recent years. Mother and I celebrated the festive season together, appropriately but quietly, and – as usual – visited our cousins.

Mother also offered me her advice, 'Try to find a less stressful job, nearer home, Willikins [cringe],' which I deflected as tactfully as I could.

While at home, I wrote lectures for the new term and devised what I hoped was a persuasive application for research funding. Overall, I enjoyed the change, but, with guilty feelings of relief, returned to Linkirk for the new term, joyously renewing contact with Beth.

When term restarted, I at once found myself in the endless grind of keeping all commitments up to date, while still managing to find some – but never enough – time to relax with Beth's companionship. The term slipped past in what I recall as endless efforts to meet deadlines, much as the first term, but with less novelty: I had seen it all before. More than once, I remembered the maternal advice to seek a less stressful job, but firmly decided *not* to abandon my academic ambitions before completing this academic year successfully. To give up sooner would be an admission of personal failure, further eroding my already low self-esteem. My hope was that the second year would surely be easier, with lectures written, and – with luck – some research funding and students secured. Finally, I could not accept defeat on the environment centre initiative. So I battled on and, with relief, found the workload slightly easing as Easter approached.

I remained reluctant to risk *any* possibility of harming my continuing happy relationship with Beth. I assumed she wished to remain in Linkirk and that it was too early yet to ask if she would consider moving elsewhere to face an uncertain future with me. Despite my preoccupations, we met regularly, even attending a Scottish country dancing class, giving us both pleasure. I visited her home fairly frequently and got to know her parents, whose company I enjoyed. During that Hilary term, our relationship strengthened, moving slowly but surely towards a more permanent arrangement, though no definite commitment had been discussed – yet.

○

Before the Easter break, I had to collect and appraise laboratory reports. This task was urgent because, before sitting the written examinations, each student had to achieve a satisfactory grade for their experimental work, achieving what was known as the 'laboratory certificate'. So far, I had received less than half the reports, shortening my time for scrutinising them. This put me under pressure, because grades and feedback had to be communicated to every student before term ended the next Friday. My three-hour laboratory supervision that day had to be devoted to urgent marking, technically breaching my employment conditions. The *LU Staff Guide* stated 'Staff timetabled to teach in laboratories must devote all their time to instructing students.' This became impossible as term was coming to an end, as it was after most of their experiments had been completed. The students were now writing up their experiments. Almost all undertook this task elsewhere, perhaps in the library, at home or even (judging by the stains) in the Student Union bar. If catching up on backlogs elsewhere was preferred by those nominally receiving my instruction, I could hardly be censured for marking their reports just then, many being seriously overdue despite reminders. Besides, it was unlikely, given the infrequency of professorial visits to teaching laboratories (the 'active coalface'), that any of the bosses would notice my rule-breaking or question my ability to demonstrate in an almost deserted laboratory.

Appraising fifty reports in three hours is less than four minutes each – an impossibility. In practice, with the inevitability of interruptions, recording the correct scores and taking my *LU Staff Guide* sanctioned tea break, I could not expect to finish today. I took the first...

An hour later, I heard activity next door, confirming Mohamed's arrival, which I took as my signal for a break. I roused myself from the semi-comatose state that invariably develops during periods of sustained concentration, brought on by reading similar reports of the same experiments. Rereading was often essential following attention lapses. I had to be scrupulously fair because these marks contributed to examination grades and, ultimately, to the students' career prospects. I stretched and got up after the tenth script, with only forty to go, plus those yet to appear.

Mohamed arrived late habitually and was slow to start work. A leisurely cup of tea was his necessary precondition to tackling things scientific. When he first started working with me, I was dismayed by this apparent lack of motivation, but soon found his *modus operandi* was misleading. Once started, he worked assiduously and for unusually long hours. The porter's late book showed he rarely left the building before 9.00pm, more than making up for late morning starts and an unwillingness, or an innate inability, to rush any task he undertook. But, by then, I knew that, despite an idiosyncratic approach to research, he was a careful, reliable and skilled practical scientist.

I went into the then fully functional research laboratory. (The unwelcome chore of detritus disposal left by its previous occupants had receded to a distant, if unpleasant, memory.) Indeed, Angus had offered to brighten the place up; this repainting was an unexpected-but-welcome bonus. At that point, we were in business at last, and most mornings started with an unchanging exchange.

'Morning, Mohamed. How're we today?' I would ask.

'Good. Thank you, boss. [My attempts to discourage this form of address had been unsuccessful so far. Happily, he used it rarely.] Cup of tea?' he would offer.

'No, thank you. I've told you—'

'That eating and drinking in the laboratory are banned on grounds of health and safety.'

'Yes, but it's *your* health and *your* safety. Why do you do it?'

'Well, *boss* [was the word slightly emphasised?], I have to wake up. I work myself up to working. It's my alarum call; ring, ring.'

While these ritual, daily exchanges were undoubtedly trivial, I welcomed his relaxed attitude, including a sharp sense of humour. I could overlook his infringements of some LU rules *unofficially* because, as a mature adult (he was about my age), he knew the risks and the reasons for these rules as well as I did. He by then fully understood the research we were doing and was contributing significant ideas of his own. This was both welcome and reassuring, and confirmed that his decision to transfer from John Bland to me was not due to any lack of ability. I accepted that he had then settled well into our collaboration, which was a situation I expected to continue. Whatever the reason, John appeared to be very much the loser by the change. Perhaps Mohamed's dissatisfaction resulted from a personality clash or an inability to communicate with Prof, rather than boredom with his work, as he had claimed. I suspected that John allocated the research to be done inflexibly, being unreceptive to student input in planning, or maybe his late start caused friction. Next, our morning ritual completed, we reviewed progress before planning the next experiments.

○

I was finishing lunch in the Staff Club when Doug arrived, bearing an unusually generously loaded tray. 'No comment, young lad! I'm keeping up my strength to face the rigors of the Easter vacation and, after that, our examination festival,' he claimed.

'I wouldn't dare comment. You'll hear no breath of criticism from me,' I responded. That wasn't strictly true, as I had intended to hint that he should moderate his food intake. While perhaps not clinically obese, Doug was overweight, but this was not a good time to raise such a sensitive subject. Continuing painful disagreements with his wife were still causing him considerable anguish; apparently, divorce proceedings were imminent. I worried that the stresses surrounding his family break-up were undermining his health, but, even so, solace derived from excess calories and drink was not the best remedy.

'I'd hoped to catch you, Bill. When'll I get the 2.12P marks?'

'It's difficult to say. I'm marking all day. Some are done, but not all are in yet.' I promised him some marks tomorrow, before threatening sanctions for further delays.

'Bill, am I right in thinking you're more relaxed now you were last term?'

I could be optimistic. 'Yes, I think so… No, I'm sure! That first term, up to Christmas, was hard. There were always too many things to do, all immediately, if not sooner. Now, I seem to be… just about coping. I won't say more than… I'm getting by.'

'I always thought you're a survivor. What's happening about the research centre?'

'It's going very slowly. Angus mentions it from time to time, and he seems optimistic that it'll start soon. I hope I'm not building too much on his hints. He sent a note about a steering-committee meeting for Wednesday. That was the first I'd heard of it; it was news to me. I assume I'm invited. My name's on the agenda. It's to discuss plans and decide on strategy.'

'Sounds ominous!' Doug's spontaneous wariness worried me. Most of his previous perceptions had been uncannily accurate, especially when he sensed equivocation.

'The fact that I'm invited means I'm involved, surely?'

'Could be. Might be. But you didn't know the committee existed. Nor did you set the agenda. As I've said before, watch your back! Where's the meeting to be held?'

'Angus's office.'

'That gives him a territorial advantage.'

I found no adequate response, but the optimism that had come with the letter was now seeping away. Truly, I must *watch my back!*

I got fresh coffee for both of us, before stating, 'It's odd that we live under the same roof and work in the same school, and yet it's here that we find the time to chat.'

Our shared flat was working well, largely because we each used it separately as a base. We lived individual lives with little interaction, except for occasional meals when we happened to be at home at the same time. Sometimes we enjoyed a nightcap together, but, after a long day, conversation tended towards trivia and gossip, or we watched TV passively, usually without much discrimination, except for Doug's sporting enthusiasms.

'I suppose so,' he concurred. 'That reminds me, may we discuss the vacation? Will you stay on after term ends? I only ask because, if you're away, I might invite my son, Owen, to stay.'

'I don't know my plans yet. I'm eating out tonight with Beth to discuss a trip south sometime around Easter. Can I give you an answer tomorrow?' I enquired.

Doug nodded.

We walked companionably to Bond College, light-heartedly exchanging unlikely strategies to encourage students to submit their laboratory reports on time. Doug's suggestions ('carrots') included, 'Open a bar in the laboratory. Reward first submissions with student disco tickets.' My ideas ('sticks') were less imaginative in awarding only half marks after missed deadlines, or locking the students in the laboratory and only releasing them on completion of their reports. This trivial banter filled the passing moment pleasantly, for once making me feel comfortable with my career decision to come here. Later, I recalled this time as the high point of my academic achievements; little did I realise that my future was much less secure than I then, so optimistically, believed. If one could put the clock back and learn from experience, that was *the* moment I would choose to restart the action replay of my life. Then, I had no premonition of the impending disastrous changes. I little thought my hard-fought battles to establish my vocation would be wrecked so quickly, that career disintegration could be so rapid and complete, or that the consequences of my later errors of judgement could be so dire.

○

The phone was ringing in my office and, expecting a return call from Albert, I answered flippantly: 'Green's Environmental Research, better known as GERRRRR.' My mood of light-hearted banter with Doug persisting, I hoped Albert might be amused by this harmless nonsense. Instead, there was silence. 'Is anyone there?'

'Is that you, Bill?' Beth's serious tone was not receptive to frivolity.

'Oh, Beth… it's you. Hello. I thought it was someone else.'

'Obviously. And you didn't think it could've been me?'

That was totally unanswerable in any way that wouldn't get me in trouble. 'We've agreed to meet this evening at—'

'Yes, yes, I know. I'm ringing to change that arrangement.'

'But we'd decided to discuss Easter plans, our trip together—'

'Yes, yes, I know. We'll still do that, but there's a problem. I can't talk now, classes are starting. Can we meet at Tom and Valerie's at 7pm? They've been let down by their babysitter, and I thought you wouldn't mind if we stood in.'

'Tom and Valerie? Do I know them?' Vague memories stirred.

'We babysat for them, months ago. Do you remember where they live?'

'I might succeed in finding it. But, we'd agreed… What about our plans?'

'I must go. I'll explain later. Bye.' She was gone.

I also was teaching and, in a distinctly irritated mood, went to the laboratory. Although aware of Beth's ability to get her own way, I felt this unilateral, late change of plans was unreasonable. I had had no choice; this unexpected 'take it or leave it' attitude, hitherto absent from our relationship, was disturbing. I could demonstrate my umbrage clearly by not going at all: 'I couldn't find the house. I had no telephone number.' On reflection, this seemed a bit extreme, but one compromise was to arrive late, signalling my displeasure. We might still discuss Easter plans for my hoped-for Sussex trip; I intended to try again to persuade her to come, despite previous inconclusive discussions.

With very few students in the laboratory, I told the demonstrator on duty that she could return to her research. 'If there's a rush later, I'll call you. Come back in an hour or so, and we'll see how things are then.' I continued marking reports, consciously suppressing my personal irritation, which must not be sublimed into unfair, harsh grading, just because Beth had annoyed me. During that last practical class, I emptied the 'report tray', though some tardy contributions had yet to arrive. A few students came to tell me their reports would be late, thereby wasting time that could have been spent more usefully on finishing their work. The final half-hour was spent tutoring informally, discussing questions from students worried about approaching examinations. Some queries, I thought, might have arisen from shortcomings in my lectures, and I noted possible changes for next year.

○

The intended protest at Beth's one-sided rearrangement was a total fiasco; my late arrival at Tom and Valerie's went completely unnoticed. This time, there was no floral offering for my hostess; babysitting was a sufficient service and an unwelcome replacement for an anticipated companionable evening. I set out just after Beth's suggested arrival time and walked slowly. Uncertain of the exact address, I reached it at around 7.30pm, earlier than I wished. Unexpectedly, Tom opened the door, making redundant my prepared response to any critical comment from Beth (a surprised 'Oh! Am I late?').

Instead of greeting me, Tom said in a hushed voice, 'Beth said you'd come. Go on through. Things are a bit fraught, just now.'

I could hear a child howling upstairs and raised adult voices.

Once we were in the sitting room, he continued, 'We're having some problems. Beth'll explain later. Meanwhile, please excuse me. Here's the paper.' He was gone before I could reply.

Without an alternative, I sat down. One or both children continued their vociferous chorus as a background to Valerie and Beth's raised voices. I could not hear what was being said, but, clearly, a serious family crisis was noisily taking place. There was great temptation to leave now and spend the evening more agreeably somewhere outside this disaster area. I was prevented only by my wish to discuss with Beth plans for our Easter vacation trip. However, judging by the continuing conflict, it seemed unlikely that this would be possible. It was obviously pointless for me, knowing nothing about childcare, to offer mediation in the action arena above, while the responsible adults in charge were being so ineffective. I decided to wait fifteen minutes, and if nothing positive happened, I would simply go home.

I turned to the diversion offered, *The South of Scotland Sustainer*, for news of local happenings. I learned that Linkirk Silver Band had won the Scottish Borders Silver Cup with a sensitive rendering of a new work, *Sweet Meggett Water*, by local man Jock Blazso. I wondered about his Scottish ancestry. The approach of Easter explained the several pages devoted to church activities. An 'eagerly awaited' (by whom?) visit to Linkirk First Church by 'the moderator' (whoever he was) outranked all alternatives by rating a feature article. The entire contents of his forthcoming address appeared to have been leaked in advance, though it was not clear whether this was to encourage attendance or to console those unfortunate enough to be unable hear it delivered in person. Very many religious organisations advertised 'special' Easter services, reminding me that I still had not thought about joining a church or discussing this possibility with Beth, though it must arise sooner or later. I reviewed 'Forthcoming Church Events' to assess whether any were sufficiently inviting for me to attend, should I be here at Easter. Most, I decided, fell short of my positive interest, while others were distinctly off-putting. Indeed, I had immersed myself so deeply in this research that I only noticed Beth's arrival when she threw herself histrionically onto the sofa with an exasperated, 'What an evening!'

I was reluctant to display sympathy in this situation, which I regarded as self-imposed.

After a short silence, she asked, 'Aren't you going to talk to me?'

'Good evening.' My tone was strictly neutral.

'What's that meant to mean?'

I shrugged my shoulders.

She continued, 'We've had a family crisis. It's now resolved, I hope. I'm in no mood for any more unpleasantness.'

'Nor me! What I don't understand is why it was suddenly so important to spend the evening here, after we'd planned a relaxed meal together?'

'We're here because Valerie's my friend. She was let down badly by the babysitter. I thought you'd agree to a small change of our plans. I think you're being unreasonable, just like the children earlier on...'

Before I could protest, a thin wail was heard, and, with a scowl of irritation, Beth returned upstairs, with the parents having departed presumably.

She came back with an unsmiling look of decision on her face. 'I'm going to tell you why things are so upset here. If you understand, then perhaps you'll behave more reasonably.'

I unbent sufficiently to nod consent.

'Irene and Babs [her finger pointed upwards towards her charges] visited Tom's mother yesterday. Irene showed great interest in Grandma's gold pendant, so she opened it to show a lock of blond hair, tied with a blue ribbon and a photo of a small boy. Grandma explained that this was Granda's hair, cut when he was the small boy, and she'd always treasured it as a dear memory of him.'

Not seeing where the tale was leading, I remained silent.

Beth continued, 'This evening, Irene came into the kitchen just before tea, with a tuft of blond hair in one hand and clippers in the other. Valerie was shocked, but became really angry when she went into the living room and saw the mess that Irene had made of Babs's hair… what was left on her head, that is. Babs was howling, and Irene was upset because something that Grandma found so wonderful had made her mother so cross inexplicably. When Tom got home, he – as I understand it – sided with Irene and a thoroughly unhappy time was had by all. Things seem to have quietened now, I hope.'

'Why was it so important for Tom and Valerie to go out?'

'Tom's big boss invited them to dinner. Tom thinks there's a chance he might be promoted at work. This could be an informal interview.'

'After such family strife, he won't be in best form to impress.'

'Tom's OK. He'll manage to keep home and work apart. It's Valerie who's stressed. She didn't want to go, but I persuaded her. I agreed to babysit at short notice *because* the occasion is so important for them. You *have* to support your friends. I'll get supper.'

The last remark gave no comfort, implying that I had slipped a notch or several down in the friend-supporting league. While this was unwelcome, I realised that an impromptu examination of my failings was unlikely to improve the situation.

Beth stood up and, as she passed, I saw that – instead of her invariably well-groomed and colour-coordinated appearance – she was slightly dishevelled, even untidy. The heavy corduroy trousers were ill-fitting, too large and did not match her jumper; I assumed that fashions had changed in ways that I, a mere male, had not yet noticed. My critical glance at her clothes, betraying mild surprise, registered with her.

'What are you looking at?' she enquired.

My flippant reply was exceptionally unwise: 'I don't know, it's not labelled!' I was forced to repeat it and at once knew I was in deep trouble. I agreed that I had been thoughtless, even rude, but had not intended to be. The rejoinder had popped out involuntarily; it was used frequently as a boorish retort when I was at school. My claim that the remark was intended to be funny, though admittedly schoolboy humour, was dismissed derisively. Apologies did nothing to soothe her pique. Attempted justification, comparing my response with the behaviour of Pavlov's dogs, was silenced with a scowl capable of souring milk. I did not hear all her reply, but it included uncomplimentary references to scientists. Since the evening was unlikely to improve, I offered to leave.

'No, we've got to talk. I'll bring in supper.' She went to walk out of the room but turned at the door. 'There was no call for you to use that uncouth… *guttersnipe* [I had not heard that word for years!] expression. If you'd any regard for me, you'd be more considerate. I should tell you, *and* this doesn't excuse *your* bad manners, that these tatty trousers aren't mine.'

'*What?*' My surprise was genuine.

'Watch what you're saying.' Her warning was sharp. 'If you must know, I'd a slight accident earlier.'

I tried to maintain an appearance of polite, emotionless interest.

She explained, 'I sat on a chair that happened to have Irene's paint box open on it beside a pot of water. My good skirt is ruined, I think. I'll try washing it. For now, Tom lent me these… his spare working trousers.'

To my relief, she left promptly, allowing my facial tension to relax briefly into a grin, before she returned with a pale-yellow skirt, held to display splodges of several bright colours from the wet paint box.

'Well, you're a *chemist*. How do I get rid of this? Is my skirt completely ruined?' she demanded.

I admitted to having no idea how to clean delicate dress fabrics and did not offer any paint-removing services, knowing I would either damage the fragile material or bleach its colour. Instead, I suggested taking it to a good dry cleaner for advice.

Without comment, she brought in supper: pizza and salad. It was tasty, but – despite slight progress towards restoring our good relationship – recent discord had taken away my appetite. Luckily, the children remained silent, presumably exhausted by the family aggravation. It seemed that just then, at last, we had the prospect of planning a few enjoyable days of freedom and leisure together.

I was still hesitating about how to open the subject, when Beth, with obvious reluctance, took the initiative. 'Bill, I know, because you've mentioned it so often, you're keen that we go to Sussex together at Easter. I'd like to too, *very much*, but, I'm sorry, it's not possible just now.' Her voice was neutral, and she ended abruptly, apparently unwilling to provide any explanation. Throughout, she studied her pizza, not meeting my eye.

It took me a while to assimilate this terrible news and accept that my (our) situation was again in deteriorating mode.

Dismayed, I reverted to a schoolboy idiom: 'You mean I'm being *chucked*? This is the *end* for us?'

I was treated to a look of shock, even horror, which seemed genuine enough, but could I be sure? I pushed aside most of my uneaten pizza and stood up.

'Bill. Please sit down! Please? Just for a moment,' she pleaded.

I did not feel like complying; my mind was in too much turmoil, trying to decide between departing immediately, collapsing on the chair or what?

'Please! Please! Just hear me out! It's not what you think. We've had a bad evening. Things are difficult for me too. I've obligations… too. I don't want us to part like this. Please listen. You're not being helpful!'

I had no ideas about how to resolve this, our first serious disagreement. We were not communicating, and I lacked any experience of defusing such a crisis situation. As an only child and the product of a boy's school, nothing in my upbringing had prepared me to cope with this type of dilemma. All my previous brief relationships had ended in irretrievable breakdown, but none had involved the serious emotional link, the *love*, I felt for Beth. Parting would bring real anguish. But, by then, I was fully convinced that she wanted to end our relationship immediately, and probably wished never to see or hear from me again. We as *an item* were over. It was difficult to take in, after a very tiring day.

Even then, if we could have shared a few words of reconciliation, our relationship *might* have survived. But, before committing myself, I needed reassurance that she wanted to continue seeing me and was still fond of me. Something needed to be done, something positive, but what? Without evidence of her goodwill, I could foresee only one possible outcome of the present row. Nevertheless, as told, I sat down, but reluctantly.

'All right. I'm listening,' I stated. I must admit that mental turmoil had closed my mind. I had firmly convinced myself that there was no value in our talking further and parting now seemed inevitable. Self-pity, frustration and anger all played their part in discouraging me from seeking common ground. I had no sympathy left to offer and only half-listened to her unhappy story.

'Since I saw you last, a friend who's just back from Aberdeen told Dad he'd met my brother Stewart there by chance and is convinced he's in some kind of trouble. He wouldn't give any details, but hinted that the situation seemed serious. Dad rang immediately, only to be told that everything's fine. Now we're all extremely worried and Dad has asked me to go to Aberdeen with him to see things for ourselves. This is urgent! It must be resolved quickly, certainly before Easter. You also know that I've promised to go to Jersey with Mum and Dad at about that time. They've managed to defer our holiday, though it seems unlikely that we'll go at all, depending on what we find out about Stewart. We can only wait and see. It's the only holiday they get, and I've gone with them for years. I thought you'd understand; after all, you've much the same feelings of obligation to your mother. With this mess, I simply can't agree to go away with you, at present. I'm sorry, *really* sorry. We'll discuss it all again later, when things get back to normal.'

Later, I realised that I should have been far more sympathetic, but tiredness and the day's frustrations, particularly Beth's 'take it or leave it' attitude over this evening's plans, had angered me. Right then, she was doing it again. 'I'd hoped, you know, to spend time with my mother *at home* and also visit my old prof. [I did not mention my sudden idea of asking his advice about other jobs, somewhere far distant from Linkirk.] The following week, presumably you'll be back at school?'

Beth said, 'Yes.'

'That's when I'm planning to attend a conference in Gothenburg, Sweden.' This excursion was invented spontaneously to signal my independence. I had seen it advertised, and this seemed as good a way as any to spend the money saved for the trip with Beth, given that we might be going our separate ways. I could also ask LU for financial support, claiming that this conference would update me on current trends in environmental sciences. With the prospect of such a bleak future, the idea seemed attractive, as I had never been to Sweden.

We sat silently. Little could be said, given that our *shared* future had become so uncertain suddenly; indeed, was fast disintegrating. I picked at the cold pizza, without appetite. Clearly, the evening's events had shocked both of us badly. Until I could work out what had gone so terribly wrong – and if possible, correct it – it was better to say nothing: least said, soonest mended. I was now convinced that Beth wanted our relationship to end, and, while trying to soften the blow, she had already made her decision. I saw no reason to prolong a parting against which I had no appeal. This realisation was painful, but I could not understand why it had come about so rapidly. In theory, I (the *academic*) accepted that if either of us decided that our friendship was over, the only reasonable action was to tell the other, as gently as possible, before going our separate ways.

At that point, bruised by the changed situation, I felt rejected, uncertain and depressed, and could not bring myself to ask, even plead, that we might still remain friends. (Though, what kind of friends *could* we be?) Continuing uncertainty would only prolong the pain and despair. With my thoughts clouded by emotions crowding out reason, I knew that nothing I could say was likely to be helpful. Invisible tears were forming behind my eyelids. I recalled all the happy times with Beth so intensely that a future without her was unthinkable, and, numb, I still did nothing and said nothing, just in case some vestige of hope remained. I supposed Beth might be equally pained, but she also found nothing to say or chose not to end our painful silence.

With our preoccupations, it took a few moments for the renewed crying from upstairs to impinge on our overworked and self-pitying mental introspections. Beth's expression changed to exasperation, and, with a mumbled comment, she stopped sawing at a tough, cold pizza crust and left the room. I set my unfinished supper aside.

I decided that her mumbled comment could have been, 'Goodnight!' Beth rarely used strong language; the few expletives I had heard her utter were the mildest. But, the alternative meaning, presenting itself more forcefully in my pessimistic mood, was that 'Goodnight!' could be an invitation for me to depart. I was already worrying about how we could end this evening without having to express sentiments that were either banal ('Have a good Easter.') or insincere ('See you soon.'). The alternative parting with words of rancour was too horrible and far too distressing even to contemplate.

'Goodnight' offered me an exit line, avoiding both confrontation and embarrassment. I decided that these conventional words of parting had been said and so I left, closing the front door quietly. I had no way of knowing how this would be received, but the responsibility was not mine, not being the official baby sitter. I made my way home to deal with my disappointments as best I could. No conversation with Doug was necessary (though, just then, I felt a particular sympathy for him having to deal with his marriage breakdown). I wished him goodnight, and went to bed early. It was a long time before I slept, and, when I did, there were tears in my eyes, for the first time since my father's death. I felt my heart was breaking...

Chapter 18

THIRD WEDNESDAY IN MARCH

ACT	a.	Implement an action
	b.	Dramatic performance to entertain

WAKING ON WEDNESDAY BROUGHT NO PLEASURE OF GREETING A new dawn. My disturbing dreams of the night transformed into an equally distressing daytime mindset, featuring failure, fault and fate. The prospect of a Bethless future might yet have to be faced. But, just then, my mind perversely preferred to avoid confronting the possibility that *that parting* had been final. Yesterday, mired in self-pity, I had procrastinated uselessly, not even attempting to repair the rift. Unreasonably, I still clung to the faintest hope that something, *anything*, might miraculously reverse *our disagreement*, restoring the prospect of future happiness. Of course, I should have tried to initiate the reconciliation, but, in a black mood of self-pity, the day was frittered away without finding the courage to take some, any, remedial action. I simply could not face the prospect of being rebuffed. Unwilling to relinquish my dwindling hope, I fantasised that somehow we might yet bridge the rift. Realistically, blotting out that nightmare evening or pretending it had never happened was a hopeless daydream.

Yesterday's busy teaching duties had been discharged adequately; at least, I noticed no disasters. Meanwhile, preoccupied with private grief, I obsessively explored all prospects of restoring our former relationship, before finally accepting that chasing hopeless fantasies only deepened depression. *Right then*, the choice was stark: take action or not. This mental dichotomy, being in two minds, might be schizophrenia, but, realistically, 'today' was '*to do or not to do day*'. Contacting Beth risked that terrible, *final* rejection, whereas procrastination pointed to perpetual purgatory. The temptation to cling to the faintest hope, and do nothing, was strong, but probably only deferred the inevitable confirmation that our romance was ended, over, gone, finished, kaput...

I was in deepest despondency!

At that point, other, urgent problems (less *acutely* painful than the ruptured romance) had to be addressed to maintain my future academic prospects. My hopes for advancement in LU seemed to depend my performance at that day's steering-committee meeting; in particular, by securing a significant role in managing the environmental centre. *My* ambition to steer *my* initiative through its formation, needed to – at least temporarily – banish *all* other distractions in a focussed, supreme effort to stake out that claim. With luck, that might even begin to repair my severely shaken self-concept and confidence.

These early-morning musings brought slight relief when, eventually, I began planning how to advance my personal agenda at that day's meeting. The most promising strategy might be to offer to undertake most, even all, of the preliminary work required to establish the centre. Setting aside the temptation to pull the blanket over my head, hoping it would all go away (*it wouldn't*), instead, I rose, garnering strength for immanent challenges. Breakfast exchanges, most weekdays, were monosyllabic.

'Tea?'

'Thanks.'

'Toast?'

'Jam!'

I finished first, mumbling, 'See you later!'

Doug roused himself sufficiently to ask, 'What about those marks?'

'Yes, OK. Is 1.00pm OK? Usual table?'

As I was leaving, Doug asked, 'Today, you've that meeting, yes?'
I confirmed.

'Take care! Good luck and *watch your back!*' There was nothing to promote self-confidence there!

Going out, my brain remained on supercharge. The *romantic-heartaches* scenario chose that moment to stage a comeback, repossessing my central consciousness. Great effort was required to switch off the mental triggers launching sequences of unwelcome *action replays* of the most painful events of Monday evening, which were vivid images invariably featuring Beth. Later, perhaps mid-afternoon, if there was still no contact, I *might* phone her and try to regain some control of my destiny (as I rather grandly hoped). Thus, again, the necessity for immediate action was deferred.

Doug's request had reminded me of my teaching obligations, another commitment in my rich and diverse tapestry of academic duties. The sentiment that troubles don't come singly seemed particularly apt, and self-doubts resurfaced, renewing my concern about my ability to fulfil all obligations. This nadir of self-confidence and despair released unexpectedly an unperceived cache of inner strength, helping me to face my predicament. Suddenly and decisively, I knew that I was *not* going to let *the bastards* beat me! While unclear about just who those *bastards* were, I personified them vaguely as the hostile Walter in adversarial mode. Angus' attitude was more difficult to judge. Though he always appeared friendly, even kind and helpful at times, I wondered what support I could expect in a crisis, particularly in any conflict involving his protégé Walter.

Self-absorption, replaced by controlled anger, strengthened my new determination not to be pushed around by Walter or anyone else at that day's meeting. My mood had brightened slightly, enabling clearer and more constructive thinking, focussing on my immediate problems, rather than continuing to wallow in a morass of egotism, narcissism and self-pity, following *that row* with Beth. Every possible aspect of our clash had been appraised in excessive detail during the last miserable couple of days. Right then, distracted temporarily, I could grapple with these alternative challenges and priorities. If things went well for me with the research centre (ever *my initiative*), then such success could build self-confidence. Eventually, I might find a way to reverse my Bethless situation (there was an optimistic thought!). So, facing this *career crunch point*, I needed to exploit this great opportunity to strengthen my ailing ego. I could not allow myself to be sidelined, if my ambitions were to be fulfilled.

○

I reached Angus' office a little early, to find the door open and Walter already seated within. I accepted Walter's somewhat *proprietorial* invitation of, 'Come on in!' confidently and pleasantly offered, and surprised myself by sitting beside him, as he gestured, while every instinct prompted me to choose a distant seat. As usual, he seized the initiative by discussing our first joint report of the tar-disposal contract, due to be sent to Albert, soon. Recognising our necessity to agree its contents, I was keen to hear his suggestions. Walter, unpredictable as ever, talked as if we had always been friends, and had never exchanged a harsh word or shared an unpleasant moment! Yet again, he had confused me into a defensive mode, making me wary about whether this pleasantry heralded an ambush that was yet to unfold. All my instincts and Doug's warning ('*Watch your back!*') counselled caution and the desirability of minimising contacts with Walter. However, our contract specified a *joint* report, requiring agreed contents (at least, in public). So, wary of pitfalls and resentful of our enforced collaboration, I was pragmatic and accepted, at face value, this superficially civilised exchange with my research partner.

We had only just begun when a red-faced Angus bustled in, dropping, with practised grace, his trademark burden of bulging, multicoloured files on his table/file-store. (He was still seemingly unaware of the invention of the brief case.) With similar aplomb, he lifted another file deftly, presumably relating to this meeting, which had been selected from several superficially identical sets. He joined us, depositing his bulk in his substantial 'chair of chemistry' at the head of the table, and faced us with an exhalation that was either of exhaustion, extremis, expectation or even exhilaration; it was difficult to know which emotions were being expressed. I was most impressed by this act of Professorial Pre-eminence (and/or Conscious/ Conscientious Chairmanship). Only then did I notice Dickey, John Bland and the others, who had followed our leader, into his office. John, after hesitation, sat beyond Walter. Dickey sat to my left and greeted me warmly, expressing his pleasure at being here as an invited observer. He enquired about Beth, though took little interest in my necessarily vague reply.

After a just-audible knock, the unsmiling Miss French arrived with a tray bearing teapot, cups and a chocolate cake, already sliced. Angus thanked her and invited us all to partake of birthday cake, made by his wife, Betsy, though it was unclear whose birthday it was: his, Betsy's or even Miss French's.

He explained, 'I thought that on this auspicious occasion, we'd have a little celebration. Term's almost over and, tonight, I'm off to Vermont for a few days relaxation before some important meetings.' He grinned. 'We'll indulge ourselves just a little.'

There was a mumble of appreciation from the members of the steering committee. However, the look of austere disapproval by Miss French certainly distanced her from such frivolity at work or, more probably, ever.

'Help yourself to cake, Lillian,' Angus said as she withdrew. Whether the use of her first name or the proffered indulgence caused her the greater woe was difficult to tell, but, visibly radiating disapproval, she left us to our decadent feasting.

While enjoying the excellent confection, Angus, between mouthfuls, called the meeting to order and, adopting his pompous mode, delivered an obviously rehearsed peroration: 'I have called this *steering-committee meeting* so that we can agree *ground rules* for the formation of the Environmental-Research Centre of Excellence at Linkirk University. We must establish its formal existence within LU before embarking on the challenges of obtaining funding for our research projects…' He went on at length before tabling, for discussion, a *draft letter* to inform the provost and the LU Council *officially* of 'our' existence and fulfil the several prerequisites required by a university centre. This was approved without dissent, as Angus had intended.

To make the decisions *official*, he asked Walter to record minutes for communication to the faculty, 'After our approval, of course.'

Dickey was asked to act as interim research manager. I was acutely aware of being bypassed in these appointments, and either Angus noticed or, more probably, anticipated my discomfiture.

He turned to me and stated, 'Bill, I know this seemingly excludes you, but these are strictly interim measures, lasting only until the centre becomes a reality and achieves financial viability. After that, a senate subcommittee will interview and appoint directors, also recognising our committee. Every appointment will be open to all applicants equally, and decided in fair and open competition.'

It seemed reasonable, but I resented Walter's apparent advancement as both unearned and something that would probably favour him later. Just then, I could think of no way of promoting my claims or objecting to the situation. Clearly, Angus (as professor) had already decided, in advance, all significant outcomes of the meeting.

Under item five, future planning, we learned from Angus that, 'A sum of £6,000 is available immediately for relevant exploratory research: £3,000 each from the Anderson bequest and the generosity of Dr Richards. These monies are to fund preliminary projects facilitating the formation of the centre.' Angus went on to ask, 'Any applications?'

Walter's response was instantaneous. He obviously knew about this opportunity in advance. 'I've talked to Dickey about an acid-rain project I'd like to start at Easter. It would investigate the weathering of limestone rocks in the Dolomite Mountains, Italy.' I was taken completely aback, though distantly recalling having discussed the idea with Walter when he had admitted his primary motivation was to help fund a visit to a friend in Central Europe. What surprised me, but should not have, was that he *already* knew about Dickey's interest in rock weathering and, consequently, hoped for his support of this research programme. So relevant a topic was likely to be funded (beside the social visit!).

I was kicking myself for having missed this opportunity. Although I was also aware of Dickey's interest in such work, I did not have the guile to try to exploit it. *And* I had given Walter all the background information necessary to underpin this request! I had been outflanked, once again, by a more skilful operator! He said that a detailed programme, including fieldwork intended during the Easter break, had been submitted to Professors McTaggart and Bland. Angus and Dickey agreed, subject to a satisfactory report on the completed work, that Walter could claim up to £350 expenses. The deal had already been struck. Walter exuded smug satisfaction.

John Bland then seized his opportunity, requesting finance for a late summer visit to two French institutes that were well-known for polymer research. He would find out about the recycling of plastic waste, to start his future research contributing to pollution reduction. Clearly, this deal had *not* been agreed in advance, and Angus was unprepared, procrastinating while deciding how to respond.

Dickey had no such qualms. 'What's fair for one applicant must be fair to others.'

Our chairman could not easily disagree with a generous fund sponsor and, slightly grudgingly, granted a similar sum, which was to be subject to the usual *LU travel expense rules*.

John started explaining his inability to go at Easter because he was moving his ageing parents into sheltered accommodation. Angus cut short this intervention and, wishing to depart Vermontwards as soon as possible, confirmed the decision quickly.

I got my interruption in promptly, in the microsecond pause following the chairman's token mention of item six, any other business, and before closing with, 'Thank you all for attending.' With nothing to lose by lodging a similar claim, I stated, 'Mr Chairman, I'd also like to apply for finance to attend the Global Warming Conference in Sweden after Easter. I haven't got the details yet, but I'll provide all information required by tomorrow. Unlike the others, I didn't know travel financing would be considered today.'

While Mr Chairman worked out how to proceed, Walter spoke up: 'I think this is outside the scope of *our* [really?] centre…' There was no surprise there; opposition had appeared.

To retain any credibility, I had to counter this argument forcefully: 'First, we've not defined the scope of the centre… *yet*… as far as I'm aware. Second, my student, Mohamed, is working on reducing emissions from power stations, which has everything to do with climate change obviously.' I paused, glaring at Walter, for emphasis. '*I* wasn't told that travel money was available today, though Dr Thompson seems to have been prepared, *in advance*. I'm applying now because my attendance at this conference will promote the centre's work.'

John continued, 'My family problems are becoming urgent. This vacation—'

The chairman reasserted his authority thus, 'We can't deal with this now, as we've insufficient information. John, I must delegate this funding decision to you, after you've seen Bill's full application.'

John nodded, which Angus took as agreement. The meeting ended abruptly after my unwelcome coda, and Angus' departure with wishes of, '*Bon voyage!*' I left with Dickey, but, due to my teaching duties, I could not discuss with him my plan to attend the Swedish conference. Instead, we walked to the car park, where he got into his familiar, highly polished Morris Minor. As I returned to Bond College, I passed Walter, getting into a red Ford Fiesta.

He enquired, 'Have you come to admire my new car? At least, it's new to me. I've wanted one for some time. See you later.'

No reply came to mind.

He drove away, accelerating unnecessarily and noisily, only to brake sharply at the exit. I noted that the registration number included the letters 'QS' and three consecutive numbers.

○

At our usual lunch table, I gave Doug the all-important marks list, and asked briefly how I might persuade the last few recalcitrant students to make a final effort.

With this topic exhausted, he demanded, 'Now, Bill, tell all! What about your meeting?'

Without comment, I twisted round to show him my back.

'No daggers visible, that I can see! Congrats! But that's not the whole story. Come clean and tell all!'

I put a positive spin on my account, emphasising that all decisions could only be temporary, until LU *officially* recognised the centre. I also mentioned, perhaps slightly optimistically, that I hoped to get funding to attend a conference in Sweden over Easter, and might be away.

He responded, 'I must race over to give the dean your marks and others. See you later. We'll talk more about the centre... then.' He hesitated briefly before handing me a newspaper I recognised as the local rag, *The*

South of Scotland Sustainer, which he read for local sports coverage. With a distinctly odd look, he left, saying, 'Cheers, for now.'

I took the newspaper, for later perusal, doubting that its contents would interest me much, being a sporting philistine. (What sports interested Philistines? Or did anti-cultural activities fully occupy their leisure time?)

○

That early afternoon was busy, starting with my last 2.57 course lecture. Having been over-optimistic about timing earlier in the term, I now struggled to finish within the allotted schedule, while still being sure I had covered the complete syllabus. Having anticipated this possibility when setting the examination questions, I already had ensured that all answers required only material from the earlier lectures of the course. (Lecturers prefer not to admit publicly to shortcomings in their presentations. I would not admit *to anyone* this timing misjudgement.) It was a gruelling hour, after which I believed I had just about fulfilled all my obligations.

The following hour was an optional feedback session, allowing the same class to raise their problems with me. More than half the students chose to remain, evidence of growing apprehension about the approaching 'examination festival'. While some difficulties were discussed, I believed that, either from my lectures or recommended reading, most of them had understood the chemical theory covered in my course.

Afterwards, approaching the coffee room, I met The Tsar outside John Bland's private laboratory, where four large gas cylinders were partially blocking the corridor.

'Aft'noon, Dr Green. D'you know where's t'Prof, please?' he enquired.

'Prof told me he's taking some leave and might not be in until after Easter,' I explained. It seemed politic not to mention that he was moving his parents into a care home.

"E's asked me to put these 'ere four cylinders in 'is lab, as soon as possible, but I can't leave them trolleys. We need 'em all the time. I don't know what to do.'

I commiserated and suggested that the cylinders be left in the room. 'That's the best idea. OK, will do!'

After the two hours of teaching, I was tired: recent stresses and strains were taking their toll. The biscuits and tepid, brown liquid (was it *tea* or *coffee?*) on offer in the coffee room did little to revive me. Afterwards, I returned to my office and slumped at my desk. *Right then, I had to* decide if I had sufficient courage to ring Beth, who should be home by now. I stared at the phone, pointlessly willing it to ring. It remained silent. So, I dialled *her* number and got an almost immediate reply.

'Yes?' The strange voice took me aback, having expected either Beth or her mother to answer.

'Er... may I speak to Miss Wilkinson, please?' I asked.

'No! She's out. Try again later. Bye.' She was abrupt, but I still had no idea who she was.

I replaced the handset gingerly, feeling as if the phone had bitten me.

Confused by this unhelpful response and with no plan B, I opened Doug's newspaper. At first, its contents excited no immediate response in my dulled brain. Then, suddenly, the reason for Doug's odd look when handing me this paper became absolutely clear. The devastating headline hit me, like an accurate, hard punch to the solar plexus. I was so angry that it took what seemed like an age to summon sufficient courage to read the offending article.

The headline was 'New Environmental Laboratory Established in Linkirk University'. Dr Walter Thompson, credited as 'speaking exclusively to our science correspondent', explained that the research undertaken in this new centre of excellence would make important contributions to pollution reductions, etc. It would be part of the LU School of Chemistry and planning would be overseen by the 'highly respected Professor Angus McTaggart'. Dr Richards, an eminent scientist, who had recently moved to the district, would add his wealth of experience to the research. The article strongly implied, without explicitly stating, that the centre would be directed by Dr Thompson, who was evidently its instigator. My name was not mentioned.

From this press release, it was obvious I could expect to take little, more probably *no*, effective role in future centre management. Walter's guile had effectively swept me aside. The timing of this article, apparently set up *before* Angus's departure, made it difficult to guess how much support he had given his protégé, but I had to assume his tacit approval of its content. Consequently, it now appeared that *the centre*, which I had proposed and promoted, was unlikely to benefit *my* career. From then on, I should expect only minor roles (if any) in its development and would be subject to the whim of Walter's decisions, as *de facto* centre director (which was a horrible thought). My ambitions at LU had been effectively destroyed by this strategic takeover, leaving me with no ideas about what I could, should, might or ought to do next, if anything.

I started rereading the article, but became rapidly too angry to continue; I was not *that* masochistic. Wistfully, I recalled Doug's words of wisdom during my first lunch in the university, which were something like, 'Be sure that *you* exploit *your own* ideas in *your own* interests and make sure that nobody else purloins *your* best inspirations.' I then saw, very clearly but too late, that my *first big idea* had been hijacked ruthlessly. I sat there dazed, as if from mild dose of anaesthetic, while those inbuilt mental-recovery processes that deal with personal catastrophes worked whatever magic they could, to comb out the knots and tangles in my chaotic brainwaves. All academic aspirations, ambitions and hopes for the future had been annihilated at a stroke, leaving my mind blank.

I have no idea how long I sat immobilised in a state of shock-induced paralysis, but, afterwards, in an ill-judged reflex, I repeated the call to Beth, without expecting a response, but I got one.

I recognised her Mother's precise tones, saying, 'Good afternoon.'

'May I speak to Miss Wilkinson, please?' I requested.

'She's not in just now. May I say who called?'

'I'll try again later. Er... thank you.' Could it be that she had not recognised my voice? Or had stress made my voice unrecognisable?

It was now after 6.00pm, but I felt no hunger. While a beer would have been welcome, drinking might have led to excess, which was unwise in this mood. Time for reflection was essential, but only after my brain had resumed rational thought processes. Perhaps going out into the fresh, cold evening air might help me to face up to recent events. Afterwards, I could start reviewing how to build an acceptable future by perhaps salvaging something from the sudden and total wrecking of both my personal life and university career. Could I bear to be 'Directed' by Walter? Did I want to stay in Linkirk – without Beth? Where else could I go and what to do when I got there? My options were few and unknown. I wondered, *Night is allegedly darkest before the dawn, but is it?*

I decided to take that walk and, without conscious intention, I found myself walking the riverside path leading to the open parkland in front of Beth's home. Realising this, I decided that a chance encounter would not be very different from the hitherto unproductive phone calls. A park seat gave me a good view of her house and prompted happy memories of past visits there, though my mind remained reluctant to address that blank future. Again, self-pity reasserted its baleful influence. I sat until, feeling cold, I decided to go home, to perhaps have some supper and if Doug felt like chatting, seek his advice. His remarkable ability to find alternative and novel perspectives on almost any problem, ideas that never occurred to me, might start me thinking positively again. By giving me that newspaper, he had shown awareness, even sympathy for my miserable plight.

Glancing again at Beth's home, I noticed curtains being drawn, but was too distant to see by whom. Stiff and cold, I got moving only slowly and chose the route directly past *her* front door as the shortest way home. The Wilkinsons' car was parked in its usual place, evoking painful memories, and just behind it was a red Ford Fiesta. *A red Ford Fiesta!* For a moment, I was convinced that I was suffering hallucinations; this must be a mirage, conjured up in an overloaded and malfunctioning brain. Inspection, however, showed its registration to be 'QS' with three consecutive numbers, leaving no possible doubt that this was Walter's 'new' car. I saw, suddenly and with a terrible clarity, that – in both personal and professional aspirations – Walter had *completely* supplanted me. I was the comprehensive loser. Unhappily, I recalled Beth's tendency to always give Walter the benefit of any doubt. She had known him since childhood and, whenever he was mentioned, she invariably had shown sympathy for his problems. Just then, I could believe that that sympathy had become, or might always have been, a deeper emotion. I was doubly defeated, in romance and in academia. I had no future in this place. The darkest predawn had just become even blacker!

The furious yapping of the horrible dog heralded the approach of the prying neighbour, making it urgent for me to withdraw rapidly and anonymously. Nobody need know I had been here, and the prospect of being seen as a stalker could not be contemplated. As I walked past *her house* quickly, the door opened, and, in the light, I clearly recognised both Beth and Walter, the latter taking her arm courteously to help her down those steep steps from the front door. An unheard comment brought laughter and they got into the Ford Fiesta together. The car started and departed, again with excessive initial acceleration; it was difficult for me to watch, now that 'the tide was flowing into my eyes', metaphorically speaking. The noisy canine and nosy owner hastened my departure. In the dark, I could be sure that nobody recognised me; I was only a solitary man on a path.

◎

My office was warm, and, back at my desk, I pushed aside the papers demanding attention that was currently unavailable. My sandwich, a supper substitute, was tasteless (it could have been filled with cotton wool), and the fizzy drink was sweet, while lacking any redeeming fruity taste. Without conscious decision, the card game appeared on the computer screen, but every attempt at puzzle-solving was spectacularly unsuccessful, confirming that logical reasoning was presently beyond my capabilities. I switched off the machine, but continued to gaze at its blank screen.

I remembered Walter saying at the meeting (was it only *that* morning?) that he intended to visit Italy during the Easter vacation. Consequently, it seemed that any further attempts to contact Beth should wait until after he had gone, although the decision as to whether or not this was worth trying could await my brain resuming its normal duties. It also would interest me to know exactly what research Walter planned to do in the Dolomites. It was, after all, my original suggestion that the area could be suitable for the type of project he outlined to me. If I could find out his exact plans, the information might prove useful later. (It was!)

Just then, in the almost deserted building, I could repeat my earlier raid on John's insecure hoard of confidential information, and perhaps learn the details of Walter's 'Italian project'. The key was still 'hidden', making my entry into this private domain, or safe archive, just as easy as previously. With the door relocked, I surveyed John's 'chamber of *chaotic* chemistry'. Unfortunately, The Tsar's earlier visit had increased my difficulties considerably. He had left all four heavy metal cylinders *unsupported* in front of the filing cabinets from which I hoped to 'liberate' temporarily Walter's research proposal. (Here, the *Staff Handbook's* regulations were of academic *disinterest*; these stated, 'Except when being moved by designated staff, gas cylinders must always be *securely* retained upright by the fittings provided for this purpose.') Mindful of the serious injury that I could suffer if one or, worse, two or more of these heavy monoliths should topple, I dragged the cylinders carefully away from the filing cabinets, onto the small remaining area of uncluttered floor. Breathless from this considerable effort, I searched the filing cabinets and easily found the papers sought. After a quick visit to the photocopier, the file was replaced precisely into its former position.

The difficult bit came next. I could not remember exactly where each cylinder had stood originally, because it seemed unlikely that anybody would ever notice relatively minor position changes (assuming my unauthorised entry remained unsuspected). Nevertheless, restoring the room to its appearance when I had entered was tricky. The badly worn wooden floor was uneven, increasing the inherent instability of these heavy narrow cylinders; standing them upright required careful manipulation. When first moving them, I had not noticed their instability, but then saw bits of squashed rubber on the floor. To return each cylinder to its former position, I had to reposition these rubber wedges beneath each, to fill in the irregularities of the floor. It appeared that this unreliable stabilisation method was often used here. It was dangerous to say the least! Nevertheless, after covering my tracks, I felt distinctly uneasy. It was possible, even probable, that my activities had left the cylinders in less stable states than after The Tsar had delivered them. Such laboratory practices were dangerous, indeed foolhardy. I had done my best, and John surely must be well aware of these hazards. After all, the risk arose directly from his flouting of safety rules.

I hid the photocopied pages, the trophies I'd obtained through great effort, beneath my filing cabinet. I did not have sufficient concentration to read them just then, but it was good to know that they were available for later examination. Physically and mentally exhausted, I was glad to go home. Perhaps this had been the worst day of my life.

When I arrived at the flat, Doug was out, which, thankfully, deferred any possibility of discussions tonight. Once in bed, I fell immediately into a deep and dreamless sleep.

Chapter 19

Fourth Thursday in March

SANCTION

a. Express approval

b. Penalty for unacceptable behaviour

For a second day, there was no joy in greeting a new, darker dawn, as yesterday's wretched memories were still persisting. *At that time*, I needed to stop indulging in procrastination and plan a future. Decisions about what to do next *had to* be taken *soon* and *implemented soonest*. My life was in such a mess, with my self-confidence damaged so badly, that it was pointless even to try discussing the situation with Doug. Without priorities, how could he help? First, my problems must be identified, and only then could suitable responses be sought. I would start this introspective exercise with a solitary walk beside Meggett Water, reviewing all aspects of my circumstances in depth, appraising all dilemmas in perspective, thinking up prospects, etc. Perhaps some progress could be achieved before my noon lecture. Doug was not up when I left, after my basic ablutions ('a lick and the hope of better later,' as Mother used to say) and some breakfast.

The bright morning was ideal for exercising body and mind. Hints of spring were in the air, with new-season blooms – daffodils in profusion – giving bright splashes of colour. On the riverside path, I soon passed Linkirk Green, which was being patrolled already by dog owners ambling about while their pets self-exercised much more vigorously by intermittently walking, trotting, running and sniffing. Involuntarily, I glanced towards Beth's home, which showed no sign of life; its stillness markedly contrasted with the surge of emotions that flooded my brain with resurfacing memories.

On leaving town, I began to think constructively about my future, considering every reasonable option before attempting to work out what to do next. Recently, vaguely suicidal thoughts had briefly flitted through my mind, but only at the times of my worst depression: I was not seriously contemplating *that* mode of escape (yet). But this lovely morning, with its spring-brings-renewal promise, helped reduce tension. Right then was the chance to apply my scientific training to appraise all problems critically – including determining what had gone wrong, what was intolerable, etc. – and afterwards confront the big question: how can I relaunch my career? In theory, this was straightforward, but, in practice, it is not easy to confront calamity calmly, coming after catastrophe.

Surveys of my predicament all converged towards the same conclusion: my situation here was now intolerable. I could not remain in Linkirk. I must move on *soon*.

The previous day's newspaper report had destroyed my confidence in LU's management, particularly the lack of fairness in appointments. If I was not competing with colleagues openly, with equality of opportunity, then I had to leave soon. The centre, my idea, had been snatched away by Walter's takeover bid, apparently with the tacit, if not partisan, support of the school director. Who had arranged the newspaper publicity, Walter or Angus? Why had it been timed to appear immediately after Angus's departure? Realistically, I had to accept that Walter, with or without Angus's connivance, had achieved his (perhaps *their*) objective. *I could not, I just would NOT* continue to work with Walter. Clearly, he was enjoying fast-track promotion, while I was apparently a slow-lane subordinate. A career with Walter lording it over me would be intolerable, as he could arbitrarily exploit his seniority at will.

If the centre prospered, could I find myself a research niche by colonising a corner of it? This was most unlikely and probably untenable, even in the short term. Alternatively, I could move from environmental research into a different field. Realistically, this was extremely unlikely to yield results sufficiently rapidly for me to demonstrate significant academic achievements *before* the forthcoming annual review of my probationary lectureship. If changing horses in midstream failed, I would thereafter be unemployed, unless I was exceptionally lucky (a commodity in short supply!). In this intolerable situation, I must depart Linkirk – soonest!

My chances of securing an academic job were negligible, with very few lectureships being available. My chances of securing one would not be improved by having resigned in my first year, which was a poor career strategy. How could I answer the inevitable question at an interview (assuming there was one!) of 'Why are you changing jobs so soon?' I had only just started independent research, published very few scientific articles reporting my own research as lead author, and had little experience of supervising students. There was also the problem of references, which perforce would have to come from my present bosses. What could John Bland say to support my applications? I preferred not to speculate. Angus, as a senior academic and a powerful force in university politics, could easily make or break my career prospects, while still smiling in my direction. I was pessimistic about the support I would get in any confidential reference that he might write, particularly after opting out from what was evidently fast becoming *his* centre.

Perhaps a more reasonable strategy would be to restart my career from scratch, admitting openly that I had found academia was not for me and move into industry or alternatively seek a job not requiring scientific training. Positions must available, but leaving LU so soon was still not a recommendation.

By this time, I had reached the end of the tarmac path, but the popular riverside walk continued as a rough and unmade rocky track, passing close to Meggettglen Castle. This building, the dark sunlit stone, looked even more menacing from this low viewpoint. Pleasant memories of a walk here with Beth last term were soured by recent events, particularly the intrusive image of Walter joking with her on the steps of her home last evening. I felt a surge of anger against my tormentor, missed my footing and stumbled off the path, sliding down steep rocks. Grasping a small tree, I narrowly avoided falling into Meggett Water, which was deep and fast flowing at this bend. With nobody in sight, my fall went unobserved. I could have injured myself on the rocks below, and been swept away by the turbulent water or even drowned. This accidental slip had come close to solving all my problems! As it was, one leg was badly scraped and bruised. I sat on a convenient patch of dry grass to recover. How easily accidents can happen!

How easily accidents can happen! Walking on rocky, uneven ground can be hazardous. Spontaneously, this truism triggered mental images of a detailed scenario (evidently lurking, already fully formed, in my subconscious) that might resolve my present troubles. If Walter was to suffer an accident during his fieldwork, many, even most, of my recent disappointments could disappear. For example, if he was seriously incapacitated, a new centre director would be required, and I already knew of one willing, well-qualified candidate! It was comforting, sitting uncomfortably on the grass recovering from shock, to indulge in a little daydreaming and muse about the possible benefits (to me) that might flow from an unfortunate serious injury to my colleague, while working alone in the Dolomites. Gone would be all the tension inherent in our strained collaboration. Also, while he was incapacitated, I could remain in Linkirk, pursuing my academic career as planned. I was overwhelmed by the possibility that one unfortunate fall could resolve so many, even all, of my problems. *Could such an accident easily happen?*

Walter had claimed experience as a mountaineer, a skill that must reduce his chance of an accident while working in the mountains. Nevertheless, his implied intention to work *alone* would increase his danger. Just then, my busy subconscious prompted that, if, by chance (of course!), I also happened to be travelling *alone* in Europe at that time, I might arrive just where and when he was doing his fieldwork (a *planned* coincidence). The likelihood of such a 'chance' encounter might, of course, be increased markedly if I could use the information already obtained, though not yet read, in my hidden copies of Walter's plans. And nobody, not even me *yet*, knew *my* plans. If I could contrive a plausible alibi, 'proving'

I was elsewhere at the critical time, while still managing a clandestine visit to Walter's worksite, I might be able to engineer an accident. That would solve most (perhaps even all) of my immediate problems! These musings left me quite light-headed. As usual, daydreaming was more enjoyable than planning. Noticing other walkers approaching, I got up.

While returning to the real world, I was horrified by the ease with which I had calmly considered the possibility of eliminating Walter. On the other hand, my own problems were real enough. With my mind in overdrive, I walked only slowly due to bruising, my uneven gait recalling Roger Master's lameness after his accident. I had not seen him since his unskilled 'help' in laboratory clearing, which was a timely reminder that not everyone survives in what I now saw as the *academic jungle*.

Despite the best of intentions, my thoughts compulsively and repetitively returned to re-examine critically 'The Walter Accident Scenario'. My portrayals were highly sanitised versions of possible events, viewed theoretically (as befits an academic), excising all pain, suffering and bloodshed. Its essential feature was that, if some fatal catastrophe befell Walter while working alone in a dangerous place, no one would think of blaming an (as yet unspecified) 'accident' on anyone (me). I would learn about it only later in Linkirk and express suitable apparent shock. Even if I had 'helped' the accident, I could not be implicated if my alibi were sufficiently robust.

When contemplating this fictitious fatal fall, my emotions were not greatly troubled by my conscience. Walter had been consistently ruthless in promoting his career at my expense, and had destroyed so recently my reasonable expectation that our rival claims for advancement should be decided on merit alone. Clearly, the academic playing field at LU was askew, and I now knew that either he or I must find alternative employment, *or otherwise vacate the scene, one way or another*.

In this imagined resolution of my problems, I justified any possible recourse to violence against Walter, because I was convinced that he was also personally responsible for ending my relationship with Beth. This aspect generated untold anguish and underlay my wish to devise the most crushing revenge I could imagine. The possibility of hiding my role in any injury I might succeeded in inflicting on Walter was an attractive feature.

Nobody else need ever know I was involved, and the prospect of getting away with it is almost a motto for morality in modern civilisation. I do not naturally resort to violence to resolve difficulties, but, this time, some *red line* had been crossed. I found myself willing to use *any* method to avenge my misery, hoping such actions would also restore my prospect of fair and open academic advancement.

I knew my plan was technically *homicide*, but if my role was effectively concealed, any 'accident' would be regarded as a just consequence of Walter's blatant risk-taking doing solitary fieldwork in a dangerous place. Before deciding to visit Walter abroad, however, I would have to devise a plan disconnecting me entirely from any possibility of direct involvement. The essential feature was the unbreakable alibi, placing me at an impossibly distant location throughout the critical time, while also maintaining the fiction that I could not know where Walter was.

When musing about fixing an incident, I never considered overt acts of murder, such as shooting or stabbing my quarry, blowing him up, or using any of the bloody methods shown in films and seen nightly (as *entertainment*) on TV. However, no detailed plan could be made in advance because the situation in which we would meet was, as yet, unpredictable. My decisive actions would have to be worked out pragmatically, at the last moment, which was clearly a planning weakness. When thinking of methods, I saw myself untying the rope that provided security for my victim while he was suspended on a cliff collecting rock samples, or triggering a landslide of heavy rocks just above his workplace. In such situations, I would not see my adversary and my actions would effectively sweep him from my view forever. First, immediately, I must decide whether or not I would seriously attempt *Waltericide* (or perhaps *Thompsonicide?*). If the answer was yes, then my first essential task was devise that unbreakable alibi.

○

The staff dining room was fairly empty, with term terminating, and I saw neither Doug nor any other friend. Instead, during lunch, I reread the newspaper article on the centre carefully, and, although I started calm, my blood pressure rose as I ingested its contents. *No*, I had not misjudged Walter's duplicity, and my wish to administer retributive justice rose by several quantum jumps. But, before attempting his ultimate downfall (literally), I had to put myself in a position to stage a convincing 'accident'. This afternoon would be a busy.

I adjourned to the library, where I considered how to conceal my movements so effectively that nobody would even *think* of connecting me with Walter's mysterious, ultimately, tragic accident or disappearance. The most effective alibi is not recognised as such. Perusal of maps showed quickly that my initial idea of attending the Swedish conference could not adequately conceal a clandestine visit to the Dolomites. It would be impossible to travel, briefly and anonymously, over 1,500 miles; do the deadly deed; and pop back unobserved. My fanciful homicidal plan seemed to be impracticable.

So, the unwelcome alternative of leaving LU was considered next. The jobs-vacant columns showed only two chemistry posts, for which my qualifications were quite unsuitable. My chances of moving to a different university were realistically zero, without strong support from whomsoever would agree to back me as a referee, which was *not* a foregone conclusion. My outlook was becoming bleaker.

Despondent, I searched the journals for notices of suitable conferences. To my surprise, joy and a surge of optimism, I learned that the First Science Initiative for Chemical Help in Environmental Restoration (1st SICHER) would take place just after Easter at the Bavarian-Munich University. The science was directly relevant to my research plans, so, my conscience clear, I could present a strong case to John, requesting his support and claiming my attendance was essential. I was less certain he would remember and implement the funding arrangement, but I must be persuasive. The essential feature of this conference (which was strictly relevant to my ulterior agenda) was the location in South Germany, not far from the Dolomites. A critical uncertainty was whether the dates coincided with Walter's planned fieldwork, which I hoped to learn later. My other problems were that the registration date had passed and delegate numbers were limited.

○

Once back in my office, Mohamed came in, concerned about some of his experiments. I was equally puzzled. We tried to work out if his equipment had malfunctioned and whether these results could be trusted. Finally (either defeated or procrastinating), I told him to repeat the experiments *exactly* as before.

He obliged. 'What I do if result is again same?'

'We talk about it tomorrow. Sometimes experiments go wrong. Take the equipment to The Tsar, if you like. An overhaul might take all day. You decide.' I was firm. I needed to plan, but only after studying Walter's research programme carefully.

Mohamed departed reluctantly, allowing me to read the photocopied schedule of Walter's intended fieldwork. Helpfully, a sketch map located his work site precisely. He would collect rock, pebbles and water samples from a small river in a remote mountain valley to analyse and find out if and how acid rain was damaging this pristine environment. Personally, I doubted whether this project would obtain any useful scientific information whatsoever. However, my views were irrelevant: he had, after all, convinced Angus and Dickey of the excellence of his idea. What he did not know was that, if my plan succeeded, his samples would never be analysed. But my imagined 'accident' scenarios were quite inappropriate; Walter was not going to climb the huge cliffs that are the spectacular feature of the Dolomites. Later, I would have to contrive another type of accident, exploiting whatever local opportunities I could find.

Happily and fortuitously, the timings of Walter's fieldwork and the 1st SICHER conference coincided. He planned to start four days of sample collecting on the day of the conference dinner. If I attended the evening event, it might be possible leave early, drive south overnight from Munich to the valley, and confront Walter on the second morning of his fieldwork. In principle, when and if I had succeeded in staging the planned (perhaps fatal) 'accident', I could leave the remote area unobserved and rejoin the conference in the afternoon. Once back, I could draw attention to myself by contributing to discussions and be remembered as an active participant. I was unlikely to know many of the delegates, so there was no reason for anyone to recall my absence. My temporary, overnight truancy would pass unnoticed. This approach offered an effective alibi that would, I hoped, never be questioned. The details could be worked out later, but, to execute this plan, I must start making arrangements at once.

I phoned John Bland, whose secretary, said 'He might be in later.' There was no surprise there.

I rang the Munich conference office, and the person who answered stated, 'The closing date for register has passed.'

I attempted persuasion: 'I know, but I'm *very* keen to come. Might I attend, if I pay a late fee and find my own hotel? Please?'

The reply was, 'I ask, but I think answer is *no*. I phone soon.'

To use the wait profitably, I prepared the necessary travel grant application. Estimating fares and hotel costs, the sum required was £350, coincidentally that allocated to Walter and to John himself. Surely he could not refuse me? I would pay any shortfall, but equally might gain a small profit. The application form filled in, I awaited the reply from Munich. To pass the idle moment, *that game* appeared (apparently effortlessly) on the computer screen, distracting me from the developing situation. The games went badly: two were won only with difficulty and four unpromising starts abandoned.

On hearing John's voice in the corridor, I followed him into his office.

'Good afternoon, John,' I said.

'Oh! Er... it's you, Green, er... Bill. I'm rather busy now on personal business,' John replied.

'It won't take a moment. This is important to me... and you did agree.'

'If you say so. What did I agree? I don't remember agreeing—'

'At the steering-committee meeting, I asked for conference expenses...'

'Yes. It's vaguely familiar. Norway, wasn't it? No! You're going to Sweden.'

'Actually, I my plans have changed to a conference in Munich—'

'That's right. I'm remembering... I think you'll enjoy Sweden when you're there. It's many years now since I've been... Was it in Gothenburg? It's expensive...'

'I wondered if you'd mind if I change my plans to Munich...'

'Yes. Yes. The art gallery's interesting...'

'Thank you, John. I appreciate your help. I wish you well with your... family problems. Would you mind signing this funding application, please?'

I put two copies in front of him, and, still vaguely bemused, he signed both. I retained one carefully for my files.

It seemed pointless trying to explain the change of plan. I could fairly claim to have told John that my destination had changed to Munich and that he had agreed. The trivial fact that he had not listened to what I said need not be emphasised later in my report. The fact that nobody knew I was going south rather than east could make it slightly less probable that any alibi I fabricated would be queried later.

Back at my desk, the phone was still silent. An impulse to call Beth, to talk things over, withered and died when I recalled her, apparently happily, going somewhere with Walter last evening. Moments later the phone did ring and I was soon confirming plans to go to Munich. It appeared that in the unexplained special circumstances, Professor Egger had agreed to register me for the conference, on receipt of a fairly large late fee (in cash). I should write to introduce myself and give my address while in Munich, and I would be a welcome delegate. It now appeared my homicide plan was potentially feasible, and Walter's fate might already be sealed.

○

Reviewing the afternoon's work, I was amazed at the ease with which I had manoeuvred myself into a situation from which I could, in theory, confront Walter during his fieldwork, while 'officially' at a conference, perhaps 200 miles distant. How to exploit that confrontation would have to be worked out later.

Meanwhile, I might discourage any later questioning of my fabricated alibi, by giving the impression that I had already definitely decided to leave Linkirk and, therefore, had no motive to pursue or, indeed, to harm a colleague. Angus was away, John had not listened to my plans and there was no point in talking to Walter! That left Dickey and Doug as friends who might offer advice, though this could raise the thorny moral problem of whether I had implicated them if later I staged that 'accident' involving my newly appointed director. Without an easy solution to this quandary, I still thought that sympathetic discussions with friends might yet redirect me towards some more moderate course of action. Helpful ideas, transforming my plight, could even make a planned accident unnecessary. It was better to examine every possibility before committing myself to the hazardous uncertainties of launching a physical attack on my enemy.

A chat with Dickey would be welcome, so I phoned him.

Emma said, 'He's just popped down to the university library.'

He seemed unsurprised when I found him there. 'I thought our paths might cross. Let me just...' He wrote furiously, checking facts in a large reference tome. 'That's all I want.' He banged the book closed. 'I know what you need to talk about. Don't look so surprised... I read the papers too.'

We went outside to sit in the fading sunshine before he continued, 'You've been treated disgracefully. I don't warm to Walter, I don't even like him much, but to make him *director* like that! It's just not fair. I guess that's what's on your mind. Before you say anything, let me say that I'm only too familiar with this sort of arbitrary treatment. I was keen to return to university research, but now I'm wondering if I want to face all that hassle. It's reminded me of the downside, *backside* more like, of academia! Perhaps I'd be better off growing massive marrows for our village show.'

At last, I was allowed to talk. 'Thanks for your support, Dickey. I don't want to cry on your shoulder, and I'm not surprised you're equally shocked by this so-called centre management. It's more like manipulation. I'm annoyed. No, I'm furious! Even so, I've asked for money to attend a conference in Munich. John signed my application, but maybe he won't remember. Perhaps you'll support me later, if necessary?'

'I'd be glad to. You deserve some benefit from your idea. Enjoy the conference.'

'That's precisely what I intend to do. I might learn something. Perhaps I'll also enquire about job vacancies abroad. I can't face the prospect of staying here much longer. I think it's time I moved on. My big question is this: where to?'

We indulged ourselves by critically reviewing the recent shortcomings of the LU management.

Responding to a direct question, Dickey agreed that I had no realistic prospect of early promotion here, finishing with, 'My view, for what it's worth, is that your best bet is to go elsewhere… and soon.'

It having become too cool to sit outside, we went our separate ways, with Dickey wishing me luck (which, for me, was in short supply). As it was too late to book my trip to Munich, I went home to see if Doug was prepared to talk. I guessed he was already very well aware of my recent setbacks, having read that newspaper before giving it to me and noticing my tendency to keep my own company. Doubtless, with his insights into the working of university politics, he had anticipated how the centre would develop and that my former optimism had been unrealistic.

I was already deep in Doug's debt as a supportive, generous friend. He had listened patiently to my many naïve attempts to make sense of the torturous, always secretive and invariably inexplicable management practices prevailing at LU, at least in the School of Chemistry. By then, I was fully aware that the Professors ultimately fixed everything important, without the obligation to justify their impenetrable decisions. Doug's cynical views of academia, based on his own painful experiences, were often unconventional and usually forthright, but his advice was always sensible. I wanted, needed, some of it right then and knew he would do his best to advise me. But could he help this time? I supposed he might review my remaining options, following Walter's takeover bid. The novel feature was that, at that point and without his input, I was already contemplating actions that must never be disclosed: *homicide had to remain my personal secret*. My discussions with Doug would have to focus on my leaving LU and what type of job I could seek. This fallback strategy offered some insurance against failure of my 'Walter-disposal plan'.

Doug's fondness for a good meal gave me the initiative I needed. I shopped, remembering his tastes, and expected him home about 7pm.

'So! It's your birthday?' he enquired.

'No. This is a sort of "early goodbye" meal,' I explained.

'Explain yourself, young Bill.' He was already pouring the Chianti. 'This isn't bad wine. Well done! It's at the right temperature, too.'

'I've not yet thanked you for giving me that newspaper.'

'Thanks are not usual for bad news. And that news was bad; *bad* for you.'

I agreed, 'I read the offending article. Realistically, I can't see any future for me here. I can't, I *won't*, work under *Director* Thompson. I've more or less decided to leave Linkirk. I'd hoped you might advise me.'

'I can't see you needing advice, if your mind's already made up. I've thought about your situation too and, to be blunt, reached much the same conclusion. You've had a raw deal here, Bill, but universities tend to be closed communities and, unless you've patronage – in other words, crawled to or slaved for one of the often distinctly mediocre deities who like being addressed as *Professor*, – you ain't going to get too far. You and me ain't got what it takes to crawl up the greasy pole.'

I was shocked that Doug accepted my total capitulation so readily. After a hard fight for this appointment, I had done my damnedest to establish myself at LU, but just then he seemed to be advising me to drop everything gained without even a token struggle. I supposed this advice to be based on his own disillusionment with the system, and, from experience, he was trying to shield me from the frustrations that had beset his career. The maxim 'don't throw good money after bad' came to mind.

He had always maintained that the promotion system here was unaccountable and impenetrable, stating, 'Decisions about academic advancement are invariably reached behind closed doors within small minds operating personal agendas.'

LU's committees made all appointments, and, because Angus obviously favoured Walter, I could like it or leave.

'My problem is to find supportive referees, if I apply for academic jobs.'

'Why do you want another *academic* job after this? Why not discuss jobs with your friend in industry? Albert, is it? You might persuade him, or rather his firm, to take you on. Chances are you'd be paid more than here. A less congenial job would reward you with a more comfortable life.'

I said I would think about it and described the jobs I'd seen advertised, which were unpromising but nevertheless available. 'May I use your name as a referee, Doug?'

'Of course. No problem. But you really need support from someone with the magic title *professor*. I can't help you much there. What about *Prof.* John?' He saw my surprise. 'I've no idea how much he'd push you, but reference writing requires effort. He's sure to have some old ones, written ages ago for other people, which he'll just dust off and, always assuming he remembers, put in your name. It's much easier than starting from scratch. Depending on the luck of the draw, you might do well.'

Doug's steak was now at the medium-rare state he favoured, and mine was well done (and disapproved of), so we sat down to eat. Serious conversation tends not to enhance gourmet delights, and, to my relief, discussion about my future lapsed.

We talked about our vacation plans.

Doug would spend a week with his parents, attacking overdue repairs to 'stop their home falling down about their ears,' as he put it. The house must be sold soon, but meanwhile his do-it-yourself skills would be tested to their modest utmost. Afterwards, exchequer permitting, he would join a geologist friend in Wales and tag along on a fieldwork course. Although he would not teach, outings in the hills with the students were deemed, '*Great!* I've noticed that places of interest to geologists are usually scenic and good walking country. The trouble is that I'll not lose weight because the food and beer are always too generous.'

I said I would go back home for Easter, but found it difficult to be consistent and avoid inventing unnecessary lies. When he asked about 'that pretty redhead you've been seeing,' I said that plans for Beth to visit Sussex had not yet been finalised due to a possible holiday with her parents. I could not bring myself to tell him that our friendship had, at best, reached breaking point.

I mentioned the possibility of going abroad to a conference, but gave few details. 'I thought about that climate conference in Sweden, but now I'm not so sure.' While avoiding outright falsehoods, I managed to hint that I had no idea where Walter intended to work, to blur any possibility that a later connection might be made between *my* travels and *his* disappearance. After enjoying too much good food and wine, including an 'end of term' whisky, neither of us was particularly receptive.

The live match on the TV was the focus of Doug's evening, and, with beer to hand, he sat snugly on the sofa to soak up sport. Having minimal interest in the entertainment value of grown men brawling over a 'bag of wind', my restless mind flitted between topics requiring *urgent* attention.

I found a map of Europe and estimated the distances between the places featuring in my plans: Linkirk, Sussex, Munich and the Dolomites. I reassured myself again that the latter two were sufficiently close for me to reach Walter's fieldwork site overnight, while maintaining the fiction of never having left the conference. Cash was short, as ever, but, on estimating expenditure and hoping for the travel grant, I decided I could remain solvent – just. I began to pack.

Right then, my *big decision* had to be made; it was my decision alone. Do I confront Walter abroad, with homicide in mind, or do I pursue the safer option by looking for a new career? The confrontation, as I envisaged it, allowed no possibility whatsoever of compromise: either Green or Thompson would prevail in any hostile, violent meeting, remote in the mountains. If my alibi failed, the consequences would be dire, but there was, I believed, the beguiling and tantalising prospect of success. The prospect of restarting my career from scratch was depressing, emphasising my failure and ambitions unachieved. Which alternative offered the better prospect of a worthwhile future?

Neither Dickey nor Doug had offered me any hope that my future career in Linkirk could prosper; they both had agreed, all too easily, that the decision to go elsewhere was my best option. Nevertheless, I found it impossible to accept failure while there was the remotest possibility of staying and prospering here. That 'remotest possibility', however, depended on *my* success in staging the 'accident' that would end forever *my* malign relationship with *my* antagonist. I self-justified these intended actions, destroying my rival's ability to harm, as arising directly from what I would describe as *his* blatant disregard for health and safety rules during fieldwork. This fiction was more acceptable than admitting I would resort to lethal violence and end permanently Walter's hostility to me or anyone else.

Walter's actions in stealing *my* ideas, crawling his way up the academic hierarchy to be the director of *my* centre and replacing me in (what I thought of as *my*) Beth's affections were *crimes* that called for a just response. I was prepared to implement the appropriate retribution myself, though amateurs are not the usual executioners of justice. The legal professionals find, in laying down the letters of the law, far-too-lucrative livelihoods to let lay practitioners participate in punishment. The damage Walter had inflicted on my fledgling career was far too personal and too hidden to give me any hope for redress by legal means. But if I could contrive a façade of disinterest and distance myself from my quarry, the cloak of ignorance would be my effective alibi, out from which I could emerge to dispense natural justice anonymously. It would be much cheaper and, for me, more satisfying than legal action. I sought no payment or reward other than the possibility of pursuing my preferred profession in peace, on a planar playing pitch.

The image of Beth, *evidently happy*, leaving her home beside Walter chose that moment to resurface, triggering mental replays of other acutely painful events. Must I accept total defeat? *No!* I would not capitulate. I suppose the critical decision, initiating the sequence of events that had led inexorably to my hostile confrontation with Thompson, was taken at that moment. I thought, *Yes! This is* my *chance to exploit* my *advantage, as Walter had, hitherto, ruthlessly exploited* his. May the best man win!

My sleep, when it came eventually, was disturbed. I imagined myself on a high ledge above a sheer precipice looking at a rope tied securely to a firmly embedded wooden peg. Sounds of hammering came from below, where – somehow – I knew Walter was collecting samples of rock while suspended precariously on the almost vertical cliff. I untied the rope, attached a heavy stone and hurled it outwards into the abyss. There was a sharp cry, scraping sounds and then silence. It was inconceivable that he could have survived the fall, and it might be a long time before anyone found the body in the inaccessible valley below. My dream conveniently avoided any need to confront the messy consequences of my action, and I supposed he had experienced a quick and painless death. By then, I knew that, with a good chance of getting away with it, I was quite prepared to *murder* my enemy, *Thompson.*

Chapter 20

SECOND TUESDAY IN APRIL

STAGE

a. Raised platform facing an audience

b. Extent of an ongoing process

THE BAVARIAN-MUNICH UNIVERSITY EXPRESSED, IN CONCRETE form, the high status assigned to scholarship and learning by successive German governments. The older university institutes – built of light-coloured stone, and dedicated to the pursuit and dissemination of knowledge – had been designed and built on the same grand scale as many other important buildings in Munich. While perhaps not quite as imposing as the Royal Residenz, this home of academia, written in stone, contrasted with many more-modest institutions familiar to me that also aspired to the title 'university'.

After my arrival, I oriented myself by strolling around the campus. The university appeared to be ideally located within the Munich conurbation, beside a main route into the city and near a large park. Some older, large institutes were set well back from the busy road and behind them were open and wooded areas: the Englischer Garten. The newer academic specialities had spilled over into the relatively narrow streets of a built-up area. These disciplines now occupied many of the substantial stone buildings, four or five floors high, which – I supposed – had once been the homes of grandees and successful businessmen. Most had since been transformed skilfully into university institutes and administrative offices. Some, particularly those housing scientific disciplines, retained their fine façades and local ambience, but had been adapted internally as laboratories and research facilities of types that could not have been dreamed of by the original owners or their architects, perhaps a century ago. Technical equipment was visible through some windows. The pavements outside were littered with bicycles, obviously a popular mode of local transport. These were chained to any and every external metal fixture, grille and lamp, despite the many notices prohibiting this. The narrow streets were filled to saturation with parked cars.

Outside one of these repurposed buildings, a prominent sign proclaimed, in large green letters, 'First Science Initiative for Chemical Help in Environmental Restoration'. This somewhat contrived conference title was presumably intended to attract English-speaking participants. My German dictionary translated the acronym SICHER as *safe* or *reliable*, which expressed succinctly the concept of saving the environment (from pollution). Clearly the organisers were exploiting their public-relations expertise, seemingly successfully, judging from the many serious-looking people, presumably 1st SICHER conferees, going towards the registration office. Supporting publicity posters, outlining 'The Mission of the Meeting' (perhaps with overtones of almost religious fervour) also included the conference logo, a *car seatbelt*. Personally, I could not accept that any symbol relating the automobile, even so remotely, could or should be associated with protecting the environment.

The large, bright entrance hall of this Institute of Environmental Sciences, the Standesamt, gave a fleeting first impression of an airport check-in area. This similarity was only superficial: here, the arrangements were strictly temporary, even amateur. Several tables, apparently borrowed from a dining area and covered with green baize, were aligned along one wall and manned, or womanned, by an already harassed-looking Welcome Team, who were busily trying to answer delegates' queries. Other equally preoccupied individuals, probably university staff, added to the confusion here, by their well-meaning efforts to facilitate the bureaucracy inevitable in welcoming the delegates. Most of these frontline volunteers were probably, by then, regretting having agreed or not disagreed sufficiently forcefully to help out at registration. Similarly, the organisers were probably wondering why they had ever decided to host a conference at all. From a queue, I watched the activity – the chaos that was being slowly, slowly disentangled – and made a mental note to avoid this particular chore, should I ever participate in organising a conference.

When my turn to register came, the middle-aged lady at the desk gave me a tired smile, doing her best to retain some warmth in her welcome. She had just answered a prolonged series of questions from my predecessor, who appeared to have little command of either English (the *official* conference language) or German. I apologised for my extremely limited knowledge of her language (mentioning a brief attempt to learn German at evening classes). Her tolerant reply, in good English, only served to remind me of my linguistic inadequacies. I gave my name and an already worn-looking list was consulted.

'You are not on the list.' An expression of weary worry eclipsed her fading smile.

'I rang Professor Egger last week and he agreed to accept my late registration,' I explained.

Another list was consulted. 'Yes, you do exist.'

'That's a relief.'

This time her smile was genuine. 'But you must find your own place to stay. All conference rooms are taken.'

I told her I had made my own arrangements, already found a hotel and was booked in.

There was, my host assured me, 'No problem,' and my registration was accepted.

A badge, displaying my name and affiliation was pinned on my lapel. When meeting another delegate whose name I do not know or, all too often, have forgotten, I find it difficult to break eye-contact to read his/her lapel badge. Should one admit to not knowing a name, by obviously reading their lapel badge, or does one imply that one already knows who they are? I just do not know. (A market opportunity exists for a book on *conference etiquette.*) I was also given the conference pack, a heavy bundle of papers contained in a large green folder emblazoned with 1ˢᵗ SICHER and the logo. This also named prominently the sponsoring firm who had 'generously' donated the folder. (It was cheap publicity. I felt less enthusiastic about their 'generosity' later when the insubstantial folder split apart, depositing its contents into the gutter on a windy day. Not all advertising is effective!)

Wearing my badge, I was transformed from an anonymous private individual into an official conference delegate. Memories and impressions from the few previous conferences I had attended flooded back. I was now an *official* member of this transitory community, licensed to consort with other affiliates of our confraternity, converse with them loudly in public places and gather to form slowly moving gaggles obstructing pavements. More importantly, groups of us would spend long sessions in darkened rooms listening attentively to lectures, or otherwise passing time by dozing, completing crossword puzzles or writing postcards home. During an allotted time interval, one of our group would talk authoritatively on his specialist subject, sometimes addressing only a tiny audience of experts capable, or even pretending to be capable, of comprehending its content. Then it would be the turn of another delegate to enlighten us on whatever different, esoteric topic had attracted his/her expertise. Each could announce important breakthroughs achieved recently in his/her laboratory by what was often referred to along the lines of 'the research school I have the honour to lead'.

Conference presentations could be about virtually any topic that related, however distantly, to the session's theme. Some such discourses purported to identify the most significant environmental problems besetting mankind, often with proposed novel and/or improbable ways of preventing or remedying them. Alternatively, speakers could share their personal views and prejudices, sometimes even betraying limited insights into whichever highly arcane and learned speciality that they claimed expertise in. Some such opinions would be already familiar to regular conference attendees, having previously been aired at one or several prior meetings. The standards of talks ranged from the polished and erudite, as expected from learned Professors who earned their stipend as teachers, to the incompetent, the ill-prepared, the inaudible and the incomprehensible, which were expounded, mumbled or simply read by diverse status-conscious or status-challenged individuals. The stage-time allotted to each speaker was strictly limited to enable most conferees an opportunity to describe – publicly, in the temporary limelight – his/her interesting research, and/or to report scientific advances or opinions to their audiences.

A chair, appointed for each session, is mandated to maintain the official timetable, and his/her most important quality is having the ability to discourage excessive loquaciousness. He/she is also expected to encourage debate after each contribution, accepting questions from the audience that the speaker may or, frequently, may not answer. When silence greets this invitation for discussion, the chair may feel it polite to offer a question themselves, thereby confirming that the talk they have just introduced as 'an important contribution to the subject' was of interest to at least one listener (himself/herself). The speaker, perhaps having travelled far to share this new knowledge with receptive colleagues, could then feel reassured that these efforts had been worthwhile and appreciated. On other occasions, questioning would be recognised easily as further, but ultimately pointless and inconclusive, jousts in long-running battles between entrenched protagonists. Vigorous, sometimes acrimonious exchanges between the speaker and questioner(s), could force a chair to intervene and terminate endless cycles of irreconcilable views. For example, concluding, 'I congratulate our contributors on this fascinating exchange of opinions. I'm sorry, but our time has run out, and everyone interested must continue these discussions in private *elsewhere*. Now, we are privileged to hear Professor [with a barely audible aside of '... pronounce your name?'] Professor Lrrkqx talk to us about...'

○

Before joining *official* activities, I found a coffee bar, thoughtfully provided for the delegates, perhaps also the organisers, to build up strength before or to recover from their registration efforts. The coffee and croissant were most acceptable and were consumed while I perused the large bundle of papers/booklets in the conference pack. A quick scan of the *official* programme (why is *everything* 'official'?) showed the two presentations of greatest personal interest were scheduled to run concurrently tomorrow from 10.45am to 11.15am in rooms A3 and C7. How was it that the most useful lectures were *always* concurrent? Again, two short talks I wanted to hear were scheduled for this afternoon and happened to coincide. I continued searching the programme, marking all items that appeared worth attending. A workshop on 'Writing Grant Applications: Presenting Your Case' was also mentioned. This could be a complete waste of time or might be immensely useful. Time alone would reveal its potential value. I marked it optimistically as a must-see. My talk, my spot in the limelight, would be tomorrow at 2.30pm. Good, I could get it over early!

The table beside me was now occupied by three conferees, who were not exploiting this chance to exchange research ideas or discuss pressing environmental issues. They were entirely preoccupied with recent bad experiences of air travel. Though without any interest, I was treated to a detailed account of the American's recent 'awrrfuul' flight. (Is it the American *voice* or *accent* that penetrates the consciousness so unignorably, or is it from early training in self-assertion?) I found some truth in the old adage that American insularity (which is a misnomer!) about foreign languages explains why English has become the international *lingua franca*. Though, as a beneficiary, I should not complain. Not intentionally eavesdropping, but more of an unwilling listener, I wondered if boundless self-confidence had been the decisive weapon in the 'language war'.

After this intrusion, I studied the busy conference schedule from my alternative perspective, beginning to plan my private excursion. This timetable was the background against which the alibi for my temporary absence to stage Thompson's 'accident' in Italy must be fabricated. Confirmation that the conference dinner was tomorrow, Wednesday, evening fitted well. Thursday would include no formal sessions, but there would instead be visits to local institutes and factories developing pollution-reducing methods of waste treatment (we were to book in advance, please). These arrangements appeared consistent with my outline plans, though the details still needed to be worked out.

O

Lunch in the conference centre promised to be a rather solitary affair. The delegate list included no one I knew personally; this could be an advantage, making my overnight truancy less likely to be noticed. Other names were familiar, but only from reading their research publications. Knowing nobody, I could only recognise individuals by going around and reading (official!) lapel badges. This did not appeal.

I was served a good meal: a flat fillet of pork fried in batter (a *Weiner Art*), with generous helpings of *Frits* (crispy chips) and peas, followed by a fresh apple. The temptation of wine was resisted; instead, there was fruit juice and coffee. With laden tray, I found an unoccupied table, but did not remain alone for long. Other younger delegates had, like me, come here without knowing anyone else and soon a group of six of us were forming friendships that could last a lifetime, or perhaps even until the end of the conference. Introductions were perfunctory; names are not particularly important in such, often transitory, conference friendships. (I refer to my difficulties with remembering people's names as '*nomenelexia*', which is a surprisingly widespread condition, but apparently incurable.) As a truly international group, we simply addressed each other by home country: the two girls came from Spain and Brazil; the other men were Canadian, Swedish and Austrian; while I temporarily became 'Scot'. Everyone spoke adequate English, and were seemingly content to use the *official* language, so I was saved embarrassment by not revealing my linguistic inadequacies.

Given the opportunity, academic groups tend to talk shop and our lively lunchtime conversation, not unexpectedly, mainly concerned our past and anticipated future research. It was highly probable that much discussed now would reappear later in the forthcoming *official* sessions. For us younger, less experienced delegates, chatting in relaxed, small groups during a meal is much more productive than addressing an audience. Such informal exchanges provide valuable confidence-building rehearsals for the real thing later. Many of the most fruitful, also enjoyable, conference discussions take place during meals, even at breakfast or over late-evening beers. Unhurried opportunities for constructive arguments and quality exchanges of ideas between friends can be more enlightening and worthwhile than in the structured formality of *official* sessions. We agreed that the conference format, particularly with large audiences, does not provide the sympathetic environment essential for really valuable exchanges of views. However, colleges, employers and financing staff at conferences, expect their delegates to announce their achievements formally in public. So, whether useful or not, there always is an *official* programme.

Our relatively youthful group enjoyed the illusion of putting the world (of our elders and betters) to rights and entering into the conferential spirit. Real pleasure and camaraderie developed rapidly within our circle, formed because we just happened to sit together for our meal here. Afterwards, it seemed natural for us to move on to the opening session as a friendly sextet. Later, because we knew one another by then, our group maintained its distinct identity, reassembling regularly throughout the conference. Secretly, I hoped that being in this group might later somehow contribute to the effectiveness of my contrived alibi, which was still unplanned.

The opening ceremony, which was to start at 2.00pm prompt, was in the university's Great Hall, colourfully decorated with tasteful displays of flowers and the conference logo. Arriving early, we found seats together in the middle of the hall, with a good view of the stage, on which some uncomfortable-looking chairs awaited the notables who were to open proceedings. These personages arrived punctually and Professor Egger *officially* commenced at 2.02pm with a long address.

He began with, 'I extend the warmest welcome to everybody here present...' and went on to, 'emphasise the importance of the contributions that we could... *No! That* I intend we *will* make to defend and save our only environment... I also hope, indeed *know*, that our deliberations will be profitable...' Opening addresses of similar platitudinous patterns and contents constitute an inevitable part of the *official* opening ceremony of most international conferences. He ended with the usual effusive praise and 'Thanks to all the Organizers', not forgetting his own modest contribution, which it seemed was in organising the organisers, rather than by contributing input himself.

It was then the turn of *Herr Professor Doktor* Feichtnicht, *rector maximus*, or University Boss. His speech reiterated most of the points already made, but in a different sequence. He finished with effusive congratulations on the excellence of the conference organisation as planned by his colleague Professor Egger, who swelled visibly with pride before returning to the rostrum to announce some changed arrangements. Finally, he invited *Herr Rector Maximus* Feichtnicht to introduce the opening lecturer, *Herr Doktor* Fuchs, who it transpired, somewhat unsurprisingly, had formerly been Professor Egger's student.

This plenary lecture was to be, and I quote the programme, 'An important, innovative and insightful presentation, revealing novel facts about the environment.' In content, it proved to be a tedious reiteration of information and ideas that had long been accepted throughout the scientific community, and virtually all its content must have been familiar to everyone in this audience. The insights claimed were not novel, though each concept was presented with enthusiasm that implied the speaker himself had only recently and single-handedly made this significant breakthrough. If he had, he was lagging rearwards of the research advancing the front line. Overall, the lecture contained nothing remotely controversial, other than a clear intention to avoid controversy at all costs, so I switched my attention away from this tedium.

Being comfortable in my seat, with interruptions unlikely and little to distract me other than the boring drone of the speaker to whom I was apparently listening, I let my mind wander. This was a good opportunity to work out how I would, finally, resolve my differences with *Thompson*. My psychological processes interested me; I still tended to avoid admitting, even to myself, that I was contemplating homicide. Was this mental block a ploy to minimise the seriousness and the horror of the actions I contemplated? More worryingly, would I be capable of executing these intentions, if and when an opportunity presented itself? I also noticed that, from this time on, I thought about *Walter* no more, my target was now *Thompson*.

My present situation would enable me, *in theory*, to carry out the dastardly deed without risk of incrimination, always assuming my alibi successfully concealed my truancy. I had chosen a Munich hotel that was not on the conference list, helpfully distancing me from the other delegates and making them less aware of my whereabouts, comings and goings. During Thursday morning, after the conference dinner, delegates would be dispersed widely across local factories and other sites, so that my absence was unlikely to be noticed. Against this background, a detailed plan was taking shape in my mind. The more I thought about it, the more it appealed, and I was thinking about the details when my reverie was interrupted by a burst of applause. Although quite certain that this sort of inconsequential lecture should be banned, rather than encouraged, I joined in the clapping with everyone else.

I was already convinced that, even if the Thompson plan failed, it had been well worth my while coming here. The scientific programme promised to fulfil my best expectations (passing over this pedestrian, pointless, plenary preamble) by widening my overall understanding of environmental science. The enthusiastic discussions with my new acquaintances had reignited my determination to make some personal contributions towards conserving our natural heritage. Already, this meeting had reawakened my academic ambitions, despite recent setbacks.

Every time I thought about my intolerable situation at LU, Thompson appeared as the single insurmountable barrier to all my reasonable ambitions. The anger, resentment and depression I had felt after he had announced himself as centre director, effectively *my boss*, returned in full measure. I would not, could not, accept defeat, with my relegation to be a permanent subordinate, without a fight. Nothing legal that I could do at LU would redress the balance. But here, remote from home, I had a real prospect of permanently removing Thompson's malign influences from my career and my life. True, my plans were potentially fraught with personal danger, but, without reasonable alternatives, the hazardous gamble that I intended to take was my very last resort. I was convinced that *Thompson must be confronted*, we *needed to* resolve our differences, and I *had to accept* the virtual inevitability that this *would* involve violence. The final outcome would be decided between the two of us, alone in that remote mountain valley where he had chosen to work.

The attractive girl sitting beside me, the Spaniard who I now knew as Evita, said 'Now tea cup, Scot? You Schottish do drink tea, like English?'

I agreed, 'Yes. Tea in afternoon is good.'

While going for refreshments before the first official session, I noticed her most attractive smile. Something in it brought Beth to mind and the memory of my recent, devastating loss almost brought on tears. This sudden despair further reinforced my decision to deal with Thompson finally, by fair means or foul, once and for all, for better or for worse – indeed, literally, in all probability, until death did us part...

Chapter 21

SECOND WEDNESDAY IN APRIL

PLAN		
	a.	Procedure for implementing an action
	b.	Map of spatial interrelationships of parts

WEDNESDAY WAS BUSY. I PRESENTED MY RESEARCH TALK DURING the afternoon session: limelight, it's my turn! Afterwards, while nominally listening to the later speakers, I continued planning the logistics of my trip to the Dolomites. My strategy had to be to maximise the advantage of surprise by confronting Thompson unexpectedly when he believed himself quite alone in the wilderness. He certainly would not encounter many people in the remote valley where he had chosen to work. I now knew its precise location, from maps in the file 'borrowed' from John Bland's insecure store. To get there, I had to hire a car, arrive and, after our conflict (assuming my success), leave rapidly *and anonymously*. I estimated the drive time from Munich as about four hours. Locating Thompson, when and if I managed to find the place, and assuming he was there, would require planning that could only be thought through later. The car must be hired that afternoon, but that should be straightforward.

Refining the details of the alibi, to conceal my truancy overnight and early tomorrow, had occupied me throughout both morning sessions. The first talk included mathematical arguments quite beyond my understanding; the endless equations obscured the science. I found nothing novel in the second presentation: *recycling* of research at conferences has been in vogue long before it became a household word and a synonym for waste disposal. So, I turned my imagination to concocting ruses whereby I could implant into the memories of colleagues in our group the certainty that I could not have left Munich during the conference. Later, if necessary, they could substantiate my unbreakable (albeit concocted) alibi, effectively excluding me from all suspicion.

Only one subterfuge capable of achieving this situation had occurred to me so far but, if successful, would suffice. I would *appear* to drink to excess at the Gourmet Dinner, so that my absence on Thursday, if noticed, would appear to be a reasonable recovery period to sleep off a self-induced hangover. However, to drive that far at night safely, I must drink no alcohol whatsoever, remaining absolutely sober after the dinner. To present the intended effect, I had to stage convincingly an overindulgence in the drinks available. This deception could be achieved if I drank only from a private source of coloured water, prepared in advance. While the taste of cold tea does not appeal, its superficial resemblance to whisky made it a suitable substitute to convey the intended illusion.

During this performance, I would appear to become drunk, with my inebriation increasing during the evening. This might not be difficult to present to an uncritical and disinterested audience, some of whom might be indulging themselves in a similar fashion. I claim little acting skill, but, long ago in a school play, I had been cast as a character who was fond of the bottle. The advice of the teacher directing us was, 'Never, never overact the part of a drunk. You'll only look silly and unconvincing. Blur your words slightly. An occasional stumble in talk or walk is permissible. Respond to questions slowly and perhaps suggest drowsiness. Don't try singing or you'll be out of my production.' I no longer recall why I wanted to be in that play, but his advice on acting the inebriate was about to be exploited for reasons that would have horrified him: he detested any form of dishonesty.

Overall, I adjudged the morning well spent. The final talks were stimulating and imaginative approaches, described modestly, suggesting novel ways to recycle waste. I asked two questions, which were only partly answered due to the short discussion times. The speaker agreed to meet me later to continue what promised to be a profitable exchange of views. This contact alone could justify my attendance here by providing ideas for future research. In my enthusiasm, I still anticipated a research future, disregarding present problems temporarily. Other talks had also been invigorating, and, despite the banal plenary lecture yesterday, there was evidence that slow advances were being made towards enabling us, mankind, to reduce the impact of our polluting activities on our already stressed environment, if we so wished. The cumulative consequences of decades of progressive industrial expansion were mentioned several times. The big questions were now political: whether, when, how and if we could live within our environmental means and find the corporate political will to curb consumption excesses, resource overexploitation, etc.

I joined in the ritual applause ending the session after the chairman's closing remarks, including lavish praise for what he called the 'excellent contributions', plus the inevitable programme changes. Participants from all the sessions hurried or drifted towards the dining area. The lunch provided was more than sufficient to sustain me until the evening; perhaps German appetites are larger than mine! Our sextet again assembled spontaneously at the same table, welcoming the group familiarity within the large conference crowd. Although strangers yesterday, and only knowing our new friends nationalities and scientific interests, we relaxed together comfortably. Everybody seemed to have benefitted from the morning and were now keen to discuss our new knowledge

As agreed earlier with 'Canadian Bob', we had each attended one of the concurrent lectures of mutual interest and exchanged information over lunch. This occupied our short break, but it had overcome the programme clash successfully.

Before returning to our sessions of choice, 'Spanish Evita' said, 'Will we all together meet for dinner this night?'

This was readily agreed.

Bob suggested, 'My hotel is beside the banqueting hall; I'm in room 427. Why don't we all go there for a nightcap, after we've eaten? If everyone brings a drink, we'll have a bit of a party.'

Again, there was unanimous agreement.

Meanwhile, the conference called and everyone went to their session of choice. My option was already decided: my talk was in room B. It was an unexpected pleasure that all our group accompanied me there to hear my offering. The chair, a courteous Indian lady, carefully confirmed my identity first, before making the customary, polite introduction. I summarised the pollution problems posed by Albert's 'tarry waste' and how we intended to dispose of it without harming the environment. All detailed information was projected from slides and accompanied by my running commentary, emphasising those features that I hoped might be of interest. This was not difficult because prompts had been included within each projected image, minimising the necessity to remember the content. I described optimistically the research that was hardly beyond the planning stage. The necessity to avoid identifying the firm responsible for causing the pollution, as Albert had insisted, only increased my difficulties. My previous critical thoughts about the poor standards of other contributions appeared suddenly unnecessarily harsh. Who was I to disapprove, when I was not doing any better myself? So, I supposed my talk could be described as 'average'; the usual polite applause at the end also sounded average.

I was very much aware that this research paper was not destined to be remembered as a memorable conference breakthrough, and wondered if it had been wise to offer it. My submitted summary contained remarkably little novel information, and I was more than a little surprised when it had been accepted. As a newcomer to the field, I could hardly claim to be contributing towards advancing knowledge, but Doug had influenced my decision to send it to the organisers by pointing out, 'Conference presentations are a good career move. You'll get known. Anyway, nobody ever listens to those talks in dark rooms.' It was also possible that LU might not pay my expenses if I did not contribute.

The first question from the audience was easily answered. The second, I did not understand, due to severe linguistic difficulties. The chair intervened to translate, so I gave what I confidently believed was a complete answer. Later, Evita told me my answer was, 'interesting, but answered a quite different question.' Conferees do not always communicate. My optimistic hope that someone more experienced in this research area might offer useful advice, or an alternative solution to the problem, remained unrealised. Tension felt before and during the presentation relaxed when I resumed my seat, rejoining the audience. The experience had perhaps made me a little more tolerant of others who, in their turn, temporarily occupied the limelight.

○

Later, I said, 'I'll slip away now, Bob. I must get back to the hotel to change.'

'Right, Bill. See you! Dinner's at 8.00pm, I think. I'm also near scientific saturation. I'll just hear this guy out, then I'm off, too,' Bob replied.

'This guy' sounded as if he could go on and on, so I left the darkened hall. I had long since lost the thread of his argument by becoming increasingly preoccupied with my plans to achieve invisibility during my Italian excursion. However, to facilitate my alibi, all necessary preparations must be completed soon. I emerged into a pleasantly mild mid-April afternoon, with my eyes adjusting slowly to the daylight. These grand buildings continued to impress, with the yellowish tint of the light enhancing the creamy-fawn colour of the stone. Fine, dry weather augured well for my forthcoming 'extra-conferential activities'. I hoped these dry, settled conditions extended south into the Dolomites. I would very soon find out!

Hiring a car was entirely straightforward, though I did not mention my intention of going to Austria and Italy. They gave me one of several similar, almost-new vehicles, ready for the approaching summer season. Before leaving, I noted the registration number of an identical car, the same colour as mine, in case this might help to conceal my movements. Having driven in Europe previously, the left-hand controls were familiar, but I set off carefully while adapting to driving on the 'wrong' side of the road. After consulting a city map, I parked the vehicle in a side street, one block away from the hotel in which our impromptu party was to take place later.

The walk to my hotel was longer than expected, but, on the way, I bought everything I needed for my evening performance, so I could complete my preparations within my room. I did not know whether the registration marks of vehicles crossing international frontiers are recorded officially, perhaps automatically. Consequently, it seemed worth falsifying the identity of my car, thus increasing anonymity, I hoped. I drew the number of the other identical hire car onto white card to affix over the number plate of my vehicle. The fake number would replace the one on my car only after I left town; I hoped the card would survive the journey to and from Italy.

Next, was my non-alcoholic dinner beverage. I had bought some Scotch whisky – Laphroaig single malt, a particular favourite of mine – and six small bottles of some fizzy, sweet drink, which was disposed of down the sink; the bottles were rinsed and the labels removed. Two bottles were filled with whisky and labelled. Appreciative of the beverage-making facilities provided by the hotel, I brewed tea, which was stored in the other empty bottles. Using a chemical skill, the ability to match colours, I mixed water and tea until the appearances of the liquids in all the bottles were identical.

I packed a haversack with warm garments brought specially from Scotland: strong walking boots, thick trousers, heavy jumpers and a waterproof outer layer. These would keep me warm in the mountains where, in April, it would probably be very cold indeed. Everything – clothes, the fake registration number and fresh food – was left in the car for my rapid departure later. Finally, there was time to shower, shave and smarten myself up, before going to the semi-formal gourmet dinner. My suit was somewhat creased, so I did my best to improve its (and my!) appearance by brushing it, along with my shoes and hair (using different brushes!). Viewing the results of these efforts in the mirror, I decided that I had cleaned up fairly well; this was the best I could manage. My preparations had taken longer than expected, so, to return to the conference, I treated myself to a taxi; this was a luxury with the hire car sitting unused nearby. The costs of this trip were exceeding all expectations, and I could only hope that my investment – more realistically, my gamble – would ultimately prove profitable.

○

As arranged, our group met in the Great Hall foyer, augmented by two friends-of-friends, who had asked to join us. I felt slightly conspicuous joining this semi-formal event with my scruffy bag containing bottles of real whisky and its lookalike-but-innocuous substitute. Many other diners were also carrying bottles; clearly, this would not be a 'dry' meal, with wines also featuring on the menu.

The Great Hall was a magnificent setting for the gourmet banquet; the pale-cream walls were adorned with paintings of classical scenes below an intricately moulded ceiling. The lines of round tables, each with a white linen cloth and fresh flowers, were set with shining cutlery and six glasses at each place. The organisers had achieved a splendour that would long be remembered by everyone present. Our, by then, octet occupied one table, which we soon found out was located strategically close to the kitchens. The waitresses, dressed in traditional Bavarian costume, served us first.

When everyone finally had found a place, we stood for a Latin grace, enunciated ponderously by a short man in black clerical dress at the top table. With much shuffling, the large assembly of 'banquetters' sat down, and the noise level of the conversation rose, registering a high level of decibels. A long time had elapsed since lunch, and the speciality pâté and toast, already served, disappeared rapidly. The wine waiter was welcomed by my thirsty friends, who then made great shows of inspecting the wine labels, sniffing the bouquet and tasting the vintage before, finally, condescending to indicate their gracious approval.

'Scot, what's this? Are you teetotal? You're not sampling the wine?' Bob seemed shocked.

'I enjoy wine as much as anyone, but, today... it's my birthday!' I responded.

Immediately, toasts were offered by my new friends.

When the congratulations had died down, I said, 'I should explain a tradition in my family is that the men drink *only whisky* on this special day. [This was, of course, a total fabrication, being part of my ploy to remain sober.] If anyone would like to try a dram, please be my guest.' I produced the half-full bottle of single malt, and it went round the table, with everyone wanting a taste.

Responses were interestingly diverse, ranging from approval, mainly from the men, to expressions of shocked distaste from two of the ladies. While this was the centre of attention, I poured cold tea into my own glass surreptitiously, and rather obviously replenished it regularly throughout the evening.

The gourmet meal came up to – indeed, exceeded – every expectation. No alcoholic appetiser was required to appreciate fully the excellent food. I concluded that – by limiting myself to cold, watery tea – my gastronomic enjoyment was probably greater than if I had indulged myself freely with the wines provided. My only problem was the generous portions, making it impossible to clear every plate. Conviviality grew throughout the evening; everyone at our table was obviously enjoying the occasion.

Once again, I found myself sitting beside the comely and vivacious Spaniard, Evita, who told me – among other things – of a recent falling-out with her boyfriend. I sympathised, mentioning my similar experience, but hinted that I was not yet thinking about other relationships. Later, without linking the two subjects, she asked me about academic opportunities in Scotland for environmental scientists. I thought it best to be vague. My recent parting from Beth had immunised me against female wiles, as embodied by Evita, who was attractive in her short skirt ('*reducto ad absurd*bum') and sexy walk, perhaps attributable to her precariously high heels.

After the first course, repeated banging reduced the conversational noise level sufficiently to allow Professor Egger to announce, 'There will be no formal speeches.'

The spontaneous loud applause greeting this news considerably surprised our host, and, as it died away, he conferred with his top-table colleagues, creating a hiatus. He returned, betraying uncertainty about what to say or do next, 'To replace... the speeches... we asked, er... that is, colleagues to relate amusing stories to entertain... that is... us.' After a short silence, he persevered by introducing the first 'amusing story'.

The audience reaction to this brave attempt to find an alternative to the usual formal speeches was distinctly unpromising. Nevertheless, a

Polish professor, claiming his story was *true*, accepted both the challenge and the microphone.

His cautionary tale, unexpected in this scholarly company, was distinctly critical of academic expertise. He described a venerable building in his hometown, dating from medieval times, which had survived World War II externally unscathed. However, after hostilities had ended, it was found that the occupying forces had built a huge, ugly bunker in the cellar, which was used formerly as an elite club. This was unacceptable to the city authorities, which wanted to restore its former glory and so asked the university to advise about the safe removal the offending concrete structure. One professor suggested the use of explosives.

'It's too dangerous,' said the mayor, 'Our ancient building will collapse.'

A council employee, a lowly manual worker, offered to do the job, not using explosives.

'At what cost?' asked the mayor.

'Seven bottles of vodka.'

'It's not possible,' said the mayor. 'How would you do it?'

'That's my secret,' said the council employee, 'But, I'll not damage the building.'

Another professor was consulted. He suggested the temporary removal of an outside wall using scaffolding.

Again, the Mayor was unimpressed: 'The ancient building cannot survive that.'

The city employee repeated his offer, but the mayor said public funds could not be used to buy vodka for his own city workers. After other fruitless consultations, the council decided that they had no alternative. With reservations, they agreed to the only reasonable proposal, from their own employee. They even agreed not to visit the area during the weekend when the work would be carried out.

On the Monday morning, the council members were relieved to see the building still standing undamaged, and made their way to the cellar, with the seven bottles of vodka for payment. There, they found seven of their manual workers standing in the now empty room, from which the bunker had totally disappeared, as if by magic, and without any visible damage to the structure. The workmen accepted their payment and were leaving when the mayor asked where the bunker had gone.

'Easy,' said the original negotiator, 'You thought it had to go, but we left it here.'

The council members were speechless.

The employee continued, 'We dug under the bunker and sank it below the floor. It was quite easy. We removed soil, not the lump of concrete!'

This story was received with appreciative laughter and applause.

The raconteur stressed the moral of his tale: 'If you can't solve a problem, make sure you're asking the *correct* questions. It's just as important in scientific research as it is in conserving old buildings.'

There was more applause.

I found this example of lateral thinking, told light-heartedly and informally, to be as insightful as many of the pompous and weighty pronouncements made in the *Official* Conference Sessions.

Next, an Australian was introduced. He began, 'My tale, also true, concerns an older couple. A man of ninety-three lived with his wife, who was a year younger, in a care home for the elderly. One day, they asked matron to arrange for them to be divorced. To say that this caused surprise would be putting it mildly. They were reminded gently that they'd been married for a long time. "Over sixty years, wasn't it? Why not remain together?" asked the matron. The unstated hint was that the situation was unlikely to continue *very* much longer. "No," said the woman, "We wish to divorce. We've wanted this for a long time. Now that all our children have died of old age, we can separate without upsetting anyone."'

This tale was greeted with a little muted laughter, but many people obviously failed to appreciate the point of the tale. Puzzled, even shocked audience members were asking neighbours to explain the humour. Jokes do not always translate readily.

After serious discussions at the top table, Professor Egger announced, 'That's the last amusing tale.' He had apparently decided that the experiment of replacing formal speeches by entertaining stories was inappropriate for the occasion. Presumably, the experiment turned out to be much less successful than the organisers had hoped.

The meal resumed, with everyone in our octet participating in lively conversation. I joined in the spirit, though my 'inebriation' was only due to the whisky substitute (cold tea). My tendency to 'doze' was noticed.

Evita asked, 'Are you OK?'

Bob said, 'Your my head will likely suffer tomorrow. I hoped you are not getting too big a thirst.'

I assured him I was OK, and contributed to the animated exchanges, then focussed on academic stereotypes and unflattering caricatures of colleagues back home. I was more concerned with making my inebriation act convincing, so that these potential witnesses would confirm later that I could not possibly have participated in an Thompson's unfortunate accident in distant Italy.

Despite the earlier promise, there inevitably had to be one, but remarkably *short*, final formal speech, expressing thanks to the banquet organisers and sponsors. Afterwards, many environmentalists, who had overindulged by then, remained in the hall, talking to friends old and new, continuing conversations contentedly and reluctant to end the pleasant social gathering. Our octet, *seven* of whom were keen to prolong the conviviality of the evening, went to Bob's hotel room, where we made ourselves comfortable in the limited space, sitting on the chair, the bed and the floor.

The first toast, using 'borrowed' plastic 'glasses', was for my health and to my embarrassment. There followed an inaccurate, tuneless rendering of 'Happy Birthday'.

I replied, slightly slurring my speech, 'A thoast to our thost, B-Bob.' And, looking round with slightly closed eyelids, I added, 'To inthernathional weelationsh,' though I was worried that I was overacting the part.

No one seemed to notice or care, with everyone making some contribution to the greetings. Evita, beside me once more, toasted the traditional links between Scotland and Spain: a tradition that was new to me, but I thought it politic not to seek explanations. The level of golden liquid in the whisky bottle, my contribution to the gathering, had dropped fairly rapidly and was almost gone by then.

I decided it was time to move on, saying, 'I musht get back home; hotel… I mean. If evr'one exchuuse me… plhease.'

Bob suggested, 'You should doss down on the floor here. It might be easier.'

My thanks were profuse, but all I could manage was, 'A thaxi… a thaxi tak me home… hotel. Thaaks. Gudd…nitth.' I was probably overdoing the speech slurring.

'You I'll find taxi': from Evita, who appeared surprisingly sober.

Help was the last thing I wanted, but, having convinced everyone that I was seriously drunk, by then I could not reasonably confess to my act. Evita helped me downstairs, coping with a couple of 'stumbles' on the way and out into the fresh air. A taxi was being paid off nearby, and Evita approached the driver.

I said a quick, 'Goooonite. Mnnn… Tanks, Evita… and bye.'

Surprised, she turned (perhaps reluctantly) back towards the hotel. I wondered unkindly if she would return to room 427 and if the 'traditional links' might now extend to Canada, with Bob in mind.

Having reached the taxi, I interrupted the driver, who was asking, 'Wo…?', by saying, 'Sorry,' in sober English, then safely ending my performance. I continued, '*Nein, nein Taxi*. I do not need taxi. *Danke. Aufwieder—*' I well understood the thrust of his irate reply, but not one of his shouted interesting-sounding German words was familiar to me!

○

It was after 11.00pm when I reached the hire car, convinced that I had contrived a virtually unbreakable alibi (if my luck held), giving me the opportunity I craved to deal with Thompson without being implicated. Just then, it all depended on whether I could locate him in that remote valley, effectively stage a fatal accident, and return to my hotel, all within the next eighteen hours, or so. There was no time to waste.

I have a good sense of direction and reached the southbound motorway easily. After historic Munich, I found Two-bridge Street (*Zwiebrukenstrasse*), thence to *Rosenheimer Strasse* and so onto the Innsbruck *Autobahn* (A8). On this clear, dry night, speed could be increased safely, and I drove steadily for an hour, covering about fifty miles easily, before stopping at a service station to complete my preparations and disguise. More rations were purchased: filled rolls, mineral water, chocolate bars and the two remaining danish pastries. It was time to replace the car registration plates with the fake substitutes, which fitted neatly over the originals, and were conveniently held in place by the transparent plastic film from the filled rolls. So, if international border posts recorded traffic, my passage would be less readily identified. Finally, I changed into the older, warmer clothes, which were more suitable for the anticipated mountain walking. Then it was back into the car and on southwards.

Innsbruck was passed at about 1.00am, after which the car slowed on the steep ascent to the Brenner Pass, though I still sped by heavy lorries labouring uphill. That triumph of bridge building, the Europabruke, was passed unnoticed in the dark, though a toll was paid for the privilege. Crossing this elevated international frontier was easy; I waved my passport to a sleepy official, who waved me onwards. Once in Italy, the motorway became a prolonged downhill sweep. Turn-off points were few in the mountains, and at only the second junction, Fortezza, I left the *Autostrada*. The name recalled former times when borders were defended more robustly and crossed less easily. At that point, I drove eastwards more slowly and cautiously along this rather narrow and winding secondary road. The road signs confirmed the way to Dobbiaco, more usually labelled Toblach, its German equivalent, which was the language that was dominant here. This small town was mentioned in Thompson's plans as his intended fieldwork base.

Less than an hour later, I reached the crossroads that went either to Old Dobbiaco or to New Dobbiaco, and turned south onto the road that my map showed leading to the *Tre Cime*, the Three Peaks, one of the Dolomites' most celebrated tourist attractions. Soon, I found a convenient, deserted roadside car park, well hidden in woodlands, and stopped under some pine trees, turning off the engine just after 3.00am. Tired, I got into the back seat, pulled my holdall into the shape of a semi-comfortable pillow and fell asleep almost immediately.

Chapter 22

SECOND THURSDAY IN APRIL

QUARRY	a.	Where stone is extracted
	b.	The hunted prey

Sleeping was not easy. I awoke intermittently, feeling cold, uncomfortable and cramped, and having to rearrange my bones to ease aches and pains before dosing off temporarily again. Eventually, the coldness and discomfort made further rest impossible; thank goodness I had brought two woollen pullovers. Rising was an equally unpleasant prospect, but, having forced myself from the car, the exertion restored my circulation, limited movement and mental functions. It was still early, and moonlight showed I was in a small car park, surrounded by dark pine trees. Between them, I could just discern a graveyard. Then, my slowly wakening brain recalled, from school history lessons, that there had been fighting here during World War I.

I eased my stiffness by walking into this military cemetery, which, a visitor notice explained, contained 1,259 graves. The burial ground was maintained immaculately; it was a memorial to past conflict and a legacy of former imperial ambitions. Two names appeared on each of the black crosses, which were set in long rows extending up a hillside. I was not the first person to contemplate violence in these mountains and, right then, some seventy years after that bloody conflict, I was here, also with homicidal intent. I wondered if my motivation was more (or less?) justifiable than the aggression perpetrated by these soldiers fighting here to defend their countries. Hardly awake, I preferred not to think about this profound moral dilemma.

When these men had been killed, long ago, their social circumstances were different: war was a heroic duty, accepted by the peoples concerned. Loyal subjects died in large numbers during campaigns that were invariably of greater value to their rulers, their aristocracy and their church back home. Such fatal clashes took place between armies of nominal volunteers, though the participants at greatest risk were often effectively conscripted men. Most of the men who had lost their lives here probably had been given little chance of opting out of patriotic wars, but, in those days, many people accepted this obligation unquestioningly. They had to confront the enemy bravely, having been led to believe that they were preserving their way of life and their freedom. My thought was that these tidy graves were being better cared for there and then than were the unfortunate soldiers who occupied them.

The historical fact of these previous episodes of death and suffering in this wilderness hardly vindicated my planned actions, though we humans are not always entirely consistent, especially when we believe our cause to be just. I was here to perpetrate violence in defence of my livelihood by removing an unreasonable impediment to my career ambitions. I wondered if this self-justification was very different from the motives of the military bosses whose armies had fought their battles hereabouts? There was no simple answer to this question, so I must not procrastinate, thereby frittering away my carefully contrived, indeed only, opportunity to win my personal war. Instead, I splashed cold water from a nearby stream onto my face, which was the only wash possible.

I returned to the car, started it, set the heater to maximum, drove off and made a dawn tour of the small town/village of Dobbiaco/Toblach (Italian/German), consisting of a single main street flanked by a few short side roads. It being between seasons, few people were about so early.

Winter skiing visitors had gone (as had the snow) and summer tourists were wisely waiting for warmer weather. Meanwhile, many hotels were closed for the vacation, and I did not find the *Gasthof* mentioned in Thompson's itinerary as his probable base, or his red car. His funding application had stressed his need to travel by car to enable him 'to reach the pristine rocks of interest and return with the many heavy samples required for later detailed laboratory examinations at LU.' (Unstated was his intention, 'With a car I will also visit my friend in Austria.')

My immediate objective was to locate Thompson as he drove to work, and his likely starting point had to be near Dobbiaco, assuming he had taken the advice I offered months ago. Presumably, he was hereabouts and had already started collecting samples in the valley of the *Rio Popena* (River Popena), as stated in his itinerary. I thought my best hope of making the essential initial contact was to see him going to work, starting south along the road to the picturesque Dolomitic scenery around the village of Misurina. This was his most likely, even only, route to his chosen fieldwork site, as the few roads in these mountains are restricted to the valleys between much higher ground. If my guess was wrong or his plans had changed, then my opportunity was lost forever and I would have to retreat to Munich, with my problems and my whole future unresolved. I accepted that this strategy was based on flimsy assumptions and the overall success of my visit depended on good guessing or, more realistically, good luck. My guesses and luck would soon be tested.

It was still early, so I parked on a minor road on higher ground north of Dobbiaco, with panoramic views of the valley, and ate a basic breakfast. The filled rolls bought last evening had, like me, lost freshness overnight, but these with cold orange juice or water were my sole sources of sustenance. Going into a hotel could be risky, and, indeed, none I saw was open. So, I forced myself to eat the unpalatable rolls to provide sufficient energy to deal with whatever stresses and exertions might take place in the next few hours. There could be rough hill walking before the anticipated confrontation with Thompson, possibly followed by physical violence. I had to be well prepared for every eventuality.

Surveying the attractive scene spread before me, at its picturesque best in the spring sunrise, was a welcome distraction from my slightly stale, impromptu picnic. Far away, across a pastoral area, the barren mountaintops were now tinged with orange by the strengthening sun. The sharply irregular rocky skyline, typical Dolomitic scenery, consisted of numerous main and subsidiary summits, which had been weathered into its present jagged skyline over uncounted seasons. Little or no vegetation clothed the highest ground, and there were irregular assemblages of pale-coloured rocks fragmented by cracks, rock falls and scree, with some places still partially covered by white snow patches, probably from recent snowfalls. Lower down, the alpine valley floor was an extensive meadow, bordered by dark, almost black pine trees extending up the lower slopes of the steep mountain sides. Parts of this forest were being harvested by a thriving timber industry, with the tree trunks being stored to season in the roadside piles that I had noticed last night. Later, it would be used here, or exported for house building and furniture manufacture. The scenic landscape harmoniously blended exploited fertility with natural beauty.

In the strengthening morning sunlight, the wide, gently undulating valley floor was a panorama of innumerable shades of green, impressing me as a pastoral idyll, with productive areas of well-tended farming countryside. Unbidden, the descriptive title of the first movement of Beethoven's *Pastoral Symphony* came to mind: 'Awakening of joyful feelings on arrival in the country'. These low grasslands contrasted with the patchworks of fields at home, being uninterrupted by hedges or walls, but instead appearing as an extended, open parkland. Scattered irregularly across this large meadow were wooden huts, presumably for storing hay, which were darkened with age and some beginning to disintegrate. Grass cultivation extended up the valley sides, ending at the irregular forest margin along the lowest mountain slopes. Despite its air of tranquil ambience, this was an intensively worked and relatively prosperous land, to judge from the many new tractors along with other agricultural machinery on the roads.

My panoramic viewpoint showed clearly that humans preferred to live on the valley floors, near the most fertile areas and away from the cold uplands that became so inhospitable and snowbound in winter. The houses, in both village and country, were large, topped by overhanging, brown-tiled roofs. The painted walls were almost invariably cream or yellow-orange, with many having large and colourful decorations, often with religious themes. Churches were also cream coloured, with most having walled burial grounds and each having its spire, either brown, slender and rising to a point, or a green, onion-shaped dome.

With a start, my reverie broke, and I remembered emphatically that I was not here as a tourist to enjoy the view, however attractive, or as a student of rural economics. My *first* priority was to locate Thompson before organising our confrontation. Even then, I could still abandon my homicidal intentions and return to Munich, innocent of all wrongdoing. But, again and for the umpteenth time, I recycled the old arguments: my hopeless situation in LU, my failing career, no jobs, etc. Then my memories of Beth brought back all the pain, as sharply as when I first realised that I had lost her love, friendship and companionship, and I felt the full impact of desolation only after she was gone. Having come so far, I *would* go on.

I still rejected compromise, such as resigning from LU, at least while there remained a realistic prospect of eliminating that single greatest obstacle to my academic aspirations: Thompson. Dismissing the temptation to review (yet again) past events and *right then* holding the initiative, I *would* implement my carefully prepared plans, hopefully resolving my problems. With my alibi in place, confrontation *must* not be long delayed, with violence as the only possible prospect of settling our differences. An ambush would give me the advantage of surprise, and *had* to be fully exploited in any forthcoming confrontation. I was certain that Thompson would be quite ruthless in a fight. However, I had to find my enemy first, appraise the situation, plan my strategy and act quickly; there could be no retreat after he had recognised me. Once I had revealed myself and/or initiated an attack, his retaliation would be merciless. However, detailed plans could only be made once I had knowledge of the circumstances of our confrontation. Would it be in a wooded area, with plenty of cover? Or on open ground, giving me no way to hide my approach? Speculation was pointless. I needed to be patient and assess the lie of the land (literally) carefully later before exploiting my advantage rigorously.

Afterwards, my objective achieved, I must leave behind a scene that would be accepted unquestioningly as a fatal accident. There must be no evidence to suggest that anyone else (i.e. *me*) had been involved. Just then, the prospect of soon resolving all or most of my problems was so attractive that my thoughts turned exclusively to the job in hand.

Privately, I still could not *entirely* accept that I was going to commit *murder*, and I found it difficult to face the harsh truth that my sole purpose here was to *end the life* of a colleague. Instead, through mental contortions, I preferred the fiction that Thompson was exposing himself to danger voluntarily by his solitary working in such a hazardous place. My only role here was to 'vary' the dangers to which he was exposing himself voluntarily. His disregard of all principles of self-preservation, isolating himself in this remote location, was obviously foolhardy. Being absolutely *alone* here, even a minor accident could easily prove fatal. And I could not be implicated because, at the critical time, I was far distant in another country, recovering from a hangover. My fabricated alibi should not even be required. Back in Linkirk, after obsequies had been observed properly, and everyone in the School of Chemistry had expressed their profound sorrow at the loss of our 'valued' colleague, I could later volunteer, or preferably be persuaded, to serve as *Director* of the Environmental Centre. Thereafter, all would bode well (for me), with my future career secured. Eventually, Beth and I might find a way to get back together; after all, we had never formally ended our relationship.

However, before realising these aspirations, my daunting task was to locate my quarry in these mountains, which was comparable with finding the proverbial needle in a haystack. Just then, I had a nasty thought: was Thompson's acid-rain research project simply a ploy to obtain financial support for the European trip he had mentioned? How could I be sure that he was in Dobbiaco? Was I wasting my time here? Who would know whether any rocks that he brought back to LU were authentic? Or was I seeking excuses to abandon my quest? No! My last-minute doubts were rejected firmly. As I was here, after considerable effort, my plan must be followed through to its bitter end, whatever that might be. I would not be deflected from eliminating Thompson; *this cat would catch his mouse*.

After having driven on, a while later, I parked beside the road to Misurina, near my overnight stop, and started my vigil. If Thompson adhered to his proposed itinerary, I could expect him to pass this way sometime sooner rather than later, along the only reasonable route to his specified fieldwork site. This narrow, wooded valley ran south from Dobbiaco between high mountains and close to the lofty Dolomite peaks of bare, largely pristine rock, which had been little influenced by human activities as yet, which was the reason why Thompson was working here.

It was still cold at this altitude, but the car had warmed, encouraging dozing and making it difficult to maintain sufficient vigilance to monitor passing vehicles. Some were German, I noticed with interest, so my car was unlikely to attract undue attention, particularly by my soon-to-be-*late* colleague. My eyelids were once again drooping, when I was roused to full wakefulness, excited and relieved, when a red car approached. As it passed, its GB number plate, including 'QS' and three consecutive numbers, transformed my hopes into relief and the need for prompt action. The greatest uncertainty in my plans was resolved satisfactorily! Completely alert, I set off in pursuit, remaining at a discreet distance. The fairly-straight-but-narrow road allowed me to follow the red car easily, without appearing to be shadowing it.

We passed a small lake, Lago di Landro, beyond which the appropriately named Monte Cristallo (Crystal or Glass Mountain), presented an unforgettably spectacular rocky panorama in the bright morning light. Some steep slopes retained bright, sunlit patches of snow. The dramatic, irregular outline of these rugged, high mountains, which are so characteristic of the region, was quite magnificent. I resolved to return in happier times to enjoy this scenery at leisure, but, just then, I absolutely could not be distracted, however memorable the view. All my attention was on maintaining contact with Thompson.

At the next junction, he took the sharp turn left, towards the mountain, and we started a steep ascent, with sharp double bends moderating the slope. The road signs informed us that we were 1,500 metres, later 1,600 metres, above sea level. (I estimated this to be about twenty percent higher than Ben Nevis.) After turning sharply left over a small bridge, I saw the red car had already stopped in a lay-by, with Thompson getting out. He glanced at my car, but not its occupant, and I continued up the road, which curved right, out of his view.

It was easy to park the car at the roadside. I got out and walked downhill to the bend, cautiously positioning myself to locate my adversary. He was carrying equipment across the small bridge, but did not look back. Giving him time to move on, I drove warily down to a second lay-by, which was conveniently close to his vehicle. The several parking spaces here identified this as a popular starting point for hill-walkers. Concealing myself as far as possible, while watching carefully in case Thompson should return, I followed him down the road, chewing chocolate for energy in preparation for whatever physical exertions might be in prospect.

The bridge spanned a small stream, with its water flow less than a metre wide and only a few centimetres deep: a sign identified this as 'Rio Popena'. The present insignificant *rio* flowed within the much broader valley floor watercourse, which contained a wide band of scattered white and light-coloured rocks of all sizes, bright in reflected sunlight. Evidently, at times of flood, such as during the spring thaw, this stream grew into a raging torrent, a large river in spate that swept downwards carrying a heavy burden of rocks and vegetation. Intermittently, this was a dangerous and violent place, but – just then, with the annual thaw almost over – it was peaceful again. The mainly dry, rocky riverbed resembled an extended, untidy quarry.

This primeval and remote landscape provided a most appropriate backdrop for my primitive, and personal, intention to execute the most fundamental and permanent method of conflict resolution. I could not hope to find a better theatre in which to stage a 'fatal accident'. Already, the harsh environment had roused my elemental survival instincts, rejuvenating the beast deep within me, which is normally overlaid by the soft decadence of civilisation. I had only just arrived here, but recognised this wild place immediately as an entirely suitable setting for the violent collision that must resolve and finally end my differences with Thompson. At that point, surrounded by raw nature, unsuspected instincts were emerging from their hiding places, and escaping from the civilised constraints and conventions of our comfortable culture. Aggressive intentions, almost invariably suppressed, were taking control of my emotions, and I was looking forward to the fight, whatever form it might take.

This lonely mountainside was still only emerging slowly out of the grip of winter, and, from a human perspective, it was inhospitable and infertile. No habitation was visible, and I saw none of the electrical power lines that disfigure so many rural areas. Apart from the road, the only evidence of mankind's intrusion were the red-and-white signs that mark challenging trails for keen hill-walkers. Nevertheless, that ubiquitous product of industrial activity, acid rain, could be causing changes even here, which made it an ideal place to assess the effects of man-made pollution on an apparently pristine environment. Later, perhaps I might embark on a more sophisticated research project here myself, but this would be possible only if my present mission succeeded. (It was my best hope!)

At last, I could begin to survey my long-anticipated theatre of conflict. Strategic advantages had to be identified quickly, to maximise my chances of success in any surprise attack or ambush I launched on Thompson. The stony river/stream bed, varying between three and eight metres wide, consisted of loose, rocky material ranging from huge boulders to fine dust. The small flow of water in the stream excluded, from serious consideration, any possibility of staging a drowning accident. It appeared that our confrontation would most probably occur within a largely dry river bed, apart from a few shallow water pools. From the road bridge, I could see only to the first bend, which Thompson had apparently passed. I supposed he was further up the valley, going onwards and upwards towards Monte Cristallo.

The sides of the wide flood watercourse were bounded by steep riverbanks composed of loose, stony soil that formed the upwards-sloping valley floor, which was covered by grass, a variety of bushes and clumps of small trees. Between these locally wooded areas were open spaces, which were thinly covered here and there by remnants of unthawed snow. The trees growing on infertile or waterlogged ground were stunted, but others that were rooted in more fertile locations were larger and thriving, forming small woods. All this vegetation had suffered damage by snow or wind in the harsh climate, with fallen branches and trunks littering the wooded areas. In places, precipitous riverbanks had collapsed recently and others, obviously unstable, would soon do so, taking with them the trees growing too close to the river. Occasional large trees, undercut by the floods and by then in various stages of decay, were scattered within the extended river bed, and others perched precariously on riverbanks would soon fall into the floodwaters.

Starting from the small road bridge and extending uphill into the valley was a recognised hiking trail, labelled 'Wanderweg 222', beside the Rio Popena. On a rock near the bridge, this black number was painted in a white square with red flanking bands, which is the traditional hikers' guide hereabouts. Thompson was visible again, and I watched him progress steadily up the continuous rise of the watercourse, his red anorak easily seen against the pale rocks. He still carried his burden and walked beside, sometimes in, the flowing stream, with the melt water from the last remnants of snow cascading over an almost continuous succession of tiny waterfalls on its downward journey.

To guard against the possibility that he might still disappear, even though he was still unaware of my presence, I followed him up the valley, starting after he had rounded the next bend. I chose to walk on the drier riverbank, along Wanderweg 222. This path was followed easily on patches of worn, grassy vegetation; the well-used trail offered an easier climb than the loose stones in the watercourse. The few scattered snow patches were not sufficiently deep to inconvenience me, though in places the ground was wet and boggy. More importantly, the track offered partial concealment behind some irregular groups of trees, so that my quarry (an ambiguous term here, among these scattered rocks!) would be less likely to notice me. This was improbable because, throughout my pursuit, I did not see him look around, even once. So early in the season, he was unlikely to meet other hikers in this remote and incompletely thawed valley. Although we were still below 2,000 metres, the prospect of unmelted snow, higher in these mountains, might deter walkers. The weather was still cold, particularly on the highest peaks, which extended above 3,000 metres.

I drew closer to Thompson, who was walking quietly, concealed by some small trees, which were more profuse here locally. He continued until we were about a kilometre upstream from the bridge. I was intrigued by his close interest in the water flow, and watched his actions to try to guess what scientific observations he was attempting in this wild place. Despite my personal hatred, the scientist within me remained curious, anxious to know what aspects of chemistry were interesting him here, and, more importantly, what, if anything, he might have achieved so far.

My time for action approached! My chances were be few. Advantages needed to be recognised and exploited effectively. My ambition to restore my career depended on successful planning at that point. Forceful, appropriate actions had to be executed without hesitation. My single window of opportunity would have been lost irretrievably if I did not act decisively *soon*. I accepted, finally, that I was about to contrive a murder, then go back to Munich *immediately*.

My options were reviewed. Surprise was my principal advantage. There I was, concealed by the riverbank, with my defenceless enemy standing on the riverbed two metres below me and only some four metres distant. He was entirely unaware of my presence. What was I to do next? He was working in the trickle of water, preoccupied with the equipment he had placed on the streambed. Crouching to conceal myself, I crept cautiously and silently to the riverbank edge. It was precipitous and unstable here. He was then almost directly below me, his attention focussed completely on his work with scientific apparatus in a water pool that had collected where he had partially obstructed the stream.

When planning my next move, I remembered suddenly the advice given by a school friend. His father, a former champion boxer, had advised his son that if he ever got into a situation where violence was *absolutely* unavoidable, the best policy was to make sure that *you* ended the conflict with *your* first blow. He was visualising his son's flying fist landing squarely on an opponent's jaw, but the same principle was applicable there and then. I *had to* act decisively *right then* and *not* regret *my* indecision for the rest of my life.

Chapter 23

SECOND THURSDAY IN APRIL (CONTINUED)

CHASE

a.   Pursue quickly and energetically

b.   Open land used for hunting

I SHOULD HAVE ACHIEVED MY OBJECTIVE WITH ONE DECISIVE throw. But things did not work out that way. One shattering blow to the top of Thompson's head by a well-aimed heavy stone could have resolved my problems. Victory would have been achieved at a stroke! He would never have known what hit him. Such a decisive strike would have been infinitely preferable to the messy conflict that followed. I was standing above him on the riverbank, ideally placed to lob a heavy rock accurately across the short distance to where it would do the most damage to his unprotected skull, exposed tantalisingly below me. But, lacking suitable missiles, I could not execute my plan immediately.

I then held the most advantageous situation that I could ever hope to achieve, but lacked the means to exploit my potentially winning, but fleeting, advantage. It was more than frustrating that thousands of suitable projectiles littered the watercourse, all beyond quick collection. I could not risk delay, nor the possibility of being seen or heard, while going up or downstream to collect suitable ammunition and carry their considerable weight back to this most effective point of attack, right there where I was then. Thompson, his back still towards me, seemed to be completing whatever he was doing in the stream. I had to act and *soon*. *Right then*. Hesitation meant this ambush would fail. I soon had reason to regret bitterly my ineffectual first attack.

Plan B was very much less satisfactory. All the suitably sized rocks nearby were tightly embedded in the hard ground and beyond my means to extract quickly. The smaller, easily collected stones were likely to be much less ineffective as lethal weapons. Over-hastily, I selected the heaviest of those readily available. Aiming at his head, I threw it as hard as I could, hoping to stun him, though perhaps only temporarily. To my intense disappointment, I learned quickly that my stone-throwing accuracy had declined badly since I used to delight in such sports (on beaches years ago, as a small child). Later, I wondered whether my poor aim might have had a psychological origin, a mental block that prevented me from hurling a stone at the unprotected head of a fellow human. Was it only lack of skill, veneer of civilisation, early training or perhaps something else that held me back?

That first missile flew past harmlessly, well above Thompson's head, and clattered across the rocks beyond; the sudden noise surprised him. While he stared towards where the stone had landed, I threw two more in quick succession. My aim had improved slightly, but my ambush still remained unsuccessful. The second projectile glanced off the side of his head, hitting him hard enough to bring a howl of pain, or surprise, but no visible damage. The final stone hit his back, before I moved away out of his sight. I heard shouted curses, but both hits had been ineffectual, serving only to anger my adversary rather than slow or disable him. My advantage of surprise had been totally squandered, leaving me to face an imminent and serious fight with an enraged enemy, who was already thoroughly aroused and would be pitiless in pursuit. In this wild terrain, the outcome of any clash was totally unpredictable. At that point, my only remaining advantage was anonymity. I believed he had not seen me.

Crouching low to remain hidden, I moved back from the elevated-but-unstable riverbank edge and thought about my deteriorating situation.

Next, I was shown that I no longer held the initiative. The counterattack was of unexpected ferocity. A fusillade of missiles, stones of just the sizes and weights that I had lacked for my first attack, flew towards me. I was shocked by the speed and numbers of projectiles that he managed to hurl in my direction, with worrying accuracy. He had judged my position with great precision, possibly as a lucky guess, more probably guided by the few stones I had thrown or he might even have noticed my withdrawal. I knew then that, whatever clues were being used, this immediate and violent counteroffensive boded ill for my future. Despite my higher elevation, I was presently in greater danger of injury than he had been up to now. As a precaution, I hid in a nearby thicket of woodland to gain some, undoubtedly illusory, protection.

Flying stones continued to appear over the riverbank, accompanied by howls of anger alternating with shouts of, 'Hey! Stop that! Who's throwing stones? You'll hurt someone! Hey, that's dangerous!' It struck me as odd that he assumed his unknown attacker here would understand English. It was even odder that he expected any adversary to stop throwing stones while his barrage continued and was more aggressive than the token few smaller stones I continued to lob towards him. Soon, his bombardment and shouting ceased, so that I no longer knew where he was or what he was doing. The silence that followed was eerie and unsettling.

The suddenness with which my fortunes had been reversed was deeply distressing, as was the violence of the counterattack I had provoked. Although still almost certain he had not seen me, I was aghast at the ferocity of the self-defence he had mounted against an invisible adversary. I wondered whether I should start a tactical withdrawal, while I still had the opportunity to retreat. I could hear only sounds of running water and wind in the trees, but no scrunch of a boot on stone or crack of a twig snapping underfoot. Not knowing where he was or what he was doing was profoundly unnerving.

Hidden within a thicket, which realistically gave no protection, I listened and watched while deciding my next move. The two options were: *To Flee* or *To Fight. Flee*: I preferred not to accept withdrawal as defeat yet, while some prospect remained of completing my original mission here. Could I have reached the car unobserved? Probably not. The steep hillsides would have made leaving the valley difficult. My alternatives were to descend the way I had come or to go on upwards, from where I *might* find my way back to the car eventually. (Unwisely, I had not brought a map.) The sparse cover around me meant that, whichever direction I went in, it was highly probable that Thompson would spot me, sooner or later. Besides, if he reached the road first, he needed only to await me beside my car, which was the only other vehicle parked near his. Realistically, there was no longer a chance to avoid confrontation. *Fight* was my only option.

The next time we met, I would have to defend myself against a thoroughly prepared adversary, and *that time* my initial assault needed to be decisive. The irony was that I had to try again to finish the fight with my first blow. Round one of 'The Battle of Rio Popena', the initial bombardment, had been inconclusive, but as Thompson was aware by then that he was being stalked, the odds in my favour had reduced considerably.

Whichever option I took, *Flee* or *Fight*, time could not be frittered away by idly standing there. (One of my father's maxims came to mind: 'Inertia in inaction inhibits initiative.') My adversary needed to be quickly located, effectively engaged and overwhelmed. I preferred, during these manoeuvres, to try to retain my anonymity in case later developments forced me into the *flee* option. I camouflaged myself crudely with my jacket's hood and covered my lower face with a scarf. Venturing cautiously from my woodland refuge, I set off to some trees on higher ground, which seemed to offer better sightlines across the valley. Making best use of the cover, I moved as quietly as possible, with my eyes and ears alert and wary. Once, I thought I heard a footstep and a twig snapping, so I hid among some bushes, but – on being reassured by silence – resumed my cautious progress, dodging among sparse patches of trees.

'He who has hesitated is found,' as I learned to my cost. The assault caught me off guard. After only the briefest glimpse of a red anorak, my adversary hurled himself upon me, grasping my waist and throwing me to the ground. Perversely, the trees I thought were hiding me had even more effectively shielded his approach. We both ended up prone, recumbent on a particularly uncomfortable patch of vegetation, where the ground was covered by prickly bushes that were apparently composed of sharp, woody spikes.

As we fell, my assailant bellowed a triumphant, 'Gotcher!'

The 'wrestling match' that followed was notable mainly for its lack of competence on both sides. Neither of us was sufficiently skilled or strong enough to force the other into submission. I had not indulged in such horseplay since my schooldays and, even then, had often come off second best, or worse, in playground skirmishes. Not that this was 'play' in any sense of the word, but anger, animosity and aggression were inconclusive without ability. For a time, we both wrestled to gain some advantage.

This undignified brawling and the urgent necessity for self-preservation prompted a long-buried schoolboy memory that I had occasionally used to vanquish a rival by using what we then called a 'neck lock'. This required me to get my right arm round the adversary's neck, use my left hand to grasp the right elbow and simply squeeze as hard as possible to close his windpipe. Whether this could suffocate a victim or even break his neck, I had no idea, but my initial attempts to get a firm grip around my opponent's neck failed. Eventually, more by luck than good judgement, I achieved the neck lock and applied maximum pressure at once in an attempt to throttle him, so discouraging the punches and kicks damaging both of us. The constraint given by this grip was much less effective just then than it had been in my youthful combat, probably because we were both swathed in bulky garments, which slipped and slid, hampering my ability to maintain a firm hold and so dominate my opponent.

I do not know how long we gripped, grasped and grunted as we grappled on the ground in a fight that was fought tenaciously by both sides, but it must have appeared more like a kindergarten brawl (had any spectators been present). To both adult combatants, round two was as undignified as it was inconclusive. Locked in my preferred grip, I was unable to exploit any advantage. I could not foresee or control what might happen next, and was worried about when and how this awkward skirmish would end. My grip on Thompson's neck began to slip eventually, I became balanced precariously on his back, when he managed to get both feet to the ground and started to run, in a crouching position, towards the nearby river bank. In retrospect, this must have presented a weird sight. I was fastened, limpet-like, on the back of a man trying to shake me off rather as a horse attempts to unseat its rider, such rodeo tactics were last used in juvenile scraps when I was about ten years old.

I doubt whether this gallop formed part of any coherent strategy, though my 'steed' might have intended to throw me over his head, perhaps onto the riverbed, if he knew it was so near. Such a fall would almost certainly have killed me, perhaps both of us, but it was more likely that he was blindly exploring every possible way of breaking my hold. However, whatever his intention, it became irrelevant when we reached a patch of residual snow that still covered this stretch of grassy ground. The sudden change of surface was a surprise. Thompson's feet, supporting both of us, skidded out from under him so that he fell face down while I remained uppermost and, having lost my grip, was then sitting on his back. I grasped the initiative quickly, as he wriggled to turn face upwards, by planting my backside heavily on his chest and using my knees to pin his arms to the snowy ground. My grasp of his wrists, held at shoulder level, restricted his movements, to bring him largely, I hoped, under my control. We both fought for breath and, for the first time, came face to face. On recognising me, his eyes almost visibly popped out of their sockets with surprise.

His shock was absolutely genuine. An initial silence allowed him to absorb the implications of this (for him) totally unexpected encounter. Then came the queries: 'Green! Green! Why the bloody hell are you here? What on earth are you up to? [He paused.] It was you attacked me? It must've been. Why would you do that?' His voice rose to a crescendo, and, though it is painful to recount, he declaimed his personal hatred of me in a stream of vituperation, enunciated precisely, which was infinitely more hurtful than his hostile comments: 'Witless Willy Wanker! Gormless Green! You nasty, useless Billy Bastard. I don't know why you're here, but, like all you do, you'll not, *not* succeed.' And so on.

I stopped listening and, maintaining my uncomfortable hold on my foe, tried to think how this unsustainable stalemate could be turned into some advantage.

My loss of anonymity suddenly had made my predicament infinitely more dangerous. The '*Flight*' alternative was no longer available: neither of us could walk away and forget that this confrontation had ever taken place. Our previous unpleasant relationship had now hardened irreversibly. I said nothing, for the good reason that I could think of nothing worth saying. Wary of any retaliation that he might mount, I watched a range of emotions – including puzzlement, pain, panic and pique – flit across his face, which was red with anger. Then, after a considerable effort, he seemed to calm somewhat. Nevertheless, I continued to restrain him, maintaining the illusion of exerting some control over the situation, while anticipating renewed violence.

When he spoke again, his voice was unexpectedly calm. 'You could've injured me, you know. Throwing stones is dangerous.'

I did not reply.

'What I can't understand is why you're here at all. [He paused.] To sabotage my work? That doesn't make sense!'

Still I was silent.

'Were you spying on my research, perhaps? That simply don't make sense either.' He thought for a while. 'You creep up and hurl stones at my head. It simply doesn't make sense. Were you trying to injure me or to hurt me? [He must have noticed some subtle change in my expression, which led to a realisation.] You're here to kill me... to kill me! That's the explanation! [A look of terror suffused his face.] Well, what'll you do now I'm at your mercy? Murder me in cold blood?'

Exactly that question was already worrying me, and I knew myself to be incapable of its execution. I was not strong enough physically, nor capable psychologically, of killing him in cold blood there and then. No alternative occurred to me and no ideas about what I would, could or should do next to resolve this frightful impasse, to which I could foresee no acceptable outcome. I wondered where, oh where we could go from here.

I had to reply. 'You also attacked me.'

'Yes, in self-defence! You attacked first! I thought you were a mugger. Some bastard wanting to rob me of my cash, credit cards or car... All alone here, I'm a soft target. I'm... vulnerable. I defended myself from attack. I *had* to respond. But, I couldn't... ever dream that bloody Bill Green would creep up and try to murder me. Why? What on earth would you gain? You owe me an explanation... always assuming you can take time out from your murderous activities to tell me!'

The mocking inflection in his voice, familiar from those many previous exchanges, once again succeeded in irritating me as was no doubt intended.

I retained my precarious uppermost position, still constraining his movements despite the discomfort, in the hope of salvaging some slight advantage, when physical hostilities recommenced. Sooner or later, a move had to be made; we could not continue this ineffectual struggle indefinitely.

'What do you think you'll gain?' he queried.

The taunt in his voice provoked my angry reply: 'You know as well as I do. Think of the centre and its history... Answer your own questions. You stole all my ideas. You... are now *director*... [I spat out the word]. Ever since I came to LU, you've been hostile and obstructed me in every way possible. Even your work here was my idea.' I was procrastinating, as talk deferred the resolution of our deadlock.

'You never saw things from my point of view.'

That was true; I had never wanted to.

He continued, 'You came to LU and tried to take over, when I'm senior... I couldn't let you.'

The situation was unreal and bizarre. We both knew compromise was impossible. There was no reasonable basis for agreement. Just then, we had interrupted a serious and vicious fight to discuss school politics.

Provoked, but attempting further self-justification, I took my last step: 'Not only did you take... no, steal... my ideas about Albert's tar research, but you later took Beth away from me.'

'What? *Say that again?*'

I did so.

The look of amazement on his face was not the response I expected; such profound puzzlement would have been difficult to fake. He declared, 'Never! You're totally wrong there. That's a lie. The Wilkinsons have been my friends for as long as I can remember. From long before you appeared on the scene. I went to school with Stewart. Beth was always... around. She's only a friend's sister and never more than that. I wasn't ever especially friendly with her. You've a vivid imagination, Gormless Green! But you're wrong... wrong ... *wrong!*'

'It looked very much like that to me, Thompson. Why should I believe you?' I queried. By then, I was completely confused; personal relationships are based on trust and when that trust is in doubt, so also is the relationship. I wanted to accept the truth of this unexpected claim, but my suspicions were too strong and my emotions too tangled to be cured by a few sweet words. Besides, my immediate problems were more pressing.

This conversation, while still bitter and angry, had moderated from our usual rancour to talking almost normally, with voices only slightly raised. The crazy feature was our unusual positions, which were more appropriate to a wrestling ring and weird, to say the least, for conversing adults. It could not be maintained much longer.

'Green, we're both uncomfortable. Why don't we try to resolve this in a more civilised way? We don't like one another [amen to that!], but we can pretend we're adults. I assume you're not going to end my life just now, or you'd have already tried. If you don't do something soon, we'll be condemned to spend the rest of our lives locked here.'

'What's your proposal?' I asked. We had to do something, but what? I could not hope to maintain this apparent-but-realistically-ineffectual dominance indefinitely.

'If you'll let me up, then we'll talk through our differences. We might even find some common ground. We don't know until we try.'

His tone sounded reasonable, and I could think of no other way to move on from this literally hopeless situation. Our recent almost-normal conversation, face to face as between colleagues, had made it quite impossible for me to contemplate cold-blooded homicide. Even if I tried, it was not clear whether I could achieve it from this position. The recent emotional tension, particularly the fighting, had fatigued me and blunted the sharp edge of my anger. His offer of parley was attractive because I wanted to believe him. I was tempted to open negotiations, though remained unconvinced that any agreement that we might reach could be trusted.

Even at the time I am writing this, weeks later and in retrospect, I cannot believe that any other realistic option existed. My uppermost position gave me no real advantage, and sooner rather than later, voluntarily or involuntarily, it would have to change. So, with uncertainty and mistrust, an unconditional truce, with violence suspended, was agreed. Round two of The Battle of Rio Popena, wrestling and fisticuffs, had been just as inconclusive as round one. But my situation had again been unimproved perceptibly.

We moved apart extremely warily, separating slowly, with each nervously watching every movement made by the other. We were both stiff after the energetic exercise; several of my joints ached, and my right hand was cut, unnoticed during the fray.

Thompson limped away towards drier ground. 'Your stone hit my leg. My knee hurts.'

Unconvinced that I had scored any hits, I hoped that any injury would reduce his agility, providing some slight insurance against a surprise attack. He moved, evidently painfully, off the then disturbed patch of snow, towards some decayed-looking trees near the unstable bank of the watercourse. Sitting on a rock, he rolled up a trouser leg and examined his knee. The lull allowed me to clean dirt from my cut hand and inspect grazes on my shin. I looked up and down *Wanderweg* 222 and was reassured that we were still apparently quite alone in the wilderness.

My relief at having escaped injury thus far was rudely replaced by dismay, when the full implications of my current predicament became clear suddenly. My carefully contrived alibi cut both ways, and it would land me in terminal trouble if Thompson noticed and exploited the fatal flaw in my plan. If, *instead of him, I disappeared*, and my body was hidden carefully, which would not be very difficult in this remote place, nobody would ever know my fate. I was shattered by this realisation. The single clue to my visit here was the car, which could be moved easily and left almost anywhere else. If it was abandoned in, say, a Munich street, there would be no indication where I had been and no connection with the Dolomites. Anyone investigating my movements could only conclude that I had hired the car, driven away and apparently disappeared off the face of the earth. Where would anyone start looking for me? By contriving such an effective alibi, I had made it equally easy to conceal a different murder (*mine!*); it was a gift to an adversary who I knew would not hesitate to perceive and to exploit every possible advantage. He had always shown great cunning in finding benefits from the weaknesses of others, as I had already discovered to my cost.

My situation was by then much more perilous than I had hitherto realised. My initial opportunity obviously had been squandered. If, *if* I could have acted decisively earlier, this irresolvable stand-off, or even *my* disappearance, need not have arisen! I could see no realistic way of disengaging peacefully from this clash, knowing that our fragile truce could only last so long as both of us retained some hope of occupying the high ground, thereby gaining an advantage when hostilities inevitably resumed. Realistically, at that point, there could be only one end, for one or the other of us.

With my urgent need to return to Munich soon, I could not defer the resumption of negotiations or hostilities for long. While walking towards Thompson, across the uneven ground, I stumbled. My instinct was to regain my footing, but, from the corner of my eye, I glimpsed something red moving rapidly and threw myself flat on the ground instinctively. A surprisingly large and precisely aimed rock flew past where my head had been microseconds earlier. So, I had been gullible – fooled. Our 'truce' was over. Thompson was on his feet, showing that his injury, pretend or otherwise, was not incapacitating. Right then, he held the initiative, in the form of a thick branch or small tree trunk that he gripped firmly to batter me into submission or worse, judging by his expression of hatred. Thus far, our unskilled efforts in stone throwing and in wrestling had proved ineffectual in The Battle of Rio Popena. Round three – horseless jousting or primitive, desperate fencing – had started.

I cannot recall picking up the stick that appeared in my hand when I faced up to my opponent, but I was disturbed to find that mine was definitely the inferior weapon. Although neither reasonable nor logical, I regarded this resumption of violence as a betrayal of my trust and experienced a surge of rage, which I controlled only by a huge effort. Just then, for the first time, I felt truly murderous. I declared, 'So, we both know where we stand.' I was aware that if this fight was lost, my situation would be worse than the fate I had planned and intended for Thompson. Nobody would ever know the reason for my complete disappearance, or the *where*, the *how* or the *who*. Thompson need reveal nothing. The stakes for both of us were now raised as high as they could possibly be, leaving no choice but for us to fight to only one final, fatal finish.

I brandished my stick, while attempting to exude confidence that certainly was not felt: 'Come on then! If you want a good thrashing, I'm pleased to oblige.'

The large improvised 'lance' moving towards me was hugely intimidating. I watched its approach with feelings of terror, but could think of no immediate or effective defence. My single faint hope was that Thompson might not have fully appreciated the vulnerability of his location. Only a short distance behind him the bank formed a raised, precipitous and probably unstable edge to the watercourse. I decided that, to have any chance of leaving this valley alive, I must gamble every effort on a maximum-impact, aggressive, frontal assault that would have to be conclusive, one way or the other. My advance must be sufficiently furious to upset his concentration, so that, in the confusion, he might be persuaded to make a brief tactical withdrawal onto the unstable, dangerous-looking watercourse edge. This sudden, all-or-nothing offensive offered my only realistic prospect of survival.

Our initial movements towards engagement were cautious, but – after some hesitation – we both changed to the offensive, each testing the other's defences. My whirling stick held Thompson at bay, while he manipulated his heavier weapon, exploiting its greater length to discourage my probing by keeping me at a distance and trying to inflict injury. To counter this, I shouted and lunged forwards with my shorter stick as aggressively as possible, and jumped back out of range as he swung his larger weapon at me. Luckily, a small projection from his lance got entangled with an overhanging tree branch, and the apparently rotten wood broke just above his hand. I caught his look of intense dismay as he threw the remaining piece of wood at my head, though it only glanced harmlessly off my shoulder. His actions became less coordinated, and he was forced to retreat rapidly in the face of my then increasingly confident advance.

His retreat was fatal. I watched with mixed emotions as, seemingly in slow motion, he moved back onto the very edge of the precipitous drop to the watercourse. The look of horrified realisation on his face will always remain imprinted on my mind, as the ground on which he stood disintegrated. Unable to help himself, he fell backwards and downwards into the river bed, disappearing from my sight.

The Battle of Rio Popena was over. Presumably I was the victor. I was still alive. I sat on the rock that my opponent had so recently vacated; I was physically and emotionally drained, and I trembled on thinking about the terrible hazards I had only just survived. Exhausted, I was coming to terms with myself. It does me no credit that I indulged myself in a period of total introspection before summoning sufficient energy to confirm the final outcome of the conflict by investigating the fate that had befallen (literally) Walter. Always having been squeamish about blood, with reluctance, I steeled myself to approach the jagged riverbank edge from which he had so recently disappeared.

My late adversary was lying motionless, face down in the small stream of *Rio Popena*. His body partially obstructed the water flow and his head, facing upstream, was positioned so that his face was below the surface of a small pond that was gathering. I supposed the hard basement rock on which he was now lying had probably broken his neck from the fall or, at the very least, had knocked him insensible on impact. He looked remarkably peaceful. There was no blood, though the water in the pool might have been slightly discoloured. I wondered if the cold water might revive him, though it seemed almost certain that he was already dead. If the impact of the fall had not been fatal, the pond in which his mouth and nose were submerged would certainly have caused death by drowning.

I returned to my rocky perch to rest and think about the day's events. Achieving my planned objective had been much more stressful than anticipated. I was now numb, with no feelings of success or triumph. I could persuade myself that our conflict had, in the end, become a matter of 'him or me'. I had not *really* killed him: the outcome of our fight was decided finally by an unfortunate accident, because he was unaware of the dangers posed by these locally unstable river banks. I knew well, in my heart of hearts, that such indefensible reasoning defied logic. This mental ploy enabled me to avoid facing the terrible truth directly: I had caused the death of a fellow human being. Slowly, my thought processes returned to normality. I viewed the body again and saw no indication that it had moved in the meantime. *Nobody* could have survived that fall of over two metres, probably ending headfirst onto hard rock! Also, with his face under water, he could not have breathed during the last twenty minutes. I could now be absolutely certain that Walter was dead.

It was then 12.30pm, necessitating my immediate return to Munich if I was to sustain my alibi through the fiction of never having left town.

After one last careful look at Walter's recumbent form, I left, being disinclined to descend and investigate his condition more closely. Touching the body might leave clues or evidence of the presence of persons unknown. This could prompt later inquiries about whether or not the death had been accidental, which was a prospect that needed to be minimised. Again, I scanned the valley and was relieved that no one else was visible. It was definitely time to go, while the going was good. My descent of *Wanderweg* 222 was quicker than my ascent, and I soon reached the road bridge. The only two parked cars were mine and Walter's, which was awaiting its owner who would never return. (I cannot explain the psychological quirk that led me, after his demise, always to think of *Walter*, in place of the former *Thompson* who had always been a threat.)

I departed quickly and, hopefully, anonymously, trying to calm my overwrought nerves and stop myself from shivering. Being tense, I drove too fast down the steep road from Monte Cristallo, just missing the safety barrier at a hairpin bend. To avoid the risk of an accident, I moderated my pace, while breathing deeply to restore my internal equilibrium. With no traffic about, it seemed a good time to stop in the car park beside the small lake, Durensee/Lago di Landro. The spectacle of the snow-covered peaks of Monte Cristallo was still attractive, but my real need was for sustenance not aesthetics: I was surprisingly hungry. The restaurant beside the road was closed, but, even if it had been open, it would have been far too risky to eat there. Instead, my scratch lunch consisted of two filled rolls, with cheese and salami, which I had bought last evening, but that were tasteless, stale and tough by then. The apple juice was refreshing and cool, but neither that nor the chocolate had much taste in my present stressed state. Finally, I walked briefly to ease my stiff joints before departing the crime scene forever. My earlier thoughts of returning to enjoy the scenery had vanished!

The narrow and tortuous road in the Rienza Valley, which ran for about sixty kilometres from Dobbiaco to *Autostrada* A22, required maximum concentration. I was no longer receptive to the charms of this fertile valley, and my interest in wood turned to irritation when timber-laden lorries limited my speed all the way. Suffering from frustration, I drove at only about fifty kilometres per hour, suppressing the temptation to overtake on the few straight stretches of road; no risks could be taken in my heightened emotional state. Suddenly, the disturbing memory of Walter's immobile body presented itself vividly in my mind – his image as I had last seen him, lifeless and face down in the water. This persistent and unwelcome picture continued to reappear unbidden, at intervals, for some time afterwards. By concentrating on driving, it could be banished temporarily – for a while.

I drove more quickly after joining *Autostrada* A22, passing the heavy vehicles labouring up the long haul to the Brenner Pass. Once across this high frontier and downward on the Austrian side, road repairs dictated a slower pace. It was only after the heavy traffic around Innsbruck that I could accelerate and use the fast lane of the Austrian *Autobahn* A12 to hasten back to Munich.

On reaching Germany, I left *Autobahn* A8 to go into a small town. There I bought a razor and, back in the car, shaved most of the stubble from my face. Next, I went into a *Konditorei*, a coffee-shop/confectionary wonderland where every item is a dieter's nightmare, but an irresistible temptation to anyone with a sweet tooth, or a taste for chocolate and cream. I indulged myself with a cup of real coffee and a slice of memorable *Sachertorte*, the cake that gives the authentic taste of Old Vienna, or so it was suggested. In their cloakroom, my face got a superficial wash, before I returned to my car, which was parked behind a hedge. There, in privacy, I removed the front false number plate. The rear one had fallen off, but this was not unduly worrying; it could be anywhere between here and Dobbiaco, and was only card bearing numbers of no obvious significance.

I continued on my journey and rejoined *Autobahn* A8, reaching Munich by early evening.

The car was returned to the hire firm a little early. The rental cost was paid in cash, after I had told the manager (as a man of the world) of a visit to a lady friend and that I preferred that my wife did not see either cheque or credit card entry. An exchange-rate bonus encouraged his agreement for this less-visible transaction.

Next, I returned to my hotel and confirmed, with relief, that there had been no messages. A shower and a change of clothes worked wonders for my morale, transforming me back into a conference delegate, who had by then largely recovered from last night's unfortunate overindulgence in the hard stuff. The incidents of the morning had receded somewhat from my consciousness, except as something akin to a bad dream that could be largely suppressed, apart from intermittent reappearances of *that* mental image of the body in the stream. While disturbing, this terrible picture could be obliterated by concentrating on other things. Before going out, I scanned the conference programme, deciding which sessions to attend tomorrow.

The size and popularity of the *Biergarten* where our group had arranged to meet surprised me. A large park was filled almost to capacity by numerous parties, large and small, all in happy mood. Noisy gatherings of friends, enjoying a sociable evening, occupied umpteen tables, where they ate from generously loaded plates and drank litres of light-coloured, frothy beer. Waiters, running literally in all directions carrying maximum loads of food and drink, ensured that the hunger and thirst of the patrons were satisfied as rapidly as could be achieved. The relaxed clientele, contrasting with the overworked waiters, gave the place a holiday atmosphere.

Soon, I located my friends.

'Scot!' one of them cried (our national identities were still the preferred form of address), 'Come and join us!'

Prompting was not needed. Everyone who had been at our table last night (by then seemingly *ages* ago) was there, plus a couple of newcomers. I noticed that Evita, rather pointedly, was much cooler than last evening, which suited me fine. She was sitting very close to a man whose name and *nationality* I had missed, but who was obviously enjoying her company.

I found a seat beside Bob, ordered a beer (like everyone else) and asked, 'What's new?' (*What was new* with me certainly would *not* be divulged!)

It seemed that rather little *was* new. Bob outlined, as being interesting, some pollution-minimisation techniques used in a factory he had visited that afternoon. With effort, I forced my thoughts back to the environmental discussions that had brought us all together here. I asked some questions, trying to contribute to an intelligent scientific conversation, but found it difficult.

'So, what did you do, Scot? You seemed, may I say, distinctly under the weather last evening. I assume you got back to your hotel safely? Evita said you took a taxi,' said Bob.

'Yes. I hope I didn't disgrace myself too badly. I've only the haziest memories of it all. The reward was a monumental headache today. It's taken until now to recover. I'm still taking it easy.' I indicated the beer. 'But I'm told it's helpful to take a hair of the dog that bit you.' My lies came easily.

Bob agreed, 'You don't look back to normal, even yet.'

This prompted sympathetic nods from the others. I was pleased with what was said and was now reasonably sure that nobody had noticed my truancy. The drunken act also seemed to have been sufficiently convincing to have been accepted at face value. It was fortunate that nobody had visited me earlier today. Evita, who might have come, had happily found a new 'friend'; genuinely and disinterestedly, I wished them both well.

I enjoyed the relaxed and convivial company during that evening together, which temporarily banished the painful introspection that included so many disturbing memories and images. My increasing tiredness, after the considerable physical exercise and intense emotional turmoil that followed my uncomfortable night, meant that I could contribute little to the jollity. Towards the end of the meal, my attention wandered as sleepiness caused my eyelids to droop, and drowsiness took over. I was the first to leave; nobody appeared surprised by my departure, but the short walk to the hotel required effort. Despite the then somewhat blurred memories of events earlier today, I was asleep almost before my head touched the pillow.

Chapter 24

Third Sunday in April

STATE

a. Condition of mental anguish

b. Enunciate a personal narrative

THE RINGING DOORBELL WOKE ME. THE ACCOMPANYING LOUD knocking banished all hope of further rest. Waking reluctantly, my rising anger was directed at whomsoever was responsible for this intrusive noise. I resented this invasion of my cosy Sunday-morning slumber, my one weekly chance to catch up on missed sleep. Who had the effrontery to breach the privacy of my home, denying me the opportunity to recover from recently disturbed nights? The flight home yesterday had been delayed, so that I had collapsed, exhausted, into bed only a few short hours ago. This rude reveille had awakened me. Why? And by whom?

To find out, I had to answer the unwelcome caller! I struggled to get up from my bed and pulled a raincoat over pyjamas, which was the first garment to hand. I supposed Doug to be away or that, less probably, he had gone out earlier. I had not seen him last night, coming in late and quietly. Surely, if he was in, he would have answered the door by then.

This untimely bell-ringer/door-knocker could only be someone looking for him; I expected no visitors.

I called, 'Coming! Coming!' to discourage yet another paroxysm of ringing and banging, and, half-awake, opened the door.

On the step was a tall man, who stepped back only when reassured that his diligent efforts with bell and knocker finally had achieved a response – me. Surprisingly, this stranger knew my name. 'Mr Green; Mr William Green?'

I nodded confirmation and noticed that my visitor was not alone: a short, portly and middle-aged woman stood beside him. Who were these people seeking me so persistently? Surely they could not be Mormons, who, on Sunday, should be immersed in their own religious observances. After all, on the other six days, they invariably preoccupied themselves with everyone else's.

As my waking mind began to function more rationally, I noticed that my tormentors, also their suits, were rather older than the average American missionary, who tends to be young and presents a well-groomed appearance. After a brief hiatus, both callers held out – simultaneously, as in a well-practised drill-movement – identity cards, which were exposed for perhaps a microsecond at most. Obviously, I was not intended to scrutinise whatever authority or information was displayed thereupon; each was partially obscured by a hand and beyond reading distance.

The significant facts of their identities were stated clearly by the taller caller: 'Police. We represent Linkirk CID [Crime Investigation Department]. I am Inspector Ross and this is Sergeant Hamilton. May we come in?'

The shock was immediate and considerable, throwing my thoughts into turmoil. What was happening? How had things progressed so quickly? Surely they could not know about Walter's death already? It was so recent. Keep calm and know nothing about it! I had anticipated the possibility of police questioning, but only much later. This was *Sunday*! I had not yet begun working out what I could and should not say. It shocked me to be sought out so soon. But their business must be urgent to justify such an early call. That they had located me so quickly was deeply worrying. My confusion increased while trying to understand the reason for this visit. Innate caution meant behaving as normally as possible; I had to let my visitors do the talking. Surprise was permissible, so I offered a welcome, 'Good morning! Excuse me, please. I've only just woken up. You'll… come in?'

We went into the living room, which was reasonably presentable, apart from my untidy luggage, which was still where I had dropped it late last night.

I explained, 'I've been abroad. I only got home this morning… in the small hours, that is. Please, sit down. Do you mind if I make myself… a coffee? And you… that is, if you'd like? Perhaps you'll let me wake up properly before you tell me how I can help you.'

Inspector Ross was a tall, broad-shouldered man in his late forties, who might have been athletic in his youth, possibly a rugby player. He was dressed in a dark suit that was far from new but had been well cared for throughout its longish service. His grey hair was short, and he had shaved carefully, apart from a tiny cut on his chin. I noticed his almost military bearing, formal speech and manner. His face was intelligent, and his expression solemn, but he looked as weary as I felt. Nevertheless, his alert eyes appeared never to rest; he continually observed, almost probing, while giving the impression that the details of everything he saw would be remembered.

In a deep, authoritative voice, he began, 'I have to tell you, sir, that we're here to inquire into the death of one of your colleagues—'

'Yes. I already know about it. I expected you. I guessed you'd want to talk about it, though perhaps not today or so early. Do you mind… if I get a cup coffee? I'll just be a few minutes?' I took their agreement for granted.

Sergeant Hamilton was a short woman, somewhat overweight and perhaps older than the inspector. She was wearing a nondescript, dark-blue suit that restrained her ample bulk with difficulty; perhaps a larger size would have been more comfortable. Her dark hair had not been styled recently, but it was made tidy by being short. Her features could have been attractive were it not for her mask of complete indifference, which she maintained or affected permanently, though perhaps only when on duty. Just then, her demeanour expressed detachment from the situation in which she found herself. She gazed out of the window, as if wondering whether it might rain or hoping to soon finish this boring chore.

In the kitchen, I found Doug recently had fulfilled his role in our domestic logistics by topping up supplies. Soon, I brought a tray bearing three cups of coffee and some biscuits into the living room. My callers accepted refreshments, expressed their thanks, and, I chose to think, relaxed slightly.

The inspector broke the silence. 'I believe you were away recently?' This was a question, rather than a statement.

'As you see, I dropped my luggage here when I got in, after 2.00am. I was at a conference in Munich… Germany, that is. My flight home was delayed. Such are the delights of air travel! I didn't expect the police to call so early.' Intended as a mild, half-humorous remonstration, any implied criticism was ignored. Then I saw the clock; 10.15am is hardly early. I also noticed that Sergeant Hamilton had produced a notebook, pen and was apparently doodling. No! *Definitely not doodling!* She was recording notes. This was serious. I had to be vigilant and be wary!

'Before you left the room, sir, you said, if I understood correctly, that you already *knew* about your colleague's death *before* we mentioned it. Is that so?' The inspector spoke quietly, without particular emphasis and almost as if he was making polite conversation, though his use of 'sir' signalled the formality of the occasion. We were *not* indulging in social chit-chat. This was an *official*, recorded interview.

Nevertheless, I saw no reason not to mention that I already knew something about the news my unexpected visitors had come to discuss. *Overconfidently*, I assumed that I could anticipate the course of the interview. Without thinking, and totally preoccupied with the events that had dominated my thoughts and actions during the past few days, I said, 'Yes and no. I heard a rumour at the conference in Munich that Walter Thompson might have suffered an accident. Are you telling me that he died?'

I saw Ross glance towards the sergeant, betraying surprise briefly.

Hamilton spoke for the first time, maintaining her impassive exterior. 'Who did you say, sir?'

'My friend, Dr Walter Thompson. We're colleagues at LU.' There was no need to stress our less-than-amicable relationship.

'Sergeant, don't we have to interview someone of that name – Walter Thompson?' queried Ross.

'Yes, sir.' She was a woman of few words, but she was consulting her notebook.

The inspector again took the initiative and, with a slight air of puzzlement, continued in his quiet and formal manner, 'There's been a misunderstanding, sir. We've come here to inform you that Professor Bland recently suffered a serious accident in the university. Unfortunately, he died as a direct result of that accident. As part of our inquiries, I have to ask what, if anything, you know about that incident.'

This news disturbed me deeply, and the silence after it went on so long that I felt compelled to say something, anything, to relieve the rising tension.

'Is this true? Professor Bland... is dead? That's difficult to believe.'

'You can accept from me, sir, that Professor John Bland's death, due to an incident in the School of Chemistry, has been established positively. I wouldn't be making inquiries on a Sunday morning if this case wasn't urgent and causing us concern. Now, sir, I must ask you the same question again. Do you know anything, anything at all, that might be relevant to Professor Bland's unfortunate and fatal accident?'

'This is the first I've heard of this accident and... er... Prof's death. I'm deeply shocked by your news... about my colleague and friend. He is... *was*... my boss. I don't... can't... know anything about what happened. As I said, I've been abroad. I'm sorry, but I don't think I can help you... with your inquiries. Can you tell me more about what... about what happened?'

The police officers exchanged what I took to be meaningful glances, though what meanings were exchanged, I had no idea. If I had understood why Inspector Ross suspended questioning just then, I would have been deeply worried. But, ignorant of the overall situation, I was relieved when he said, 'Thank you, sir, for now. You've been most helpful. I need to know all the circumstances surrounding Professor Bland's fatal accident. You say that you knew nothing about the incident until we told you. We'll note your reply, but it's likely that we'll have to talk again about this. Thank you for the coffee. We'll go now.'

At the time, I assumed that the matter was closed, at least, as far as it concerned me. *I was as wrong as one can possibly be.*

For breakfast, I had porridge and fresh coffee. My attempts to make sense of this morning's news and to anticipate what might follow *totally* dominated my thoughts. I had the distinctly uneasy feeling that I had not handled the interview in my best interests, which was a deeply worrying doubt. In particular, it could be that by revealing prematurely that I already knew of Walter's accident had been extremely unwise. This early and unprompted disclosure could ultimately prove dangerously damaging. Two apparently concurrent fatalities in the school were a shocking, even unbelievable, coincidence. So everyone, however remotely involved, would be questioned intensively to establish, in detail, all relevant aspects of the deaths of both our late colleagues. To remain beyond suspicion, I must remain exceptionally wary, but wondered how – and, indeed, if – I could manage it. Time would (*and did*) tell.

After breakfast, I started preparing for the busy teaching week ahead. Maintaining a façade of normality by continuing all usual activities was essential. The phrase that came to mind, 'life goes on', was unfortunate; it hardly applied here and now.

My mail was in a neat pile on the hall table (thank you, Doug!). Discarded immediately and unopened were special offers for credit cards, cars (oh, that I could afford one) and diverse invitations to spend my scarce cash on unwanted goodies. This already wasted paper was consigned directly to recycling (from which it would, in time, reappear in other guises, courtesy of a thriving junk-flyer industry).

This purge left only two items: Mother's weekly letter and, unexpectedly, this week's *Linkirk Reporter*, a newspaper we did not normally take. It was folded to display its dominant headline: 'Mystery Death of Linkirk University Professor'. Doug clearly wished to attract my attention – and he had. (Yet again, *thank you*, Doug!) This was of compelling interest, and I wished I had read it before Inspector Ross's questioning. There had been an accident in a LU laboratory on last Thursday evening, resulting in the death of Professor John Bland. The police were interviewing everyone in the School of Chemistry and pursuing several positive lines of inquiry.

Was I one? Further bulletins were expected soon. The report hinted that the police were withholding information; it stated that 'some facts remain undisclosed at this stage' (which explained the 'Mystery' in the headline).

The article went on to say, 'Mr Stair, laboratory professor, who was interviewed after the accident, said he was working late on the fatal evening and, when he was leaving, noticed a light in Professor Bland's room. This was unusual at almost midnight, and, on investigation, he had found Professor Bland collapsed on the floor, trapped under heavy cylinders that had apparently fallen on him. After his resuscitation attempts had proved unsuccessful, Mr Stair had called the emergency services.' Later, Prof had been pronounced dead on arrival at the local hospital. The error in his name and the spurious title (perhaps self-awarded), made me uncertain about the reliability of this report. Nevertheless, The Tsar's pervasive interest in everything that was going on (otherwise known as nosiness) was entirely in character, and had been vindicated this time. But, and to his credit, he often worked late; no office-hours routine would prevent him from completing repairs to sustain his claim that, '*My* apparatus *always* works.'

Disregarding the reporting inaccuracies, there could be no doubt that Prof had been fatally injured by heavy cylinders falling on him, when working late and alone in his dangerous laboratory. In this situation, waywardly and by his own choice, John had exposed himself to risk. By chance, The Tsar had found him, but it was too late: his first-aid skills had failed to save John's life. The incident appeared to me to be an unfortunate accident and, despite two re-readings, I could not see it as being a 'mystery'. Certainly, the situation required extensive inquiries, but why should *everyone* have to be questioned, urgently? What other positive lines of inquiry needed investigation?

I could give the police *no* useful information about John; of that, I felt certain. Worryingly, it was highly probable that Inspector Ross could know nothing yet about Walter's accident, and, from my point of view, it remained to be seen whether my reference to this unrelated fatality had been unwise or worse. Moreover, when it became known that there had been two fatalities, it was likely that both the intensity and scope of police inquiries would be extended. I began to feel less confident about my future. The only hope of hiding my direct knowledge of Walter's 'fall' was to behave normally and keep calm. *Say little, and volunteer nothing to nobody, never ever.*

Then, I had a further a nasty thought: the selfsame cylinders that had killed John *could* just as easily have fallen on me! John's private laboratory was a disaster area; within it, accidents were just waiting to happen! And then, one had. I had not appreciated the seriousness of this risk during my clandestine visits to find out about Walter's research. John had exposed me to danger or worse! I recalled moving those unsupported, cumbersome and heavy objects, not fully aware of the hazards they posed. I had been lucky, without knowing it, but could this good fortune continue?.

Some diversion, calming me temporarily, came from Mother's always-welcome letter. Similar, handwritten accounts of her activities arrived each week, extending to four closely written sides of the pale-blue notepaper she favoured. The familiarity of the contact was comforting, though I learned little that was new or interesting. I was pleased that she was in good health and the routines of her mundane activities continued as she wished. In response, I replied immediately, telling her that my visit to Germany had been stimulating, but I gave little detail. I reassured her that I was safely back in Linkirk, without mentioning the travel delays (or the Italian excursion!).

Filial duties fulfilled, I went to my office where I found my school pigeonhole tightly stuffed. The papers included examination regulations, minutes of meetings, health and safety rules and other topics, informing everyone about everything, irrespective of need or wish to know. I recoiled instinctively, regarding such circulations as counterproductive. Did staff simply shelve such papers for reading later (perhaps after retirement?) or discard them unread, for recycling? As a comparative newcomer, I felt obliged to scan, at least superficially, all documents so generously sent by the school office, as the all-too-tangible precursor to the new term.

However, before launching into this labour of lugubrious literature, I started the computer and, compulsively, played that electronic game. All attempts to solve the familiar puzzle proved unsuccessful. Experience had shown this mental challenge to be a fairly reliable barometer of the acuity of my current cerebral abilities. Usually, I won about half the attempts, when fresh and bright, early in the day. Successful outcomes became fewer later, as I tired. This indication of fatigue or stress further depressed my flagging spirits, so, dejected, I accepted defeat and switched off the computer.

My reading of the school papers was delayed no longer. Some of the content did not concern me directly, but, nevertheless, had to be speed-read, to know (*officially*) about all school activities. With lacking two staff members by then, their duties would have to be shared among those of us remaining. This was a good reason to familiarise myself with everything. If well-informed, I might deflect some of the extra work that could come to me and, perhaps, avoid receiving a larger-than-fair proportion of the reallocated tasks. Less-welcome duties might even, with luck and anticipation, be redirected to my colleagues. I settled down to this reading and was relieved to complete it. Next, I prepared my honours lecture for 9.00am tomorrow.

Keeping going, I started marking the first-years' laboratory reports, and had finished only one-third when the door burst open, accompanied by a tardy knock. Doug had arrived, red-faced and hyped-up.

He stated, 'So, you're back! I take it you've heard our news? I've never seen anything like it! What a to-do! The provost and boss cops have been crawling all over the place. I believe the chief constable himself has taken charge.'

'Hello, Doug. This is terrible news! Thanks for the paper. What's happened since?' I was keen to hear his version and, more importantly, his views of events.

'Welcome back. I don't know that I've much that's new. But… we need to talk about this frightful accident. Tell me what you know.'

'Remarkably little, except that two police called at our flat earlier to question me, but I couldn't tell them anything. I don't know what happened, do I? I was far away when John died.' The image of Walter, face down in the stream, which appeared suddenly in my mind's eye, was most distracting. 'Tell me what you know. Please.'

Despite Doug's extended account of the events, I decided quickly that he knew little more than the newspaper story.

He was, however, more upset by John's death than I expected. 'He was a reactionary old sod, our John, with his divine right of the profs to rule and all that crap. He did little to raise the scientific reputation of the school. His death was tragic. I wouldn't have wished that end on anyone. He didn't deserve it. He was a pain in the butt to most of us, but this… is… not good.' Although usually hidden beneath a direct and acerbic manner, Doug nevertheless had a surprisingly soft centre and was sufficiently affected by John's death to reveal this sympathetic streak. When he turned his attention to discussing The Tsar, his caustic opinions were exactly as I expected: 'Who or what kind of creep is a *"laboratory professor"*?' The error of his name attracted similar derision: '*Stair*way to the *Starrs*! Indeed!'

After the analysis of the school tragedy had run its course, constrained by lack of hard facts, Doug told me, in sober tones, why he had been away. His father had been taken into hospital as an emergency. 'I went to see my old ma. She and Da got a right shock. The medics said the attack was mild and a warning. I hope they're right, but you're never sure. When Da gets back home, he'll find a new regime. Ma'll veto his evenings in the pub. The darts team'll need a new member.'

I listened while Doug rambled on. While sympathetic, I preferred to discuss the school's problems. 'What do you think will happen here, now?'

'What? About John's accident? Goodness knows; I don't.'

'The police must suspect something or they wouldn't be so persistent. Inquiries continuing… and all that. Is there any suspicion of foul play?'

'You mean did someone bump off John? I'd have thought not. It wouldn't make any sense to me. As I've often said, the old bastard was a pain in the backside, but why should anyone want to do him in? Why risk your neck, or rather your freedom these days, by arranging for tons of ironmongery to fall on him? It'd be an unreliable sort of booby trap, I'd have thought. Why do you ask?'

'What's the reason for all the questioning?'

'We'll know eventually, I've no doubt.'

Having told me all he knew, Doug was disinclined to speculate further. We agreed to eat in this evening.

'We might even open a beer, old son,' he suggested. There was no surprise there!

The mention of food reminded me of a missed lunch, which I had forgotten during my preoccupation with the terrible situation here. But I was not hungry.

Doug, worried about his parents, John and the school, looked weary as he left, saying, 'See you later.'

I returned to marking, but my mind kept reviewing recent events. My unguarded, potentially inexplicable revelation to Inspector Ross that I had already known about Walter's accident, worried me increasingly. I could have avoided this mistake, if mistake it was, if I had been able to read the newspaper that Doug had left so helpfully. What more could I find out about John's fatal accident? Abandoning the scripts, I went to The Tsar's workshop, where he sat surrounded by his equipment.

'Good afternoon. Are you doing some overtime?' I questioned.

'Who? Oh, it's you, Bill. There's no overtime for me. Just the usual.' He put down a soldering iron and met my gaze. 'I take it you've heard our awful news?'

'Yes. I read the local paper and talked to Doug. I believe you found Prof.'

'Yes. I couldn't save him.'

We marked the moment with a short silence, in respect for the loss of our colleague.

'I did my best, you know,' he stated.

'I'm sure you did. What happened?' I asked.

'I don't know that I should talk about it. That inspector chap... Ross, is it? He told me not to talk to nobody.'

'I'm not asking for any secrets, but I was... am... interested to know what everyone else heard while I was away.' Feigning a lack of interest seemed the best ploy to encourage him to share confidences.

'I knew you was away. There's little to tell. I don't know if you was ever inside that laboratory?'

I shook my head to imply ignorance.

'Well! It were a scientist's nightmare; he'd no call to ignore all safety rules...' Strong views were expressed forcibly and at length. The Tsar, once started, was pleased to list – with examples – every way that John had flouted all known safety conventions, and ranted, 'such practices wouldn't never be tolerated by me, nowhere else in this school.'

I let him ramble on, knowing that – later, rather than sooner – he would share most of what he knew.

On that fateful evening, The Tsar had gone into the lab to see why the lights were still on, near midnight. Immediately, he had seen Prof on the floor, pinned down by two large cylinders across his back and with a third alongside him. I listened to his account of the rescue and the ultimately unsuccessful attempts to rouse John. Among the details, I learned that three metal chains, used to secure the heavy gas containers safely to the bench, were not in place.

The Tsar told me, 'Must have been mad, he were, to leave them off.'

Also, and significantly, a rubber tube from one cylinder had detached, leaking poison gas into the room. This was just the sort of hazard that The Tsar would notice.

He explained, 'It could've been why Prof were overcome. It were carbon monoxide, so he were likely poisoned. I put on the fan, so I could breathe, while trying to get fresh air into Prof's lungs.'

I listened to a long account of his first aid, the arrival of the ambulance and police, and later actions, without learning anything new. When he *finally* ended, I thanked my loquacious colleague and returned to my room, where the phone was ringing.

The voice explained, 'Biggar House porter. Someone 'ere wants to speak to Dr Green; is that you, sir?'

'Yes. Who wants me?' I enquired.

Then came a recently familiar voice: 'Mr Green? This is Inspector Ross. We talked this morning. I wonder if you could spare a short time to answer some more questions about Professor Bland's accident?' His words were courteous but his authoritative tone was more like a command.

'Certainly. Of course. When and where would suit you? Here?'

'It would be more convenient if you'd agree to come to Linkirk Police Station. We'll drive you there. We'll be outside Bond College shortly.' Again, his tone implied that refusal was not expected, and I did not put it to the test.

I duly went outside to wait for the car. I did not recognise the car driver, and the inspector said little. Soon, I was ushered politely but firmly into interview room 2 where Sergeant Hamilton was already seated, maintaining her aura of detachment. Her muttered greeting was about as welcoming as the bleak room, which had the lower wall painted in 'institutional brown' and the upper wall in 'sickly green'. I sat, as invited by her gesture, on the hard chair opposite and awaited developments, which were not long delayed.

Inspector Ross entered briskly and said, 'You met Sergeant Hamilton, earlier.'

I nodded.

'We wish to ask you some questions about the events surrounding the unfortunate death of Professor Bland.'

The sergeant was already taking notes.

The inspector continued, 'This interview is only a preliminary investigation. You are here voluntarily and free to leave at any time. [Once more, his words and tone conveyed contradictory messages.] I should also state that it's in everyone's interest, including your own, to clear up this matter as soon as possible. I hope you'll cooperate.'

'May I say something?' I interjected.

The inspector paused with obvious reluctance, so I took his silence for assent. 'I understand that Professor Bland's accident took place on Thursday evening last, is that correct?' After this was agreed by a just perceptible nod, I continued, 'I was in Germany from Tuesday to Saturday, and only got back here early this morning. I cannot understand how this can have anything to do with me. You can make inquiries in Munich to confirm these facts.'

'Yes, sir. We probably will do that, but at the proper time. [The 'probably' stressed the effective dominance of my interlocutor.] However, I'm obliged to inform you, sir, [there was no indication that he noticed my wince] we are not yet satisfied that Professor Bland died due to a simple accident. Everyone must be convinced about that before the matter can be closed.'

'You mean... someone... *intentionally*... killed... Professor Bland? Who'd do such a thing?' My surprise was genuine.

'The answers to both questions, at this time, are that *we just don't know*. But homicide has not yet been ruled out, and if homicide remains a possibility, then we must continue our investigations. If we find any evidence, we will pursue all leads found.'

I could think of no suitable response.

After a pause, Inspector Ross resumed his initiative doggedly, 'I can tell you, sir, that fingerprints, other than those of the deceased, were found on the equipment we believe he was using before his accident. I understand that this was Professor Bland's private laboratory, which was not normally used by other people. Consequently, we must establish who else had been in the room recently and why they were there. We intend to screen all chemistry staff and, if no fingerprint matches are found, our inquiries will be extended.'

This was a devastating revelation. During my visit to John's laboratory, to 'borrow' Walter's plans, I must have left my fingerprints everywhere. Just then, the realisation that I could be a suspect in a case of homicide appeared as a terrible threat. From the detective's point of view, it was conceivable that I had set up a booby trap, which had killed John Bland. I needed to keep calm and act normally. I, alone, knew that I was innocent of harming John, but how could I prove it without compromising my alibi for the Italian excursion by confessing to my filing-cabinet raid? I could not refuse to provide fingerprints; I was sure that if I objected, force could be used, even as a last resort.

While thinking, I procrastinated, asking, 'What was the nature of the accident?'

'We cannot disclose details other than stating, as already reported in the press, heavy cylinders fell on the professor, inflicting injuries that proved fatal.'

My situation was deteriorating rapidly. During my last visit to that fatal laboratory, I had moved the cylinders to access the filing cabinet, undoubtedly leaving fingerprints all over the place. At that point, I could not remember whether I had replaced the all-important safely chains afterwards to secure the moved cylinders. The irony of the situation appalled me. After carefully fabricating an evidently unbreakable alibi for Walter's accident in Italy, I was now in danger of appearing to have set up a clumsy, ill-concealed and, ultimately, lethal booby trap for John Bland, here in Linkirk!

With limited time to work out a plausible story, I wondered what arguments I could possibly devise to distance myself from involvement in *both* incidents. My only realistic option was to adhere to the truth as closely as possible using a consistent, plausible and simple story without incriminating myself. That was not easy. I might admit to entering John's laboratory secretly, claiming an interest in Walter's research but knowing nothing about when and where he intended to work. Lies would have to be told. Could my skill as a liar withstand police questioning? Hitherto, it had never been tested. Professional interrogators would not be fooled as easily by the amateur acting that, so far, seemed to have succeeded in concealing my absence from Munich.

Dreading the immediate future, an unexpected distraction appeared in the attractive form (I noticed) of Constable McKee, who asked Inspector Ross to, 'See Superintendent Wilson, immediately. Please!'

This welcome interruption allowed me time to review my disorganised thoughts, to appraise what could and what should not be admitted about my recent activities.

The sergeant broke the silence with, 'A cup of tea, sir?'

I accepted gladly, Constable McKee fetched it, and we sat in unsociable silence, sipping the hot-but-tasteless drink and awaiting developments.

My query about how long we might sit here received the trite reply: 'You are, of course, free to leave at any time, sir. But it would be helpful if Inspector Ross could complete this interview. Meanwhile, with your consent, I'll record your fingerprints, saving time later.'

I raised no objection and, after washing off the surplus ink, we resumed our silent vigil, with Sergeant Hamilton's disengagement discouraging discourse.

Inspector Ross rejoined us, appearing preoccupied, and continued the interrogation. 'I believe we've recorded your fingerprints.'

I nodded.

'Thank you, sir.'

Disconcertingly, he expanded his questioning to include *both accidents*, his experience and expertise easily outflanking my novice attempts to retain some control over our exchanges. His first question, posed deceptively in the quiet style of polite conversational interest, was so unexpected that he upset my planned strategy completely to make minimal admissions about my less-serious misdemeanours.

He asked, 'I think I'm right in remembering you saying, sir, during our earlier talk, that your colleague, Dr Walter Thompson, recently suffered an accident?' Thereafter, the course of the interview was totally determined by the inspector.

'Did I say that? I don't remember. I heard a rumour at the conference...' I responded.

'I think you said you'd heard he'd suffered an accident. What do you remember, sergeant?'

Hamilton searched her notebook, betraying a brief interest in the proceedings. 'Yes, sir. [Here, 'sir' conveyed respect.] As I've recorded, the inspector mentioned the death of an unnamed colleague before we had coffee. I also remember that Mr Green did not appear surprised at that time, and later mentioned that he had heard of an accident relating to "Walter", whom he later identified as Dr Walter Thompson. But Mr... Dr Green was *very* surprised to hear about Professor Bland's death.' The bored pose camouflaged an alert mind, capable of almost verbatim recall of conversations.

'That agrees exactly with what I remember. Now, sir, would you please tell us everything, *everything* you know about Dr Thompson's accident,' requested the inspector.

'I thought you wanted to talk about Professor Bland.' I was becoming confused.

'All in good time, sir. First, please tell us *all* you know about Dr Thompson's accident. What did you hear about this and who told you?'

'Perhaps I was mistaken.' Ignorance was my only possible refuge. The silence from my questioner disconcerted me, so I added, 'I don't remember how the subject arose.'

'You must have known *something* about an accident. You were *not* surprised that a colleague had suffered an accident and you mentioned Walter. Later, you were *very surprised* when we told you of Professor Bland's death. This doesn't make sense.'

I had obviously made serious errors of judgement, and damaging truths were bound to come out if I continued. Accordingly, I denied having any detailed knowledge of an accident involving Walter. I explained that I had heard, in Munich, an unsubstantiated rumour about an injury to

Dr Thompson, but no longer remembered how I had heard this news. Realistically, it was too much to hope my interrogators would believe these answers.

We had reached a state of deadlock; my answers were inadequate. Aware that I had lost control of the situation, I expected the inspector to press his undoubted advantage, and, just as I started to panic, he changed the direction of his questioning suddenly and unexpectedly. He asked me, as if genuinely interested, about my relationship with John. This was hugely welcome, though I was very much aware that leaving the unfinished business could only be temporary. Reviewing his tactics later, I concluded that he did not then know the details of Walter's accident and could not risk going any further. But, by implying an awareness of inconsistencies in my story, he showed his strong position, thereby softening me up for later questioning.

With some welcome relief, I answered these questions truthfully, emphasising that I had always worked harmoniously with Professor Bland. 'We never had any disagreements; indeed, I found him to be a good boss. I'd always carried out, to the best of my ability, all the duties he assigned to me. I had no idea whether he found my work satisfactory – the subject never arose – but, as far as I know, he had no reason to complain about my contribution within the school.' I agreed that, 'On one occasion, by chance and on a Sunday, I talked to him in his private laboratory.' I also admitted I had entered his laboratory clandestinely later to consult some papers, as I expected this to come out later. My motive was only to learn about Walter's scientific work and thus avoid possible future research clashes. My statements were recorded without comment, and I believed this part of my story, at least, was consistent and plausible.

Inspector Ross ended the interview in a neutral tone. 'That is all that I need to ask you at this stage. We can expect to continue these discussions later, as our inquiries continue. I can also tell you that the reason why I left the room earlier was because Superintendent Wilson had a communication from the *Carb... Crab...* er... Italian police authorities. Some hikers found a body, appearing to match the description of Dr Thompson, in a valley near Cortina this morning. They found his name from papers he was carrying. There was also a car with a UK registration number parked nearby. Inspector Chincarini, of the...'

'*Carabiniere*,' I supplied.

'Whatever...' he responded. 'I talked with the inspector, and he said the victim had apparently died as a result of a broken neck, possibly resulting from a fall. Inquiries there are still at an early stage, but I must ask you to remain here, in Linkirk, and remain available for further interview. Do you intend to go anywhere in the near future?'

'No. I have university duties. Our teaching term starts tomorrow.'

'Then our interview is over, for now. Thank you, sir.'

◎

I was delighted to breathe the cool, fresh evening air as I set off home, able (at least temporarily) to walk the fairly deserted streets towards the anticipated evening meal, including the beer (or two) suggested by Doug.

Chapter 25

THIRD SUNDAY IN APRIL

LAST

a. Keep going continuing prolonged activity

b. Final event completing a sequence

MY INITIAL RELIEF, VERGING ON EUPHORIA, DISSIPATED RAPIDLY after my release (or was it escape?) from interview room 2. My reflex actions, rather than conscious effort, guided me home, oblivious to people, traffic and the weather. As a wounded animal seeks its lair, I sought the familiarity, the comfort and the haven of home.

My mind continued its obsessive activity, appraising my precarious future from every angle. Comforting and optimistic thoughts did not feature, and indications that my memory had become less reliable boded ill for my outlook. I no longer recalled exactly what I had said, or should, could or might have said, during either interview. Consequently, I could not plan what I should, could or might say next, and *what must not be said*, whenever interrogation restarted, and restart it would, soon. Too many uncertainties about the recent past overloaded my brain, rendering it less capable, even incapable, of separating the important from the trivial. Any missed details and significant inconsistencies in my statements would render my accounts of events increasingly implausible as the interrogation advanced. The cumulative effects of a lack of sleep and stress from helping the police with their inquiries was eroding all hopes of offering rational explanations for my actions. But my brain still would not relax, and was persistently scanning the tangle of problems besetting me. Intermittent replays of that last distressing image of Walter in the stream also distorted my normal and rational thought.

My capricious mind's eye recalled repeatedly the most worrying aspects of recent events, particularly the interviews. Being vulnerable, I might be easily led, persuaded or trapped into making damaging admissions. My outlook appeared literally *hopeless*. It was possible that, after forensic examinations of both crime scenes – John's laboratory and *Rio Popena* – the accumulated evidence against me would be overwhelming and damning. Perhaps the police would manage *to prove conclusively* that I was responsible for one or other fatality. Would I ever be allowed to present my version of events? Even then, what could I say that anyone would believe? My Munich alibi was likely to be scrutinised critically, after the details of Walter's accident reached Linkirk. With my depression deepening, the bleak possibility that 'they' would conclude I had intentionally contrived *both* 'fatal accidents' occurred to me for the first time. Worse, any suspicion of my having caused one fatality would make it all the more believable that I was responsible for the other. I was in serious trouble, and I could see no way to avoid or deflect suspicion.

But why had I been released? Presumably because, so early in the investigations, the police did not yet have sufficient grounds to hold me. Soon, forensic scientists would find *my* fingerprints all over those fatal cylinders, providing evidence of *my* involvement in the laboratory incident. Undoubtedly, a man of Inspector Ross's intelligence and experience had already anticipated this possibility; his case would be strengthened when his surmising was confirmed by forensic facts. He could then resume the questioning he had started so successfully, building on his already dominant position. For me, the growth of tension during this brief respite must inevitably erode my resolve further. My consequent loss of self-confidence would make his job of establishing my guilt all the easier. By obliging me to remain in Linkirk, he had little to lose; I could be recalled for further interview to suit his convenience.

Hitherto, I had not considered going on the run, but a quick review of possible disappearing acts suggested no suitable hiding place. If I went home to Sussex, I could be picked up quickly there with no more than a short delay. (Explaining my predicament to Mother brought a new dimension to my anguish. I could not imagine what I could tell her; that was yet another problem for the future.) If I attempted to go abroad, I would be stopped at the port or airport; my details had probably already been circulated. With nowhere to hide, what could I achieve by putting off my fate?

Nevertheless, the idea of a period of respite had taken root strongly in my mind, and, once implanted, was not easily dislodged. I began to think seriously about how I might achieve a break (and *play truant* again!). Exploring this possibility brought welcome relief from my endless unsuccessful attempts to concoct consistent accounts of recent actions; all my hopes of demonstrating my innocence were receding. Chronic weariness made me dread the prospect of further questioning, knowing how likely it was that I would accelerate my downfall. But I hoped that if I took a break and put off the evil day, I might recover sufficiently to withstand interrogation and perhaps even devise a plausible defence. Rest and recuperation were essential to restore any faint hope of extracting myself from this imbroglio.

If I disappeared, the police and forensic services would have to work out for themselves exactly what had befallen John, by obtaining no clues from me, given unwillingly or unwittingly. Their conclusions would then, perhaps, be more objective and nearer the truth, being based only on tangible evidence. Nevertheless, my unfortunate advance disclosure of knowledge of Walter's accident before *anyone* else knew about it was going to be difficult, more probably impossible, to explain. However, if I could find out how my alibi had fared, I could then try to concoct an edited version of events abroad.

On balance, the case for an immediate, though perhaps temporary, 'disappearance' seemed quite strong. While such a convalescence might not achieve much, facing immediate interrogation might be worse. That day's catastrophic deterioration in my situation had totally devastated me.

However much I might wish to abscond, the real problem was where I could find a suitable refuge. I surveyed my options again. I had little cash remaining after the expensive German trip. I could afford few hotel nights. These were not suitable hiding places anyway, unless they were distant, which would require train fares. There must be a cheaper alternative, if I could think of one.

Then came a sudden ray of hope: a distinct possibility appeared. I just might be able to disappear locally and within budget, if I could persuade Dickey to give me the essential and considerable support. His cottage (The Bothy, was it?), near the Grey Mare's Tail Waterfall, was the perfect hiding place; it was outside town but not too distant. Its disadvantages included my need to depend on an accomplice and whether we could conceal my whereabouts. Would Dickey go so far as to aid me by incriminating himself as an accessory after the fact, or some such legal jargon? The Bothy was an attractive secret refuge, but it was practicable only if Dickey would contribute positively throughout. That was a *big* 'if'! He would be taking serious risks. How much could I tell him about my predicament? Would he be prepared to assist me as a fugitive from the law? I knew very well, from our conversations, that Dickey had a taste for the mysterious, and I saw him as the *only* potential accomplice in whom I could risk placing my trust. We would, of course, have to ensure his role remained our secret, never divulging afterwards where I had hidden, though there was no obvious reason why he should be suspected. But would he willingly accept me as a temporary tenant? Without any plan B, the only way to find out was to telephone and ask. I had little or nothing to lose and possibly much to gain.

Conscious that the authorities could trace phone calls, it seemed safer to use the public callbox on Bridge Street, though it seemed unlikely that there could yet be surveillance of our phone. (Were phones tapped in homicide cases? I had no idea. Perhaps I had read too many detective novels. Was I becoming paranoid?)

I went to the aforementioned phone box and made the call. With relief, I recognised Dickey's voice.

'Hello, Hello,' he answered.

'Dickey, it's Bill here…' I said.

'I was thinking about you earlier. You're back then? Have you heard about—'

'Dickey, I'm sorry to interrupt, but I'm in deep, deep trouble. *Really serious trouble.* I'll tell you more later. Just now, I desperately need help. Your help, if you'll give it.'

'If it's a loan, that's no problem, just say how much?'

'No, nothing like that. It's far, far worse.'

He must have caught the anguish in my voice because he remained silent.

I continued, 'I'll tell you all about it later, but it's about John's accident. The police think I set it up.' It seemed best to be honest and direct.

'No. That's not possible, surely? You were away. Why do they think that?'

'I don't know. It's a long story, and I haven't time to explain now. The point is that I want to disappear for a time.'

'Disappear?'

I sympathised with his difficulties in following my logic. 'I want to *hide*, just for a short time. Until… I see how things develop…'

'I'm not too clear about… what you want? It sounds odd and… I don't—'

'Please, *listen*. I'll explain later when we meet. May I ask a favour? A huge favour. In fact, it's more than a favour; I desperately need your help.'

'You certainly may ask a favour… But help? I still don't understand what you want.'

'I want to hide during the police investigates of John's fatal accident. They seem to believe I'm involved in some way. I don't understand their reasons, but I want to avoid suspicion while they work out whether it was an accident or not…'

'You mean they think…'

I understood why he hesitated.

'You're… somehow involved?'

I was getting my message across slowly. 'I think so. I wasn't involved at all, but once inquiries start there's suspicion…'

'What exactly do you want me to do?'

I had *finally* communicated my urgency. This was the crunch question. 'I'd like to rent or borrow your cottage; isn't it called The Bothy? To stay there for a while. I don't want anyone, *anyone*, to know where I'm hiding... except you, of course. It'd be strictly temporary, until the police back off. Then I'll return to normal life, I hope.' It was not the truth, or the whole truth, and certainly not nothing but the truth, but it was the best argument I could devise that might persuade Dickey to give me the urgent help I sought.

'It would only be temporary... for a *short* time?'

'Yes.'

'It would be our secret? Between you and me? Concealed from the police?' This was another big question. Dickey was being cautious.

I had to be honest. 'Yes.'

'Exactly... what do you want me to do?'

'Agree to my living in your cottage, incognito, for the next month or so. You can deny all knowledge to everyone forever. I'll stage a break-in and pay for the damage later, if you prefer it that way. I'll deny you knew I was there, if anyone ever asks. I don't want to implicate you *at all*. I just want to disappear for long enough to think my problems through. It might save me a lot of hard questioning, because the police would then have to investigate John's accident without my help.'

'How'll you get there?' This was a chink of light. The idea had not suffered immediate rejection. Progress was being made.

'I'll find a way. I'll probably walk there after dark, then nobody'll see me.'

'But it's nearly twenty miles!'

'That's what I want. They'll not find me, if they search.'

'Are you serious about this?'

'Absolutely.' I managed to avoid saying, '*Deadly* serious.'

There was a long silence. It wasn't an easy decision for him. My request was unreasonable. The answer, when it came, was a welcome surprise and a relief; I had been anticipating rejection. However, some hope for the future remained.

'Yes, I might agree, but there'd be conditions. You must promise me it's a strictly secret, short-term arrangement and you'll not be there long.

Also, we must agree that I know absolutely nothing about your being there. Do you agree?'

'Thank you…'

'It's not your thanks I need, it's your agreement. You promise?'

'Yes. Yes, I agree to all your conditions; I promise and… Dickey… thank you.'

'Good. Now we must plan. If you're going to get away with this escapade, you'll need support.' He deflected an interruption. 'You can't do this alone. Secrecy is as much in my interest as yours. If you're found, I'll be in loads of trouble. They'll blame me for hiding you. I'll have to answer nasty questions or worse. On the other hand, if I help and you're not found, then I'll not be a suspect. I prefer that. [His logical mind was now working overtime and soon his planning was ahead of mine.] You'll need clothes, food and things. If you'll get those together, I'll pick you up somewhere outside the public gaze. Let me think… what about behind the School of Chemistry, in the delivery area. Late? Say, 9.00pm?' Again, my thanks were deflected. 'A friend needs help. I'll do what I can. See you at 9.00pm, agreed?'

I agreed wholeheartedly and ended the call.

Walking home, I hoped I had regained temporary control over my destiny. A friend was helping me in my hour of need. Unhappily, this slight feeling of reduced tension was brief. I recognised a familiar figure walking in front of me on High Street, with her auburn hair set off to perfection by the golden light of the setting sun. This cruel chance sighting of Beth brought back a torrent of memories of pleasures shared but, suddenly, ended so painfully. The jolt felt was like a painful physical blow; my heart missed several beats. One brief glimpse of her had added new depths to my despair. An impulse to throw myself on her mercy was seen quickly as hopeless, knowing that the almost-certain rejection of my advances would be even harder to bear. No approach could be contemplated while my future was in jeopardy, and so compromised. Moreover, I remained uncertain about how she *really* felt about Walter, despite his claim that she was only the sister of a friend. All this was far too complicated to confront just now and too fraught. We must *not* meet, so, assuming she was going home, I varied my route to avoid any possibility of her noticing me. This poignant reminder of our so-recent and so-optimistic past only increased my despondency.

I must not indulge in self-pity; my disappearing attempt, by then hatching with Dickey's help, required immediate and decisive action. I judged it best not to tell Doug that I would be away for a while. The more people who might guess I was hiding locally, the greater the possibility that an unguarded remark could alert the police to my presence somewhere near Linkirk. I hated having to be so duplicitous, but regarded effective concealment as my top priority, even if it had to be contrived by convoluted arrangements, including support from friends, knowingly or otherwise. So, that evening, I would give Doug the impression that everything was normal, so, later, my nocturnal flit would be inexplicable. Hopefully, and maybe soon, opportunities might enable me to make peace with whichever friends I might still hope to retain. But if things turned out badly, my foreseeable future would be out of my control, possibly *constrained* in ways I preferred not to contemplate right now.

◎

Doug's and my domestic activities followed our usual weekend pattern, and we prepared our evening meal together from the *sufficiency* of food bought by Doug. He had spent a pleasant afternoon watching a rugby match, in which he claimed his son had contributed heroically to a narrow victory over local rivals. I was glad for his joy and listened to his perhaps critical analysis of the game as a welcome diversion. His preoccupation allowed me to plan my immanent disappearance, at the cost of a few questions about the sporting action being replayed vividly in front of our cooker. There, Doug was frying (as ever!) two generous steaks, while I prepared vegetables and chips (in small and large helpings, respectively).

The wine was open, but I declined. 'I don't feel much like wine just now, thanks. Perhaps later.'

Doug's response was predictable. 'Don't let the bastards get you down. A little alcoholic refreshment revives… It'll do you the world of good!'

The problem was that 'The Bastards' were already well on the way towards getting me down. My judgement could not be allowed to become clouded at this critical time; the forthcoming departure required the maximum effort from those of my thought processes that remained functional. 'My innards seem a bit upset,' I lied.

'You've been eating foreign food again. It causes guts ache. When you get stuck into this traditional fare, your thirst'll return. The steak's coming along nicely!'

Later, during the meal, Doug's cheerful mood faltered and he became almost morose. Unusually, we ate in silence before he stated, 'I'm trying to decide what advice to offer Ma and Da. Naturally, they want to stay in their home…'

So did I! But the reasons for my forthcoming temporary (*oh, please, let it be temporary!*) change of address were quite different from the problems facing Doug's ageing parents. I made few comments during his précis of their plight, and instead listed the essentials I needed to subsist while isolated in Dickey's cottage. It was not easy to decide which basics were required to live frugally, until things improved (how long would that be – a month?). Was The Bothy stocked with bedclothes, including sheets and blankets? I hoped so, because I had none of my own. As for clothes, what should I take? Some were packed or, more realistically, not yet unpacked after Munich. These needed washing, but there would be plenty of time later for this chore. I needed to remember toiletries, including soap. As for food, I'd need to discuss that with my new landlord, including shopping. I should bring the small radio for the news. (Though did I want to hear the news?) Music and books were *must haves!*

I became aware that the grave tone of Doug's introspective monologue was gradually returning to his usual, lively conversational style, as he cheered up. I deferred the compilation of my essentials inventory.

He said, 'What about your problems? I've rambled on while you, I'm sure, wished I'd shut up so we can talk about the school and where we go from here.'

The wine seemed to have hit him harder than usual, and I wondered how much he had drunk before I got home.

He continued, 'I simply have no idea. Whaddo… do… you think?'

'I don't know either. I talked to The Tsar… after I saw you.' I waved my fork to defer the expected denigrating remarks and aired the booby-trap theory to find out what Doug thought of it. 'He suggested John might have walked into some kind of trap. The fatal cylinders, I think he was hinting, could have been left unstable deliberately so they'd be likely to fall on anyone in the lab... John! He also mentioned that the carbon monoxide release, poisoning the atmosphere, might have been deliberate. He seems to think John had little chance.'

'Silly bastard! Who'd want to do away with *John*? Who'd go to all that trouble and risk their neck? [Doug *did not like* Mr Starr.] What he thinks is that if he makes enough fuss, he'll be made *professor* of health and safety. Empire-building has got him where he is, wherever that is, and empires are never complete while the likes of The Tsar remain at large...'

Doug was clearly embroiled by imbibition, so I let him ramble on and continued my planning. The meal finished, and each preoccupied with our own personal problems, we cleared the table.

'Do you want to watch TV, Bill?' he asked.

'No. No, thanks. I'm tired. I got little sleep last night and have a 9.00am lecture tomorrow. [I did not mentioning that I would not be giving it.] I'll just turn in,' I stated.

'Mind if I watch this tape of yesterday's match between—'

'Enjoy it! You'll not bother me. I won't hear it.' This was true. If only he knew!

I went to my room, where I filled a holdall with everything I thought necessary to sustain me throughout the time in hiding. To be fair to Doug, I wrote a cheque for my next rent. It was the best I could manage at present, while wondering, with a qualm of conscience, if my university salary would be banked at the end of this month, to meet it. I put £20 into the drawer where we kept our joint household accounts, to repay my small, outstanding debt. Then, hearing an excited commentator shouting, while noisy supporters urged their teams to greater efforts, I left quietly.

The sky was cloudy, so it was dark when I walked briskly across the LU campus to Bond College. I saw few people, and recognised none, while trying to keep my bulky luggage inconspicuous.

Dickey, as good as his word, was already waiting in his wife's car. He explained, 'It's less likely to be noticed than the Rolls or the Morris.'

I put my luggage in the boot and got into the car. We set off purposefully, not wasting any time.

'Bill… you can tell me as much or as little as you wish… but sometime later. First things first! If you're going to live undetected at The Bothy, you'll need food, etc. I've made a list to give you a basic, if not very imaginative, diet. You'd better look at it.' He gave me the list.

I read the list, appreciating his kind thoughtfulness, and added a few items.

We arrived at the local supermarket, where we parked in the darkest part of the car park.

'You'd better not come in. It's best we're not seen together while you're hiding. I'll do the shopping,' confirmed Dickey.

At my insistence, he accepted some cash, headed to the supermarket and, remarkably quickly, returned with bulging plastic bags. We set off rapidly on the road heading south-west, but I was too tired to take much interest, unwinding after the stressful day.

Dickey declared, 'Bill, I'm prepared to let you stay at The Bothy, without understanding your reasons for hiding. No, hear me out. I don't want to know about it now. You can tell me later, if you wish. For now, I'll know the absolute minimum. It must be clear between us, sorry to repeat myself, but I *will* say, if asked, that I had no idea you were there. Also, I must be quite sure your occupancy will last only about a month. *That's the absolute maximum*. Is that fully understood and absolutely agreed between us?'

'Understood, yes. Absolutely agreed, yes. Thank you. I hope we'll talk about my future later, if you'll listen. I'd appreciate your advice, but not just now. I fully accept all your conditions and your kind hospitality, and I'll say a heartfelt thank you!' I confirmed.

'Good. That's fixed then.'

There seemed to be nothing more to say.

Soon, we turned off the road, opened some gates and bumped our way down a track, between unruly hedges that made the isolated cottage invisible from the road. We got out of the car and walked to the house, where Dickey unlocked the door and handed me the key before turning on the electricity and water. There was the slightly musty smell of an unoccupied building, but this did not diminish my delight at entering my new, if temporary, home. Dickey soon left, without saying when he might come back.

Afterwards, I buried myself in The Bothy's own bedclothes and, exhausted, fell at once into a deep and dreamless sleep.

Chapter 26

FOURTH MONDAY IN APRIL

CONCLUSION   a.   Termination; completion of a sequence
    b.   Judgement from analysis of facts

ALTHOUGH WISHING FERVENTLY TO REJOIN THE NORMAL WORLD, the sound of a car approaching my hideaway was profoundly disturbing. Anticipating just this situation, I planned to avoid unwelcome visitors by disappearing into the forested area around The Bothy. After identifying any such visitor, I could then decide whether or not to make contact. Nevertheless, and realistically, I had minimal control over my destiny. I lodged here temporarily, with my limited freedom depending entirely on my host's generosity and his complicity in shielding me from the long arm of the law. So, believing *they* were searching for me, I awaited Dickey's next move with interest, hoping this was his car. Undoubtedly, procrastination was beguiling, but decisions about my future must be made soon; remaining a fugitive indefinitely in the borrowed The Bothy was not an option!

Soon, I would need a top-up of supplies: the larder was low, after my solitary, wasted week. I wanted a news update, particularly about police inquiries, to help plan my next moves. Also, I hoped for Dickey's views on how long the present impasse would last. Ironically, I was an effective, if voluntary, prisoner in solitary confinement, which was exactly the situation I was trying to avoid. I should, by then, have devised a defence strategy to minimise my guilt, but, instead, my mind preferred to focus inflexibly on the imagined-but-definitely-unpleasant fates in prospect. Unstimulated, I was now torpid and unable to devise plausible responses to the probing questions undoubtedly awaiting me when the interrupted police interrogations resumed. I needed some incentive to push myself towards effective answers. I then wondered if it had been a mistake to come here at all, perversely accepting self-incarceration. In my literally hopeless situation, almost any action seemed preferable to being alone and moribund, moving to morbid.

Hitherto, nobody had seen me because I remained indoors during daylight, venturing out cautiously only after dark. Perhaps I should have surrendered gracefully right then and faced the inevitable consequences of my past actions. It was unreasonable to continue implicating, even incriminating, Dickey as an accomplice. The more time wasted in this stagnant situation, the more difficult it might be to extract myself later. and, no doubt, the more dire my final fate. By then, police searches might have already found clues suggesting my whereabouts, and the approaching vehicle could herald a closing net. Was I already surrounded with the stark choices of stay and submit, or attempt absconding again? Although (in theory) I preferred submission, when facing immanent arrest, my instinct was to hide in the woods, which was my remaining escape strategy.

On hearing the car, I put out the light immediately to maintain a strict blackout and 'blackin'. I listened intently. Yes, it was definitely a car arriving. Should I adopt my evasive strategy *before* identifying my caller as friend or foe? Pushing aside the thick curtain, I peered through the crack between shutters. In the fading evening light, I could just discern the familiar Morris Minor. Its unlit headlights and the confident way the car crunched to a halt on the gravel driveway, exactly at the door, were both reassuring. I relaxed, sure by then that my visitor was Dickey, not the constabulary, which – if the media are to be believed – execute arrests before dawn rather than early evening. This visit might, of course, be a diversionary tactic using a vintage car to allay suspicion, so I remained silent and wary in the darkened house. Only the driver's door opened, and I began to hope Dickey and I would soon be discussing my unsustainable situation.

After the solitary week, the joy of renewing human contact was greater than I could have imagined, even though the pleasure was muted by my concern about the news he might bring; would it be good or bad? Had the progress of police inquiries dashed all hopes for my future? With mixed emotions, I went to the door, but a key was already grating in the lock.

Dickey called, 'Hello!'

At last, there was the prospect of constructive discussion, which might rouse my brain from its recent torpor, with its endless recycling of the same few ideas, some practicable, others impossible or even bizarre. Then, perhaps, with Dickey's sympathetic advice, based on common sense and good will, I could break these cycles and bring some optimism about my future.

'Well! How's the hermit?' Dickey seemed cheerful.

'I'm as well as can be expected. Thanks!' This was an inadequate reply, I knew. My long, enforced silence and introverted thinking had slowed down my ability to communicate. I had so much to say, but how should I start? I wanted clues about Dickey's ideas before deciding the best line to take, and he probably felt similarly about me. But his future was not so fraught: I was the one in the mess. So, we stood, saying nothing for a long moment.

Dickey spoke first. 'I couldn't give you advance warning that I'd come this evening. Sorry about that, but it's high time we discussed your future. I know you're anxious for news. I can't stay long. If anyone notices my absence they might associate it with your disappearance, and we don't want that, do we? You've been thinking?'

I agreed strongly, 'Yes. Yes. That is, I've been thinking, but I've no plan... yet. Your advice and help would be... helpful. I seem to have become quite incapable of helping myself... out of my mess.'

'Right, let's sit down. We must start somewhere. How about some wine?'

'Sorry, I haven't any. I'm a poor host.'

Dickey went out to fetch some bulging plastic bags, perhaps evidence that I was not, as yet, facing immediate eviction. Most welcome was the Chianti wine he produced. I watched, seemingly bereft of initiative, as he drew the cork and poured the dark liquid. With the door and curtains closed, we were now *in camera*.

'You've had some supper?' he asked.

My reverie was broken. 'Yes, thanks. Sorry... I seem to have switched off.'

'It's probably surprise at my arrival. Sit down and tell me what you think of this *red*. I'll update you with the little news I've been able to glean. I assume you'll want to know...'

'Yes... please. I've heard brief comments on the radio about the... situation. I thought it best not to shop for a paper... I've been indoors... a lot.'

'Good thinking. Now, I'll tell you what I've learned, though I've distanced myself from the inquiries. Also, we've got to review your next moves. I'm not offering advice... yet. Obviously, it's best you make your own decisions. Sorry to remind you, but we've agreed your time must be limited. No! No! I'm not evicting you. It's just that sooner or later someone'll notice you're here. You can't hide forever. You really do need to have a good reason for staying on longer here.'

'I accept all that... but I don't seem capable of planning for myself. I do appreciate this respite... but...' Starting a meaningful exchange of ideas was difficult.

'We'll come to that later. First, I'll bring you up to date. What about the wine?'

'It's most welcome... and good. You've no idea how welcome—'

When required, Dickey could be peremptory and limit himself to the essentials. He interrupted me. 'Good! Now, like it or not, I think you should hear what little news I have.' Newspapers were produced. 'Look at these later, or not, that's up to you.'

I nodded my thanks. Unless drastic changes were decided now, I would have plenty of time.

'I hardly know how to start, but, being honest, I must say... things don't look good for you. I'm trying to be realistic, but it... it's highly unlikely that you'll be able to return, anytime soon, to your life as it was… before recent events.'

'I'd already guessed that. I'm having trouble facing… I just don't know what.'

'I can't help you there. I don't know the official line, but the police seem to think you were involved, one way or another, in *both* John's *and* Walter's… er… er… accidents. I don't know enough about the way they, or the law, work, but I think we should prepare for the worst. We can't talk about the future unless we're realistic about the present and… er… the past.' Dickey's repeated use of 'we' lessened marginally the anguish of having my worst fears confirmed. My outlook was about as bad as it could possibly be: I was facing a charge or, even worse, two charges of *murder*.

'All the chemists and some others at LU have been interviewed. I spent an uncomfortable half-hour with a junior officer, which was one of the shorter interviews. I told him I wasn't abroad when Walter was in Italy. I didn't know John Bland had a private laboratory, was certainly never in it and was in Yorkshire when John had his "accident", as my interviewer chose to describe it. I agreed that I worked in chemistry part-time and mentioned you as a colleague. I said you'd never expressed any wish to harm anyone in the school. I knew you'd been to a conference in Germany, but knew of no possible ulterior motive for that trip. It had never occurred to me that you might want to harm Walter. I didn't know why you disappeared afterwards… and still don't want to know, unless you want to tell me. I got the impression that I'd convinced the police that I have no information of the slightest value to them. I told no lies, but said as little as I could.'

'I appreciate your support. You've allowed me recover some equilibrium. Unhappily, I've not yet decided what to do next, except to keep you out of this. Thanks, again.'

'Yes. Yes. As I see it, police inquiries have stalled. At intervals, they issue requests for information about you and your whereabouts. The sudden loss of teaching staff in the School of Chemistry is causing difficulties. Angus is just about tearing out what remains of his hair. He has had to lecture to first-year classes himself, which is an unwelcome chore (as he sees it) that he's not endured for years. It seems he's not making a great job of it.'

'I don't know what to say...'

'Hear me out before you say anything. This last bit may be unwelcome, but I think it should be said.'

My apprehension grew while he sipped wine.

He continued, 'It's about Bet... Beth.'

My concern grew to shock.

'Emma met her, by chance, in the supermarket yesterday. She looked tired and worn... even ill... and most reluctant to talk. At first, she seemed to pretend she hadn't seen Emma. Their conversation was strained, and no reference was made to LU or... or... to you. Beth said that Stewart, her brother, is unwell and he'd come back here. He's supposed to have had a mental breakdown, but Emma got the impression that drugs were involved. The family is trying to help him recover, apparently with little success so far. Beth said that she'd taken Walter to visit him in some clinic or other, because he and Stewart had been friends at school... and after. She'd hoped that bringing them together again might stimulate and help Stewart. The chaps' meeting, just before Walter went to Italy, was cordial but brief. Beth thought it was probably a wasted effort.'

I took in the full implications of this news only slowly, being forced to accept reluctantly that it confirmed what Walter had said during our confrontation in Italy. At that point, I was forced to accept that my jealous suspicions of Beth's apparent close friendship with him were groundless. The thought I had made so frightful a misjudgement was a terrible blow and horrible to confront. I felt numb. It seemed that my anger and frustrations – with LU, *the system*, Walter, Angus, John and everyone else – had twisted my judgement so badly that I had become distrustful, and suspicious of anyone and everyone. I was particularly upset by the thought I had harboured the completely unjustified belief that Beth had developed a relationship with Walter. How could I have been so wrong? I was ashamed to admit, even to myself, that my insane jealousy had absolutely no foundation. I had failed to trust the one person who might have successfully dissuaded me from all my excesses.

'What's wrong. Should I not have brought up... so delicate a subject?' queried Dickey.

'No, don't apologise.' I took a gulp of wine. 'I knew Stewart had problems, possibly... involving drugs, though that was only a guess. I appreciate you telling me this, and I'll be OK in a minute. [I paused.] Now, might we talk about me... please?'

'Yes, of course. Perhaps you have some ideas about yourself? It's your future...'

Starting was difficult, without having any practicable plan in mind and while also avoiding possible later conflicts with the advice Dickey might offer. I decided to list the possibilities, hoping that, together, we might agree upon the least worst option. Even so, I was fully aware that, realistically, I had little chance by then of escaping my self-made mess. Feeling that I was not *totally* to blame did not help, so I began, 'One way of keeping my freedom would be to emigrate, perhaps clandestinely. But I have no idea how I'd get a fake passport with a new identity or even where to go. Frankly, I don't know how to disappear and start a new life elsewhere. Similarly, I don't want to live on the run in this country; I'd be an illegal worker without papers. I'd be underpaid, an unskilled labourer without prospects, and always looking over my shoulder for pursuers. That's not for me, I think.' I preferred not to mention the black feelings that were occasionally surfacing at night: thoughts of despair or ending it all. Suicide was one alternative to indefinite incarceration, but, at least during the daytime, I had not seriously considered this escape route. My situation was not *quite* that bad *yet*.

Dickey remained silent, so I assumed his tacit agreement. We deleted these unprofitable possibilities from the agenda with sips of wine, the treat I was still appreciating.

I continued, 'Dickey, I know my actions caused tragedy. I've inflicted terrible pain on innocent people and wish *most sincerely* I could wipe the slate clean. That's not possible, I know, but I do feel genuine remorse. If I could do anything, *anything* to undo past actions, I'd do it. But I can't and I don't know whether I can explain...'

'Try me!' he offered.

'I sincerely believe I'm not nearly as culpable as might seem to... everyone.'

'Explain. And... finish off the wine.'

'I'd certainly no intention of harming John Bland. I found him hard to like, it's true, but the fatal toppling of those cylinders was not *entirely* my fault. Against all the rules, he maintained his workplace as a death trap, *and that has now been confirmed... for him.'*

'But you were there... You went into that lab to find out Walter's plans?'

I nodded my agreement.

'And moving those cylinders *may* have caused—'

'But it was a pure accident. If the place had been safe... *He chose* to work in a dangerous place, flouting all health and safety rules. I could just as easily have been injured by those cylinders falling. I was lucky; he was unlucky. I feel I shouldn't be held *totally* responsible.' Put like that, my case sounded stronger than I had imagined.

'Not being a lawyer, I can't apportion blame, but I see what you're getting at. They – the police, maybe also the university bosses – do seem to have come down against you, but without having heard your version of events... you didn't stick up for yourself.'

'Point taken. I mentioned John's accident first, because I genuinely believe it was an accident and not altogether my fault. I certainly never *intended* to harm him. Even so, I suppose that, by moving those cylinders, I might have contributed to, or even unintentionally increased, the danger to him. I was genuinely shocked to learn of his death. Also, I'm sincerely sorry for the loss and grief it's caused everyone.'

We observed a short silence before I went on, 'Walter's case was different. I admit to you that I must accept some, *but not all*, of the blame for his accident. I don't know if you'll agree?'

'Again, try me!'

'I believed the alibi I concocted *proved* I couldn't have left the Munich conference. It seems now, in retrospect, that my watertight proof may have become leaky. I did go to Italy unofficially, and it's fair to say that, for a time, *I did intend to harm Walter*. But... later... when it came to actually performing the act, I found myself quite incapable of carrying it out.' The horrible events of that fatal fight with Walter flooded back, with painful emotions blurring my memory.

With an effort, I continued, 'At first, Walter and I threw stones at each other. Then, when I tried to get away, to save my own skin, he pursued me relentlessly and became quite ferocious. I believed him fully capable of homicide, so that I could justifiably claim self-defence, if he could be connected with my death, although I was supposed to be in Munich. Then I realised that my carefully contrived alibi equally protected Walter and so the boot was now *definitely* on the other foot. Throughout our subsequent chase, you could call it a fight or a hunt, Walter pursed me aggressively and ruthlessly up, down and across the wide river valley while I tried to hide or escape.

'Somehow, he always prevented me from getting away. Truly, I feared for my life. I'd squandered my initial advantage by being too timorous, which was a weakness Walter exploited effectively by seizing the initiative and mounting exceptionally aggressive counteroffensives. After several inconclusive skirmishes, during a messy running fight, he retreated onto unstable ground, apparently not aware that the river was so close behind him. He was some distance from me when the undercut riverbank on which he stood collapsed beneath his feet. He fell backwards onto the rocks of the river bed, two metres below. [Once again, I was pained by the vivid memory of his look of utter terror as he disappeared from view.] I think the fall killed him outright... my immediate feeling was relief. His aggression had been his downfall... we couldn't disengage. Believing my alibi still held, I returned to Munich... where my truancy hadn't been noticed.'

'You make a persuasive case. Though admitting *you did intend to harm Walter* sounds damaging, even if that final fall was... accidental. However, my ignorance of such matters is profound, so I won't say more. A clever lawyer might argue mitigation because you were defending yourself and didn't intentionally cause his final fatal fall.'

'If I hadn't said, in my first police interview, that I already knew Walter had suffered an accident, I might never have come under suspicion. My comment about an *accident of a colleague* was my greatest mistake. They didn't even need to test my *unbreakable alibi*, as I'd destroyed it myself! Later, I said that I "thought" I'd heard Walter was involved in an incident, and, because there was no legitimate way I could have known, that raised questions to which I had no answers. I'd presented myself as a suspect!'

'Interesting as this is, I wonder what we'll do next, Bill. I think it's unwise for you to stay here much longer. Your "invisibility" depends on how thoroughly the police search. In summer, hikers use the lane nearby, and you can't remain indoors forever. Also, for July, I've rented this cottage to our LU colleague, Tom Cox. Tom said he wants to, "get away from it all, to write". Cancelling that deal might attract suspicion. We've only got away with this arrangement because so few people know I own this place. My coming here frequently might be noticed because it's usually unoccupied. We're living on borrowed time. Do you have any ideas about what comes next?'

'I have only one idea… which is strictly for discussion… but I hope you might agree. I mustn't impose too much on your generosity when I'm already so deep in your debt. I'd like to pay rent, but… using my bank account might attract immediate, pressing invitations to accept the hospitality on offer from the authorities…'

'And the point of this preamble is…?'

'Explaining my predicament to you has helped me to realise, to my surprise, that my defence case could be stronger than I'd supposed. Just by listening, you've helped me get my thoughts into a more logical order. Thank you for that. Now, I've a tiny bit of hope that I might convince other people I wasn't *totally* and *directly* responsible for causing either fatality. I'm sure I could answer the accusations, at least partially, if I had time to prepare a convincing defence case. I'd welcome the opportunity to get everything clear in my own mind before setting it all down on paper. When I've written the true account of recent events *from my point of view*, a lawyer could be asked to advise about my best defence strategy. Have I got a case worth presenting? Do you think this is worth attempting? Would you allow me to stay here long enough for me to write *My Story*? I know it's a lot to ask, but, after our discussion, I'm really keen to try.'

'How long would you take to write *your story*? It could take months… even years?'

'I don't think so! It's so recent, and all still fresh in my mind. I'd write fairly quickly and easily, if I had a computer. I'm guessing, but is a month or so unreasonable?'

'It's risky and longer than I'd like. But… we might chance it. You have more to lose than me. I might be persuaded, but I've a suggestion of my own. You might, while you're doing your own job, do something for me.'

'Certainly. I'll do anything you ask. It'd be my pleasure to return your generosity. I'm sorry I didn't suggest it earlier. I've been too preoccupied with my own problems.'

'You might think about the research I'm so keen to start. Your ideas could well help me to begin. Regard it as a business deal or payment in lieu of rent, if you like.'

'Sort of earning my living?'

'You could say that.'

'What could I do? Recently, chemistry has become a bit remote, but I'll try to help. I'd welcome a scientific challenge to distract me from my own problems.'

'As you know, I'm an honorary research fellow of LU School of Chemistry, which is a temporary, unpaid position and the lowest form of academic life. My chances of doing worthwhile research are limited by not being a full staff member. Having only a toehold in the school, I could be let go at any time. When the environmental centre was being formed, I had the prospect of embarking on long-term research, but, just now, the School of Chemistry is facing, at best, an uncertain future—'

'All because of me...' Dickey ignored my interruption, but I persisted. 'They might appoint you onto the staff, perhaps even as my replacement. The examinations are due soon, and they still must give the remaining lectures, mark course work...'

'Yes. Yes. I've thought of all that, but writing and giving so many lectures at short notice would be a full-time job. I've always spent a lot of time on preparing teaching material. Maybe that's why I never became a *professor.*'

'I've already written notes for all my lectures. You could... er... use them as a start.' Remembering the effort I had put into them, I was reluctant to let all that work go to waste.

'Thank you, but what kind of notes do you think John Bland would have left?'

Confronting these consequences, arising directly and indirectly from what I had done, left me speechless. I was shattered by the full extent of the chaos caused by my accursed actions.

Meanwhile, Dickey answered his own question: 'They could be a meticulous and exemplary account of his topics, right up to when he wrote them, perhaps two decades ago. But I'm not serious; I just don't know. On the other hand, after all those years, he may have become word-perfect and not required any notes.'

This, I could not accept. '*Word-perfect* is not a quality I associated with John.'

'Anyway, there's no need to speculate. I've never been asked officially, or even informally, to join the school, and certainly not to teach.' He changed the subject, his voice taking on a new urgency. 'Throughout my academic career, I've nursed the ambition to research what I adjudge to be one of the most important topics on which a scientist can work. So far, other obligations have always interfered, or I've just procrastinated. Now, at last, I have the leisure time to think and the spare cash to invest, but time is running out as the years pass by. I've just never got started.' He stared at me with such intensity that I felt as if I was preventing him from achieving his life's ambition.

'What do you want me to do? You've mentioned your interest in soil science?'

'Could you come up with one or two ground-breaking research suggestions about how I might begin? I'd appreciate any, *any* ideas about how I could start that work.'

'Yes! I'll do whatever I can… to *figuratively* break the new ground for you.'

With smile of real pleasure, he talked almost confidentially. 'I believe we – that is, all mankind, though some more than others – are exploiting all the earth's resources too greedily, damaging our only environment and changing nature in ways we don't understand. Most people neither notice nor care. If future generations of humans are to go on inhabiting this planet in any comfort, we must maintain a suitable climate, which also must be acceptable to the food crops on which we depend. Already, global warming and its effects are being studied in detail. It's important research, but outside my skills.'

He finished his wine. 'I'd better not drink any more, as I daren't risk being caught over the limit.' Refreshed, he got to the crux of his peroration: 'What far, far too few environmental scientists are doing, in my not-so-humble opinion, is working out just how soil is formed naturally. Soil, 'dirt', the ground, clay – call it what you will – is essential for growing all the plants we eat and those eaten by our domestic animals. Even sophisticated urbanites and remote, star-like so-called *celebrities* feed on products grown in the humble clods below their haughty feet. Yet we treat soil as if it was in unlimited supply and to be exploited without a care. *But* we still don't know the *details* of how soil forms and, more importantly, how fast it's being replaced in nature, though we could, if anyone wished, measure how quickly it's being lost in our intensive farming methods. If we understood nature's ways of forming it and how to replace those losses, then we might reverse some of the heedless damage we inflict continually. Until we know more about nature's capital, the soil that is ultimately underpinning our prosperity, we can't take it for granted, as we do today. It's literally the bedrock of our lifestyle. Nature invented soil long before man invented money. Economic viability is quite different from environmental sustainability. Quite different! I suspect politicians, and I might list these in a different order of priorities... Yes?'

'Since it's getting late, and I don't want to hold you back... [The impromptu lecture was showing every sign of reaching innumerable conclusions, but not of finishing in the foreseeable future.] Perhaps you'd explain how I might contribute?'

Accepting that the remainder of his monologue had to be deferred, Dickey returned to business, 'Yes, I do go on a bit. Hobby horses are pleasurable mounts! I'm asking if you'll think about how soil forms in nature. How do we investigate the chemistry of the ground beneath our feet? What goes on *underneath* our cultivated fields?'

'I've no idea. I'm willing to read and to think about your research ambitions, but I can't promise to contribute much. I'll view the countryside around here through "new eyes", venturing out only after dark... Me! A fugitive from the law! If I'm seen and suspicions are reported—'

'To the police. Yes, I agree. Take no risks. Turn night into day, if you like. With the shutters closed, it's dark enough to sleep in here.'

'I'll need equipment. Can you lend me a computer?'

'Yes, that's no problem, as I have a spare that works reasonably well. I'll bring it tomorrow.'

'You've got articles about soil formation?'

'Yes, I'll also bring some books and articles to get you started. Anything else?'

'Only the worrying problem about how I can pay some rent, overheads, etc.'

'I'm happy to spend some of my unearned and unexpected Lottery winnings on worthwhile causes, but only on projects that interest me! On reflection, the most likely reason why I never got this research off the ground was being unable to decide how to begin. By giving me imaginative ideas about how to initiate that research, you'll be the first *Richards'* *researcher*. I supply board and lodging, and you do some digging into soil-formation science and suggest novel ideas for me to work on later. You'll be part of the Environmental-Research Centre of Excellence at Linkirk University, through a uniquely informal and anonymous contract.'

I thought it was a fair bargain! I responded, 'I'm worried about my debts. My bank balance, like that of many academics, is often in the red. And… I can't get at it until… when?'

'If you help launch my research, while writing your personal memoir, *My Story* or whatever you're calling it, we'll call it quits. You're costing me almost nothing. In fact, for me, it's an excellent investment. If I had to buy your expertise through LU, they'd charge far more and impose overheads on that inflated price to keep the administrators happy. I'm sure I'm getting much the best part of this particular bargain. If the provost knew of our deal, I bet he'd try to relieve me of even more cash.'

'Are you sure? I have no money to repay my debts.'

'It's OK by me, but it has to be temporary. One month max. Longer becomes too risky. I don't know if you'll complete your record of recent events by then, but that's up to you. I'm more interested in your bright ideas to start my research.'

'Yes, a month or so. I'll try to keep to that. Then I'll have to surrender to whatever fate awaits me. If I decide to do something else, and I have no alternative plans yet, I'll simply disappear. If I leave without notice, then you won't… can't be involved. If I'm ever traced back here, you can tell them I broke in unbeknown to you. Dickey, I do appreciate your help. Thank you.'

'OK. We'll leave it like that.'

Before he left, we planned our next meeting; the delivery of the computer, books, etc.; and how to replenish supplies. Then I walked down the lane and signalled when the road was clear. With a wave, he was gone, his car lights coming on at the first bend.

I returned to the cottage with mixed emotions. The time spent in Dickey's company had boosted my morale wonderfully, but made the renewal of my solitary confinement even harder to bear. Perhaps I would indulge in a little nostalgia while writing *My Story*, but knew it might later appear to have been time wasted. Nevertheless, there was a prospect I might convince a defence lawyer of the merits of my case, thereby perhaps reducing the severity of penalties from the charges I could face. Unfortunately, my present truancy could easily offset any benefits achievable from *My Story*.

○

Dickey's pet ambition, to investigate soil-formation chemistry, appeared to be a huge, vague and immensely daunting project. Modesty aside, I wondered if I were capable of thinking up any ideas of sufficient merit to allow their later exploitation. Lacking his motivation, which was almost religious in fervour, I wondered if I could contribute anything, without having a clear understanding of what he wanted, needed or expected. The problem was quite beyond my ability to confront that night, but I hoped that, without much optimism, the task might appear more tractable tomorrow, when I was fresher.

Thinking about the chemistry of countryside creation meant getting out and about, with an open mind, to recognise the relationships between nature and science; that is, *how both function*. Having to spend daytimes indoors meant walking the hills at night, when potential hazards meant careful planning! My next month would be busy!

The Grey Mare's Tail Waterfall was about two miles away, where the effects of water, ice, wind and weather, acting together, had cut deep into the hard Scottish rock over millennia. Its top layers had somehow been broken down progressively into fine particles, ultimately forming the soil that now covered much of the countryside; this is called 'weathering'.

First, I must identify which slow, natural processes disintegrated the solid bedrock first into stones, then through sand and silt, and, finally, to clay. With ingenuity and without preconceptions (exploiting my ignorance!), I just might find insights into ways that rocks are weathered over prolonged geological timescales.

Somewhere inside me persisted a nucleus of optimism for the future, but only a tiny fragment of the high hopes I had brought to Linkirk, and LU, not so long ago. The mess in which I was now so deeply embroiled had resulted directly from my unwillingness to conform to the conventions and practices imposed by an inflexible university hierarchy. I had been naïve in my futile and ultimately pointless attempts to *level the academic playing field, making the rules fairer*. Being unwilling to accept the existing situation, my actions had become totally irrational and irresponsible. I might then, at last and far too late, have learned bitter lessons and be a little wiser, by recognising the damage I had caused so many people, and for which I, alone, was responsible. However, before regaining the luxury of planning my own future, the due processes of the law would decide the price I must pay for the harm inflicted on those who had suffered, so tragically, from my intemperate actions. Sooner or later, judgement must be faced. My choice right then seemed to be either endless, hopeless hiding or institutional incarceration. Meanwhile, I could retain briefly the illusion of limited freedom and enjoy it as best I could.

I locked the door, checked the closed shutters and adjusted curtains so that no light was visible from outside before going to bed. My serious work, racing against clock and calendar, needed to begin the next day, early. Before drifting off to sleep, I wondered whether *my story*, as related to Dickey this evening, was over-optimistic. Not for the first time, I hoped to be able to tell the truth, the whole truth and nothing but the truth. Lawyers who dispense justice, or perhaps only do a job, would decide my fate in due course. The next day, I would start recording the facts, the whole facts and nothing but the facts, *as I recalled them*. Whether *My Story* might (or even could or should) help in my defence, mitigate my punishment, etc., would only emerge later…

Newspaper Articles

CLIP	a. Item cut from newspaper
	b. Device to hold papers together

From *The South of Scotland Sustainer*, Linkirk's Weekly Newspaper.

It alliteratively, and immodestly, described its contents and policy as, 'Timely, thought-tingling, trustworthy and tireless in tracing the total truth.'

The following is dated the third Tuesday in April.

MYSTERY SURROUNDS THE DEATHS OF TWO PROFESSORS
Police Seek University Colleague

As we reported last week, John Bland (62), professor of chemistry at Linkirk University (LU), died recently in unexplained circumstances. The provost, Professor Sir Thomas Carruthers, described the death as, 'resulting from a tragic accident in a laboratory on the university campus.' He also said, 'This is the first fatal accident in our entire history. Everyone at LU offers our deepest sympathies to Professor Bland's widow, family and friends.'

We understand that Professor Bland was working late and alone in his personal laboratory on Thursday evening last when some heavy equipment fell, fatally injuring him. The alarm was raised by Mr Simon Starr, laboratory professor, who noticed a light in the laboratory in the late evening. On investigating, he found Professor Bland injured badly but still alive, trapped under large, metal cylinders in his own workplace. Although he started resuscitation immediately (Mr Starr is a qualified first-aider) his efforts were unsuccessful, and, unfortunately, he was unable to save Professor Bland's life. He was later pronounced dead on arrival at Linkirk Park Hospital.

Following this fatal accident, the police have imposed a news blackout on the incident, while 'inquiries continue into the circumstances of the death, which may be suspicious' according to Inspector Frazer Ross of the local police constabulary. He also stated, 'The media will be informed of developments in due course.'

The Rev. Roy Kerr, of Linkirk 2nd Presbyterian Church said, 'Professor Bland was an elder, a staunch supporter of his church, and an outstanding scientist. Our deepest sympathy is offered to his wife Alison and his bereaved family, who will be remembered in our congregation's prayers.'

The Sustainer is doing everything possible to investigate the unexplained aspects of this tragic event and will keep our readers fully informed of all developments.

Second Death

Today, we further report the accidental death of Dr Walter Thompson, lecturer at the School of Chemistry of LU, who was working in the same department as Professor Bland. It is a remarkable coincidence that this fatality, which occurred while Dr Thompson was undertaking scientific fieldwork in Italy, occurred on the same day that his colleague Professor Bland died: Thursday last.

Dr Thompson has contributed recently to the establishment of the Environmental-Research Centre of Excellence at Linkirk University, and had been appointed its first director. Professor Angus McTaggart, head of chemistry, said, 'At the time of his tragic death, Walter was starting research on the very first project supported by our new centre. His skills and enthusiasm for environmental research will be sorely missed.'

Police Appeal for Information

Detective Inspector Ross, of Linkirk Police, has since issued the following statement: 'The occurrence of two unexplained accidents, apparently on the same day, both proving fatal and both involving staff from the same university school is unprecedented. The police are investigating fully the individual circumstances of both accidents and also the possibility that the incidents may be linked.'

He continued, 'I would appeal to Dr William Green, a colleague of both of the deceased, who has recently and unexpectedly left Linkirk, to come forward as soon as possible to assist police inquiries. It is hoped that he may be able to clarify the circumstances of one or both of these sudden and apparently accidental deaths. Anyone knowing Dr Green's current whereabouts is asked to communicate immediately with the Linkirk Police detectives. The next bulletin will be issued only after progress has been made towards resolving these tragic and unusual cases.'

Dr Green, also a chemistry lecturer at LU, attended a conference in Germany recently. It is believed that he returned to Linkirk late on Saturday evening last, two days after Professor Bland's demise. The police have talked to him briefly, but he has since absented himself, apparently voluntarily, from the apartment he shares with Dr Douglas Montgomery, senior lecturer, also at LU School of Chemistry. Dr Green's present whereabouts is unknown.

Help Required

This newspaper strenuously supports Inspector Ross's appeal. It is the duty of everyone with any relevant knowledge, however trivial, to assist with police inquiries.

Both bereavements are tragic losses to the families concerned: two lives have been cut cruelly short mid-career. We offer our sincere condolences to everyone afflicted directly.

These distressing events also seriously impinge on the reputation of LU School of Chemistry, which has lost two valuable and scholarly staff members. Continued publicity arising from these fatalities can only cause further harm, damaging morale and possibly discouraging students from coming to LU, which has hitherto enjoyed an excellent academic reputation. Any incident injuring our university must also reflect adversely on Linkirk. The sooner the present uncertainties surrounding these fatalities are resolved, the better for us all. The public are asked to help in any and every possible way.

We cannot yet judge the role of Dr Green in these events. However, we council his immediate return to Linkirk to clarify, as far as he is able, these situations reflecting adversely on LU and everyone connected with it, including the people of Linkirk. As always, this newspaper will assist in any way to facilitate contact between the police and anyone having useful information. In the interests of the whole community, we earnestly hope that the dark cloud hovering over LU and Linkirk can very soon be dispersed.

From the Desk of Your Editor:
Health and Safety in Universities

The tragic events reported on page 1 are a cruel blow to all the people most directly concerned – the family, friends and colleagues of the deceased – but also, indirectly, to everyone who lives in or is connected with our university town of Linkirk. To all of those immediately concerned, we offer our most sincere condolences and sympathy. We can only hope that better times will return after this frightful shadow is lifted from us all. It is essential that thorough police investigations are completed as soon as practicable. This might be achieved more quickly if the public can provide the police with the essential information necessary to resolve all the present uncertainties.

That said, we have received intelligence that some aspects of the health and safety regulations applying to science laboratories have recently been ill-enforced in Linkirk University (LU). We trust this is not a widespread practice in that respected institution.

Accordingly, we strongly urge that possible breaches of these codes of practice should be rigorously and rapidly investigated, enabling instances of non-compliance with all statutory rules to be corrected immediately. Staff health and safety must remain a top priority for *both* employers and employees.

It seems possible that one of the accidents (if accidents they were), arose directly from violations and/or lax enforcement of the rules. Ongoing police inquiries will, in time, establish the circumstances leading to the fatal incident in Professor Bland's laboratory. However, the seriousness of the current situation and the consequences that can result from ignoring safety rules mean all areas of possible danger should be identified rigorously and unacceptable practices rectified. Decisive action is now urgently needed to reassure LU staff, students and the public that all their interests are, and remain, fully protected.

Chapter 27

EPILOGUE

a. More than a few words of conclusion: completing *My Story*

b. By Brian 'Dickey' Richards

Bill Green died as the result of a tragic fall at the Grey Mare's Tail Waterfall. This 'accident' poignantly paralleled Walter's remarkably similar demise. Bill's lifeless body was found, one morning in early June, in the pool just below its first cascade, some six weeks after the final evening described in his last chapter of *My Story*. The post-mortem examination confirmed that Bill's death was 'consistent with having sustained fatal injuries by a fall from the rocks above the waterfall pool in which his lifeless body was found'. At the subsequent inquest, the procurator fiscal recorded his official verdict as 'death by misadventure'.

The discovery of Bill's lifeless body, as reported in our local newspaper, *The South of Scotland Sustainer*, is reproduced later, but this account is incomplete. Although it is still strongly suspected that Bill may have had information about the fatal accidents of his two colleagues, such a link has never been confirmed. Accordingly, the newspapers wisely have avoided speculating about The Chem-Mystery and the possible interrelationships of the *three* fatal 'accidents', at least while police investigations continue. As far as I know, nobody has ever questioned why the fugitive (re)appeared on that dangerous waterfall. As owner of Bill's nearby bolthole (The Bothy is about two miles west), I was relieved that this line of inquiry was never pursued.

After learning of Bill's fatal fall, *my* first priority (to minimise the possibility of being charged with hiding a fugitive from justice) was to remove *all* evidence of his recent sojourn in The Bothy by performing a meticulous spring-clean. A competent forensic scientist could have proved easily and conclusively that Bill had been there, but, without such suspicion, no such search was ever made. To my relief, I remain uninvolved.

While packing all Bill's belongings into plastic bags, I wondered how to dispose of these artefacts without implicating myself. Then, I recalled a news report about a fugitive on the run who had managed to live undetected for some weeks in woods close to his home village. His base camp had been located skilfully in a depression screened by thick vegetation. This successful camouflage prompted my copycat scheme to place a similar 'camp', which would be recognisable as Bill's bolthole, in Craik Forest, a few miles east from where he was found, but in the direction *away* from The Bothy. The details no longer matter because it seems that nobody has ever found this planted cache of Bill's identifiable belongings. Presumably, all his personal effects are still concealed within the dense vegetation where I hid them. This fugitive's hideaway, included a small, old tent, found in the roof space of my home, left by a previous owner. I even lit a campfire for authenticity and added camping utensils: plates, mugs, etc. Because this lair was never found, my diversionary tactics were never scrutinised. For me, this was the best of all possible outcomes: I disposed of all incriminating evidence, evaded suspicion and remained untroubled by any inquiries.

Next, in the borrowed computer's memory, I found Bill's valuable legacies. His revealing account of his time at Linkirk, presented in narrative style, gives us this book. Unexpectedly, *My Story* more closely resembles a novel than the legal arguments that I understood he was preparing for his defence against possible charges of manslaughter or, worse, murder. Its length is greater than I believed him capable of writing during the six weeks or so of his incarceration. Alone and uninterrupted, he must have worked throughout most nights, recording his recent and vividly recalled experiences into readable text as fast as he could type. Because the contents are so candid and provide such detailed insights into the trials and tribulations of a young, aspirant, but overambitious university teacher, I decided that *My Story* merits publication as a record of Bill's personal-but-ultimately-disastrous efforts to achieve the status of an established academic. It is, of course, quite different from *Mein Kampf*, but may, nevertheless, be of wider interest due to describing a recent struggle. After some editing, *My Story* appears here as Bill's *auto-obituary*. (This personal history, written under pressure and remarkably quickly, is evidence that his literary skills could well have been exploited as an alternative career. As a writer about science, or perhaps fiction, he might well have prospered without the stresses and strains that, so disastrously, overwhelmed his personality in the academic environment. Alas, it is too late now, and we will never know.)

My second (and personally more welcome) legacies in the computer memory were Bill's significant contributions towards initiating the soil research programme, which I then, finally, got started. His ideas are more valuable than I could have expected, adequately fulfilling his agreement with scientific suggestions that have certainly 'paid his rent in full'. His imaginative and clearly explained research concepts, bequeathed to me, were investigated actively and developed more rapidly than I had hoped initially. After the proposed environmental centre in LU foundered, following the crisis related in *My Story*, I was appointed to a research chair in another university. Being able and willing to finance my own research (using Lottery money obtained without effort and certainly not providing any evidence of my scientific skills or merit!), I achieved *professorial* status during the eventide of my academic career. Thereafter, I retired to live quietly in Linkirk. This research is not described here because the scientific results will soon be published in reputable academic journals. It is a poignant, though, that Bill's greatest contribution to environmental science had to be posthumous. Nevertheless, full credit will be given to his original and valuable scientific insights by including his name as a principal author of our significant and original refereed research articles. (I wonder if the ability of a wanted-but-*late* fugitive from justice to contribute positively to scientific advances will ever be noticed and subjected to police scrutiny? Somehow, I doubt it.)

I deduced, from Bill's final jottings, which were handwritten shortly before his final, fatal fall, that he had been exploring the area above the Grey Mare's Tail Waterfall to investigate the high ground there. Presumably, this was after nightfall to minimise his chances of being seen and recognised. This accounts for his accident in such a dangerous place, which is exceptionally hazardous after dark. I will always bitterly regret that my scientific ambitions might have encouraged Bill to take such risks. Certainly, I would never, *never* have approved of his visit to the top of a high waterfall after dark.

During our last meetings, in my irregular visits bringing essential supplies to The Bothy, I adjudged Bill to have regained a little of his former optimism about his future and to be in fair spirits. He mentioned once, in a moment of candour, that he had come to terms with his fate and accepted that, very soon, he would have to surrender and face the music. For this reason, I would prefer to believe, but can never know for certain, that Bill's final tumble was an unfortunate accident rather than an expression of his final despair. Nevertheless, Bill Green has paid his 'green bill' finally by making significant contributions to the advancement of environmental science: his account is now closed terminally.

The other victim of the events recounted at the end of *My Story*, whom Bill did not adequately (in my view) recognise directly, was Beth. My personal opinion (for what it is worth) is that, after that ill-fated babysitting evening, Bill should have made much greater efforts to heal their breach. It would have been difficult, of course, for someone inexperienced (as he made clear) in resolving the stresses that occur in romances, but not insuperable, even for someone without much self-confidence.

Beth was undoubtedly another loser in these events, and her situation was made much worse by her brother Stewart's problems. Neither Emma nor I had any further contact with the Wilkinsons. Later, I heard that the family had moved to somewhere near Glasgow, where a clinic was providing care and treatment to rehabilitate Stewart. Mr Wilkinson must have been transferred there by the bank, retired or resigned, because now there is a different manager where he once worked in Linkirk.

POSTSCRIPT

DURING MY OWN ACADEMIC CAREER, I ALSO EXPERIENCED THE frustration (and worse) resulting from the secretive and unaccountable workings of university administrations. My problems resembled some of those described by Bill. However, despite such provocation, I never intended to murder any of my colleagues. (Though, on occasion, temptation was distinctly... tempting!) I have, therefore, some sympathy for the sentiments expressed in *My Story*, which can be read as a confession but also identifies serious reasons for the disinterested appraisal of some management practices and priorities tolerated within our imperfect higher education system. Staff cannot challenge arbitrary decisions, without the risk of seriously compromising their own career prospects. While my own academic career has ended recently, I believe Bill's experiences and views (also mine!) merit wider critical analysis and that this story of our time is worthy of wider interest. Perhaps the external and impartial scrutiny of academic career structures could identify and improve the unacceptable and, more importantly, unaccountable features of university administration attitudes and practices surviving from their perhaps past times with ivory-tower status.

We might feel some sympathy with the frustrations of this young and inexperienced academic, but did his perceived predicament justify his intended actions? In every legal and moral respect, *certainly not!* However, we can all guess how we ourselves might respond on finding our situation to be *absolutely intolerable*. If the reader is angered by the attitude of this 'hero' telling his own story, in which he was culpable and literally got away with murder, this opinion can only be academic because no legal action against Bill or anyone else (including me, I hope) is practicable now.

After my chance meeting with Bill Green on that windy hilltop, we became good friends and, sharing concerns about the stresses that mankind is imposing on our environment, we looked forward to collaborating to try to reduce, or possibly reverse, some of the damage that we are all inflicting increasingly on our fragile domain. However, later, I recognised that Bill was finding it difficult to establish himself in his first university post and came to believe he was not temperamentally capable of achieving success in his chosen profession. He was a 'nice guy', but lacked the self-confidence, the political acumen, the single mindedness and even the ruthlessness that are the personal qualities necessary for achieving academic success.

I admired his undoubted commitment to his chosen vocation, and genuine attempts to fulfil every obligation and duty allocated. Nevertheless, I sensed his growing disappointment, felt keenly, when his best-intentioned efforts received little or no recognition or encouragement from his superiors. He did not fully understand some inter-personal problems that he encountered, which are likely to be a stumbling block for any newcomer who joins an established and competitive group of colleagues who do not welcome – indeed, can tend to exclude – outsiders. Being inexperienced and, certainly, naïve, Bill became disillusioned gradually by his lack of tangible achievements, as he saw it, despite his best endeavours to meet all targets set and to overcome the various pitfalls encountered in his challenging career choice. I became aware that, as time passed, he became disillusioned progressively, even angered, by the belief that his senior colleagues were ignoring his best efforts to further the work of the school.

When his discontentment grew, he told me that he might have to quit the job. I now regret bitterly, with hindsight prompted by the later tragedies, that I did not then mention my concerns to the professors. I had failed to fully appreciate the depth of Bill's despair. Unjustifiably perhaps, I hoped that if he could complete his first year satisfactorily, he might regain some of that lost optimism during the summer vacation. My inadequate excuse for inaction was my concern that unwelcome intervention, by an outsider, might further damage his already weakened self-concept.

Bill's problem, I am convinced, was his conviction that Angus, John and others were at best unsympathetic and at worst hostile to him. He also perceived, with real justification, that some school management decisions were both arbitrary and discriminatory. His colleagues (most notably Walter Thompson) received preferential treatment in resource allocation and career advancement. The cumulative effect of these perceived injustices pushed Bill Green finally to breaking point – and well beyond. I believe that, briefly, he did intend to commit homicide (of Walter), but, in execution, his plans misfired. As in his academic career, his aspirations exceeded his ability to deliver. The revenge he intended, and the tragic consequences for others and also himself, are clearly evident and admitted in *My Story*.

The pressures on university staff are multiple and considerable. Academics are contracted to teach (theory and practical skills), to undertake research (entering testing and time-consuming competition to raise the essential financial support) and to administrate. The perception fostered generally (or, at least, *never* denied) by universities is that teaching excellence is a top priority. High-quality instruction is claimed to be supported by good research because 'good researchers make good teachers' (I wonder what 'research', if any, underpins this highly debatable generalisation?). In practice, however, the ethos prevailing within most academic institutions encourages an entirely different hierarchy of priorities. More usually, it is the amassing of *research* money (which is definitely not for *teaching*) that attracts the greatest kudos, because this is perceived as raising the profile of the university, in that more research money means more research excellence. This type of logic disregards the *non sequitur* that one *cannot know* the excellence, or otherwise, of predicted 'discoveries', 'breakthroughs', etc. when their value is '(pre-)measured' by the *amount* of money invested in the university *before* the work is actually started! In the race to raise research resources, undergraduate teaching can be a casualty.

I have no wish now, having retired from the fray, to debate the relative merits of ways that university staff might achieve academic excellence (however *that* can be defined). Nevertheless, I recall acutely the stresses I experienced when working diligently to deliver acceptable performances across my complementary FRART (finance raising, administration, research and teaching) commitments. These duties were allocated across their staff by a set of self-important, uncriticisable and unaccountable professors who also were required to satisfy themselves that their minions (my colleagues and I) were carrying out all their assigned multiple tasks adequately. 'Prof power' resides in their decisive control of both school finances and the career paths of their juniors (promotion, references, etc.). Professors, directors, consultants, managers, etc. (i.e. school bosses) are, in turn, theoretically but equivocally, subject to control by the university officers and central administration. This large bureaucratic phalanx usually manages to keep itself sufficiently remote from the research and teaching coalfaces to give the appearance of being an entirely separate organisation (almost as if situated in a distant galaxy).

University administrations tend to maintain themselves at a safe distance from the academic schools within which all the scholarly and creative work of the same institution take place – that is, the research and teaching – and also including much administration – that is, the self-regulation within each school). This structure, with the effective separation of bureaucratic administrators from learned academia, might perhaps have been appropriate in medieval times, but is it still relevant? Certainly, the collection of separated, distinctive parts that together constituted *my* university never appeared to function as a single, unitary organisation in which one could take a corporate pride. Even so, despite my disillusionment with the system, I never seriously contemplated homicide. Perhaps my fascination with Bill's tale, *My Story*, set in such a familiar context, is a safe proxy situation, through which I can relate to my unfulfilled or successfully suppressed aspirations.

I have taken the liberty of adding chapter titles to Bill's text. I hope he would have approved. Each single word title has been chosen to have two 'alternative but distinct and different' meanings, both of which resonate with some aspects of the chapter's contents in the unfolding story. This illustrates one type of imprecision in language and problems in the telling of *My Story*.)

Professor Brian Bernard Richards, Linkirk, Scotland, 2018.

Newspaper Article

THE FOLLOWING IS DATED THE SECOND TUESDAY IN JUNE.

DEATH OF MISSING LECTURER
'The Chem-Mystery' Remains Unresolved

The police have confirmed that a body was recovered on Monday morning last from a small river, Moffat Water, beside the A708 road from Moffat to Selkirk, at the Grey Mare's Tail Waterfall, about ten miles north of Moffat. The deceased is described as an adult male, but his identity has not yet been confirmed. A post-mortem will be carried out to establish the cause of death. A police spokeswoman declined to speculate as to whether this body could be the missing Dr Green, but added that inquiries into his recent whereabouts would continue.

If this identity is confirmed, would bring an end the unexplained absence of Dr Green, who absconded very soon after the deaths of two other staff members of Linkirk University (LU). In April, the accidental deaths of Professor John Bland and Dr Walter Thompson were reported; the exact causes of their deaths still remain unresolved.

It had been hoped that Dr Green would be able to provide information about unexplained features of the situations whereby two of his colleagues from the LU School of Chemistry lost their lives, apparently in quite distinct and unconnected accidents. By a strange coincidence, both colleagues died on the same day but in widely separated locations: Linkirk and Italy. Now, following the death of the only possible witness, it seems that 'The Chem-Mystery', as it was referred to in the national press, may never be resolved.

Body Found by Hiker

The body found at the Grey Mare's Tail Waterfall, possibly that of Dr Green, was first noticed at about 8.30am by Mr Peter Barnes (35), a hiker from Leeds. He was starting early on an extended hill walk, and stated, 'We don't know this area, but wanted to see where this path led. First, we got above the big waterfall; a hard climb it were [sic], but with good views and worth the effort. Then we reached the smaller upper waterfall. In the small pond underneath the drop of about fifteen feet, I saw what I thought were [sic] a bundle of old clothes in the water. I thought, *Scotland's National Trust* – I think it's their land – *won't like people dumping their rubbish here.* I said to George here, who was walking with me, "I'll do them a favour and pull 'em out to clean up the place." The countryside is being polluted all over, and we must all do our bit to keep it clean. It were [sic] my good deed for the day. Then I saw that it were [sic] a body. Such a terrible shock, it were [sic]. I saw a man's face under the water. There was no way he was alive. I didn't try to revive him; his neck were [sic] too bent. There were [sic] no way he could be alive, with his face under water. Gave us a right turn, it did. So I called the police. They were here right quick. They took over, and we told them all we knew, which weren't [sic] much'.

Two Earlier Deaths

Six weeks ago, we reported the death of Professor John Bland of the LU School of Chemistry. It is known that he died from injuries in his research laboratory that were sustained when several heavy metal cylinders collapsed on him. The results of an internal university inquiry into this fatal accident have not yet been made public, but we believe that some health and safety rules were being flouted blatantly. The same source said that there were 'unexplained features' of this accident. It appears that some unauthorised person, not yet identified, may have entered the laboratory and departed, leaving the heavy equipment in such a dangerous state that its later collapse could have caused this fatality. Aspects of the incident are still under investigation, but the police are withholding the identity of the suspected intruder.

On the same day, Dr Walter Thompson, another staff member of the LU School of Chemistry died, also apparently in a tragic accident. At the time, he was undertaking environmental scientific research in the mountains of northern Italy, and it is believed that he fell to his death from unstable ground, landing on the rocky bed of a small river. Again, the exact circumstances of this fall have not been made public and the case remains open.

Dr Green has not been implicated directly in either accident. However, his university office is near the laboratory in which Professor Bland was injured, which, seemingly, he could have entered easily. We also know that, at the time of Dr Thompson's untimely death, Dr Green was attending a conference in Germany, not very far from the scene of the other accident. These facts should not be taken to mean that Dr Green was in any way involved in either fatality. Nevertheless, his sudden, unexplained departure from Linkirk, immediately after a preliminary police interview, requires urgent explanation. He has failed to respond to repeated calls to come forward, giving the impression that he is unwilling, for unknown reasons, to help resolve The Chem-Mystery.

Dr Green's death, again apparently the result of yet another 'accident', is a further coincidence. One explanation is that, after absconding, Dr Green hid somewhere near Linkirk. This reasonable possibility requires rigorous investigation. No doubt, the police will redouble their efforts to locate where Dr Green hid, to find any remaining clues that may relate to his and/or both other fatalities. However, it is now hard to believe that the many outstanding questions about these three 'accidents' will ever be fully answered. This newspaper hopes that the authorities will succeed in allaying the understandable public concern. We are also pleased to offer all possible help towards resolving the many unanswered questions. However, even with optimism, it now seems unlikely that The Chem-Mystery will ever be fully, finally resolved.

Chemistry at LU

The unexpected, tragic and almost simultaneous, losses of three staff members from the School of Chemistry have caused numerous problems. Professor Angus McTaggart, head of chemistry, recently said, 'All our staff have rallied round magnificently and we have now got the situation totally under control. It has been a struggle, but we are succeeding. Our most important objective is that none of our students will suffer in any way.' We wish them well in dealing with their considerable challenges.

Statement by Mrs Green

Mrs Roberta Green, Dr Green's mother, speaking through her solicitor, has said she had no information about the recent tragic events reported from Linkirk, and declined to speculate about them. She was well aware that her son was working hard in his new job and had high hopes that he would make a success of his university career. She stressed that it would have been quite out of character for him to act dishonourably or to have contributed in any way to the tragic accidents suffered recently by LU staff. She intended to travel from her home in Sussex to Scotland to help the police inquiries, as requested, but has no plans to make further statements now or in the foreseeable future.

The Future

These tragic events still remain unexplained, and many outstanding questions still require answers. The public will continue to follow the progress of all three cases and any movement towards solving them with the greatest concern. They will seek reassurances that everything is being done to investigate fully these three so-far-unexplained fatalities in our Linkirk community. As always, *The Sustainer* will keep everyone up to date with developments, as soon as they are made known, and, where appropriate, press the authorities to adopt policies that will uphold the good names of the town of Linkirk and its university. The sooner the unwelcome publicity that has soiled the good name of Linkirk can be consigned to the past, and normal, decent life resumed, the better for all concerned. Watch this space!

ACKNOWLEDGEMENTS

It is my real pleasure to record my sincere appreciation of the help provided by the Staff at Troubador in guiding me through the publishing process. In particular, I would mention Fern Bushnell (Production Controller), Hannah Dakin (Customer Service), Andrea Johnson (E-books), Sophie Morgan (Marketing), Jonathan White (Sales and Marketing).

AG.

JEERING B

"Hey, look at Petey," yelled Jasper MacMillan. "Petey's in a ring full of girls!"

Hump started hooting, "What's a boy doing in the *Maiden* class?"

Pete was so upset that he dug his right heel into the horse's ribs. All he could think of was getting away from the heckling voices. Casper took the bit in his teeth, and bolted. All Pete could do, in the crowded ring, was try to avoid running anyone over.

"Petey!" His mother shrieked in horror, seeing her son's horse out of control. Casper shied and bucked. Pete went flying.

At that moment, Peter realized that there was something worse than being THE ONLY BOY IN THE RING

THE DUTCH MILL STABLE STORIES

Kids who love horses: rich kids, poor kids, good kids, spoiled kids, girls, boys—you'll meet them all at the Dutch Mill Stables. Where young people have wonderful, heartwarming adventures and learn important lessons about riding, horse care, friendship, values—and, above all, about life.

Don't miss the other
Dutch Mill Stable Stories
published by Tor Books

IF WISHES WERE HORSES
THE JUDGE IS SEEING DOUBLE
A LEG UP FOR LUCINDA

A Dutch Mill Stable Story

THE ONLY BOY IN THE RING

NANCY WRIGHT GROSSMAN

Illustrated by
MARY DAMON

TOR

A TOM DOHERTY ASSOCIATES BOOK
NEW YORK

THE ONLY BOY IN THE RING

A TOR Book
Published by Tom Doherty Associates, Inc.
49 West 24 Street
New York, NY 10010

Cover art by Tim O'Brien

ISBN: 0-812-56506-1   Can. ISBN: 0-812-56507-X

Library of Congress Catalog Card Number: 88-50993

First edition: January 1989

Printed in the United States of America

0 9 8 7 6 5 4 3 2 1

For Seamus
My One and Only Boy!

Chapter One

Lazy Daze
Comes to Stay

Pete Draper stuck his head out the window as his Uncle Will's big red and white horse van turned the corner and lumbered up the driveway toward Dutch Mill Stables.

"Hey, Tracy, I'm back! And wait'll you see what I brought with me!" Pete yelled to his friend, who was out sitting on the fence in front of the office.

Tracy jumped down and came running. The truck pulled up by one of the barn doors. The lettering on its side read, ELEVEN OAKS, ROYALTON, NORTH CAROLINA.

Pete hopped down from the cab and ran around to the side of the van. As soon as he and Uncle Will had opened up the doors and pulled out the ramp, Pete raced up it and into the huge nine-horse transport. Inside was one very lonely pony.

Pete threw his arms around Lazy. Lazy Daze had been Pete's to ride for the summer, and now he was Pete's for the rest of the year as well. He still couldn't believe it.

"Hey, Lazy!" Pete boomed. "You poor old thing, all by

1

yourself back here for all these miles. But it's okay now, we're here!" Lazy neighed in response to the good news.

Tracy came bounding up the ramp to see what all the fuss was about. "Wow, a pony!" she exclaimed. "Oh, she's cute! What did you call her?"

"Lazy. *His* name is Lazy Daze," Pete corrected her. "But I call him Lazy. Keith—he's my cousin—he calls him Crazy Daze because he used to drive Keith crazy. Keith has a horse now, so I got to ride Lazy this summer. Finally!"

Pete made a face. "I was getting real tired of Midget— you know, that little tiny pony I told you about, the one I outgrew ages ago. He was so short my feet would drag on the ground.

"Lazy and me, though, we get along great. I couldn't believe it when Uncle Will called up Mom and Dad and told them I could bring Lazy home with me if I wanted to—and they said yes!" Pete, barely able to contain his excitement, led the pony out of the van.

A few minutes later, Pete's parents rolled in and parked next to the truck. "Petey, Petey!" Mrs. Draper called to her son before the car had even stopped. Pete, like any normal ten-year-old boy, rolled his eyes.

"Hi, Mom. It's Pete, remember?" He dug the toe of his boot in the dirt. "Peter, if you have to. But, please, Mom, no more Petey, okay?"

"My, look how you've grown! Look, Bob, look how tall Petey's gotten!" was his mother's only response to his usual complaint. Then she exclaimed, "Oh, why look—is that your little brown horse?"

"Pony, Mom," Pete explained, patiently. "He's a pony. And he's not brown, he's a bay. He's a bay pony."

"Well, he certainly looks brown to me," Mrs. Draper insisted. "Looks awfully young, too."

"He's full grown, Mom. He's a full-grown pony. Good grief, he's fourteen years old. There's no way he's going to grow any more. And he's got a black mane and tail, so that makes him a bay. That's just the way it is, Mom," Pete tried to convince her. "Tell her, Uncle Will," he ended, lamely.

"Y'all listen to the lad, Eileen. He should know. He's been trained by the best—me!" Uncle Will said with a laugh.

"How are y'all?" he went on. "My, it's good to see you! Martha sends her love. She sure is gonna miss the boy." He put an arm around Pete. "Me, too, Pete," he added with obvious affection.

Pete had been spending his summers at Eleven Oaks in North Carolina with Uncle Will and Aunt Martha ever since he was five years old.

"It's a pretty weird sort of farm," Pete had tried to explain to one of his friends once. "The only things my Uncle Will raises are ponies and horses. He's always saying, 'Hmm, mighty fine crops of foals this spring' and 'Would you look at that crop of yearlings over there' like they were corn or carrots or something!"

The best thing about Pete's summers was learning how to ride well enough to keep up with his cousins, Keith and Kelly. Keith was four years older than he was. Kelly was a year younger than her brother, which made her three years older than her New Jersey cousin. All three had their own ponies to ride, and they spent many warm summer days playing cowboys and Indians, galloping through the undergrowth of Eleven Oaks's wooded pastureland.

Coming back home in September had always been hard for Pete, at least until this year. Last year he had discovered Dutch Mill Stables, the barn where several of his classmates kept their horses and took riding lessons. You didn't have to own your own horse to ride there. You didn't even have to be taking lessons to spend time at Dutch Mill, and Pete soon became a familiar sight around the barn, making himself useful wherever he could.

But this year everything was different. This year he was returning with a pony to ride! He would be able to take lessons with the other kids and maybe ride in shows. He'd go out riding on the trails, and, best of all, he would learn to jump. Uncle Will had been teaching Keith to jump this past summer. Now Pete would be able to learn, too.

Betsy Ingersol, the head trainer at Dutch Mill, came out to greet the new arrival. "Hi, Pete. Welcome back!" she called out warmly. "Looks like you're going to be one of our gang, now! We can always use another hand around here!"

She offered Lazy a hand to sniff and then ran her hand up the pony's face and scratched between his ears.

"So this is Lazy Daze, eh? You don't look so lazy to me," she commented with a chuckle. The pony's ears pricked up as he took in his new surroundings.

"No way! He's not lazy!" Pete stated firmly. "He's a lot of pony, right Uncle Will?"

"Nobody needs to speak for Lazy, lad. Or for y'all, I've noticed! Lazy'll make a name for himself 'round here, y'all see if he don't. Why, he'll be a reg'lar gentleman before ya bring him back next summer." He looked over at Pete. "Miz Ingersol tells me she's going to make a proper rider out of you, so's Keith and Kelly won't even recognize ya come next June!"

Pete smiled proudly. "You sure won't."

Chapter Two

Crawling Lessons

Pete became one of the most enthusiastic of Dutch Mill's many young riders. He was usually the first one there after school. He always ran all the way.

"It's a wonder you don't wear that pony's coat right off of him, laddie," old Mike, one of the grooms, had said more than once. Like everyone else around the barn, he marveled at the energy Pete put into the care of his pony. "There's nothing much I can be teachin' you on the subject of groomin' a horse, that's for sure!"

But there were many things Betsy could teach Pete on the subject of horsemanship. Pete had a *lot* to learn. She knew she had her work cut out for her from the first time she watched Pete ride.

"Young man, this is *not* a rodeo," Betsy called, laughing good-naturedly. "Come here and let me give you a few pointers."

Pete trotted over to where Betsy stood in the middle of the ring. "What's the matter?"

"Oh, just about everything, if you want to know the

truth! But don't let it bother you. How about we tackle one problem at a time, okay?'' Pete nodded.

"Let's start with your legs. When you've got them where they belong and doing what they're supposed to be doing, we'll go on to the next thing.''

Betsy came around, stood beside Lazy, and took Pete's leg and positioned it properly. "Okay, *this* is where your leg belongs,'' she showed Pete. "You've gotten used to riding with your legs too far in front of you, and that throws off the position of your upper body.'' She put a hand firmly in the middle of Pete's back and moved his upper body forward.

"Good. Now, let's see a little arch in your back. That's it, sit up really straight. Oh, does that ever look better!'' she encouraged her new student.

"Okay, now that your leg knows where it should be, let's see you drop your heel. Heels down, toes up.'' Pete did as he was instructed.

"Can you feel that in your calf muscle?'' Betsy asked.

Pete nodded. "I sure can. It feels weird.''

"You'll get used to it. Okay, now, I want to see you stand up in your stirrups.''

That's easy, Pete thought until he tried it. It took three tries before he got up and steadied. When he was finally standing, Betsy pointed out why it had been so hard.

"Look at your leg, Pete. See? It's where I showed you it should be. When you tried to get up, your leg went back to your old forward position and you fell backward, didn't you. Your leg has to be under you like this to give you a base of support. Can you feel it?''

Pete wasn't sure. "Move your leg forward like you used to and try to stand up,'' Betsy instructed. He couldn't. "Now, bring it back.'' Up he went with no trouble. A big grin spread across his face. "I learned something!''

"You bet!'' Betsy smiled. "And you're going to learn lots more. Now, go out to the rail and walk.''

"Walk?'' Pete questioned.

"You have something against walking?'' Betsy asked him.

"Well, no. I mean, I like to canter and gallop. I already know how to walk. Walking's boring," Pete complained.

"Walk!" Betsy commanded. She watched as he guided Lazy out to the rail. "Hey, Pete," she called to him, "do you remember how *you* learned to walk?"

A girl Pete didn't know trotted by him and giggled.

"No! I was a baby," Pete answered indignantly. This lesson felt pretty ridiculous all of a sudden.

"But you have a little sister, right? How old is Jenny?"

"She's five."

"Do you remember when she learned how to walk? How did she do it?" Betsy prompted him.

"She just got up and walked, I guess."

"After a lot of crawling and pulling herself up, and practicing holding on to somebody's hand or the furniture, right?"

"Yeah."

"Well, for the next few weeks, that's what you're going to be doing. Just think of it as crawling lessons. Don't be embarrassed. We all have to start somewhere!"

Chapter Three

Good Riding, Good Grades

"I think he's cute," Meg Walsh stated flatly. "Kind of young, but definitely cute." Meg was eleven.

"I think he's cute, too, and I don't think he's too young at all," ten-year-old Celia Mason said with a giggle. "Actually, Pete looks just exactly the right age."

Julia Jackson and Mel Hollister, who were both ten, nodded. They both liked Pete and always had. He had helped Mel on a lot of projects around the barn. Mel worked for Betsy to help pay the board bills for Streak, the pony she had leased from Julia's parents. Working for Betsy meant anything from pitching hay to painting jumps, and Pete was always ready to lend a hand.

Pete brought the number of boys who rode at Dutch Mill to a grand total of three. First there was Jonathan James Fitzpatrick III, who was thirteen and a serious show rider. Alexis Appleby, who turned twelve that year, considered Jonathan to be her own private property. As yet, however, she hadn't succeeded in making Jonathan aware of her feelings. He seemed to be more interested in Tracy Field. Bobby Williams, the only other boy, was seven.

9

Pete was surprised to find out how popular he had suddenly become. Being one of the three Dutch Mill boys was practically a full-time job.

"Want to come with us out on the trails?" offered Meg's twin sister Morgan. "We're going over to Murdock's Pond and back. And Julia and Mel are coming, too." She thought for a moment, then added, "We've got candy bars."

"I can't," Pete answered with a groan. "I've got a lesson with Betsy in fifteen minutes. Some other time, okay?"

He continued on down the aisle toward Lazy's stall. "Hey, Pete!" came a voice from behind him. He looked back to see Loretta leading her horse, Crazy Eddie, down the corridor. "Hiya, Loretta." Pete responded.

"Hey, Jody and I are going out for a ride on the Country Club trail. Want to come?" Loretta asked.

"Sorry, can't." Pete told her about his lesson.

"Well, we could wait till you're finished. It still stays light till about seven, so there's no big rush, right?"

"Gee, I'd like to, but I have to be home early tonight. It's my older sister's birthday."

Before he reached the ring, Pete had been invited on two more trail rides and on a ride and picnic for Saturday. That invitation he accepted.

Most afternoons, however, Pete spent his free time working—hard. He was determined to win Betsy's praise.

Betsy had lots of different ways of working with the kids she taught. With some she went slowly, concerned that they might quit if she pushed them too hard. With others, she bullied them a little bit, sensing that they responded well to being challenged. Pete was definitely the type who did his best when he was pushed.

"I'd say that was good—if I didn't know you could do better," Betsy told him after he'd executed a figure eight for her. His next one was faultless. "Yes! Yes! *That's* good riding!" She rewarded him with an approving smile.

Pete grinned ear to ear, collapsed on Lazy's neck and patted the pony vigorously. He never forgot that Lazy put in one-half of every good performance.

Pete's parents were concerned about another kind of

performance—Pete's school performance. His grades in school had never been great, and his mother feared that having the added distraction of the pony would make it just that much harder for Pete to concentrate on his schoolwork.

Lazy, in fact, had just the opposite effect on Pete.

"Petey, would you come in here please," Mrs. Draper called grimly to him one evening in November. Pete appeared at the door quickly, wondering what had prompted her serious tone of voice.

"Can you explain this to me, young man?" she asked, pushing a computer printout toward him. He looked at it with alarm.

"It's my midterm grades, isn't it?" he said, nervously.

"Yes, and they're excellent. What exactly is going on here?" She looked at him sternly and then started to smile, unable to keep up the pretense any longer. "I've got to admit, if anything Lazy seems to be having a good effect on your schoolwork. I'm really proud of you, and so's your Dad."

Pete let out a sigh of relief and decided to ignore this one "Petey."

Chapter Four

"It's Not Who Wins . . ."

Pete's days with Lazy flew by. The warm September afternoons had become crisp November afternoons, and evening came earlier and earlier. Before Pete knew it, it was Christmas.

"A show coat!" Pete let out a whoop, as he opened the biggest present under the tree first. Ever since he'd brought Lazy home with him, he'd been thinking about the day when he'd be ready to join all the other Dutch Mill kids who took their horses or ponies to the shows.

"Betsy gave us a few hints!" Mrs. Draper said as she hugged him. Pete jumped up to try on the navy blue coat, and Sarah, his older sister, surprised everyone when she admitted that she thought he looked sharp.

Santa also brought Pete a new pair of breeches, a pair of gloves, and a hunt cap. Pete was especially glad about the hat. His old one was looking pretty worn.

"All I have to do is give my boots a good polishing, and I'll be ready!" Pete crowed. He couldn't wait. He was over at the barn the next morning at eight o'clock, looking for Betsy.

"Hey, Betsy," Pete yelled when he finally saw her. "When's the next show? I got a coat for Christmas and I'm ready to roll!" He ran breathlessly up to her.

"Whoa there, pal!" Betsy answered laughing. "It's not quite that simple. It takes more than clothes to be ready for a show!"

"You mean I'm not ready yet? After all those lessons? Just two days ago you said I was doing great. Now I'm not?"

"You are. It's almost 'all systems go.' It's just that a few things still need some polishing up. Not your boots—they look terrific!"

Pete hardly heard the compliment. He tried to look in-different, but he couldn't hide his disappointment.

"Oh, come on now, Pete. I'm not talking about years. A few more weeks. Anyway, the next show is the Green Tree, and that's a big one. That's no place for your first show." Pete still looked dubious. "Trust me," Betsy added.

The next several weeks taught Pete a lot about pa-tience. He also worked harder than ever. Betsy drilled him mercilessly on lesson days, and instead of going out on the trails, he used his other afternoons to drill himself. One day in mid-February Betsy called him into the office.

"Now?" he asked expectantly.

"Now." Betsy nodded and grinned. "You're good and ready. You're *more* than ready, which is what you've got to be. You've really proven to me that you want to show and that you know your stuff."

Betsy handed him a prize list that described all the clas-ses. Four Springs Farms was having a local show in three weeks. Pete's entries would have to be in by this Friday. He and Betsy talked about the classes he would try.

"I'm going to be honest with you, Pete," she told him seriously. "Lazy is a cute pony, but even braided up, he's not much to look at. He's what he is—a cute, fat pony.

"The fact is, you're going to have to work darned hard to even get noticed in the show ring. This may be just a local show, but I've got to tell you, kiddo, a lot of kids around here have some really flashy horses. I don't want you to be disappointed if you get overlooked, okay?"

Pete was sure that wouldn't bother him at all. "I just want to show. I don't care if I don't win," he insisted.

Betsy complimented him on his good attitude and started her usual pep talk about sportsmanship.

"I know, I know," Pete interrupted her. " 'It's not who wins . . .' My dad says it all the time."

Pete found himself repeating his father's words all that spring. "It's not who wins," he muttered to himself as he lined up in front of the judge in class after class, show after show, and each time he heard six other riders called out to receive their ribbons. By the time Uncle Will's van pulled into Dutch Mill that June, Pete had seven shows under his belt—and not a single ribbon on his wall.

Chapter Five

Green Horses
and Old Ponies

"Y ou're back!" Kelly yelled as the Eleven Oaks van pulled up the driveway. "Hey, Ma, Pete's back! Lazy's home!" Kelly ran across the gravel to meet her father, who stopped to let her step up on the running board and give him a welcome-home kiss. She rode up to the barn hanging tightly onto the door frame, bubbling over with questions.

"How's Lazy?" she shouted to Pete across her father. "Did everyone like him? Was he good? Did he miss us?"

"Everyone liked him fine, except the judges at the shows," Pete grumbled. "None of them even noticed him, not in a ring full of horses."

"But did he do good? Were ya good?" Kelly wanted to know.

"Yeah, we were great. Only it's the best kept secret in the entire state of New Jersey."

Pete and Kelly got Lazy out of the van, walked him around for a while to get the stiffness out of his legs, and then put him in his old stall. Lazy sniffed at the feed tub, the water bucket, and in the corners and then settled down.

Pete threw a handful of hay in for him, and pretty soon Lazy was chomping away contentedly.

Keith showed up as Pete and Kelly finished putting away Lazy's saddle and bridle. He had just finished riding and was still in his boots and breeches.

"Hey, Pete, how's it goin'," he drawled, sticking out a hand. Pete couldn't help thinking how tall Keith had gotten since last summer.

Keith seemed to read his thoughts. "Grew four inches. I'm fifteen, after all. I've jes' 'bout outgrown Ghost." Keith laughed. His voice was a lot lower now, too.

"Ghost?" Pete asked, confused.

"Ghost Story. The horse I've been ridin' this year. Him," he said, pointing down the aisle to a beautiful gray whose head was out its stall door. "That's Ghost."

Pete walked down and greeted Keith's horse. Keith came up behind him.

"He's okay. I've been showin' him since January. Took reserve junior hunter champion at Tryon. He was jumpin' real good there. He's not real consistent though. Jumps good some days, not so good other times. But Pa's watchin' out for a jumper for me. Somethin' a whole heck of a lot bigger. I want to show jumpers. Nobody cares what you look like—you jes' have to get over them fences."

Pete had seen a few junior jumper classes at the shows he'd entered back home. The Dutch Mill kids didn't ride in many of them. The jumps were big, and Betsy didn't want anyone picking up bad habits riding jumpers. Just as Keith had said, proper horsemanship didn't matter—all that counted was making sure your horse cleared the jumps.

"Hey, Pete, maybe Pa'll let y'all take Ghost home with you the end of the summer," Keith said slowly. "Yeah, if we find me a horse soon, maybe ya can get started riding Ghost before you go."

Pete's eyes got big and he found himself looking at the gray with much more interest. "How old is he?" Pete asked.

"Six. He was pretty green when Pa got him."

"He looks better gray," Pete joked.

Keith laughed, grabbing Pete and wrestling him into a

hammerlock in a matter of seconds. "Okay, okay," Pete gasped. "You win! He was green." It was the oldest joke in the horse book—a young, inexperienced horse was always referred to as 'green.'

"Think *you* could ride a green one?" Keith challenged his young cousin. "Lazy's no spring chicken. He's no big deal."

"You're telling me," Pete agreed glumly. "I've been showing him since the spring and nothing."

"Nothin'?" Keith was surprised.

"Nope," Pete admitted. "He didn't stand a chance in the middle of a bunch of classy horses."

"Didn't you show him in any pony classes? He always did okay in the pony division 'round here."

"Oh sure, pony classes too. Nothing."

The two cousins had wandered back over to Lazy's stall and were looking in on him. "He's showin' his age, that's for sure," Keith commented. "And he's gettin' fat. I guess his show days are 'bout over. It's lazy days ahead for ol' Lazy Daze."

Chapter Six

A Good Idea

I t didn't take Pete any time at all to get settled back in at Eleven Oaks. After one of Aunt Martha's great lunches, he galloped upstairs to unpack. Afterward he threw his jacket on the extra bed in Keith's room—which would be his for yet another summer—pulled on his boots, and ran back down to the barn.

Kelly and Keith were both in the tack room. Kelly was working away at a bridle that hung on the cleaning hook, and Keith was just getting down a saddle that needed attention. He swung it onto the saddle-cleaning stand and started soaping up a big sponge.

"So, you and Lazy didn't exactly take New Jersey by storm, eh, twerp," Keith kidded Pete. Pete grabbed another sponge from under the cleaning stand and let it fly at his cousin.

"Hey, buddy, you're playin' with dynamite now!" Keith grinned, dunking his sponge back in the bucket that stood beside him. He held up the dripping mass and started advancing toward Pete.

"No!" Kelly shrieked from behind him.

"Oh, so you're standin' up for the little guy, eh?" Keith called, not taking his eyes off Pete. "Y'all on the same team? It's the midgets 'gainst the men, is it?" Suddenly another wet sponge caught him on the back of the neck. Keith spun around, confronting Kelly in mock rage.

"So the pipsqueak wants to get into it. Okay, get into it!" His sponge flew.

Kelly ducked and the sponge sailed out the tack room door, landing squarely at Uncle Will's feet. He picked it up and raised his eyebrows questioningly.

"Uh-oh." Keith, Kelly, and Pete gulped in unison.

"Hmmm." Stepping into the tack room, Uncle Will barked, "If I didn't know better, I'd say that maybe a little less than a whole lotta work's gettin' done here today.

"Pete, whadaya say we take us a little walk and leave these younguns to their chores. Then when they're finished, you kids can go on down to the swimmin' hole and cool off." Uncle Will's broad wink made it clear that he wasn't half as angry as he had sounded.

Pete and his uncle wandered out of the barn and across the courtyard in front of it. Eleven Oaks's main barn was a beautiful brick structure shaped like three sides of a huge square. There were big planters trailing with red-flowered vines by all the doors and a pair of cast-iron jockey hitching posts stood guard by the main entrance. Their jackets were painted white with red sleeves, and their caps were red as well.

"Remember the first summer I came down here, Uncle Will?" Pete reminisced. "I wasn't any taller than those two jockeys!"

"You sure are taller now, lad," Uncle Will said with a twinkle in his eye. "Taller, and a lot smarter. You always was a smart one, though. You picked up everythin' there was to know about horses like you was born to it, boy.

"And your Miz Ingersol, she was tellin' me y'all're ridin' like a pro these days. She was tellin' me how hard it was for you at first, and how ya stuck with it and worked like a demon. Yep, that's what she told me," Uncle Will answered Pete's surprised stare.

"She said that?" Pete marveled. Betsy's compliments were so hard to come by that it even felt great getting one secondhand like this.

"That she did. And she also told me how frustrated you were gettin', what with tryin' to show that tired old pony we saddled you with. Don't worry—y'all don't have to be polite with your Uncle Will now. I know Lazy's fun for knockin' around the woods, but I also know he's no show pony anymore. But from what Miz Ingersol told me, you learned a whole lot on that little guy. I'm lookin' forward to seein' what kind of a rider y'all're becomin'!"

Pete took a deep breath. "Uncle Will, Keith said you're looking for a jumper for him and that he's outgrowing that gray horse, Ghost Story. He said maybe I could ride Ghost this summer . . ." Pete's nerve failed him and his voice trailed away. He gulped nervously.

Uncle Will looked the boy up and down. "Hmmm . . . Y'all are gettin' some size on you," he mused, half to himself. "And you're long 'nough in the leg. Hmmm . . ."

Uncle Will took his cap off and ran his hand through his hair. He always did that when he was deep in thought. Pete stood his ground and looked Uncle Will square in the eye.

"Yep," he nodded suddenly to the boy. "Good idea."

Chapter Seven

Send Betsy Back
to Jersey

Pete held his nose as he jumped off the boulder and into the "swimmin' hole." An old rock quarry—the hole, as they'd come to call it—had served for many years as country club, secret headquarters, and proving ground for all the local kids. Boys and girls for miles around would long remember those first death-defying leaps into the hole's chilly waters.

Pete came bursting to the surface, whooping from the sudden cold.

"Whatsa matter, twerp," Keith taunted him from high up on the opposite wall. "Water not quite warm 'nuf for y'all? Shall I have the maid draw ya a hot bath?"

"Come on, chicken. Here, little chicky. Come on and jump off the little ledge and into the warm water, little chicky," Pete jeered in return. "Bok bok-bok-bok-bok!"

Keith launched himself into space, pulled his legs up and blasted the far reaches of the quarry with water as he landed in a perfect cannonball not a foot and a half from his nervy little cousin. He surfaced quickly, reached out, and pushed Pete under. Pete came up ready to take him on.

"Why, young man, don't you have any idea how dangerous that kind of behavior can be?" Keith acknowledged the danger by pushing Pete back under.

"Oh, please, kind sir, please, please don't do that to me again," Pete pleaded, grinning gamely as he came up again.

"I'm going to tell your mother on you," he said the third time.

The fourth time, Pete shot himself up into the air and came down with arms out and hands flat, sending a spray of water splashing in Keith's face. Then he struck out fast for the shore. He was lying back sunning himself on a rock and talking to Kelly when Keith came out of the water a few minutes later.

"So, Pa tells us ya went and learned how to be some fancy-pants rider," Keith started in again as he found himself a comfortable spot to sit. "Have ya gotten too big for yer fancy breeches, or are ya gonna keep on talkin' to us home-grown equestrians?"

"Oh, I'll probably keep talking to you," Pete said condescendingly, "if you try not to embarrass me *too* much. And if you're real polite, maybe I might even give you a pointer or two."

That was too much for Keith. He jumped to his feet, strode over to Pete, picked him up, and carried him to the water's edge. Pete nonchalantly crossed one leg over the other and acted as if being dumped back in the water was what he wanted to do more than anything else in the world. When he came sputtering to the surface, he said very politely, "Thank you, young man."

"You know, sometimes your legs are too far forward when you jump," Pete told Keith the next morning. "That's why you sometimes fall back over the fences, which is probably why Ghost doesn't jump real consistently. He's waiting to see what's going to happen over the next fence."

Keith glowered at his cousin. Pete was really beginning to get on his nerves. However, he did try adjusting his leg position to match Pete's. "That's it," Pete said.

Pete urged Lazy into a canter and stood up in his stirrups

in jumping position. "See, you need to keep your legs like this all the time. It helps keep you forward. Try it."

Ghost followed Keith's cues into a smooth canter and Keith attempted to mimic Pete's position. He found it very hard to maintain his balance for more than six or eight strides at a time.

"I don't see where's all this standin' up and bobbin' around's gonna make much difference over a jump course," Keith drawled.

"Betsy won't let you even try jumping till you can do this for hours without falling back. She makes you go around like this for weeks—for years! You feel real stupid, but she says it's important."

"Yeah? Well if Miz Betsy said it, it sure as shoot must be true," Keith said sarcastically. He'd already heard as much about Betsy as he could take. The way his father had been going on about Pete's lessons and Pete's trainer had really gotten to the older boy.

"You don't believe me? Hey, that's no skin off my nose," Pete said. He had heard his father use that expression many times. To his surprise, it seemed to work on Keith just as well as it had ever worked on him. It shut Keith up, anyway.

Pete continued to canter around, still standing in his stirrups. Finally Keith called out, "You sure can do that for ever, can't you." Then he tried it again.

After falling back several more times, Keith was about to give up in disgust. Pete rode up to him.

"Hey, don't quit. Try this. Grab a handful of Ghost's mane and use that for balance." Keith tried it and found it worked. Pretty soon the two cousins were challenging each other with circles and figure eights, all done standing in their stirrups. They looked like jockeys breezing their young colts as they galloped down the sides of the ring.

Keith tried jumping a few little crossbars. To his amazement, he felt steadier. Ghost seemed steadier, too. Pete sent Lazy over the same jumps and then pulled him up. Lazy and Ghost were heaving and sweaty from all the work, in spite of the early morning chill.

"How did that feel?" Pete asked.

"Not bad."

"It looked good. It looked smooth and steady and balanced, like—"

"Like Miz Betsy says, right? Look here, midget, I've gotta tell you, I sorta feel like this Betsy person's invaded this place, you know what I mean? Thing's was goin' along jes' fine till this Betsy showed up with you yesterday. How's about we send ol' Betsy on back up to Jersey, if it's all right with you, okay?"

Chapter Eight

Private Lessons

"What else am I doin' wrong?" Kelly wanted to know. Keith hated having Pete point out his faults, but Kelly didn't mind at all. She looked on Pete as her own private trainer.

"Your feet are sticking out too far," Pete yelled to her. "Turn them so they're pointing forward. Yeah!" Kelly was standing in her stirrups just like Pete had showed her.

"Now get your elbows in, too. And your shoulders back."

Kelly circled the ring twice at a trot and once at a canter. Then she popped Max over a two-foot post-and-rail jump. The pinto pony hardly broke stride. Kelly patted Max on the neck as she slowed him to a walk.

"You sure have picked up on how to teach folks," she observed as she and Max pulled alongside of Pete and Lazy. "You don't look like you used to, neither. Ya make me feel like a know-nothin'.

"I never really cared much before. But with Keith goin' to shows, and y'all ridin' like some kinda professional . . .

well, it makes me want to learn. Pa never taught us much— he jes' put us on the ponies and gave 'em a slap on the rear!" She gave Max an affectionate pat.

"I sure enjoy ridin'. I can't imagine not havin' a pony or a horse in my life. But now I think I'd like to be better at it. Would you teach me?"

"I'll teach you everything I know—which you'll see really isn't all that much," Pete admitted freely. "You're getting a real amateur, I'm warning you!"

"Will you give me real lessons, like every day?"

"Uh, well, sure. How about nine o'clock, Monday to Friday? Rain or shine."

"Rain or shine. Now what about Saturday and Sunday?"

"Hey!" Pete complained. "When are we supposed to have fun? Remember, this *is* summer vacation!"

The next morning, Pete was standing in the middle of the ring trying to look as official and professional as he could manage. It wasn't easy. His pupil was the same cousin he had clowned around with for six summers in a row, and at this moment she was sticking her tongue out at him.

"I said get your heels down further!" he hollered at the impudent Kelly.

"And I said they don't go no further," Kelly shot back, giggling.

"Okay, okay. But keep them down as far as you can. Now, instead of kicking Max, I want to see you squeeze him into a trot. No, I mean, I *don't* want to *see* you squeeze him into a trot. I shouldn't be able to see anything. At the moment, it looks more like pony abuse than horsemanship."

Kelly made another face at him but followed his instructions well. Max moved into a slow trot.

"He won't do nothin' but poke along if'n I don' give him a good kick, Pete," Kelly insisted.

"Oh, yes he will. You just have to squeeze harder. Really squeeze, and push him along with your seat. See?"

Max cooperated by picking up his pace. Kelly was con centrating so hard she looked like she was going to burst

"Y'all don't really mean I've gotta do this all the time, do you? Kickin's a whole lot easier."

"It may be easier, but it's not what they want to see in the show ring, that's for sure. Betsy says it's supposed to look like Max can read your mind."

"I sure hope he can't read my mind right now. He wouldn't like what he was readin', I can tell ya that!"

Keith never let Pete know he hung around for these nine o'clock lessons, but he was always within earshot. Later in the day, when Kelly and Pete had finished their chores and would take their ponies out on the trails, Keith would saddle up Ghost and go into the ring to practice everything Pete had told Kelly that morning.

Uncle Will chuckled, looking out the kitchen window. Keith was trotting figure eights in a perfect imitation of Pete's jumping position. When he settled back down into the saddle, his posture was erect, his hands were in the proper position, and his legs were under him where Pete insisted they should be.

"That boy's goin' to make rider of 'em both," Uncle Will whispered to himself.

Chapter Nine

Bubbles

"Well, would you look at that!" Kelly crowed. Keith was jumping Ghost as Pete and his cousin rounded the end of the barn. "Fancy-pants ridin'!"

The Mangy Midgets, as Keith had taken to calling them, had announced that they were going all the way out to Dawson's Mill to hunt for old bullets today. Dawson's Mill was a Civil War battlefield, and you could still find all sorts of treasures if you looked really hard.

The sky had clouded up, however, so Pete and Kelly decided instead to go over to the Simpsons' house to see Kate and Deena, who were friends of Kelly's. The Simpsons had a whole farm full of animals—goats, sheep, chickens; the works, as Pete liked to put it—so he didn't mind going along, even if he was going to be the only boy. If it got too boring, he could just go off and visit the cows or something.

But Kate and Deena weren't home, so after wolfing down the milk and cookies Mrs. Simpson offered them, Pete and Kelly headed back home. Big drops of rain were just beginning to fall as they cantered along the path that ran between the two lower pastures and back to the barn.

Pete realized he hadn't actually seen Keith on a horse in weeks. The change was instantly obvious. Keith's rangy home-trained style had given way to Pete's "proper" methods.

"He's ridin' Betsy-style!" Kelly exclaimed.

"So?" Keith glowered back at her. "What's it to you?"

"Hey, it looks great!" Pete quickly interjected. "You and Ghost look terrific. Really!"

"Well, I gotta admit, Ghost sure is jumpin' better'n ever. That's all *I* know," Keith admitted begrudgingly.

"That's all that matters," Pete pointed out. "You know—riding the way you do now you could enter an equitation class. And you'd win!"

Keith pulled Ghost to a halt. "Ya mean that?"

"Yep."

Two days later, Uncle Will announced over breakfast that at noontime he was heading over to the Milfords' place to look at a jumper for Keith and asked if anyone wanted to come. They all did, and ten minutes before noon three excited kids packed themselves into the van.

"Bubbles is what we call her. She's big, but she's jes' so light and perky, and there's somethin' 'bout the way she jes' floats over 'em fences. Named herself, she did," Jeb Milford told Keith.

Uncle Will ran a knowledgeable hand down the gray mare's legs, under her belly, across her flank. He opened her mouth, checking her teeth, then picked up her feet and inspected each hoof. Jeb led her off a bit and then trotted her up and back in front of everyone.

"Y'all can see fer yourselves, she's sound as a dollar. Never had an off day, this 'un. She's gonna make someone a fine show horse, she is. Ben," Jeb called to his stable hand, "throw a saddle 'n bridle on her and put her through her paces for the folks."

It was just like Jeb had said. The fine-boned Thoroughbred really did seem to float. Trotting, she covered ground without seeming to touch it. Her canter was smooth and elegant, and her jump looked completely effortless. Jeb kept raising the fences, and Bubbles kept jumping them.

"Want to try her?" Jeb asked Keith. Keith grinned as Jeb gave him a leg up.

He was still grinning fifteen minutes later as he slowed the tired mare back to a walk. Jeb came up to them and gave Bubbles's sweaty neck a pat.

"She could be fitter, that's the truth, but the boy's been on the road showin' the young horses, and I jes' don't have enough hands 'bout the place anymore to keep all the horses workin' out like they should. You could have her ready to show with a few weeks o' work, though." Jeb stepped back and took a long look at Keith and Bubbles. "Your boy sure does look good on her. Nice picture."

Uncle Will nodded in agreement. "You'll let us take her on trial?" The two gentlemen farmers discussed a few details, stood admiring the horse a moment longer, and then shook on the deal.

Chapter Ten

Mounting,
the Hard Way

"So Ghost is yours now, Pete. And if y'all get along good, you be plannin' on takin' him up north with you like last year, okay, boy?"

"You mean it, Uncle Will? Boy is that ever okay!" Pete was tingling with anticipation. He couldn't wait to get back to Eleven Oaks to ride the big gray. It seemed like hours before the van made the last turn and the old house and big brick stable came into view.

Uncle Will brought the van to a halt under two of the farm's eleven oaks, and Pete and Kelly scrambled out. Pete started to help unload Bubbles, but Uncle Will shooed him off. "Go and throw a saddle on your new horse, lad. I know that's what you want to be doin'." He gave Pete a playful clap on the shoulder and sent him on his way.

It didn't take long for Pete to notice some very basic differences between Lazy and Ghost Story. Size, for starters. He could look Lazy straight in the eye. Ghost might not be as big as Bubbles, but he certainly was a whole lot bigger than Lazy.

Pete brought Ghost out of his stall and put him in cross-ties to groom him. He scratched the horse's nose and ran his hand up the gray's face. "How about if I call you Casper, Ghost? You're friendly enough." Ghost snickered his approval of his newest stable name. "And you can call me anything you want," Pete rambled on.

Pretty soon he began to laugh. "Good grief, you're no horse—you're a giraffe," Pete said, reaching to brush the horse's forelock. He was surprised at how far he had to stretch to get to Casper's ears, and he was really amazed when he went to put on the bridle. "Now this is ridiculous," he gasped, tiptoeing like a ballet dancer as he tried to reach the bridle over the top of the horse's head.

Fortunately, no one was watching as Pete attempted to mount Casper. He just couldn't reach his foot up to the stirrup. He looked both ways to be sure there were no witnesses and then lengthened the stirrup leather as far as it went. That was a start, but it still left Pete with a real scramble to get his other leg up and over the saddle.

Once on the horse, Pete had to adjust the strap on his left stirrup, moving it back up to where it should be. Casper began to dance a nervous jig, realizing that a stranger was on his back. Tossing his head with fear, the horse began to back up while Pete was still collecting up the reins. Before Pete could stop him, Casper had backed squarely into one of the planters. Terrified, he leaped forward, and Pete went flying.

Casper took off at a gallop, the empty stirrups hanging at his sides. Pete groaned and got to his feet, more shook up than hurt. He started after the horse but hadn't gotten far before he found Keith leading Casper by the reins. The horse, nostrils flared, was panting and dancing around in fear.

"Y'all okay?" Keith asked, with genuine concern. "You don't look so good."

Pete brushed himself off and tried to laugh. "Hey, no problem. Ghost just taught me a lesson is all, didn't you, boy?" He took the reins from Keith and gave the horse a pat. "Calm down, you ol' spook."

"You're the one who looks like a ghost, little cuz,"

Keith commented. "You're white as a sheet. What happened, anyway?"

"I was just trying to mount him. He's big! It was a job getting up there. A totally screwed up job."

"That's what mountin' blocks were invented for, dummy," Keith reminded Pete, who smacked himself dramatically on the forehead.

"Oh, how could I have forgotten?"

"Beats me. Well, hey, look on the bright side. There weren't any girls around to see you sprawled in the dirt. Or guys, for that matter. That's even worse."

Pete walked Casper around for a while to calm him down and then led the gray over to the mounting block and climbed up on him gracefully. As he slipped his feet into the stirrups, he grinned over at Keith, who gave him a thumbs up in return.

"That's more like it, twerp," Keith chortled.

Chapter Eleven

Bubbles vs. Terminator

After all those months of anticipation, riding Casper was nothing like Pete had expected. Riding Casper was just plain hard.

For starters, Pete was light compared to Keith. Pete was about average size for his age, but he barely weighed seventy-seven pounds. Casper wasn't impressed. Keith weighed 124, and those extra pounds seemed to make a big difference.

Pitting his seventy-seven pounds against a thousand pounds of young horseflesh was Pete's biggest challenge. It wasn't so bad when he rode in the ring, but the minute they left its confines, Casper seemed to remember he was a Thoroughbred and would take off like a racehorse.

The first time it happened, Pete had no choice but to just ride it out. He had never run into this particular problem before, so he had no tricks up his sleeve to help him handle it. That evening he told Uncle Will what had happened.

"What can I do? I couldn't stop him. He just ran and ran and ran until he ran out of gas. I couldn't stop him, I couldn't steer him, nothing. It was his trip."

"Don't despair, boy. I'll tell ya what the jockeys do

about it. They're not a whole lot heavier than you are." Uncle Will turned his chair around and assumed a riding position on it.

"Okay now, say your colt's got it into his head to take you for a ride. You take up your left rein real short and plant it on his mane, right in front of you. Then you pull your right rein up toward yourself and you cross right over the mane as you're doin' it. You're goin' to turn his head that way and pull him 'round in a tight circle, that's what you're goin' to be doin'. An' you jes' keep pullin' him 'round till he comes to a stop."

Pete listened attentively. "Left rein planted, right rein pulled over his mane?"

"That's it. Or the other way 'round, whichever suits you. I've always preferred clockwise, m'self. See if'n that don't do the job. If y'all are still feudin', I s'pose we could try out some tougher bits, but I'd rather see you handlin' him with jes' a pelham." Pete was anxious to give Uncle Will's suggestion a try.

"Okay, Casper, here's your big chance to do your worst," he whispered to the gray the next morning. "I'm ready for you. Today, it's gonna be a fair fight."

Casper took the challenge, but Pete came out the winner. After several attempts to take off, Casper finally seemed to accept the fact that running away was going to get him nowhere. "Nowhere but dizzy, you dumb horse." Pete laughed.

"Bubbles, she's a jumpin' fool, she is," Keith announced to no one in particular over dinner one evening. No one disagreed. Keith and Bubbles were getting along great.

"So, Pa, when can I let the rest of the world in on the secret?" he wanted to know. "Can I take her to a show before Pete has to go on back home? I sure could use the pipsqueak in my cheerin' section. Lemme hear y'all cheer, kid."

Pete let out a couple of good hollers.

"Yep. Can't let talent like that get outa the state, now

can we? I sorta had my eye on the big show over in Greensboro for Bubbles to make her debut."

"What's a day-bue?" Pete asked.

"What's a debut?" Keith looked suitably horrified. "Hey, don't they teach y'all no French up there in Yankee land? A debut? A debut is, um, well it's like a first time out—the first time on the stage, or the first time playin' in a baseball game . . . a first for any ol' thing."

"Hey, yeah, I'd like to see Bubbles's first show. I could help and everything. And yell."

"Well, Pete, y'all practice your yellin' then, and I'll see 'bout entries. If that's what you've got your heart set on, son," Uncle Will told Keith, "it's okay with me."

The Greensboro show was the biggest show Pete had ever been to. It was a five-day event, and temporary stabling had been put up under several big green-and-white tents. Over four hundred horses were entered.

"Aren't you totally terrified, Keith? Shaking in your boots? Sick to your stomach? I mean, aren't you scared to death?"

"Thanks, Pete. Believe it or not, I was doin' jes' fine till you started in on me. Like they's always sayin', with friends like y'all, who needs enemies?"

"Gee, I'm sorry," Pete started to apologize. "But, gosh, did you know there're forty-four horses in the preliminary jumper division? And that's just what's listed in the program. Who knows how many late entries they got! That's one heck of a lot of horses."

Keith made a menacing face at Pete. "Shut up or beat it, kid, you hear me?"

"Okay, okay, I won't say any more. I promise." Pete quickly set to work making himself useful.

Pete was on the rail for Keith's first class. Seventeen horses had jumped by the time Bubbles entered the ring. Of those, only three had gone over clearly. Bubbles put in a perfect trip, becoming the fourth. Pete yelled his head off. By the end of the first round of jumping, only eight were still in it.

The jump crew raised the fences and the eight jumped the course for the second time. Bubbles again put in a clean performance, with Pete whooping it up after each and every fence. This time, only one other entry went clean, a huge black horse called Terminator. The fences were raised again.

Keith and Bubbles jumped first. They made a big circle at the end of the ring, and then Keith headed Bubbles for the first fence, a white gate with three red-and-white striped rails above it. Pete gasped as he clearly heard one of Bubbles's hooves graze the top rail as she went over. His heart sank as he watched the rail roll slowly, lazily off the standards. He hardly breathed as Bubbles continued on around the course. The horse went over every other fence perfectly.

"That's four faults on Bubbles, Number 232," boomed the announcer. "Next to jump is Terminator, Number 344."

Terminator entered the ring. Pete watched stony-faced as the big horse cleared the first four jumps. On the fifth jump, a large spread fence coming off a sharp turn, his rider misjudged his takeoff. The horse brought down the entire jump, costing Terminator four faults.

It's not fair, Pete thought to himself. Keith only took down one measly rail. This guy totaled that fence. He should get more like a *hundred* and four faults.

Terminator continued on, over the wall and the coop, and down to the three-fence combination that ended the course. Pete suddenly saw that Terminator's timing was off as the horse approached the first of the three fences.

"He's doomed," Pete whispered to himself as the horse took off too early on the first jump. He should have taken two strides before the second jump, but ended up putting in three choppy ones instead and brought the top rail down as he somehow scrambled over it. He never even tried to jump the third fence but plowed into it anyway, scattering rails in all directions.

Keith had just won his first class with Bubbles.

Chapter Twelve

Casper Meets the Iron Lady

It was one of those amazing shows—Bubbles could do no wrong. Class after class, day after day, he just kept putting in one excellent performance after another. After the last of the preliminary jumper classes was over, points were tallied. Keith and Bubbles were called into the ring to accept the blue, red, and yellow championship ribbon, a large silver bowl, and the applause of an audience that recognized a great young horse when it saw one.

The show over, an elated and weary Eleven Oaks crew packed up and headed home. Keith was sitting by the window and fell asleep before they had even left the show grounds. Pete was sitting next to Uncle Will. They kept their voices low so they wouldn't disturb the snoring champion.

"That championship is part yours. Ya know that, don't you?" Uncle Will asked his nephew. Pete shrugged. "Hey, I didn't do all that much. Maybe I helped with the grooming and stuff, but I was glad to. It was fun."

"You did more'n you know, boy. Why, Keith wouldn't be half the rider he is if'n it weren't for your trainin'."

"What do you mean? I taught Kelly the stuff I know, but Keith wouldn't have anything to do with it."

"Maybe not in front of you, but I happen to know he worked jes' as hard at it as Kelly. Harder. He sure never learned that kinda ridin' from me."

Pete basked in his uncle's praise. The two fell silent as Uncle Will drove the van on through the night. Now that the Greensboro show was over, Pete started thinking about his trip home. Would Betsy be impressed with his new horse and how he rode him?

They pulled out of the driveway at Eleven Oaks well before dawn. Pete had made the trip home from Royalton many times, but it had never seemed as endless as it did today. The van crawled up through Virginia, past Washington, D.C., and across little bits of Maryland and Delaware. Pete and his uncle both let out big sighs as the "Welcome to New Jersey" sign finally flashed by.

Even the Jersey leg of the trip, as Uncle Will always called it, seemed to take forever. It was well after sunset when the van rolled up to the stable door at Dutch Mill. Pete was disappointed that none of the kids would be there to greet him. At least the light in Betsy's office was still burning.

"Well, now, that's what I call a horse!" Betsy exclaimed, as Pete led Casper down the ramp.

"Betsy, I'd like you to meet Ghost Story, alias Ghost, alias Casper. Casper, this is Betsy—alias the Iron Lady."

Betsy couldn't find enough nice things to say about the gray, and Uncle Will enjoyed her enthusiasm every bit as much as Pete did. She was just as impressed the next morning as she watched Pete put him through his paces for her.

"The way he moves is wonderful! He's beautifully built, and he's really supple. It looks like you've really been working hard with him. Has he been shown at all?"

"Keith showed him last year in junior hunters," Pete shouted over his shoulder as he trotted a tight circle. "Did pretty well. Won a bunch of ribbons and took one reserve. But he said Casper was inconsistent. I think he's going pretty good now." Pete brought Casper into the center of the ring where Betsy was perched on the top rail of a fence. He gave the horse an appreciative pat.

"*Pretty* good? I'd say very good! I can tell he's a handful for you, but you seem to have things well under control. What's he like on the trails?"

"Like Secretariat," Pete joked, referring to the Triple Crown winner. "Only Uncle Will could teach me how to hold him. I call it a jockey-stop. You run him in circles till he gives up. It works."

"Pete, I am so pleased for you. You've really got a show horse now!" Pete's face glowed with happiness. "Let's do a little polishing, and then let's find you some shows."

Pete's friends were just as enthusiastic about Casper. Alexis decided he was "awesome." "Great" and "gorgeous" were Meg and Morgan's words for him. Mel offered to braid him for free for his first show. She called it her "get acquainted offer" and hoped Pete would like her braiding well enough to ask her to do it for him all the time.

Chapter Thirteen

Can You Tell Me What My Number Is?

"I didn't know Uncle Will was going to let you bring home such a *big* horse, Petey," said Mrs. Draper nervously when she first saw Casper.

"He's not that big, Mom. Anyway, you don't have to worry. This one's full grown, too. At least he won't be getting any bigger."

Casper tried to make friends with Mrs. Draper by sniffing at her neck just as she turned to answer Pete. She stifled a scream and rushed out of Casper's stall faster than Pete had ever seen her move.

"Oh, Petey! I'll—I'll never understand what you see in horses," she stammered as she tried to collect what was left of her dignity. "I'm sorry, Casper. I'll come and watch you at horse shows, but I don't think I'll be paying you any more visits in your stall!"

True to her word, two weeks later Pete's mother was sitting in the grandstand waiting for Pete's first class to begin. It was a local schooling show at Saddle Park. Mrs. Draper was just about the only mother in the stands, probably because of the light but steady rain that was falling. Over the loudspeaker, the announcer had assured everyone that unless things got worse the show would be proceeding right on schedule. The first class would be the Fourteen-and-Under Novice Over Fences. Pete's mother sat under her golf umbrella and tried to remember what that meant.

All the riders had put clear plastic rain jackets and hat covers over their show clothes. Betsy held Casper as Pete tried to tie his number around his waist. His hands were shaking.

"Hey, relax, kiddo," Betsy told him. "Weren't you the guy who was complaining that this wasn't a big enough show to bother with? Weren't you the one who wanted your first show with Casper to be at Madison Square Garden?"

Pete looked at her sheepishly and tried to calm down. "Hey, just think of it as a warm-up class, Pete. Do what I used to do—pretend this one doesn't count!" Pete grinned and Betsy continued.

"The fences are small, no worries there. The footing is getting a little heavy with the rain, but really, that's probably for the best. Casper's a little excited. Working his way through the stuff will slow him down a bit."

"I'll be okay if I just don't go off course," Pete joked. The course was simple—twice around, over four, two-foot three-inch fences.

"Just remember, this may be a novice class, and I know you've never won three blues, but you've got more experience in the ring than most of these kids. It's just that you spent so much time showing poor old invisible Lazy. They're going to see you this time!"

Pete was jumping third. He watched the first two riders go, took a deep breath, and then headed into the ring. He moved Casper into a trot and then a canter, making a big circle. The horse swished his tail nervously and then settled down to business as he headed for the first fence.

Pete kept the refrain "This one doesn't count, this is just a warm-up" running through his mind, and suddenly he felt himself relax. A smile actually came to his face. Just as suddenly, a new thought hit him. This was going to be fun!

Pete's round was excellent—proof that positive thinking

helps. It seemed like only moments had passed when he found himself pulling the gray back to a trot and heading for the Out gate. Even before he saw Betsy's grin, he knew he'd ridden very well. He was immediately surrounded by several other Dutch Mill kids, all congratulating him noisily. He felt terrific.

The rain had tapered off and it almost looked like the sun was going to break through the clouds. Pete walked Casper for what felt like hours, waiting for the rest of the riders to jump. There were twenty-four in all.

"Would the following riders please return to the ring . . . ," the loudspeaker finally announced. Pete froze. What was his number?

"Numbers 118, 56, 39, 88, 17 and 106. I repeat, 118, 56, 39, 88, 17 and 106, to the ring, please."

Pete grabbed the rider next to him, turned his back to him, and asked him to tell him what his number was.

"Boy are you out of it! It's thirty-nine."

"Third!" Pete grinned and trotted quickly into the ring. The six horses lined up and the ringmaster awarded them their ribbons. Pete thought Casper looked great with the yellow ribbon pinned to his bridle.

Chapter Fourteen

Jasper, Freddy, Lucius, and Hump

"**D**o you know who that is?" Jonathan whispered to Pete and Julia as one of the judges walked by them.

"No," Julia answered for both of them.

"I didn't think so. That's just Greg Mersio, is all," Jonathan informed them.

Jonathan had been showing at all the big shows for years and was considered Dutch Mill's resident expert on who was who on the show circuit.

Julia finally made his day by asking, "Okay—who is Greg Mersio?"

"Only one of the top trainers in the country. What he's doing judging at a rinky-dink, leaky-roof little show like this, I don't know. He's the only reason I decided to come, myself."

As soon as Jonathan left, Julia and Pete looked at each other and cracked up.

"That guy is such a stuffed shirt," Julia giggled. " 'He's the only reason I decided to come.' Did you hear that? I'll tell you the only reason *I* came. This is a small enough show that I have half a chance of winning some ribbons. I never even looked at who was judging."

"Me either. Besides, the name wouldn't have meant anything to me even if I had. I came because Betsy said I should," Pete said with a laugh. But he found himself looking at the famous judge with interest and just a little nervousness.

Pete's second class of the day was the Maiden on the Flat, a non-jumping class for riders who had never won a blue ribbon. He felt like he had a good chance in this class, considering the amount of time he had spent over the last few months working Casper. He was as ready as he'd ever be.

What he wasn't ready for was the combination of seeing Greg Mersio standing in the middle of the ring and Jasper MacMillan sitting in the stands. What was a big-shot trainer like Greg Mersio doing judging a beginners' class like the Maiden? And why did Jasper have to be there. Pete felt close to panic.

The second time he came around by the grandstand, he understood Jasper's presence. He was sitting with Tracy Field's brother Freddy. Freddy was there to watch Tracy ride. Freddy and Jasper were both in Pete's sixth grade class in school, and they hung out together a lot.

"Oh, no," Pete gasped under his breath. True to form, Freddy and Jasper's shadows were there, too—good old Lucius and Hump. Hump had to be the unluckiest kid ever named. There weren't many other possible nicknames for Humphrey, and his middle name was Rutledge, one of the best kept secrets of the twentieth century. The only thing he could thank his parents for was not producing any sisters or brothers to spread the word around.

"Hey, look at Petey," came the unmistakably low-pitched voice of Jasper MacMillan. "Look at Petey in a ring full of girls!"

Pete felt his face go beet red as he suddenly looked around him and realized that he was, in fact, the only boy in the ring. The voice on the loudspeaker announced, "Trot, please. All trot."

Pete tried to stay as far away from the railing as he could the next time around, but he could still hear loud and clear when Hump started hooting, "What's a boy doing in the *Maiden* class?"

Pete tried to force his concentration back on his riding, but the third time he came by the stands, all four boys were rehearsed and waiting for him. "Petey's not going to be a maiden for long, not in that ring full of girls," they sang out in unison. "Canter, please. All canter," came the announcer's call.

Pete did something he had never done to Casper before. He was so upset that he dug his right heel into the horse's ribs, almost viciously. All he could think of was getting away from the heckling voices.

Casper suddenly took the bit in his teeth, bolted, and ran. Pete realized too late what he'd done and hauled back on the reins, but Casper was beyond noticing. Pete groaned as it hit him that the ring was way too crowded for him to use his jockey-stop. If he turned in a circle, he'd run into a million girls.

All he could do was try to avoid running anyone over. He watched for openings as Casper galloped uncontrollably through the crowd of cantering horses and ponies. Pete was doing okay until he and Casper blazed by the grandstand one more time.

"Petey!" his mother shrieked in horror, jumping to her feet as she realized that her son's horse was out of control. Casper saw her out of the corner of his eye, shied, bucked, and came lurching to a halt. Pete went flying.

At that moment, Pete decided that there was definitely something worse than being the only boy in the ring.

Chapter Fifteen

"You've Got Talent, Kid"

Casper sent a nervous shudder through the crowd as he took off through the ring full of riders—his reins trailing on the ground.

Only luck kept the panicked horse from stepping on them, or worse yet, catching a foot in them in his headlong gallop. As it was, he finally came to a halt and allowed one of the jump crew to approach him and lead him over to the Out gate. Pete fought back tears of humiliation as he accepted the reins and led his horse from the ring in disgrace.

Silently, Pete took Casper back to the Dutch Mill van and untacked him. Not speaking to anyone, he put a halter on the horse, sponged him down, and walked him until he was cool. He put Casper back in the van, struggled out of his jacket and tie and unbuttoned the collar of his shirt.

The van was pulled up alongside a rock wall. Pete went around to the wall. He climbed over it, sat down, and leaned back against it. The rocks poked into his back, but somehow it just felt right. His head sagged and he covered his eyes. He tried to make his mind go blank, but all it would do was show him instant replays of the Maiden class.

51

He didn't know how long he'd been sitting there when he heard a voice ask someone by the van, "Has anyone seen Pete Draper? He rides with you all, doesn't he?"

Pete heard Celia answer. "Yeah, he does. At least, I think he still does. He may have given up riding altogether by now."

The voice asked, "Do you know where I could find him?" It was a man's voice.

Pete cringed as he heard Tracy tell him that she'd seen him back behind the van, on the other side of the wall. So much for privacy. He was still sitting with his head in his hands when a pair of tan loafers and brown corduroys came into view in front of him.

Pete looked up reluctantly and recognized the weathered face before him. He scrambled to his feet in confusion.

"Hi, I'm Greg Mersio," the judge said with a friendly smile. He put out his hand. Pete shook it dumbly.

"And you're Pete Draper, right?" Pete nodded. Greg could tell he was going to have to conduct a one-man conversation until Pete recovered his composure.

"Pretty embarrassing, what happened back there," Greg went on. "I really felt for you, kid." Pete blinked.

"I could hear those guys heckling you. Nothing worse. I know, it's happened to me a few times, too. I don't think I'll ever forget what it felt like. Seeing you go through it today really brought it back."

Pete felt like he'd never speak again, but he somehow managed to choke out, "You?"

"Yep. Once when I was nine, and then, let's see . . . when I was fourteen, and then again the next year, I think. The one when I was fourteen was the worst, the absolute worst.

"You know what happened? This girl I was crazy about was sitting in the bleachers. I was riding in a hunter hack class, on the flat, just like you. I was riding this chestnut mare, a wonderful horse named Red. Great horse.

"Anyway, here I was, warming up, feeling good—you know, that feeling you get when you can actually imagine yourself winning the class? And I noticed DeeDee in the stands. I started getting all self-conscious and nervous. And then I noticed that she wasn't by herself, that this guy I knew was sitting by her. He had his arm around her, as a matter of fact.

"That was bad enough, but then I clearly heard him saying to her, loud enough for the whole county to hear, 'You don't have to worry about Greg. Look at him. He's got a whole ringful of girls to himself.' People heard him, too, because the next thing I knew a bunch of little kids had started saying it." Greg paused and then sat down next to Pete.

"You're probably wondering what happened then . . . oh, nothing much. I went scarlet; Red went purple and took off with me. Spooked a bunch of other horses and the whole ring went crazy. Three people ended up on the ground. I was so mortified that I found myself wishing I was one of them. They got to leave the ring. Me, I had to finish the class. Needless to say, I didn't get anything but a whole lot more embarrassed. I almost gave up riding that day."

Pete started to giggle in spite of himself. "That bad?"

"That bad."

"But you didn't quit."

"Nope."

"I might."

"Aw, come on, Pete. It's just one of the knocks of being a guy who rides. I've never heard what the statistics are, but I'll bet you there must be ten thousand girls for every guy who rides. Hell, maybe not quite ten thousand, but there sure are a whole slew of 'em.

"But you want to know something interesting? Out of all those girls, probably ninety-seven percent of them'll quit before they finish high school. Or college, anyway. But— here's the interesting part—most of the boys who're good riders at your age stay with it and go on to become pros."

Pete looked up at Greg, surprised.

"Yup, professionals. You know what else? I think *you're* a good rider. I get a kick out of spotting good new riders, especially if they're boys. And you're definitely good!

"Don't get me wrong. I'd never give you a ribbon just

because you're a boy. But I'll tell you, you're one kid I plan to keep an eye on. You've got talent, kid. And you know something else? Someday, I bet you'll even learn how to speak!" he teased.

Greg got to his feet and dusted himself off. "I've got to be getting back to the show. See you later?"

Pete looked up and grinned. "Yeah. I'll be there."